MAYBE

THE COMPLETE SERIES

ELLA MILES

Copyright © 2018 by Ella Miles

EllaMiles.com

Ella@ellamiles.com

Editor: Jovana Shirley, Unforeseen Editing, www.unforseenediting.com

Cover design © Arijana Karčić, Cover It! Designs

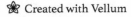 Created with Vellum

FREE BOOKS

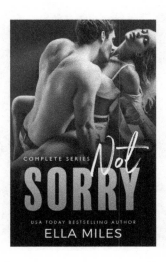

Read **Not Sorry** for **FREE**! And sign up to get my latest releases, updates, and more goodies here→EllaMiles.com/freebooks

Follow me on BookBub to get notified of my new releases and recommendations here→Follow on BookBub Here

Join Ella's Bellas FB group for giveaways and FUN→Join Ella's Bellas Here

MAYBE, DEFINITELY SERIES

Her future is already set, all she has to do is marry a complete stranger.

Kinsley Felton has everything. Money, a loving family, and a modeling career. She graduates from Yale in just days, but unlike a typical college student she doesn't have to spend hours looking for a job when she graduates. Kinsley will inherit the multi-billion dollar gaming and hospitality company her great-grandfather started. The only problem is she has to do everything her family asks for in order to get that money. That includes marrying a man of her family's choosing. That's not a problem since Kinsley has been following her family's orders all her life. Until a phone call from her grandfather changes everything.

Will she marry the man her family chooses or will she decide her own future?

MAYBE, DEFINITELY SERIES:

Maybe Yes
Maybe Never
Maybe Always

Definitely Yes
Definitely No
Definitely Forever

MAYBE YES

1

—————

"WHERE THE HELL HAVE YOU BEEN?" I hear as soon as I walk into my apartment.

I smile. "Good morning."

"Don't *good morning* me! I have been worried sick and trying to fend off your father all fucking night. Where the hell were you?" Scarlett, my best friend, says.

I ignore her and walk to my closet to put my shoes back in their correct place. The closet isn't really a closet. It's more like a changing room overflowing with gifted clothes from various designers after doing shoots for them. The other half of the room is filled with every kind of makeup, jewel, and accessory I've ever worn. It's every woman's dream. I'm just not sure it's my dream.

I slip off the crop top and pull on a comfy T-shirt instead. Scarlett storms in before I've finished changing.

"Well?" she asks again. Her arms are crossed over her chest, and her foot is tapping slowly on the hard floor as she waits for my answer. Her ombre brown-colored locks flow down her back in thick curls unchanged from last night when she persuaded me to go out to a bar instead of my usual routine of hiding in my apartment to study and wait for my father to call.

"I was with Brent."

"You were with who?"

"Brent."

"I heard you the first time. You couldn't have been with a guy!"

I laugh. "Too late." Although I think I have to get further than second base to actually say I was 'with a guy.' I puked before things got too far.

"Kinsley Elizabeth Felton! You were supposed to get drunk, flirt with some guys, and then come back here with me to sleep it off—not go home with a complete stranger without telling me."

"Calm down, Scar," I say, brushing past her and heading to the kitchen to get a glass of water.

"Don't Scar me. You...you can't just..."

I laugh, seeing Scarlett so flabbergasted. She didn't think little ole me had it in me to have a one-night stand. Well, I did—sort of. I've had one boyfriend before. Scarlett is the one who dates. She's the one the guys are always after.

We are both models and both beautiful in our own right. But while I model for Seventeen magazine, Scarlett models for Victoria's Secret. I look seventeen, and she looks twenty-five. Guys find my thin frame, long legs, and blond locks attractive, but guys want to sleep with Scarlett.

It's for the best guys never want to sleep with me. I shouldn't date anyway.

I sigh. "Calm down, Scar. Nothing happened."

"What do you mean 'nothing happened'? You went home with him!"

"Yeah, well...something almost happened, but then I threw up, and he passed out on the couch while I was in the bathroom."

Scarlett's body visibly relaxes at my words, but it doesn't stop her questions. "Why did you go home with him though?"

"I don't know." I fill my glass with filtered water. "I was drunk."

Scarlett shakes her head. "Just don't do it again."

I take a long gulp of water as I stare at Scarlett in disbelief. "You were the one who pushed me to go out."

"Yeah, and you are supposed to listen to every word I say, not go off and make your own stupid decisions like that."

I roll my eyes at her change from wild friend to motherly concern even though she has every right to be concerned. The last time I did anything remotely crazy it ended badly.

"Why are you here anyway, Scar? I thought you'd be at your apartment shooing a man out of your bed." Scarlett rarely stays over at my place. She has her own luxury apartment a block from mine. If it weren't for our parents' pocketbooks, we would have been roommates. Sometimes, I wish we had been anyway so we could have gotten the real college experience. It would have never worked though. Our clothes alone would have been too much to fit into one apartment together.

A phone vibrates, and Scarlett reaches into the pocket of her jeans. She pulls out my phone, and a worried look crosses her face. "I think you'd better answer it. Your father has been calling you nonstop, every twenty minutes, all night."

I stare at the phone, afraid to take it from Scarlett's hand. I know what's waiting for me on the other end of that phone—yelling. Lots of yelling and lecturing about my responsibilities, how immature I was last night, and how my parents should take everything away and give it to someone who will respect their terms. I can already hear my father's stern voice now.

"I'm surprised they haven't already shown up here," I say honestly. I've never missed a phone call from my father. He calls every Friday evening, and I answer instead of going out and partying with my friends. But I turned twenty-one this week. I deserved to have some fun, but now it's time to deal with the consequences.

Scarlett's eyes grow wide with fear as she thrusts the phone into my hands. "Answer it before they do show up. I don't think I could survive getting a lecture from your father."

I smile weakly as I stare at the still vibrating phone. It's not my father I have to worry about though. Our relationship has always been good. It's my grandfather's lecture that terrifies me.

"Hello?" I say, finally answering the phone. "I'm sorry I didn't answer earlier. I accidentally grabbed Scar's phone instead of mine. You know how we have the exact same phone. I was so focused on studying last night I forgot it was Friday. I fell asleep before I remembered. I'm sorry if I worried you, but I'm ready to talk now," I lie. I've never lied in my entire life. It doesn't feel natural, leaving my lips.

"Kinsley, shut up. I don't believe a word coming out of your mouth anyway. I need you to come home to Vegas immediately. I sent a jet to come pick you up," Granddad says.

"Wait...what? I have finals all next week. I need to be studying." I move my phone from my ear to make sure I saw the number correctly. It's my father's, not my grandfather's, number. *Why is my grandfather calling me on Dad's phone?*

"It's an emergency," he says grumpily into the phone. "Your father's dead."

"What?" I say, not believing his words.

He wouldn't say that to me over the phone.

"Your father's dead," he says, repeating his words. "He had a heart attack, probably due to the fact his only daughter never called him like she was supposed to. You need to come home for the funeral, and so we can decide..."

I don't hear the rest. I drop my phone and watch it clank against the hard floor. I slump to the floor. Tears stream down my face as Scarlett, my only friend, rushes to my side and holds my body in her arms.

It can't be true. It can't be.

"What happened?" Scarlett keeps asking as she holds me firmly in her arms.

"He's gone," I finally say between sobs.

And it's my fault. If I hadn't gone out last night, if I had called him, he might still be alive. If I hadn't gone out last night, I could have had one last conversation with him. I could have heard one last piece of advice. I could have heard one last 'I love you.'

I didn't though. Now, I'll never get to hear my father say those words to me again. It's all my fault. Another mistake to add to my list of flaws.

I never realized how one mistake could ruin your life.

Except, I already knew one mistake could. That was five years ago. This is nothing like that. This time, it's worse.

I thought the day I found out my father had died was the worst day of my life. I thought nothing could get worse than that.

I was wrong.

I thought the funeral might be the worst day because I had to say goodbye to the only family member who had understood me at all.

I was wrong.

Today, the day after the funeral, is the worst day. Today, everything has become real. The tears are gone but not the pain. The pain is worse, much worse than I could have ever imagined. I have no one here who can comfort me or steal my mind for just a minute.

Scarlett came to Las Vegas for the funeral, but she's already gone back to Connecticut to finish her finals. She won't move back here until later this week.

My mother is a mess. We got into a fight after the funeral. It was about something petty, like what to do with the donations made in my father's honor. She can't comfort me.

And my grandfather...I wish I could stay far away from him right now.

I love my grandfather. He has done a lot for me and our family. Without him, the Felton Corporation might never have reached the heights it has. We wouldn't have more than enough money to take care of ourselves for dozens of lifetimes without even having to lift a finger. Granddad was the one who turned a simple casino into the almost twenty properties we own now. He was the one who grew the empire to what it is today.

He has given me direction in my life. He was the one who got me the modeling jobs. He was the one who decided I should go to Yale. He was the one who decided I should major in theater. He was the one who chose my whole future.

And I know why he has brought me here—to decide what comes next.

I'm usually thankful for his guidance. He's always right. He's even right about what he's brought me here to tell me. I'm just not prepared to hear it yet. I'm not ready to hear it on the worst day of my life. Today, I need to go back downstairs and finish watching the Harry Potter marathon and drown in a tub of buttered popcorn. I need to feel sorry for myself. I need to feel angry with the world. I don't need to deal with this.

"Take a seat, princess," Granddad says, indicating for me to take a seat opposite him.

But I can't. I'm frozen in the doorway. He called me princess. Only my father ever called me that.

Tears I didn't even know still existed threaten to fall as my eyes fill with moisture. I thought I had cried all the tears out.

Granddad immediately realizes his mistake. His arms are quickly around me in a hug, but it doesn't stave off the tears. They fall fast and hard. My body moves from a frozen statue into uncontrollable trembles. I feel my grandfather guide me over to a chair. My body collapses into the chair, but it doesn't stop the trembling or the tears.

He hands me a handkerchief before moving back to his seat across from me. I wipe my eyes, and then I stare at him. Nobody would know he is eighty-five years old. He looks sixty, tops. It's the lucky Felton genes. He doesn't work out or eat any better than I do.

"We need to talk about your future."

I nod, expecting this.

"We need to figure out who is going to run the company in your father's place."

I nod again.

"As you already know, your father and I argued a lot. We never agreed on anything." He sits back in his chair, smiling a little at a memory.

When he looks back at me, he frowns. He thinks I'm the reason his son is dead. I don't think he'll ever forgive me.

Maybe he would if I gave him everything he ever wanted?

"But we did agree on one thing," he continues.

I already know what that one thing is.

"That you want the company to stay in the family," I say, completing his sentence.

His frown deepens. "Yes. Your mother isn't capable of running the company. And, frankly, neither are you."

Now, it's my turn to grimace. Although I already knew how he felt, it hurts to hear my father felt the same way. He didn't have any more confidence in my abilities than my grandfather did. It stings I was never even considered for the job even though I'm family. I'm the only heir to the empire.

"We all agreed the best thing for the company is for you to marry someone who *is* capable of running the company—a man your father and I would choose after years of scrutiny."

I nod. I already knew all of this. It's why I never really dated. It doesn't matter whom I want to be with. It only matters who is best for the company. I'll marry for my family, not for love.

It's always been years into the future though. I'm only twenty-one. I haven't even officially graduated yet. I haven't even met the guys my father and grandfather have been considering. I haven't tested out the men myself to at least make sure whomever they might choose would be a good fit.

"Well…" Granddad pauses like it's hard for him to say the next words because he knows how much I'll hate them. "We found him."

My mouth falls open. I wasn't expecting that. I didn't know he and my father had already chosen a man for me. I thought I still had time left.

"You'll meet him tomorrow."

I nod. It's all I can do.

"And then you'll marry him in six months."

My eyes grow wide at his words. *Six months?* I can't marry someone I've never met in six months. I don't even know if I'll be able to tell if I like the guy in six months. I won't even be over mourning my father in that amount of time.

"I can't…" I whisper. The words feel strange falling from my mouth. I don't think I've ever said those words to any member of my family, even my mother. I've always been the good girl following their every order. I've always been their princess who never disobeys. Right now, I don't know if I can ever be that girl again.

Granddad walks over to me and rests his hand on my shoulder. It's meant to be comforting, except it's not.

I can't get married in six months. I just can't. A few years, maybe. That was always the plan—do the modeling and acting thing for a little longer, and then in my late twenties, they would match me with a guy who they felt was capable of running the company but would also be a good match for me. We would date like a normal couple and then marry by the time we were thirty.

I'm only twenty-one. That's nowhere near thirty. And I can't focus on anything right now except my father being gone.

"Oh, sweetie, you can."

I incredulously stare up at him. I don't know how he can focus on anything except his son being gone right now, but I guess the company comes first. It always comes first.

"I...I don't think so." My eyes beg for him to change his mind, to understand I'm not ready to get married. I don't even know who I am yet or what I want in life.

"I'm sorry. I know we all wanted to wait until you were older, but it's time. I'm not getting any younger. I need to know the company is in the right hands before I go."

I tuck my long strands behind my ear. I can't believe he is talking about his death right now. I nervously run my hands through my hair over and over.

"I'm not ready," I say without meeting his eyes. I can't face disappointing him again.

"Yes, you are. You're beautiful. You were born to marry a man who can run the Felton empire. Once you are married, you will see it was the right thing to do. You will feel taken care of. You will finally feel like you have found your place in this world."

I let my eyes glance up at him for just a second. I see honesty. His eyes are filled with honesty.

"Maybe," I say weakly.

His face brightens. "Yes," he says.

"Yes," I repeat on autopilot.

"The meeting is tomorrow at eleven a.m. at the Felton Grand on the strip."

"Yes," I say again. I stand up without looking him in the eyes. I walk out of the door without looking back.

I walk back to the basement, back to my haven. This time, when I slump into the chair, I don't feel an ounce of comfort. In fact, I feel nothing. Sitting here and watching movies the rest of the day isn't going to help anymore. I won't be able to zone out on them again. I just promised my grandfather I would marry a total stranger in six months. I've never broken a promise before, and I don't plan on starting now.

I just don't know what I want.

I think of everything I've been told I want—money, clothes, a modeling career, an acting career, and an intelligent husband who will run our company to give me even more money. But not one of those things has ever made me happy. I try to think about things that have made me happy—my family and Scarlett. But that leaves me with fewer answers.

I know what I don't want.

I don't want a modeling career.

I don't want an acting career.

I don't want to marry a complete stranger.

I try to think of my happiest memory with my dad. It was on my eighteenth birthday. It coincided with my high school graduation. He took me to a casino in California, one I could legally gamble at. He taught me how to play blackjack and how to count cards. We won—a lot. It wasn't the winning that made it fun. It was learning something from my father. It was the confidence he displayed in me when he gave me high amounts of money to place a bet I would win because I was capable. It was one of the only times I felt he was proud of me for something other than my looks.

The line I will never forget my father saying to me is, "No one would ever suspect you of counting cards. You're too pretty."

It was that day I learned my beauty was a weapon I could use to my advantage. I just never learned how to harness it.

I head to my room to grab my shoes and purse to head to a casino, to find a happy memory...because tomorrow I'll meet the man I'm going to marry. Tomorrow I'll have to face the fact I don't get to decide my future. I don't have to face it today though. I still have a chance to make today better.

I was wrong. Today isn't the worst day of my life either. Tomorrow probably will be, so I'm going to make the most of my last night of freedom.

2

I PLACE five hundred dollars in chips on the table—my maximum bid. The true count is up to plus-six, so I need to bet high since a positive true count tells me I have an advantage over the dealer. I watch as the dealer deals out the cards. In my head, I silently keep track of the cards being laid out. I look at my cards—a jack and a ten. I smile at the twenty, just one short of twenty-one—the number I want to match without going over. The dealer turns to me on my turn, and I signal I want to stand.

I watch the dealer flop an additional card to add to his fifteen. It's a king. He's busted at twenty-five. I smile as he hands me a thousand dollars in additional chips bringing my winnings up to five thousand for the night.

I should stop soon. Not stopping is always the chance you take when you play against the house. The house always has the advantage, even when you count cards, even when you know the odds. There is always a chance you will lose the hand, you will lose track of the count, or you will get cocky and bet too much.

But I didn't come here to win. Although winning feels good, I came here to escape. So, I'll keep playing, no matter what.

"You're good. You should teach this old man to play. I'm having terrible luck," an older gentleman sitting next to me says.

I smile at the sweet old man. He's been sitting next to me for over an hour now, and I don't think he's won more than a couple of hands. He is down well over a thousand dollars.

I bid my maximum five hundred again. I keep my eyes on the cards as the dealer deals. I silently keep up the running count while still giving attention to the older gentleman.

"It's just beginner's luck. I haven't played in years."

The man smiles at me. "It looks like more than luck to me."

I shake my head as I smile back. I watch as the man takes his turn. He has seventeen. He should stand. If he hits, there is a good chance he will bust. He hits and busts. I knowingly shake my head.

It's my turn. I get a blackjack. I smile as the dealer pushes more chips my way.

The old man sitting next to me shakes his head in disbelief of my winning streak. I try to act innocent by twirling the long blond hair of my high ponytail with my fingers. I don't want to draw attention to my card counting, not that anyone would expect a young woman in jeans, a ripped comfy sweatshirt, and no makeup to be counting cards. But if security does catch on, I know enough about casinos to know I'll be kicked out.

I silently divide the running count by the decks left in the shoe. I get negative four indicating I'm at a disadvantage. I place a low bet this time, expecting to lose. I do.

"Guess my winning streak can't last forever."

The older gentleman chuckles. "Maybe your luck has passed to me."

I glance up from the table when I see them—the most intense eyes I have ever seen. The eyes belong to a man in a suit. The kind of man who knows designer clothes and only wears the best. A man that demands attention wherever he walks because of his mere presence. The kind who spends all day in a boardroom but still looks like he spends all of his time at the gym. I can't believe I haven't noticed him before. I've been sitting at this table for over an hour. In that time, many people have come and gone. None of them were the least bit intriguing.

There is something about the way this man is looking at me that sends goosebumps all over my body. I'm not sure what the look actually is. *Is it lust? Interest? Anger? Frustration?* I don't know. All I can feel is the intensity of his eyes. And they are staring at me. His eyes don't leave me as the dealer begins dealing.

I glance back at the table to continue counting the cards, but I still feel his eyes burning into me. I lose track of the count, not really caring anymore. I hit even though I'm at nineteen, and it doesn't make sense. I bust.

"I think I've pushed my luck too far at this table. Good luck," I say to the older gentleman next to me. I stand from the table, taking my chips with me.

I make it a point to avoid looking at the man in the suit with the intense eyes, but I still feel his eyes on me. I'm not ready to leave yet. As soon as I leave, my world will no longer be in my control—*not that it ever was in my control*. I need more of a distraction.

I walk to the bar in the center of the casino and take a seat. I relax as my butt hits the cushion of the barstool. I know I can't sit here for long without ordering a drink, which is the last thing I want. Maybe I'll try my hand at pushing the buttons on the slots. I know I'll end up losing all the money I just won, but I don't care.

"So, you're a pro."

"What?" I turn left, toward the direction of the voice.

That's when I see them—the same piercing eyes. It's the same man who was watching me at the blackjack table.

I flip the chips over in my hands at the bar.

"A pro card counter," he says as he takes a seat next to me.

Shit. I'm about to get thrown out of here.

"I don't know what you're talking about." I turn back to the bar. I try to get the attention of one of the scantily clad bartenders, but the closest one to me is busy flirting with a man.

Out of the corner of my eye, I watch my visitor as he raises his

15

hand, and the bartender immediately smiles and begins walking over to us.

"Yes, you do. Don't worry. I'm not going to turn you in."

I exhale a breath I didn't even know I had been holding. "Do you work here?"

"No."

I don't know how to respond to that, so I don't. I have no idea why this complete stranger followed me. It's not like the other night at the bar when I was dressed to pick up a guy. Tonight I look like death. No one is attracted to that. So, he can't be here to hook up with me. He's not here to kick me out. That leaves...I have no idea.

"What can I getcha?" The woman leans over the bar, pushing her cleavage closer to the man's face.

I watch his lips move, but I don't register his words. He doesn't ask me what I want. He just speaks to the bartender, while keeping his eyes on me.

I stupidly assumed his eyes would be on the pair of boobs in front of him giving me an opportunity to check him out. I was wrong.

Now, I can't take my eyes off of him even though my cheeks are burning red with embarrassment. I notice his suit conforms to his body, making it obvious he doesn't work here. His dark brown hair spikes slightly to one side, and I think there is a little red in it if I look closely. He has a hint of a five o'clock shadow outlining his down-turned lips that seem just as intense as his eyes.

The whole time I'm taking him in, he doesn't move. His expression never changes. I'm used to men at least smiling at me, but his lips don't curl upward even a hint.

He's older. I know that much. He has lines around his eyes that hint at him being older than me. I have no idea how much older though—maybe ten years, if I had to guess. Closer to thirty than twenty.

He's intimidating.

His eyes don't shift from mine until the bartender returns with our drinks, and he reaches into his pocket to hand the woman his shiny platinum credit card.

I glance at the bar and see two glasses of wine sitting in front of us. The bartender returns his credit card having opened his tab.

"Thanks," I say.

He nods and takes a sip of his wine. I do the same. As soon as the liquid touches my lips, my whole attitude toward this stranger changes. The liquid is exquisite. No, it's better than exquisite. It's the best thing I've ever tasted. It puts the Cosmo my almost one night stand got me the other night to shame.

"This is delicious." I hold up the wine to my lips and take another sip.

"Good," he says, seeming satisfied with my response.

I curiously look at him. "Why are you here?"

"Because I'm like every other person on the planet who likes to drink and occasionally gamble his money away while looking at boobs."

I smile bashfully when he says 'boobs' even though he isn't talking about mine. Mine are completely covered up, if you can even call what I have boobs.

He, on the other hand, still hasn't cracked a smile.

"I meant..." I shake my head. I'm not going to ask.

"I'm intrigued by you. You're beautiful, yet I detect a bit of insecurity in you for reasons that don't make sense. You are obviously intelligent if you are able to count cards, but you are used to your beauty helping you to cover up that intelligence, just like you did with your card counting. You seem sad, yet you've chosen to come to one of the most alive places on the planet. You have every reason to be confident, yet you act like a scared, innocent little girl. I'm just trying to figure out what *you* are doing here."

I narrow my eyes at his rude comments. *How could he have formed such a strong opinion of me in such a short amount of time?* "Thank you for the drink," I say as I stand. I'm not going to sit here and listen to a stranger insult me, not tonight.

He grabs my arm as I get up. "I didn't mean that as criticism."

"Seemed like it to me," I say cautiously as I stare at his hand holding my arm. I feel the heat transfer from his body to mine. It feels overpowering, like everything else coming from this man.

"Let's try again. I'm Killian. You seem like a nice woman. I would love to hear over another drink how you became so good at blackjack and hopefully get some tips because I sucked back there." This time, after he speaks, his lips curl up slightly.

It's not quite a smile, but I can tell it's pushing it for this man.

I smile brightly, hoping that if I smile, he will too.

"I'm Kinsley," I say, extending my hand and returning to my seat.

Killian shakes it like it's a business arrangement. I suck in my breath at his touch. His handshake is powerful and strong. It's practiced, like he has shaken a million hands. I bet he can close business deals with just the strength of his handshake.

"And I would love more wine." I take another sip of my wine, finishing it off.

He nods to the bartender this time, and she immediately comes over to him even though the bar is now full, and it's not our turn to be served.

"Another?" the woman asks him, smiling brightly.

He nods.

She winks at him before she goes to retrieve our drinks.

My mouth stays open. "How did you do that?"

He raises an eyebrow. "Order drinks?"

"How did you get her attention like that? Are you a regular or something?"

"No. Bartenders just know where their biggest tip lies. And that's with me."

I nod although I'm not sure if that's completely it. He definitely has the sex-appeal thing going for him. And the intense almost lust-filled look he gives would make any woman say yes immediately.

I find myself wondering what it would be like if he asked me to go home with him tonight. *How different would it be from Brent, my almost one night stand from hell?* I shake my head, getting that thought out of my head. I can't have sex with this man—not that he is asking me anyway.

The bartender places our drinks in front of us. I immediately grab the glass and bring it to my lips to taste the sweet, smooth liquid again. I moan quietly as the liquid pours down my throat. The taste is magical. I've never had anything like it.

"My father."

His eyes find mine, but he doesn't say a word.

"My father taught me how to play blackjack."

He nods.

"He taught me how to count cards." My cheeks flush slightly from my admission.

I think I see a hint of a smile forming, but I don't know how to keep that smile on his lips. I don't know how to flirt and show him I need a distraction.

"He passed away..." I blurt out, but can't add that he died this week. Then, I wait. I wait for the *I'm sorry*. I wait for the *Is there anything I can do for you?* I wait for the *How are you doing?*

"Let's get out of here."

My eyes widen. "What?"

"We are leaving." Killian stands from his seat, throws a hundred dollar bill on the bar as a tip, and begins walking in the direction of the exit.

I laugh. *He's got to be kidding.*

When I glance at him, I realize he's not. His face is stoic as he waits just a couple feet from me to follow him.

"What?"

"This isn't what you need."

I laugh again before I glance back up at his eyes. "How do you know what I need?"

Killian walks to me until his body just grazes mine. His eyes stay on mine as his hand tucks my hair behind my ear. His hand doesn't stop there though. It trails down my neck as he pushes my hair back until he is gently holding the nape of my neck. My breath catches. Shivers form all over my body. An ache for more forms in my belly, but I don't let my need show. A complete stranger can't turn me on this much. It took Brent most of the night to get me this filled with lust. *How has this stranger done it with barely a touch?*

I watch as he bends down. For a second, I think he's going to kiss me, but he doesn't. Instead, his lips move inches away from my neck so I can feel his hot breath there. I can't move. I can't breathe.

"Your body tells me. Your eyes are begging me to kiss you," he whispers into my ear. His deep voice causes fluid to soak my panties. "You're wet."

I suck in a breath, proving him right.

"You want me to take you to my hotel room down the strip and fuck you until you scream." He moves away from my neck. "That's what you need."

He cocks his head and grins for the first time. It's a beautiful sight, and it's a side of him I doubt he displays often.

I nod, and he smiles brighter.

"Come," he says, holding his hand out to me.

I blush at the double meaning of the word. I bite my lip as I debate on what to do. I reach for the phone in my pocket, but I let my hand fall to my side. My father isn't here to guide me. Scarlett can't give me any advice. I have to decide this one on my own. And my body is begging me to go with this stranger. I have no doubt he will know how to handle my body.

But I can't. I tried it once, and I ended up puking alone in a stranger's bathroom while my father was dying.

"I ca—"

His lips stop me from speaking as his tongue slips into my mouth in one motion. The kiss is long and slow. His tongue takes complete control as he explores my mouth. Owning my tongue with complete authority. When he breaks from the kiss, I'm panting, unable to catch my breath.

"Come with me. You need this."

I stare at him, still panting hard, while I try to decide if he is a serial killer or not. Based on that kiss though, I'm not sure if I care. I would die happy, kissing this man.

I grab my glass of wine and down the last few drops, hoping the liquid will calm my nerves. It does.

"At least let me take you to get another bottle of your favorite wine."

"It's not my favorite."

"Yes, it is."

I turn back to the bar, expecting him to order another glass of wine.

"They're all out."

"I doubt it." I try to flag down the bartender, but she won't stop for me. I sigh.

"Don't trust me?"

"No, I don't."

He flags her down. "Another round," he says without glancing at her breasts.

"I'm sorry, sir. We are all out of that wine. Can I recommend another one?"

"No, thank you, Clarissa."

My eyes grow wide at the mention of the bartender's name. Her name tag sits across the left side of her blouse just above her cleavage. So, he did check out her tits.

"Come split a bottle of wine with me."

"Maybe," I say. I can't help but smile. I need this. I need to have one night to sleep with whomever I want before I never get to choose again. I need to finish what I never got with my last attempt at a one night stand.

"I'll take that as a yes."

3

_____

KILLIAN'S HOTEL room is impressive. It's one of the most impressive hotel rooms I've been in, and I've been in a lot. It's large and spacious, and has more rooms than any hotel room should. It's also in the Felton Grand, one of my family's hotels. I didn't want to come here yet. Not so soon after my father passed away. Not when this is the place I would miss him the most. But I didn't want to tell Killian the truth when he brought me to this hotel, so I came.

I shake nervously on the couch as I watch him pour two glasses of wine. The nerves at least keep me from thinking about my father. He hands me my glass of wine, and he takes his and sits in a chair opposite to me. I hate that he is sitting there. I want him to sit next to me. I want him to kiss me. I want him to sleep with me, like he promised.

Instead, he sits, patiently watching me, as we both sip our wines.

"What do you do?" I ask, trying to distract my nerves.

"Do you really want to know? Or would you prefer, when I make you come, you don't know anything about me? That way, when this is over, you can go back to whatever you are running from without any attachment."

"How do you know I'm running from something? Maybe I'm just missing my father."

"You are."

I just nod. I don't know if he means, I'm running from something, missing my father, or both.

"What about you? What do you do?"

"I thought we weren't going to talk specifics."

"No. I'm not going to tell you about me. The more you know, the more it's likely that you will get attached."

God, why am I here when this man keeps insulting me? I frown. "I won't get attached."

"No?" He raises his eyebrows.

Killian's probably right. If I fall for him, it will only give me more of a reason to run from whomever my father and grandfather have chosen for me.

"Fine." I sigh. "But I don't want to tell you about me either."

If I don't get to know anything about this man, he doesn't get to know anything about me.

He nods and takes a slow sip of his drink.

"When are we going to..." my voice says shakily.

"Fuck?" he says, finishing my sentence.

Wine slips from my mouth at how easily the word rolled off his tongue. He probably says *fuck* daily. He probably fucks daily. *I'm never going to live up to the women he's had before.* I try to push that thought out of my head. *He chose me.* And he doesn't have to know how inexperienced I am.

"Come here," he says, motioning for me to come to him.

I place my glass on the coffee table and walk to him. When I reach him, he remains seated. So, I stand awkwardly in front of him. I fidget with my hands, not sure what he wants me to do.

Killian chuckles in a deep raspy voice, like he hasn't used his voice to laugh in a long time. His hand grabs my wrist, and he pulls me hard onto his lap.

He strokes my cheek. "Don't think, princess."

I try to listen to his words. I try not to think as his mouth kisses down my neck, leaving warm, wet tingles. I can't help the tears that begin welling in my eyes. Of all the terms of endearment he could have chosen to use, I can't believe he chose the one that reminds me of my father, the one nickname my father always used to call me.

When he sees my tears, he softly kisses them with his lips before licking up the salty liquid with his tongue.

"What's wrong, princess? We don't have to do this." He tucks my hair back behind my ear before his hand softly rubs my back. "I just thought you might need it."

"Why did you call me princess?"

He smiles weakly at me. "Because you are one."

"What do you mean?"

"You're beautiful." He softly kisses my hand. "You're intelligent." He kisses my other hand. "You're used to being taken care of." He softly kisses me on the cheek. "You're a little too sweet and naive." He kisses the other cheek. "Your clothes are simple yet expensive." His kiss brushes softly on my lips. "You should be worshipped." He runs a hand through my hair. "You're a princess in every sense of the word."

I smile at how intuitive he is. He's picked up a lot about me in the short amount of time we have been together.

"Okay."

"Okay?"

"Okay, you can call me princess."

He wipes my remaining tears on my cheeks. "It's going to be okay, princess."

I suck in a breath as he grabs the nape of my neck and kisses me hard on the lips. I moan as his tongue massages mine. His kisses are deep and intense. His kisses are full of purpose.

I hold on to his neck as he kisses me. I'm too unsure of what to do with my hands to do much else, even though my hands are desperate to rip off his suit jacket and buttoned-down shirt to see what lies beneath them.

Instead, he lifts me and carries me to a room with a lavish bed covered in throw pillows. I land softly among the pillows. I watch as he removes his jacket and carefully places it over the back of a chair in the corner of the room. He removes his tie before he unbuttons the top couple of buttons of his shirt.

I watch as he climbs over me, but his body doesn't touch mine. My heart pounds erratically in my chest as I stare up at the thick, muscle of a man above me. I squeeze my hands into fists to prevent myself from running my hands all over his body.

Killian squints his eyes at me before he takes my hand and presses it against his chest. "You can touch." He smirks at me.

He leans down and kisses me again, hard. It's so forceful he sucks all the air from my chest. His hand slides up my shirt, massaging the exposed skin of my stomach. His eyes occasionally open to study my reaction when he takes everything a step further, but he doesn't slow down or hesitate. The intensity of his stare is there every time he opens his eyes. I can't help but keep my eyes open, needing to take in every moment of this man.

I let my hand slip into the opening of his shirt to feel his hard chest, but I don't let myself explore beyond that. His hand mimics mine, except his moves with more confidence and surety. I gasp when his hand expertly finds my nipple beneath my shirt. He slowly rubs the peak between his thumb and finger.

"Don't think, princess. Just feel," he whispers into my ear.

This time, I do what he says. All I feel is the intensity building inside me. He releases my lips, and his tongue discovers my other nipple as he lifts my shirt up.

"Oh, wow," I moan when he flicks his tongue.

"You're beautiful, princess."

His words barely register. I can't focus on anything but the sensations on my breasts.

His hand slips down my pants, and my heart rate increases in anticipation. He takes my pants off in one fluid motion, and then I'm exposed. My shirt is lifted high above my breasts, and my pants now lie in a pile on the floor while Killian is still completely clothed. *Why the hell is he still clothed?*

When his mouth sinks lower until his tongue touches my clit, I

26

no longer care he is still clothed. All I care about is that he keeps doing that.

"Oh my god!" I moan louder than I probably should.

I feel his mouth curl into a smile, but his tongue never leaves my clit.

"God, don't ever stop whatever the hell you are doing." I breathe fast as he swirls his tongue faster and faster over my bud.

When he sticks two fingers inside me, I almost lose it.

"Killian!" I scream as he stretches me.

The sensation is beyond words. His fingers seem to fill me completely. I can't imagine how it will feel to have his cock pushed deep inside me.

His fingers move faster inside me as his tongue moves in rhythm with them.

"Come for me," he commands in between thrusts inside me.

"Oh, fuck," I moan as I come, just like he commanded.

His fingers slowly and reluctantly move out of me, but I can't move. I'm too exhausted.

I just came on a man's fingers while his mouth tasted my juices. That's a first. I've had sex before, sure, but no man has ever made me come before. Maybe that's why I never went to seek it out. If I knew orgasms could feel better than the ones I give myself with a vibrator, I would have sought out men who could give orgasms like Killian sooner. I wonder if he is as good at making a woman orgasm when he's thrusting deep inside her.

"Be right back, princess," he says. He gently kisses my lips. It's a stark contrast to the kisses he was giving me just moments earlier.

I exhale deeply for the first time in a long time as I sink into the bed. I close my eyes as I wait for him to come back. I don't bother with covering my naked body. Modeling has taught me not to be shy about my body, and I want more.

When Killian comes back, I'll be brave. I'll show him what I want. I want him to fuck me like I'm sure he has with countless women before. I want to feel slutty and dirty. I want to feel wild. For the first time in my life, I want to fuck a complete stranger.

4

I WAKE up suddenly as I'm thrown from another nightmare about my father's death. I try to wipe the tears streaming down my cheeks, but I can't move. I'm pinned to the hotel bed by a hot stranger's arm.

His arm feels nice, stretched across my body—that is, until I realize we are both naked. Completely naked. Not I'm-wearing-underwear-and-a-bra kind of naked. No, I'm utterly naked. He is, too. I know because his leg is draped over me, and his erection is pressed against my hip.

I lie in the bed, frozen, not sure what to do. I don't want to wake him, but I can't stay here in bed all day although it does feel good to be wrapped in a hot stranger's arms.

I know how this goes though. As soon as he wakes up, I'll awkwardly try to get dressed while he tries to find the best way to kick me out as fast as possible. I can't handle that—not today, not ever.

Maybe if I just slowly slip off the bed, I can get out, get dressed, and escape the hotel room before he even wakes up to avoid the tension bound to happen if he wakes up. Then, I can go back to my own bed and forget this ever happened. Except, after a night like last night, I don't know if I'll ever be able to forget. I've never orgasmed so hard in my life. My only regret is not actually having sex. I have no idea why Killian is naked.

I gently begin moving his arm off my chest, already feeling the cold the second his arm falls to the bed. I wince, afraid he is going to wake up, but he doesn't. I run my fingers harshly across my cheeks, flinging the tears from my face. Now, I just have to get out from beneath his muscular leg. I try to shimmy off the bed, but I can't. His leg is holding me in place. I try lifting—

"What are you doing, princess?"

I glance over at Killian. His eyes are still shut, and his five o'clock shadow has grown slightly overnight.

"Um..." I swallow hard. "I need to pee, and I have a meeting in five hours I need to get to."

Killian leans over and softly kisses me on the lips. "I'll order breakfast then."

He moves off of me and gets out of bed. I watch his bare ass as he walks to his suitcase. He pulls out a pair of jeans and slips them on without putting underwear on first. I curiously look at this man. His body is even better than I imagined, his muscles are sculpted into thick strands of hard steel along his back down to his cute butt I want to squeeze. I just wish I could have seen the front of his body.

He leaves me alone in the bed.

Weird. My experience after my almost one-night stand is that the guy wants you out fast. If not that, then I would assume he would be looking for sex. But Killian did neither of those things. *Maybe he doesn't find me attractive?*

I shake my head. *It doesn't matter what he thinks. Today will be the last day I ever see him,* but it still stings. It hurts that he doesn't even want to have sex with me.

I get dressed quickly, but linger in the bedroom because I'm embarrassed. He has seen me naked and done untold things to my body while I barely even touched his.

Maybe he wanted a blow job, and I didn't even offer?

Maybe he has a girlfriend?

Maybe he was drunker than I thought and has a hangover?

Maybe he's into guys?

When I hear the door to the hotel room open and shut, followed closely by the smell of bacon, I can't hide out in the bedroom any longer. My stomach rumbles loudly as I open the door.

Killian, still shirtless, is pouring coffee at the small table in the dining room. He stops and looks at me as I enter the room. He doesn't smile. He doesn't have to. His eyes say everything—that he's attracted to me, that he wishes I were naked again and back in bed—but something is holding him back from doing what he really wants. I wish I knew what that was.

I let my eyes drop to his body as I make my way over to the table that is large for a hotel room, even for a suite. From the looks of his muscles, it's obvious he works out but not in the obsessed-with-the-gym sort of way, simply in the I-care-about-my-body-and-want-to-be-healthy-and-look-good sort of way.

My mouth is gaping, I realize, as I stare at his body. "I, uh...your body...you look good," I say, trying to make up for why I'm gawking awkwardly at him.

He chuckles at my broken words. I quickly bite my lip to keep it from falling open again and saying anything more embarrassing.

"I didn't know what you would want for breakfast, so I ordered two options. There is a healthy option or an I-want-to-die-happy option."

I take a seat opposite him and grab the plate with the pancake, eggs, and bacon before I change my mind. His eyes grow wide, but he doesn't say anything.

I smile. "It wasn't what you thought I would choose?" I slightly raise my eyebrows, waiting for him to respond.

Killian frowns, shaking his head. "No."

That's when I look at the plate in front of him. A majority of the plate is fruit and vegetables along with an egg white omelet. He's not drinking coffee, only water. He's a health nut. Maybe I shouldn't have shown my true colors in front of him, but I don't really care. After breakfast, I will never see this man again.

"How are you feeling this morning?"

I bite into my pancake, the food immediately settling my stomach.

"Hungry," I say.

I dig more into my meal so I don't have to talk. I don't know what you are supposed to say when having breakfast with a man you almost had sex with. And he doesn't seem like a huge talker anyway. So, maybe he will enjoy the silence.

"When did your father die?"

I was wrong. He's a talker. I stare awkwardly up at this stranger, not sure I want to confide in him. *But I need to confide in someone, so why not him?* He's already told me he doesn't want me to get attached, so he's not looking for anything beyond whatever happens this morning.

"He died four days ago." I don't look at him. I just shovel more food into my mouth.

"That's what I thought," he says, his voice sounds sad, withdrawn. "Were you close?"

"Yes, he was the only person in my family who even remotely understood me."

"I'm sorry," he says after a long pause.

I give him a weak smile as I glance up from my food. He seems genuine. I nod, but words like that never make me feel any better, no matter how genuine they are.

A few seconds pass as we both make huge dents in our breakfast plates. Neither of us speak. I barely even breathe.

"I've never lost anyone like that. I can't imagine the pain you are going through..."

"It's not something I ever thought I would go through. And I'm not sure how I'm going to get through it right now. The pain is unbearable. I know I have to find a way...for him."

He nods and waits for me to say more, but I don't.

"His death is what you're running from," he says.

I stare off into the distance. *Is that what I'm running from? His death?* I think for a moment. *No, it's not his death I'm running from. It's my future.*

"No," I say firmly. "I'm running from family obligations that have been sped up now that he's gone."

His mouth turns upward into a slight smile. I have no idea why my statement would make a man who hardly ever smiles, smile.

"Now, that's something I can understand."

I run my hands through my hair, trying to read into that sentence's meaning. *What family obligations could a man almost in his thirties have?* He can't still be following his parents' orders, like I am. That could only mean one thing...

"Oh my God! You're married, aren't you? You probably have four or five kids at home you're responsible for." I push away from the table and begin searching the hotel room for my purse, but I don't see it. *Shit*, I silently curse. I'll have to leave and get a new ID and credit cards later. I don't care about the cash I will lose. It's not worth staying around to find out I was the other woman—even if it was only for one night.

"Whoa...slow down there, princess." He grabs my arm so I can't move. "I'm not married," he says slowly, like if he talks slower, it will somehow make his words more believable. "And I sure as hell don't have four or five kids."

He cocks his head to the side, like he thinks I'm crazy. Maybe I am. I swallow hard, watching his desire grow in his eyes as he looks at me.

"You're not married?" I ask hesitantly.

"No," he says, smirking at me.

"You don't have kids?"

"No."

I stare at his lips until they move so close to mine that I can barely breathe. His hands move up to tuck my blond hair behind my ear. I shiver at his touch. He doesn't kiss me though. He just hovers, obviously wanting more but denying himself what he wants for some reason.

I don't know what comes over me. I don't know if it's the fact that this man has already kissed me, and I already miss his lips. I don't know if it's the fact his desire for me is so obvious I can basically feel his heart beating fast beneath his chest because of me. I don't know if it's because today is the last day I get to choose who I can and can't kiss.

Whatever the reason, I kiss him. I grab his neck as I do, so he can't pull away. My kiss is defiant and carnal. It's wet and deep and everything a kiss should be—except this time, when I kiss him, he barely kisses me back. *Maybe I'm doing it wrong?* But I know I'm not. I can feel his erection growing as it presses into my stomach. So, I don't stop.

It only takes a few seconds more until he is kissing me back with as much hunger as he was before. I smile against his lips as he does. Maybe we will be having sex after all.

Our kisses quicken as we both become more and more desperate for more, for unfulfilled promises from last night. We stumble backward until my body is trapped between him and a wall behind me. It feels nice to be possessed in such a way. When he lifts my body, I wrap my legs around his waist and moan because it's exactly what I wanted him to do.

I don't stop kissing him as he carries me back to the bedroom. I don't stop until he roughly throws me onto the bed.

I smile as he stares at me with those intense eyes that say so much when his mouth doesn't. I watch as they turn from lust-filled to empty. I run my tongue over my lip, trying to look sexy, but the moment has passed, and I have no idea why.

"You should go," he says.

My eyes widen, but I don't ask why. I'm not going to beg someone to sleep with me when he obviously doesn't want to.

"Okay, help me find my purse." I must look disappointed as I stand and gather myself from the bed.

"Don't. Don't think that. I want you. I'm desperate for you..." He looks down. "I just can't. I'm not going to be the guy you lose yourself in because you are running away. When I fuck you, it will be because you want me as much as I want you right now."

I laugh nervously. "I thought we were done after today."

He looks at me even more seriously, if that is possible. "No. Today is the beginning."

I try to smile, but I can't. This man is insane. No, he's bipolar. One minute, he can't keep his hands off of me, and the next, he's a knight in shining armor. I just wish I knew which was a facade and which was the real Killian.

I walk out of the bedroom and back into the living area. I hear Killian following me, but I don't turn to face him. I just walk.

"Here," he says, holding out my purse.

I take it from him. I see he is also holding my phone in his hands. He types something in before handing it to me as well.

"I put my number in your phone."

"What makes you think I want that?"

He cocks his head to the side as he stares at me. "You will. I have a feeling you will want it really soon."

God, this man is arrogant, but his confidence is alluring. I could use an ounce or two of his confidence, if only for a day. Maybe then I wouldn't be marrying a complete stranger in six months.

I walk to the door. He follows.

I open the door and stand in the doorway. "Thanks for the wine and—"

His lips crash with mine before I can say anything. He's promising more, I realize. With his tongue pushing further into my mouth, he's demanding I call him.

When we finally break away, my breathing is fast, much too fast. I touch my hands to my chest, trying to calm my breathing. I stare at him for a second longer before turning to leave without a word.

"Don't run anymore. You're stronger than you think."

I pause at his words, but I don't turn around. He doesn't follow me or say anything else.

He's left me his number to call. And I will. I'll call. He knows it as well as I do.

I walk into the elevator alone. I touch my fingers to my lips still tingling from his kiss, a kiss I want more of. Maybe he's the answer. He's smart, probably a businessman. He's older and responsible.

There's not a tattoo or piercing on his body—at least not one I noticed.

What if I found someone capable of running the company on my own? What if I found my own love? Then, I could marry who I wanted while still making sure the company would be in good hands.

I have to find a way to convince Granddad. I need to find a way to buy myself some time. And introducing Granddad to Killian might be the way. I could show him I am capable of dating strong, intelligent men.

Killian might not be the best choice, but right now, he's my only choice. Maybe he's the right choice.

5

I step foot back inside the Felton Grand. Even though I was just in the hotel earlier when I was with Killian, this is the first time since my father's death I've really let myself take in the casino. Last night I let Killian rush me to his room as fast as possible. Now, I'm walking slowly, taking in everything.

I notice the gentle calming sound of the expansive fountain at the entrance to the hotel. I see the light twinkling off the water from the large crystal chandelier overhead.

I walk through the long hallways filled with shops and restaurants. The hallways are calm. It's early, and only a few people have woken up to enjoy breakfast at one of the many restaurants. I smile as I look up and see the details of the arched ceiling overhead. When I was a kid, I used to lie on a bench in the hallway and stare up at this beautiful ceiling.

I walk to the casino floor. I take a deep breath. I feel my father all around as I walk past the flashing lights of the slot machines. This is where my father spent most of his time—here on the floor of the casino, mingling with guests and making sure everything was running smoothly.

I walk off the casino floor to a door that says *Employees Only*. I flash my card on a sensor and watch as the light changes from red to green before I open the door. I enter and take the stairs up to the second floor.

I take a right and head down to my father's office at the end of the long hallway. I take the key out of my pocket and unlock the door. I push it open, and the smell immediately overwhelms me. It smells like expensive cologne and cigars. It smells like my father.

I miss you, I think as I walk in and close the door behind me.

Tears fall fast as I make my way over to my favorite couch on one side of my father's office. I let them. I cry. I let everything out. I let go of the pain. I let go of the guilt. I let go of all of it. It all comes out.

When the final bits of pain and guilt have washed away, all I'm left with is anxiety over speaking to Granddad. I begin pacing back and forth in my father's large office while I wait for my grandfather to arrive.

I can do this. I can do this. I can do this.

I try to keep my eyes on the ground instead of looking at the numerous reminders of my father.

I don't have to look up to know a picture of Dad and me is sitting on his desk. I was five, riding on his shoulders. There's another of the whole family sitting beside it.

I don't have to look up to know the most comfortable couch on the planet is leaning against the far wall. I have fallen asleep on it countless times while reading a book, waiting for Dad to take me out to dinner.

I don't have to look up to know a considerable stack of every magazine I modeled in is piled in the corner.

I don't have to look up to know a picture of my first modeling job when I was twelve is in a frame on the wall.

Instead, I try to rehearse what I'm going to say when my grandfather gets here. *Granddad, I love you and respect you, but I'm an adult. I can make my own decisions in the best interests of myself and this company. I've already found someone who I think would make a good candidate, and with time I know I can find the perfect man...*

I keep repeating the speech I practiced all night, but my mind quickly goes back to Killian. I bite my lip, remembering how his lips felt on mine, how he pulled every emotion out of me. I tuck my hair behind my ear, recalling how his touch against my neck sent shivers all over my body. My heart speeds up as I think about how I had the most explosive orgasm of my life with his tongue buried inside me.

I try to stop thinking about Killian, but I can't. I haven't called him yet. It's only been a few hours since I saw him, but I have a feeling I'll be looking for something comforting after this meeting, and I will need someone to talk to. No, I'll need someone to help me forget. I'll text him this afternoon. It won't hurt to ask if he is free.

"You're on time," Granddad says as he walks into the office.

"Yes," I say as I stop pacing. I immediately forget about Killian. I know my face is flushed, so without having to look up, I walk to the corner of the room where there is a container of water. I take one of the white plastic cups and fill it with water before walking slowly to a chair in front of the desk.

I slowly sip my water, trying to drain my face of its overly pink color, while stalling from giving my speech. *I'll wait just a few minutes longer—no need to rush the speech and get it wrong.*

"He should be here soon," Granddad says, staring at his watch, as he sits behind the desk my father used to.

I don't think I could ever sit there. That's Dad's chair, not his.

"Last time I spoke with him, he was just wrapping up a meeting."

I nod and drink my water faster. I don't have much time then.

"Granddad, I've been thinking. I, uh...?" I start talking, but I have no idea what I'm saying. "I, um...I don't think marrying whoever is going to walk through that door is the best idea. I think...I think I should have a say in who I marry." I make the mistake of looking up to see Granddad frowning at me with his eyes raised, but it doesn't stop my mouth from spilling every dumb thought on my brain. "I think I've already found someone whom I could fall for. He's smart and handsome, and I think you will like him. He's a businessman. And he's a great kisser." *Damn it, why did I say that?*

"Hush, girl," he says.

But I don't hush. I keep talking. "And I don't think I even want to get married anytime soon. I want to find more men to kiss. I'm young, much too young to get married this year. I need to live a little first. And if I'm honest, I think I could run the company by myself without a husband by my side. I think that's what Dad would have wanted."

"Hush," he says more sternly this time.

I stop, mainly because I can't believe the words that just came out of my mouth. *What the hell has come over me? I don't want to run the company myself, do I?*

I grab my cup of water sitting on the edge of the desk with shaky hands. I take a long sip, waiting for the lecture.

But it never comes.

I hear a deep voice clear his throat from behind me. I don't have to look up to know the man I'm supposed to marry is standing in the doorway. I just hope he wasn't standing there long enough to hear that embarrassing speech.

"Come on in, son," Granddad says, standing from the desk with a massive smile on his face.

I'm screwed. He just called this man son. He's probably more in love with this guy than he is with me. And after my epic speech, I have no doubt I'll be marrying the man behind me.

"I would like to introduce you to my granddaughter, Kinsley," he says, as he walks toward the man behind me.

I take one last sip of water before I plaster on the biggest fake smile I can manage while I turn to meet my future husband. I wonder if he knows. *Has he already been told to get complete control of the company, he is going to have to marry me? Or is he blissfully ignorant to that fact?*

I bring my eyes up to face my future husband. The man standing in front of me isn't my future husband. He isn't a complete stranger. It's Killian.

I choke. That's what stupid thing I do in response to seeing the man who had his tongue down my throat only hours earlier. I cough and choke on the remnants of the water still clinging to my throat. That's what I do while I watch my grandfather place his hand on the shoulder of the man who just gave me my first orgasm that wasn't given by a vibrator.

"Are you okay?" Killian asks.

I nod as I choke again. I grab my throat, trying to get it to stop. It doesn't, not until I get three more coughs in, causing my cheeks to turn an even brighter shade of pink.

When I finally lift my eyes back up, I see two pairs of eyes intently staring at me. One pair looks at me with concern, the other looks at me with shame.

I try to recompose myself by bringing back the smile I wore moments earlier.

"Let's try that again," Granddad says. "I would like to introduce you to my beautiful granddaughter, Kinsley Felton."

"Kinsley, this is Killian Browne."

Killian steps forward and extends his hand to me. I slowly place mine in his, already anticipating how his firm handshake is going to start tiny fireworks inside me. It does the second his hand touches mine.

"Pleasure to meet you, Ms. Felton."

I narrow my eyes but nod anyway. He's not going to let on we have already met. I'm grateful.

I notice Granddad smiling brightly behind him at our encounter.

"Please take a seat. We have lots to talk about," Granddad says as he retakes the seat behind the desk.

I walk back to my chair, aware of Killian's eyes taking in all of me from my high heels to my knee-length high-waist pencil skirt to my magenta top.

I sit down and glance at him sitting in the chair next to me.

Killian looks much the same as he did last night. He's in a nicely fitted suit with a blue tie. His hair is gelled slightly to keep it spiked to the side. The only difference is his five o'clock shadow is gone.

I look back to myself. I look entirely different from the last time he saw me. I'm no longer wearing casual attire. Makeup covers every flaw I showed him before. My long, hair is perfectly curled into flowing locks free of the frizz from our night together.

Does Killian know why he's here—to marry me? Is that what he was referencing this morning when he talked about family obligations? Is he being forced to marry by his family? Did he know when he saw me at that table last night I was whom he was going to marry?

No, there's no way. He would have said something. He wouldn't have led me on like that.

"You both know why you're here, so let's get started on some of the details."

I nod and see Killian nodding stoically next to me. *So, he does know he's here to marry me?*

"My son and I thought you two would make a perfect match. Kinsley is about to graduate from Yale. She's an experienced model. She's beautiful."

Killian nods, but he doesn't say anything as Granddad tries to sell me to him.

Granddad turns to face me now. "Killian has been working for the company for five years. He graduated from Harvard. He is our current VP of Casino Operations. He's intelligent, ambitious, confident, focused, decisive, and professional."

I nod at my grandfather, disappointed he's listed several positive personality traits of Killian's, while I only got beautiful. That's all I am to these men.

I watch as he digs in the desk drawer before pulling out a stack of papers. He hands one stack to me and one to Killian.

"These are the terms of Robert's will. It includes everything the two of you need to do to inherit his shares of the company. There is also a copy of my will and what you will need to do to get my shares as well. It includes what we expect before we'll make you CEO, Killian," he says, staring at Killian now.

Killian nods.

"Both of you need to read it over in the next couple of days, so you understand everything." He focuses his attention on Killian, like he is the only one who gets a say in any of this. "You have one month to decide. That's all I can give you. I'll need an answer then."

"Of course," Killian says. He glances down at his watch. "I'm sorry to cut this meeting short, but I have another meeting I need to get to."

Granddad stands, smiling. "Don't worry, Killian. I'm having Tony cover the meeting today. Instead, I have a reservation for you two at a restaurant downstairs."

"Sir, I'm not sure Tony is the best man for the job. He's not up-to-date yet on the new systems."

"I agree, but this"—Granddad points to me and then back to Killian—"is a more pressing issue at the moment."

Killian glares at my grandfather but doesn't argue again.

He turns to me. "Would you like to have lunch with me?"

"Yes." My answer isn't forced. I want to have lunch with Killian.

I have a lot of questions for him. *Why the hell did he agree to marry a complete stranger? Did he know who I was when he stared at me from across the blackjack table? Did he know when he got me into his bed and fucked me with his tongue? I'm afraid Killian's answer to all those questions will be a resounding yes.*

6

I STARE DOWN at the menu. I haven't said a word since we left my father's office. Killian hasn't either. I think he's giving me time to process everything. I try to look at the menu to at least make up my mind on what I'm going to eat. Then, I can focus on what just happened.

"What can I get you?" the bubbly waitress asks.

"Um..." I say. I take a deep breath, trying to decide what wine I want. I want wine—no, I *need* wine to get through this, but I have no idea about wines. I eye a delicious-looking cheeseburger as a waitress passes by with it before placing it on the table next to us. A cheeseburger sounds good. Or maybe I should eat something a little lighter and healthier. Or maybe I'll have the pizza. That's what my father and I would always share when we came here.

"We will both have a glass of Chateau Margaux Bordeaux '61, if you have it. If not, then '82. We will have the vegetables and hummus appetizer. And we will both have the salmon with asparagus."

I glare at Killian as the waitress takes our menus away.

"What was that?"

"What?" he asks innocently.

ELLA MILES

"Why did you order for me? And why did you order the salmon? I'm not a health nut like you. I wanted the burger." *Yes, definitely the burger. Or the pizza.*

"Health nut, huh?" He casually leans back in his chair. "I didn't want to give you too much to think about right now. I knew you liked the wine, and after the breakfast you had, you need some vegetables and healthy protein to keep you going today."

I shake my head. "You have no idea what I need."

The waitress quickly brings the wine, and I'm at least thankful he ordered my favorite wine.

"I'll have the cheeseburger and fries, actually." The waitress gives me a disapproving nod before leaving.

I sigh as I sip my wine and try to process what just happened, so I'll know where to start with my questioning. My brain immediately goes to the moment in my father's office. I literally choked. *God, that was so embarrassing.*

What was surprising was *Killian's* reaction. When he saw me, he didn't seem the least bit surprised. Not even the best actor in the world would have been able to hide some sort of reaction of surprise when he saw me. I've studied enough actors' reactions to know a truthful one from a fake one. His was truthful.

I deepen my glare. "You already knew who I was. Last night, when you saw me at that blackjack table, you already knew who I was."

"Yes," he says.

"Why would you do that? Why would you lead me on like that when you already knew? You lied to me! You made me believe I could find someone on my own. Instead, you were prearranged. Did my grandfather put you up to it? Did he want you to seduce me before we met? Did you two think I would be happy then, if I already liked you when I found out it was you?"

My face flushes bright red again, but this time, it's mostly out of anger and only a little bit from embarrassment. Everyone knew, except for me.

46

"I didn't initially go to the casino seeking you out last night. I went there for the same reason as you, I'm guessing. I was mourning a man I deeply cared about, and I thought gambling like I used to with him would be the best way to honor that man."

"Wait, my father went gambling with you?"

"Yes. I worked very closely with your father over the last five years. He was a great mentor to me. When we flew to different cities for meetings, we would gamble at various casinos. It was the best way to learn from the competition. Robert was a great man. I miss him."

"Don't," I say, my voice trembling. "Don't. You don't get to miss him. You don't get to mourn him like I do. He's not your father."

The guilt immediately comes back. This man spent time with my father when I didn't. I should have been there for him when he died. I should have gone to college closer to home so I could have spent more time with him. Instead, I was happy to get as far away as possible when my family suggested Yale.

"Oh, princess, I could never miss him like you do, but I still miss him."

I freeze when he says the nickname he has adapted for me... except he didn't come up with my name. My father did.

"You got it from him."

His eyes narrow in response, but he has no clue what I'm talking about.

"You got the princess nickname from my father. That's all he ever called me. I'm sure if you hung out so much together, you heard him talk about me in that manner. Don't call me princess—ever again."

He looks sad when I say that, but I can't deal with this. I can't deal with the fact that he got to spend so much time with my father in his final years while I was away at school and got so little time. My life isn't fair.

I feel the tears welling in my eyes, but I don't let them out. Killian doesn't deserve any of my tears. He doesn't deserve to see me mourn a man who was mine, not his.

The waitress places our appetizer in front of us. It looks disgusting. A mush of stuff sits in the middle with raw carrots, cucumbers, and celeries lining the outside. I don't touch it. Instead, I lift the wine glass back to my lips.

I have so many questions. I don't even know where to start. So, I sit and watch as Killian fills a plate with hummus and vegetables. Then, to my surprise, he places the plate in front of me before filling another one.

"Eat," he says.

My stomach grumbles, so I do, but it's not because he tells me to. I try the carrot in the mush. It's not half bad, I realize, as I crunch on the vegetable, but I'm not going to let him know that.

"Ask me," he says before taking a bite of his food.

"What?"

"Ask me everything."

"When did you find out?" I ask hesitantly.

"When did I find out that your father wanted me to marry you before he would make me CEO?"

I nod, unable to say any words.

"Three years ago. It was when he promoted me to VP."

My eyes are wide. He's known for three years that he's going to marry me. He could have come up to me at any point in those three years and told me. He could have at least introduced himself to me. He could have done anything, but he didn't.

"Why didn't you tell me?"

He runs his hand through his hair, slightly messing it up, but somehow, it looks even better. "I wanted to. I learned a lot about you from your father. I stalked you on social media. I quickly realized your father was right. You weren't ready to meet me. You were too young and naive to meet whom you were supposed to marry. You're still too young."

"I am not!" I protest.

He smiles a smug smile. "Yes, you are."

"Then, why did you agree to marry me if I'm so young and naive?"

"I haven't yet."

My eyes grow wide at his response.

"What do you mean, you haven't yet? I thought..."

"I told your father I would think about it, but I've never really had any intention of marrying anybody—ever. I'm perfectly content as I am."

"Then, why are you here? If you are not going to marry me, why are you here?"

He looks smugly past me as he contemplates his answer. "Because I want to be CEO. I've earned it. And I'll marry you, if I have to, to get it, but I think there is another way, a better way."

His words sting. It stings a lot to hear him say he doesn't want to marry me even though I don't want to marry him either.

"What was last night then? Why did you almost sleep with me if you didn't want to marry me?"

He cocks his head and smirks at me. "I can fuck a woman without marrying her. And, if I recall, we never got around to the fucking."

I wince every time he says the word *fuck*. I'm not used to men using language like that around me. Although it usually sounds sexy when falling from his lips, right now, it feels like a punch to the gut.

"Why were you at the casino last night?" I barely whisper.

"As I said earlier, I didn't go into that casino seeking you out. I saw you at that table, and I thought it would be fun to mess with you. After watching you for a while, I found you were almost a complete contradiction from everything I had known about you. You seemed confident at that table, sure of yourself. You didn't seem like the naive young girl I'd thought you were."

"And now?"

He sighs. "I still think you are a naive young princess."

I glare at him when he says the last word. "You're wrong."

The waitress interrupts us, bringing us plates of salmon with asparagus and my cheeseburger. I dig in. Otherwise, I might do something stupid, like climb over the table and ring Killian's neck.

"I know you went to Yale to study theater. Who does that? You don't go to Yale to study theater. You go to Yale to study business or economics or finance—something useful."

He pauses to take a bite while I continue shoving my own food in my mouth, trying my best to remain calm and poised, like I've been taught to do.

"I know you modeled for *Seventeen* magazine along with a slew of other teenage magazines. You're beautiful; it comes easily to you."

I take another bite. I feel the tears welling again, but I hold them back. *Do not cry.*

"I know you haven't been on a date in three years. That's why you needed a release last night. I know you have never made one goddamn decision by yourself. You want to know how I know that? You texted your father every five fucking minutes, asking him for advice."

A tear falls, just one single tear. I hate him. I loved my father and would do anything for him. Even marrying this asshole in front of me if my father thought it was for the best. And Killian is using my love for my father to hurt me.

"I know because you are the reason this has gotten this far. If you had stood up to your father before he died, you wouldn't be getting forced into a marriage you didn't want. And don't tell me you want this. I know what you were running from last night. It's *this*. You were running away from being forced into an arranged marriage."

I wipe the tear from my eye. "Stop!" I say a little too loudly. I notice the stares from the table closest to us, and I try to adjust my voice to not bring any more attention to us.

"Well, you were running, too. I don't have to have studied everything about you for three years to know everything I need to know about you. You're an arrogant, bossy ass. Everything in your life revolves around work. You don't date because you don't have time. You find any attractive woman you can at bars to pick up and take home for one night. And, worst of all, you must not be that good at your job if the only way you can get the CEO position you are so desperate for, is to marry the previous CEO's daughter. The only reason they chose you and not someone more qualified is because you are the only man in an executive position who's anywhere near my age," I say, having no idea where those words came from. I've never been this outspoken in my entire life.

I stare at my now empty plate I didn't even realize I had been eating.

"Feel better now?" he asks calmly.

He stares at me, completely unaffected by my words, which makes me even angrier.

"Yes," I spout.

He eyes my empty plate as my stomach rumbles again. "You should have stuck with the salmon, and then you wouldn't still feel hungry."

"I'm not hungry," I say, acting like a defiant child as my stomach growls again feeling bloated and hungry. *God, no wonder he thinks I'm like a child. I act like one.*

His bottom lip twitches in a smile.

"So, what do we do now? What's your fabulous plan?"

"My plan is for Lee to realize how valuable I am to the company —so valuable he will want me to be CEO whether or not I marry his granddaughter. I already had Robert convinced. I can convince your grandfather, too."

"That's not going to work. They want the company to stay in the family."

"That's where you come in. You need to tell him that you are so devastated by your father's death you don't want anything to do with the company. You don't want it. You'll marry someone else who your grandfather wants when you are older but not now. And, no matter what, you want nothing to do with the Felton Corporation. All you want is what you already have—plenty of money to live by."

I stand up and throw my napkin on the table before I storm off. I'm so tired of listening to what other people tell me I should be doing. Killian doesn't say a word, and he doesn't stop me from leaving the table.

I wander down the hallways of the largest casino and hotel in the Felton empire. It's the original one, the one that started it all. This one isn't my favorite though. My favorite, Crystal Waterfalls, is farther down on the strip. It has a river and a waterfall flowing through it. But Felton Grand has its charms, too. It's flashy and brings the hustle and bustle of the city inside.

It could work. I know it could. I'm already devastated. I could convince Granddad I'd lose my mind if I had to step foot inside one of the casinos again. *But is that what I want? Is that what my father would have wanted for me? Did he really tell Killian he wanted him to run the company without marrying me? Don't I want at least some small part of the company for myself?*

I try to think about what I want, but all I come up with is what I don't want. I don't want to marry Killian. At least, I don't want to be forced into marrying him, especially now I know he doesn't want to marry me either.

I don't know what *I* want. So, instead, I try to think about what my father would have wanted. *Did he ever give any indication he didn't want me to marry Killian? Did he ever give me any clue of what he did want me to do?*

One memory pushes into my head. The memory used to seem so unimportant, but maybe it means more than I know.

"What does my princess want to be when she grows up?"

I think for a minute as I put another block on top of the one my father placed. "A princess!" I shout.

He laughs. "Of course! You already are a princess. And when you're old enough, I'll make sure you have a castle and a whole empire to run, if you want it. But what else do you want to be?"

My five-year-old self thinks harder this time. What else do I want to be, other than a princess? "I know! I want to be a CEOOOO, like you, Daddy!"

He smiles and thinks seriously for a second. "If that's what you want someday, it's yours. You can be anything you want, no matter what Granddad or I tell you."

"Yay! I'm going to be a CEEEAAA, like you!" I squeal.

"Shh," he says. "You have to keep it a secret though."

I pretend to lock my mouth with a fake key, like I do whenever anybody else tells me a secret. My father laughs again. He's always laughing at me, and I love to make him laugh.

52

"For now though, let's just say you want to be a princess."
"Princess Kinsley and King Daddy!"

I've never thought about that memory—until now. I don't even know if my father was serious when he said I could be CEO. And I never thought to ask. I never thought I wanted to run a company. I don't have the talent, the skills, or schooling. But maybe it's what I want—to follow in my father's footsteps. It's all I've ever wanted—to be just like him.

I make my way back to the table and find my plate has been taken away. In its place is a piece of chocolate cake and ice cream. Confused, I look up at Killian.

He shrugs. "To make up for not letting you order your own food and for telling you what to do. I was wrong. I'm sorry. Don't all girls love chocolate?"

I smile. Killian does have some good qualities to him when he's not being a bossy, arrogant ass. I dig in and melt in my seat as the ice cream melts in my mouth. I forget about everything, except for how good this tastes in my mouth.

"So, you'll agree to the plan then?" Killian asks, seeming slightly nervous for the first time since I've met him.

I take one more bite. Chewing slowly, I savor every last drop in my mouth.

"Maybe," I say on autopilot.

He smiles, thinking he's won.

"I mean...no," I say, realizing my screw-up. "I don't think your plan will work."

"Then, what do you propose?"

I wince at the word *propose*. That's what will happen if I don't find a way out of this. If my plan fails, it will end with Killian proposing to me. It's not that I wouldn't want to look at a handsome man like Killian for all of eternity, but he doesn't want me in return.

"I propose you find a new company that will make you CEO because the current position is already taken."

"By whom?"

"Me."

He laughs, hard and uncontrollably. And then he laughs some more while I sit in my seat, frowning. When he finally stops, he seriously looks at me. "You can't be serious?"

"I am."

"You can't make a decision to save your life. You can't even choose what you want to eat in a timely manner. You have no skill set. You don't have a college degree. The only thing you have going for you is..."

"My beauty."

"No." His eyes meet mine. "I was going to say that you're family."

I shake my head. He's wrong about that one. Granddad doesn't care I'm part of the family. He already thinks I will make a terrible candidate for CEO even though the company has been passed down to members of the family for three generations now. He's only willing to pass it down to my husband. My beauty is the only thing I have going for me.

"Well, this should get interesting. But go ahead and try. This week is going to be amusing."

"I will." I stand from the table while digging into my purse to throw some cash on the table.

He grabs my arm again, keeping me from walking out. He pulls me close to him so he can speak into my ear, but this time, there is nothing sexy about the move. "And when you realize what a mistake you've made, call me, and then I can work out a real plan to save you from marrying an arrogant, bossy ass like me," he says, repeating the names I called him earlier. "Because trust me, princess, nobody wants that."

"I don't have..." That's when I remember I already have his phone number.

"Although you should probably change the name in your phone to arrogant, bossy ass. I kind of like that." He winks at me.

I pull away from his grasp and run out of the restaurant. He's right. I don't want to marry him, not now after the conversation we just had. I wouldn't marry him if he were my only choice.

I don't know what to choose. One, marry Killian and be everything my family has always wanted. Two, refuse and be shamed by my family forever. Or, three, convince my grandfather I can run the company—just like my father, just like my grandfather, and just like my great-grandfather. I'm not sure. The only option I'm convinced I don't want is number one. I don't want to marry Killian.

7

"REALLY?" I ask into the phone.

"Yes. Your grades were high enough you could graduate without making up your final exams. Of course, if you would like to make them up, your last semester grades would improve."

"No. The grades can stay as they are." I release a sigh of relief.

"Okay then. We will mail you your degree. Congratulations, Ms. Felton."

I end the call as I hear the door open to my childhood bedroom. I turn and smile at Scarlett.

"Hey, bitch," Scarlett says as she makes herself at home on my bed.

"Hey," I say, shaking my head at her words. "Are you all moved in?"

Scarlett sighs. "No. The movers are impossible. They have been at my new house all day, and they've only moved in half of my stuff. They said it would take them another day to finish. So, I'm stuck at my parents' house for another night."

"I don't know how you'll survive," I say sarcastically.

"You really have no idea how bad it is. All I hear about is how I don't have any jobs lined up. I don't have a serious boyfriend. What am I going to do with my life?" She sighs again. "It's exhausting. I don't know how you can stand to stay here with your mother and grandfather. Why don't you find a house or at least an apartment to move into?"

I glance at Scarlett, who is now flipping through the papers Granddad gave me. I walk over and snatch them out of her hands.

"Those were boring anyway."

I shake my head. "I'll move out soon. I just haven't put much thought into where I want to live."

"So, how did it go, meeting the future Mr. Felton?"

I put the papers back on my desk. I spent all night reading every detail of my father's and my granddad's wills. I'm screwed. If I want any equity, any money, the only way is to marry Killian.

I bite my lip as I turn to face her. "Not well."

Scarlett sits up in my bed. "Why? Is he ugly? Or, no...is he, like, fifty years old or something? Does he have a disgusting mole on his face? Is he bald? Doesn't speak English? Fat? What?"

I pace my room, occasionally stopping to stare at Scarlett. "No."

"What is it?"

"Remember that guy I told you about? The one I met at the casino the other night?"

Scarlett crawls forward on my bed until she is lying on her stomach. "You mean, the mysterious, sexy man who gave you the only orgasm of your life?"

"Best, not only." I pace. "And, yes. It was him."

She scrunches her nose at me. "What?"

"The man I'm supposed to marry is Killian, the same man who gave me the orgasm the other night."

A sly smile spreads across her lips. "So, what's the problem?"

"He doesn't want to marry me."

"That's crazy. Everybody wants to marry you. Why doesn't he want to marry you?"

I grab my forehead that is pounding from her insane questioning.

"I say, fuck him!" she says after a few minutes.

"What?"

"Have sex with him. Once he gets a taste of Kinsley Felton, he will want more and more. He'll be begging you to marry him."

I chuckle. "I don't think that is going to happen. He thinks of me as a child."

"Ew. He does not, or he wouldn't have done what he did to you the other night."

"He was just messing with me."

"No, Kins, he wasn't. He was into you."

"Whatever, I don't want to marry him anyway."

"What? I thought you said he was sexy. I thought..."

"I don't want to marry him because maybe I want to be CEO. I don't want to have to marry someone else in order to have anything to do with the company. Or maybe I don't want anything to do with the company."

Silence. That's the answer I get.

"Scar?"

"Yeah?" she says hesitantly.

"Well?"

"I don't know, Kins. Running the company is a lot of responsibility. Are you sure you are up for that?"

"I don't know."

She laughs. "See? You can't even honestly answer a simple question. How do you expect to run a huge company where you are going to have to answer, like, a million questions a minute?" She pauses. "I don't know, Kins. But if I were you, I'd fuck the guy. That's what I would do. It's a lot more fun."

"Thanks, Scar. You're a real help," I say sarcastically.

"Kinsley!" my mother screams from downstairs.

"That's my cue to leave," Scarlett says.

I nod. "I'll tell you how it goes later."

Scarlett quickly hugs me. "I know you are still sad about your dad. And I know you don't want to deal with everything right now, but I'm always here for you if you need me."

I nod, and then she slips out of my room.

I grab my purse, so I can get out of here as soon as I deal with my mother. I take the stairs down two at a time and find my mother in the kitchen.

She's slumped over the bar. She's not crying, but she doesn't exactly look her best in my father's old robe. Her hair is matted on her head. She's a mess, but at least she left her room.

"Morning, Mom," I say as I open the pantry to find a granola bar.

"Where's the alcohol?"

I take a deep breath before answering, "What do you mean?"

"The alcohol we always keep in the bar. Where is it?"

I shrug. "I don't know, Mom. I think everybody drank it all after the funeral." That's not true. I know exactly where the alcohol is because I'm the one who took it.

It's been years since my mother relapsed. She's been sober for almost five years now. She cleaned up when I almost destroyed our family.

Dad dying must have pushed her back to the alcohol. I don't blame her. We all miss Dad. And we all deal with losing him in different ways. I just can't handle the way she has chosen to deal with his death.

I glance at my phone. Her old therapist and AA sponsor should be here soon to help her since I can't. I know from experience. I don't have the patience to help her.

"I need the alcohol, damn it!"

I calmly walk over to my mother. "I'll make sure to have someone pick you up some alcohol on their way in today. But, right now, I think you need to eat. Can I make you something?"

She grabs the closest vase of flowers and slams it to the floor. I jump at the sound of the glass breaking on the floor. I don't react to her tantrum. Even though I've wanted to do the same thing to the stupid vases of flowers, I can't show her it's okay.

"Hi, Mrs. Felton. Let me make you some breakfast," Samantha, one of our cooks, says as she enters the kitchen, seeing the mess.

I go over and clean up the glass while Samantha has my mother's attention.

When I'm finished, I whisper to Samantha, "Just keep an eye on her until Dennis and Kirsten get her. Half hour, max."

She nods and smiles before going back to cooking my mother some pancakes. I walk out of the kitchen to the front door. I need to move out of here. I don't know how much more of this I can handle.

"Where are you going?" Granddad asks as I try to leave.

"To the Felton Grand."

He curiously looks at me even though it's not that strange for me to go to the casino. I used to go all the time before I went off to college. It should be understandable I would want to mourn my father there.

"I'm sorry," he says as he looks at me. For the first time since the funeral, I see tears in his eyes. "I'm sorry for blaming you. It's not your fault. I need you to know that."

I walk over and hug him. I know he needs me to forgive him for blaming me just as much as I need to stop blaming myself for my father's death. But I'm not sure I can do either of those things yet. I'm not ready to forgive.

"I miss him," is what I say instead.

"Me, too, sweetie. Me, too." He gently rubs my back, like a grandfather should. "Do you want some company?"

"No, I just want to spend some time by myself," I lie.

I try not to look him in the eyes, so he won't know I'm lying, but somehow, he does. Everyone can always tell when I'm lying. It's one of the reasons I would make a terrible actress.

I don't want him to come with me though. I need some time to interact with everyone at the casino, to begin to form real relationships with them, to begin to understand how the business runs. That way, when I tell him I want to run the company, I will have some ammunition to do it with.

Then, Granddad smiles, like he just realized something. I stare at him with a blank expression.

"Ah, you're going to see Killian. That's why you don't want me to come with you."

I blush at his words, bringing more truth to them in his eyes.

He smiles wider. "Have you fallen for that boy already?"

"No, Granddad. I just need some time to myself."

He nods knowingly. "Just let me know when he's wrapped around your finger so I can set the date."

"Granddad!"

He winks at me before heading into the kitchen to be with my mother. I sigh. But, at least, if he thinks I'm into Killian, he won't think anything of me spending time at the casino in the upcoming days, which will come in handy since I plan on spending lots of time there. It'll be enough time to make up my mind.

The only problem is, I haven't been able to get Killian out of my head. Anytime I'm not missing my dad; I'm lusting after Killian. I miss the taste of his lips. I miss his hands on my body. I miss his tongue on my clit. I miss screaming his name when I come. Most of all, I miss that I never got to feel him inside me. And, now, I'm never going to.

8

I'VE SPENT the last three hours sitting behind my father's desk, reading anything I can find that will catch me up on the direction of the company. The only problem is, I haven't learned much. Most of the files that would be of any importance are locked away in the file cabinet or on his computer, which is also locked.

There are a couple of reports showing decreasing sales in two casinos, but when I look at the numbers, it's easy to see the most important figures haven't been plotted. With just a few changes, the reports would show the casinos had been increasing in sales from month to month. At least, that's what makes sense to me, but maybe I'm missing something.

I sigh when I look through the last piece of paper that has anything to do with the company. I just wasted three hours and am no better off for it. I'm not sure I'm going to be able to do this, not unless I find the key to my father's filing cabinets or his password for his computer.

Granddad would know, but I can't ask him. I guess I'll just have to learn about the company elsewhere. I don't know how though. That's probably why I've been hiding out in my father's office for the last few hours.

I get up from the desk and poke my head into the hallway. It seems relatively empty for a Thursday. I'm surprised no one has come into my father's office all morning. It's probably because everyone is too sad to think of him as gone. I know everyone loved him. He was a great boss, a great friend, a great husband, and a great father. At least, that's what the minister said at his funeral. I choose to believe that.

I step into the hallway and start walking. I don't know where I'm going. I just go.

"Hi, Ms. Felton."

"Tony," I say before hugging the man who is practically a member of the family. He always seemed like a brother to my father.

"How are you doing?" he asks the token question.

"I'm holding up."

"You visiting your father's office?" He nods in the direction of the office.

I nod.

"I haven't built up the courage to go in there yet. When I do, I know I'll end up crying like a weepy old man."

I smile. "We can't have that."

"I should get back to work. I hope to see more of you around, Ms. Felton."

I smile and start walking again. "Wait," I say, turning around. "Do you mind if I hang out with you today? I want to be around people who knew my father. It feels like home here, not like at the house."

Tony looks at me with confusion. "Are you sure? It's going to be pretty boring. I have some phone conferences, and then I really need to get the numbers ready for the expansion Mr. Browne asked for."

I smile. Tony has already given me more information about the company than I found all morning.

"Yes, I'm sure." I take his arm and walk with him to his office. "And call me Kinsley, Tony. We are practically family."

———

Oh my God! This office is a mess. It looks like a tornado came in here and blew papers into disastrous piles all around the room.

Tony, on the other hand, walks into his office with no surprise on his face. He doesn't react like someone just came in here and ransacked his office. He actually seems to relax when he enters his office.

I walk over to his desk as Tony takes a seat behind it.

"I have to take a quick phone call, but make yourself at home. Then, I can show you some of the stuff your father and I were working on," he says.

I nod and do my best to smile as I glance around the smaller-size office, but I'm afraid it comes across as a frown or a horribly disgusted grimace. I cover my mouth with my hand, hoping he didn't see. He brightly smiles back at me. I guess he didn't.

He begins dialing his phone. I wait until I hear him chattering away at someone, paying me no attention, before I take a seat on the floor in front of piles of paper.

I feel bad for Tony. He's my father's age. He's worked for the company almost as long as my father, but he will never become CEO, never even be given a chance. Instead, he will always be just the Assistant to the VP of Operations. He's Killian's assistant, I realize, even though Killian has only worked for the company for five years, and Tony has worked for the company for thirty. To a company this big, it doesn't matter who is more loyal. It matters who is more likely to get results. And after I look around this office, I know why Tony will never reach a higher position. His office is a mess. There is no way he can be organized in a mess like this.

I still feel sorry for him though. Even though I know Tony gets paid generously to do this job, I still feel sad. I have a better chance of becoming CEO than Tony ever will.

And if I am CEO, I will have to make tough decisions, like promoting a less experienced, younger employee over a loyal and mature employee. That is probably an easy decision compared with the choices my dad made on a daily basis. I'm not sure I can do it.

I swallow hard and push the thoughts out of my head. I'm not here to think about if I can make the tough decisions required of the job right now. I'm here to learn as much as I can about the company and the job. Then, I can make decisions about my future.

I dig into the pile, trying to figure out what I'm looking at. There are hundreds and hundreds of more charts and graphs with the same incorrect information on them as the ones in my father's office. *Shit*. I hope my dad wasn't relying on them to make decisions about the company. I hope Killian isn't either.

I look at the name on them, trying to figure out who made the graphs and who wrote the reports, so I can tell Killian he needs to fire them. Then, I see it. It's Tony. He created these graphs. If anybody ever found out, he'd be fired. My dad was the only one who would care if Tony still worked for the company or not.

I sigh. Now, not only do I have to learn about the company, but I also have to find a way to make sure Tony gets better at making graphs, so he isn't out of a job.

I give up sorting the mess of papers when I hear Tony end the call. I stand and walk over to his desk with a smile on my face. He looks stressed as he shuffles papers around on his desk before switching on his computer.

"Mr. Browne and Mr. Felton wanted to expand this hotel and casino to allow for more high-roller rooms."

I nod as I walk over to stand behind him. "Makes sense. So, what's the problem?"

Tony sighs as his elbow knocks some papers off his desk. He watches them scatter onto the floor of his office, but he doesn't bother to pick them up. He turns to his computer instead. "The numbers don't support doing an expansion."

"Do you mind if I take a look at them?" I bat my eyes and smile as sweetly as possible at him.

"Be my guest," he says, getting up from his chair.

I take his seat, but I don't want him here when I change everything. I don't want him to know how badly he screwed up. I need to find a way to teach him. But that isn't right now. Right now, I need to fix this before he passes it along to Killian or anyone else who might fire him.

"Tony, do you mind getting me a coffee?" I ask. I yawn, bringing more credibility to my lie. *It isn't really a lie*, I reason with myself. I could use a coffee. I didn't sleep much last night, and I woke up earlier than I'm used to in order to have a full day here.

He smiles and nods. "I'll be right back."

As soon as he leaves, I turn my attention back to the screen. Everything is a mess. Everything is wrong. I pull up a new spreadsheet to start over because it's not worth fixing what he's already done.

I let my fingers fly over the keys as I type in every figure that I can find into the new data points. I love the rush I get as I enter in all the data. I love how it feels to use my brain for something other than deciding what my next pose should be. When I'm finally done, I press enter and watch the numbers turn from just numbers on the page into pretty graphs.

I lean back in the chair with a broad smile on my face as the graphs now represent a need for expansion of the casino and hotel. In less than twenty minutes, I just did what would take most people several hours to do.

"Here's your coffee," Tony says, entering the office with a coffee in each hand and sugar packets tucked under his arm.

I notice a small coffee stain on his shirt. *God, the man can't even get coffee without making a mess.*

"Thanks," I say.

I get out of the chair to allow Tony to have his seat back. I take one of the cups and add a sugar packet to it before drinking it. My eyes dart to Tony as I watch him stare at the screen.

"Holy shit!" Tony says. More coffee spills onto his lap from him being startled by the numbers on the screen. He covers his mouth when he realizes he swore in front of me. "I'm sorry, miss. I just...this is just...how did you do this?" Tony points to the screen.

"It's okay, Tony. I just rearranged one little thing. You did most of the work," I say.

"I need to get this to Mr. Browne right away." He hits print, and the paper begins shooting out of the printer next to the computer. He grabs the paper and moves quickly to the doorway. He pauses at the doorway and turns to me. "Come on, Ms. Felton. You need to take some of the credit with me."

I shake my head. "No, I didn't do anything that you wouldn't have been able to figure out on your own."

Tony shakes his head. "I've been working on this all week. I would never have reached this conclusion without you. Plus, you should meet Mr. Browne. Word is, he is in the running to take over your father's position."

I blush when he speaks about Killian. "We've already met."

A wicked smile forms on Tony's face as his eyebrows rise deliberately. "Ah, Mr. Browne is a very good-looking man."

I stare at Tony in disbelief. He did not just accuse me of being attracted to Killian. "I am not attracted to him," I say, answering a question that was never asked. "I'm just not a big fan of Killian. He's cocky and self-centered and..."

"You don't have to convince me of those things, Ms. Felton."

Great, now, we are back to Ms. Felton.

"I have worked for Mr. Browne for the past three years. He is all of those things, but he is also a good man. Give him a chance before you dismiss him."

I swallow hard and nod even though I don't agree with him. I don't want to give Killian a chance. I already did, and instead of being honest with me, he played with my emotions just because he could. A man like that doesn't deserve second chances.

I just don't know why all the men in my life keep pushing me to be with Killian. My father is pushing me, even in death. My grandfather is, and now Tony. *Don't they trust me to find my own man? To find someone better than Killian?*

Tony moves his head to the side, indicating for me to follow him, so I do.

I bite my lip as I watch Tony knock on Killian's door. *Please don't be here.*

"Come in," Killian shouts from inside.

Tony gives me a knowing smile before he pushes the door open and enters Killian's larger office. I enter slowly behind Tony, keeping my eyes down. Maybe Killian won't notice I'm here if I don't say anything and don't look at him.

"I have those numbers for you," Tony says.

"Thank you," Killian says. "I..." He pauses.

I know he's spotted me. I let my eyes drift up, and there he is, staring at me with the same intense eyes. He's wearing another dark suit, and another grim frown covers his face.

I try to move. I try to say something to make this less awkward. I can't though. It's like his eyes have captured me and glued me in place. I lose all my thoughts when I see him, except for how it felt to have his lips pressed against mine. I think about how it warmed me to see him smiling at me and no one else, something I realize he rarely does. I think about how it felt when his tongue finally touched me *there*, and I already feel desire forming deep in my belly from just thinking about it.

I blush. That's when I notice Killian's reactions change. It's just slightly. I notice, but it's not enough for Tony to notice. Killian's eyes turn from intense glaring to intense lust, and his lip curls up slightly into the tiniest of smiles at my reaction. *He knows*. He knows what dirty thoughts I'm thinking about, making me blush more.

Tony chuckles and shakes his head as he looks from me to Killian.

Killian glares at Tony. "What's so funny?"

"Nothing. Nothing's funny. I just think Robert is smiling down right now, seeing the two of you together."

"There is nothing going on," Killian and I both say in unison.

This makes Tony chuckle again. "Not yet." He winks at me. He takes a step closer to Killian. "Anyway, I have another call I need to get to. Have a look at the numbers. I think we finally have the data you need to present tomorrow to get the expansion you and Robert wanted."

I watch as Tony leaves, leaving me alone with Killian. I turn to go as well.

"Wait..." Killian says.

I don't know why, but I wait. When I turn back to him, his mouth has dropped open slightly as he stares at the papers in his hand.

"These numbers...they actually work," Killian says. He runs his hand through his hair. "How did he do it?" he asks himself. Forgetting I'm there, he begins typing on the computer again. "This is genius."

I smile. *Good for Tony.* I take another step, but the heel of my shoe clicks along the floor, bringing Killian's attention back to me.

Killian stands then and walks until he is blocking my exit. "How did he do this?" He holds up the papers.

I try to scrunch my face in a quizzical look, like I have no idea why Tony wouldn't be competent at his job. But again, I make a terrible actress, a terrible liar. I shrug and look down, avoiding Killian's eye contact.

His hand lifts my chin until I'm staring back at him as he furrows his eyebrows, searching my face for the answer.

"Who did this?" he says slowly while holding the papers up.

"Tony," I say quietly.

He shakes his head. "Tony sucks at numbers. He couldn't have done this, not even by accident." He moves his body closer to mine so that we are almost touching. "Who did this?"

"I don't know." My voice is shaky.

I don't know why he cares who did it. Killian moves closer, and I take a step back, unable to hold my ground any longer, but he grabs my elbow, holding me in place and keeping our bodies pressed together. I can feel his body breathing slow and easy against my chest, compared with my fast, quick breaths. I even think I feel his heart beating in his chest in a perfect, steady rhythm, unlike my now erratic heartbeat. He's not affected by my body, like I am by his. It disappoints me.

He raises his eyebrows at me. His lips graze mine, and I stop breathing.

"Who did this?"

I close my eyes. "Me."

I feel him suck in a breath. It wasn't what he had expected. When I finally open my eyes, he's gone. He's back at his desk, looking everything over again, like he must have missed a mistake. If I created this, it must be wrong.

"What are you doing?" I ask when I have caught my breath again.

"How did you know how to do this?"

I roll my eyes. I hate that he just answered my question with another question.

"It's not that hard. I just took the data Tony had and started over. When it was organized, it was obvious to see the trends over the last six months. But based on the numbers, you should add a thousand rooms to the expansion, not five hundred. It's a waste of money to do such a small expansion. You'll reach positive cash flow faster with one thousand. It's sustainable in the long-term, too, even without the holiday spikes. And one good holiday season would more than triple sales with the additional guests staying in the hotel. So, the casino expansion looks spot-on with the data."

Killian is frowning at me. I nervously run my hand through my hair as I bite my lip. I should have kept my mouth shut. He thinks I'm wrong. He thinks I'm an idiot.

"What was your major in college?"

I narrow my eyes. "You already know the answer to that."

He raises his eyebrows though, waiting for me to answer.

"Theater," I say.

He nods. "You didn't take any business classes on the side? You didn't minor in anything?"

"I minored in French, but I didn't take any business classes."

Killian cocks his head to the side, trying to decide if I'm lying. I'm not.

"What jobs have you done, other than modeling?"

I have no idea where he is going with this. "I've only ever modeled."

"I don't know how you did this." He shakes head before running his hand through his locks. "I spent all morning working on the numbers. I knew whatever Tony gave me would be useless."

I sigh. I wish I had known that before. I wouldn't have worked so hard to try to save his ass.

"But I never came up with these numbers. I never came up with anything half as good as this."

I smile.

"You're a walking contradiction, princess."

My face falls. "Don't call me that."

He stands and walks over to me. "I can't stop, princess. That's what you are. It feels weird to call you anything else."

I glare at him, but I'm not really angry, so I know it doesn't come across as the angry girl I want to be.

"I want you," he says when his body is close to me again.

I quizzically look up at him. "You want to marry me?"

He laughs. "No, I want to fuck you."

I stare at him, wide-eyed. I don't move as his lips come down on mine, showing me just how much he wants to fuck me. His hands find the nape of my neck, firmly holding me against him. I moan as his tongue sweeps between my lips, easily parting them. I feel his hard erection pushing against my belly.

Does he expect me to fuck him right here in his office?

Killian pulls away, but I don't open my eyes. I'm still lost in that kiss. When I open my eyes, I'll realize this is all a dream. He's just toying with my emotions again. He doesn't care about me. He might want to fuck me, but only so he can destroy me.

"You're not ready yet."

"Ready for what?"

"For me to fuck you. I told you, when I fuck you, it will be because you want me as much as I want you, not because you're running. You're not there yet, but you will be."

I shake my head. "You're wrong. What makes you think I will sleep with you? I don't even like you."

He smirks. "You're a terrible liar, princess. Plus, if you are talking to Tony about me, that's a good sign."

"Tony needs to mind his own business."

He turns away from me to walk back to his desk. "You need to stay out of the business. Go home to your comfy house and modeling career before you get hurt."

"What is that supposed to mean? I am capable of running this company, if that's what I decide I want. I just showed I could make decisions and run numbers. I just need a chance."

He sits in his chair and stares at me for several minutes. I don't know why I bother with trying to convince him that I can do this.

"Okay," he says.

"What?"

"Okay, if you think you can do this, then prove it. There is a meeting tomorrow afternoon to present the data and to give my recommendation for the expansion. You can present in my place. And if you convince everyone you are right; then I'll stop hounding you about giving up. I'll even help you get up to speed on everything with the company."

I suspiciously eye him. "And what if I don't?"

He smiles widely now. I'm afraid he's going to tell me I'll have to stop trying to be CEO, that I'll have to give up. I'm not sure I can.

"Then, you go on a date with me."

I relax. I can handle that. "Deal."

"Good, I'll send you my notes for the meeting."

"Thanks," I say before turning to leave. But before I do, I have one more question for him, one that's been gnawing at me. "Why haven't you fired Tony yet?"

He looks up at me, like I'm crazy.

"We both know he is terrible at his job. So, why haven't you fired him?"

"Because I respect his loyalty. That man would take a bullet for this company. I know I'm going to have to work harder to do things, like create graphs he should be doing, but that's okay. He cares, and he is a hard worker. He would never jump ship to a competitor's company. We need more people like him around here."

His words shock me. I thought Killian was ruthless. I thought he would have fired Tony the second my father died since the decision was now up to him. I was wrong. It makes me wonder what else I'm wrong about when it comes to Killian. Too bad I don't have time to find out.

I need to spend the next twenty-four hours doing everything to prepare for tomorrow. I need to impress the other executives. I need to prove to my grandfather I can do this. I need to prove to myself this is what I want. It might be my only chance.

9

I MOVE my hand to rub my eyes, but I stop myself. If I rub my eyes, I will ruin my mascara. I yawn instead, the exhaustion getting to me. It will be worth it though when I see Killian's smug face turn into one of his classic frowns when I win. I have no doubt I will. I've been up all night, going over everything Killian sent me along with seeing if there is any more data I need to prove my recommendation.

I was surprised actually when I got the email from Killian. He sent me everything he had on the project, including his personal notes and email exchanges between him and my father. Those were hard to read, but I read them anyway. He sent me hours and hours of material. I don't know why he would do that if he wanted me to fail. Maybe he wants me to succeed.

"Ready?" Killian says as he pokes his head into my father's office.

"Yes," I say.

I gather my things and follow Killian. I do my best to stand tall and confident even though everything inside is trembling. I follow Killian until we get to the conference room where the meeting is going to be held.

"You'll do great," he says, winking at me, before he holds the door open for me.

I walk in, but I have no idea what he is doing. *Is he trying to give me fake confidence? Is he trying to distract me?* I have no idea. I push the thoughts from my head and instead walk into the room with an intense expression on my face. I try to pretend I'm Killian walking into the room. He wouldn't be smiling and happy. He would be glaring at everyone, forcing them to do what he said with just one look.

I can't keep the expression up long though as I walk in. I'm a little in shock at the number of people in this room. There is close to thirty, and the room isn't even filled yet. I was expecting to present to a small intimate team of ten people, max. Instead, I'm going to be presenting to what feels like the entire company.

Killian puts his hand at the small of my back, guiding me to the front of the long table in the center of the room that has at least ten chairs around it. Those are probably for the most important people. On either side of the table, there are three rows of chairs holding at least ten more people, and they are all staring at me.

"Killian, why didn't you tell me there was going to be so many people at this meeting? Who are they?" I hiss between clenched teeth.

He smiles brightly. "I didn't want you to be nervous, but no need to worry. You'll do great. You are completely prepared. The main table here is the execs, which is where you will need to focus most of your attention when you talk. The rest are their assistants and staff who will be in charge of helping to implement the expansion. They might have a few questions for you because they are more familiar with what the day-to-day operations will look like."

I stare, wide-eyed, until we get to the end of the table where we each take a seat. I realize now why he's being so nice to me. It's not because he wants me to do well. It's because he has fed me to the wolves, and I'm about to get slaughtered.

I've never given a speech in front of this many people. The only thing I have done in front of this many people is model, and all that involved was looking pretty while walking down a catwalk without falling. It was nothing compared with this.

Killian leans over to me. "You wanted a chance. I'm giving you a chance. This is what it's really like to run the company."

He grabs my hand and gives it a quick squeeze before he stands. It does nothing to reassure me. Instead, I feel my palm growing sweaty from where he just touched it.

"I'm Killian Browne, VP of Operations. Today, I'm supposed to present the plans for the expansion of the Felton Grand. I'm not going to do that." He pauses while people uncomfortably shuffle in their seats at his statement. "Instead, I'm going to let the person who ran the data explain. I would like to introduce you to Kinsley Felton."

I stop bouncing my foot under the table and stand. The room has fallen silent now that they know Robert's daughter is the one who will be speaking. I smile weakly around the room as I get up from my chair. Killian winks at me again before taking a seat.

"Hi. I'm Kinsley." I can feel my heart beating out of my chest with every word I'm saying. "Today, I would like to show you my thoughts on the expansion and what the data shows." I walk to the computer that is already set up with my slides. I press the button for them to turn to the first screen.

I realize I've been staring at the ground the whole time, so I look up. Dozens of eyes fall on me, but to my surprise, all the faces are smiling. A few of them are trying to check out what's underneath my pencil skirt and pale pink shirt, but for the most part, I'm getting friendly faces in return. *I can do this.*

"As you can see from the graph, the numbers show a steady increase from month to month in the hotel and casino revenue. This shows there is a need for expansion because we can't keep up with the demand."

I continue talking, uninterrupted, for thirty minutes, explaining every reason we should do the expansion and why it is in the best interest of the entire company. I feel good about my presentation. It seems to be going well, and everyone is giving me their undivided attention. I even glance over at Killian a couple of times, and he seems to be nodding his head in approval.

I click the computer to get it to move to the last slide, the one where I give my recommendation. I feel good throughout my speech. Maybe I can do this. Maybe this is where I belong. "After looking at all the data, it is my recommendation that we increase the expansion to one thousand rooms. That would also allow us to increase the number of slots and the high-roller rooms by fifty percent. It..." I don't continue though. As I glance around the room, there are about a hundred hands in the air. At least, that's what it looks like.

"Yes," I say, pointing to the closest gentleman at the center table.

"I'm sorry, but it would be ridiculous to spend that amount of money on an expansion where we will never get our money back out of it. If we put those kinds of resources behind the Felton Grand, we aren't going to have enough resources to keep the others from failing."

I freeze at his question. "I, um...I'm not sure."

I point to the next man, hoping he will say something positive to save me.

"The data you used doesn't make sense with the data we already have. I just went through the numbers again. They don't line up. Can you explain why we have different numbers?"

"I don't know."

"What metrics did you use?" another man says.

"I...I'm not sure." I have no idea what he is talking about, and I can feel my face getting redder. I try to gather myself. "If you would just turn your attention to this slide, I can better explain to give you more confidence in the plan."

"Wouldn't expanding to just five hundred give us the same amount of profit in just a month longer with less risk?"

"Maybe, but—"

"Then, why don't we just do the five-hundred-room expansion?"

"I—"

"Killian, why have the plans changed?" a man sitting less than five seats from me asks.

Shit, now, they are addressing Killian instead of me.

"Killian, I think you'd better finish the presentation," Granddad says.

I didn't even realize he was in the room. I'd thought if he heard how great of a job I did from others, he would believe I could do this. Instead, I've just fucked up, proving him right.

I swallow before nodding at Killian to finish. He seems reluctant to get up, but he does. I brush past him as I walk. I walk past all the stares. I walk past all the embarrassing murmurs. I walk out of the room until I find my father's office.

I fall onto my father's couch, and then I cry.

I've failed.

I can't do this.

I was wrong to even try.

Killian knew that. My grandfather knew that. Even my father knew that. They all knew I wasn't strong enough to handle this.

I should just marry Killian. Or better yet, I should just let him have the company. I could go back to modeling where nobody ever asked me any questions that were difficult. Instead, I got praise daily for how beautiful I was. I felt important. Now, I feel broken.

"What were you thinking?" Granddad says.

I sit up and wipe my tears. "I just wanted to prove I could do it. That I could be a part of the company and not just sit on the side-lines while Killian runs it. I want to be more than a trophy wife."

He sighs before walking over to me and taking a seat next to me. "I know you do, but you have to know your strengths. That doesn't include giving big speeches or making decisions. Your beauty is your strength. If you want to help and be a part of the company, then agree to do some modeling for our ads. Be the face of the company, not the voice."

"But I want more. I want to be more than just a pretty face."

"You don't need to be though. You're beautiful. You have a perfect life. There is no need to throw that all away just to try to feel more useful. If you're not careful, Killian won't even want to marry you, and then you'll be out of luck. I'm afraid I'll have to make that man CEO whether he marries you or not. He's too good at his job to let him go to our competition."

He stands. "If you were smart, you would be focusing on getting him to fall for you instead of thinking of how you can be more useful to the company. You are most useful as Killian's wife. You need him to fall in love with you before he figures out I will promote him whether he marries you or not."

I watch my grandfather as he walks out of my father's office without saying another word. Killian already knows he's invaluable to the company. He already knows he will become CEO whether or not he marries me. That's why he proposed what he proposed.

Maybe my grandfather's right. I should be focused on getting Killian to fall in love with me instead of focusing on getting my grandfather to believe I can do this.

"I figured you would be in here," Killian says.

"Do you ever knock?"

"No. You find out the best stuff if you don't knock."

I do my best to casually wipe my eyes, so he doesn't think I've been sitting here, crying, but it's no use. He knows that's what I've been doing.

"Here to gloat?"

He narrows his eyes. "No, I figured you would be the one who was going to do the gloating."

"Why would I do that? I failed. I lose. You win."

He smiles. "I would call it more of a tie."

I watch as he walks over and casually takes a seat on the sofa.

"What do you mean, we tied? I did horrible in there. They were practically laughing at my plan."

"I wouldn't say that. They ended up agreeing with you in the end."

"What? How?"

He sighs. "I should have told you there was pushback for even doing the smaller expansion in the first place. Nobody wanted to do it. There was no way you were going to convince them we should spend that kind of money and take that kind of risk, no matter what the data said."

"You did! It took you less than twenty minutes to convince them!"

"Ten actually," he says, smirking.

I hit him with a throw pillow.

"Sorry, just thought you should know it was a joint effort. You supplied the information and got them warmed up. I just closed the deal."

I roll my eyes. "No, you win. I didn't close the deal, as you say. I couldn't even answer their simple questions."

His smile widens. "I was happy just to call it a tie, but if you want to go on a date with me that badly, you can just ask."

I roll my eyes for a second time. "So, what happened after I left?"

He shrugs. "I answered their questions and told them it was happening whether they wanted it to or not, and it would be better if the company as a whole were behind it."

I frown when he puts his arm around me, but I admit it does relax me a little to have it there.

"Who has the ultimate decision then about if the expansion will go on or not?"

"Right now, your grandfather."

I nod, realizing the only reason they even had a meeting with half of the company was to get them behind the decision. It was never for them to decide the fate of the company. My grandfather was always the one who was going to make that decision. If I had just gone straight to him with my speech, maybe things would have been different. Maybe then, he would have realized I was more than just a pretty face. *Too late now.*

"So, when is this date I have to go on?" I sigh.

He tucks a loose strand of hair behind my ear. His touch sends chills down my arms.

"You are eager."

"No," I say, shaking off the chills. "Just ready for it to be over."

"Tomorrow, then."

I nod although I have no idea why I agreed to go out with him. All he wants is another chance to fuck me. I don't plan on giving him that pleasure, but as his eyes travel over my body, stopping at my chest, I don't know if I'll be able to resist his temptation.

Maybe fucking him is the only way to get over him?

10

KILLIAN IS LATE, thirty minutes late. He hasn't called. He hasn't texted. Nothing.

I pace back and forth in the living room of my new room that feels more like an apartment than a hotel room. It's the presidential room. It's the room Dad and I would stay in when we stayed at the hotel.

I had most of my stuff moved into the hotel this morning. I couldn't live in the family house any longer. I like living by myself. And hotel rooms feel more like home than my own house ever will. It will also help to be closer to the offices below. If I'm still committed to figuring out how to convince my grandfather I can do this job, then I need to learn from everyone in the casino—from the maids to the card dealers to the managers. I need all the help I can get to learn this business.

And if I'm honest with myself, I didn't want Killian picking me up from my parents' house. I wanted a place of my own, however temporary.

I pace again. I should have had Scarlett stay. She would have known what to do when he didn't show up. I should call her and tell her to come back, that we should just have a girls' night instead.

I hear a knock on the door. I open the door, and my jaw drops. Killian is standing there. That, I expected. What I didn't expect to see was him dressed so casually. He's in dark jeans and a T-shirt. His hair isn't gelled like usual. Actually, it looks a little unkempt. And a five o'clock shadow completes his look.

He grins at me when he sees my expression. I look down at how I'm dressed. *Shit!* I'm in a dress, a nice dress. I was expecting formal Killian. All I've ever seen him in is suits. I thought that's what he would wear since he came straight from work to pick me up. He's not.

"What's wrong, princess?" he asks smugly.

"I need to change," I say. I turn to run back into my bedroom to change.

He grabs my arm. "No time. My meeting ran late."

"You should have called and let me know you were going to be late."

"I should have, but I'm an asshole. And I like seeing you squirm."

He pulls me into the hallway, and I hear the hotel door shut behind me before I can protest. We enter the elevator, and he presses the button for the ground floor. I can't look at him. I'm too embarrassed.

Scarlett helped me decide what to wear. She told me to wear this black, slightly see-through, lace dress, so I did. I shouldn't have.

"I like your hair like this." His thumb caresses my exposed neck, thanks to Scarlett for putting my hair up.

I quickly forget why I'm supposed to be embarrassed when he is looking at me like this. I lick my bottom lip, preparing for the kiss that always follows that look.

"I like that it gives me better access to your neck." He softly kisses me on my neck but doesn't do anything further.

Instead, he grabs my hand, and when the doors open, we walk out of the elevator and onto the casino floor. I let go of his hand as we walk through the casino. Several employees nod their heads at us in recognition—except they don't recognize me. They are acknowledging Killian. I'm surprised to see a smile on most of their faces when they see him. They seem to like him. He's probably a good boss, firm yet fair. I might be making a huge mistake, trying to take that away from the company, but I'm not trying to take it away. I'm just trying to improve upon that—whether that's with me or someone else.

We exit the casino into the warm Vegas air. Killian comes to an abrupt stop. I expect him to have changed his mind. I expect him to decide we should spend the whole date back in my hotel room or go to his place, wherever that is.

"I should have let you change. Can you walk in those?" He points to my black high heels.

"Yes, I can walk just fine in these." I'm surprised that he didn't order a car.

He raises his eyebrow. "You couldn't walk in them the other night."

"I had too much to drink that night. Trust me; I'll be fine. I've walked enough catwalks with heels twice as high and tighter dresses than this, all while being blasted with flashing lights. I'll be fine." The first part isn't true. I didn't have too much to drink that night. My body was just reacting to Killian's stare as he walked me to his hotel room that night.

It's the same stare he has on his face again as his eyes travel over my body before landing on my black bra that is visible beneath my dress.

"What are you doing?"

"Trying to imagine you with fewer clothes or tighter clothes. I can't imagine it. I'm going to need a show later."

"This was a mistake."

I turn to go back to my room, but he stops me.

"I'm kidding. Relax, princess." He breathes slowly in and out, trying to get me to imitate him.

I roll my eyes at him.

"I'm just trying to make you smile, and apparently, I'm doing a terrible job. I'm a bit out of practice." His eyes stay transfixed on mine.

I laugh. *This guy is unbelievable.*

His lips curl up slightly at the sight of me laughing. He looks around to find the cause of my laughter. "What's so funny?"

"You are. You don't expect me to believe you haven't taken a different girl out every night. I bet you have had a different model or actress or showgirl in your bed every night this week." I raise my eyebrows at him, waiting for an answer.

"I don't date. At least, I haven't in a long time. Yes, I occasionally take a woman home to my bed, but even that happens rarely."

"Define *rarely*."

He shrugs. "Once a quarter. Lately, less than that."

My eyes widen at his response, but I'm not sure I believe him.

"You are telling me you only sleep with a woman once a quarter or less?"

"Yes, I only fuck once a quarter or sometimes less."

I wince again when he says *fuck* although it's less apparent this time. That was not what I had expected.

"Why? You could have any woman you want on any night you want. You're good-looking and intelligent. You make more money than ninety-nine percent of the population. Sure, you act like a cocky ass most of the time, but your looks more than make up for it." I stop talking when I realize I'm rambling about all of Killian's qualities. This is the opposite of flirting. I should just shut my mouth.

He smugly takes my hand back in his. "Come on; we have a long walk ahead if you are wearing those shoes. And I want to get to dinner on time."

I sigh and go with him. "Why?" I ask again.

He pulls me around a group of people dressed up like the band Kiss. They are followed by a woman who's dressed up as Dolly Parton.

I relax a little though because I'm sure, wherever we are going, I'll be dressed appropriately. Vegas isn't known for its tame looks. People wear whatever they want to wear here, no matter where they are going.

"Just not interested in more than that, and women always want more after I fuck them. At night, they promise they don't want anything more than one night, but the next morning, they are begging to go out again. I hate having to fend them off. Once every couple of months is the max I can handle."

"Why haven't you found *the one* yet? I'm sure you want to settle down and get married. Most people your age have been married for years with several kids, old man."

He glares at me. "Just how old do you think I am?"

I shrug. "I don't know."

"I'm thirty. Thirty isn't old."

I smile. "It is to me."

He sighs. "God, you're such a child."

I feel his grasp on my hand loosen. I frown. I want him to hold my hand tighter. I want him to want me. I don't like him thinking about me as a child...except I shouldn't want him to want me. I shouldn't even be on this date.

"So, when is the last time you went on a date before tonight?"

Killian doesn't look at me when he answers, "Three years."

My jaw drops. "Three years? That's a long time." It's also the same time my father told him he wanted Killian to marry me. *Coincidence?* I don't know, but I'm too afraid to ask.

"When is the last time you went on a date?"

Eli, my high school boyfriend, was the last person I went on a date with. We dated for one year in college before he broke it off.

"It was...three years ago," I say as I realize it.

I stare up at him, and we stop walking.

He's looking at me like he wants to ask me the same question I want to ask him.

Did I stop dating because of him? I didn't—well, not exactly. I didn't know he existed yet. I didn't know my father had already chosen. I just knew it would eventually happen.

When I don't ask and when he doesn't answer, he turns us to the building we have stopped in front of.

"We are here."

Now, I really wish I had changed.

"What can I get you to drink?" the waitress says.

She looks tired, but when she looks down at my attire, I swear, she smirks at me.

I stare back down at the menu, hoping to God some drink will pop out at me so I will know what to order, but there are no drinks listed on the menu. I glance around the diner. From the looks of this place, I doubt they have the wine he's bought me before. Actually, I doubt they have any wine. I should order a beer, but I don't even know where to start. So, instead of answering the woman, I stare intently at my menu.

"What do you want to drink, Kinsley?"

I look up to see Killian staring at me with a small smile tugging at the corner of his lips. It's weird to hear my name fall from his lips. I can't recall him using it before, but I realize what he's doing. He's giving me exactly what I said I wanted. He's not going to help me, not unless I beg. And I'm not above begging right now if he will help me.

I plead with my eyes for him to just order a drink for us. I pucker my lip, like Scarlett taught me.

He rolls his eyes at my look and sits up straighter, turning his attention to the waitress.

"I'll have a Miller Lite. Bring her a Blue Moon. We will have your mountain onion ring appetizer with extra sauce. And we both want your special burger, hold the onions."

Killian takes the menu from me and hands it to the lady, who rushes off, glad to finally be done with us.

"You really can't make a quick decision."

"I can." I take a deep breath, ready to reveal something embarrassing. "I just haven't had a lot of experience with drinking. I've only drunk a handful of times in my life."

"Well, that explains a lot."

"You didn't have to order my dinner for me though."

"I was afraid if you took any longer, the waitress would end up spitting in our food. She's obviously swamped tonight, and you were taking half an hour just to order your drink. What did you want? I'll make sure she changes the order."

I sigh. "I was going to order exactly what you ordered me." My cheeks flush at the admission that he was right—again.

Killian smiles and shakes his head.

"So, what made you choose this place? I'm guessing you don't come here often. Doesn't seem like it has the healthiest of menus."

"Just wanted to get you the best burger in Vegas after I almost denied you one the other day."

You denied me more than just a burger, I think as I bite my lip.

The beers and appetizer are thrust onto the table. I take a sip of the beer. It's definitely not the Chateau Margaux wine that Killian ordered me before, but it's drinkable. I take an onion ring off the tower before me.

"Tell me something about yourself. You might be my future husband one day, if we don't figure a way out of this mess. I might as well know more about you."

He shakes his head. "I've already figured a way out of this. You have yet to agree to it. But, okay, I'll play. What do you want to know?"

I take a bite as I contemplate what I want to know most. I really want to know what it would be like to be fucked by him. But I can't go there. I fidget with the wrapper on the silverware, trying to think of a tame question.

"Where did you go to college?"

"Yale."

"Really?"

"No," he says, laughing. "I went to Harvard. I majored in business and then started law school there, but I didn't finish. Instead, Felton Corporation snatched me up, and I've been working here ever since."

"Did you grow up in Vegas?"

"Yes."

Hmm, that surprises me.

"What about you? Why Yale? Why theater?"

89

I take a long sip of my beer. I don't want to answer that. Instead, I try his trick. "What part of Vegas?"

"No, it's your turn. I answered your question. Now, you answer mine. That's how the game works."

"This isn't a game."

"Whatever, I'm not answering any more questions until you answer me. Why Yale? Why theater?"

I take another sip of my beer, stalling for as long as I can until I can't anymore. His stare pierces through me, forcing me to let go of whatever I'm hiding.

"My father. He chose Yale for me. He chose the theater major. I haven't chosen anything that's important in my life. Nothing of this life is mine."

"Why?"

I pause for just a second before I answer, "Because I loved him and could never disappoint him. Because family comes before everything."

There's a long pause as he lets my words sink in. He finally has the tiniest understanding of what my life is really like. Although if he was around my dad as much as he said, he already knew. He just wanted to hear it from me.

"I'm sorry."

I quizzically look at him.

"I'm sorry your life has never been your own."

I shrug as I keep back tears threatening to fall. "It's okay. It's been a good life."

His eyes are intense, as intense as I think I've ever seen them, as he says the next words, "But it's not *your* life. That's what I'm trying to give you—a chance to find your own life."

"What makes you think I want that?" I let my eyes drift to my lap as I tuck a fallen curl behind my ear.

"Because I do."

My eyes immediately go back to his. I don't know if he meant he wants that for me or he wants that for himself. But I feel like he just poured his heart out to me while sitting in a grungy diner.

"Two specials," our waitress snaps as she thrusts two plates of the biggest burgers I have ever seen in front of us.

When I glance back up at Killian, the moment is gone. It's passed. It doesn't keep me from wondering what Killian is hiding as I dig into my burger.

11

"I CAN'T BELIEVE you ate that entire thing," Killian says while knocking on a hotel door.

"I was hungry, and that was delicious. I can't believe you didn't eat the entire thing."

He scrunches his face in disgust. "It was a pile of grease. We will probably both be sick tomorrow because of it."

I laugh. He's way too serious to relax. I bet he eats every nutrient his body needs and nothing more.

"What are we doing here?" I ask.

But I'm too late. The door opens, and a man slaps Killian on the back.

"Kill, you made it!" The man glances to me and then back to Killian. "Who is this?" he asks Killian while staring at me.

"This is my date for tonight, Kinsley."

I notice Killian intentionally leaves off my last name.

I appreciate it. Enough people in this town know my name I don't want to be stereotyped before this person even gets to know me.

"Kinsley, this is Grant Brampton, my best friend and one of the best poker players west of the Mississippi."

Grant tips his hat as Killian talks, making me giggle. He takes my hand and softly kisses it, eyeing Killian. I laugh harder as I notice Killian glaring at Grant. He knows exactly what he is doing—pissing Killian off. I like Grant already.

"Come in. The game is about to start," Grant says.

I follow Killian into the hotel room, except this room has been turned into a makeshift poker room. There is a large circular table in the center with decks of cards and chips stacked perfectly on one end. The kitchen has been turned into a mini bar. I notice three other men standing around with drinks in their hands.

"Everyone, this is Kinsley," Killian says.

Everyone says, "Hey," back with obvious curious stares as to why Killian has brought a date to a boys' night.

I'm curious about that myself. My hands are shaking slightly. I'm beginning to feel more confident around Killian, but a roomful of guys I don't know makes me uneasy.

"Killian, I can go home. I didn't mean to intrude on boys' night."

"Nah, they don't care. They'll be happy to have someone good-looking to gawk at while I take all their money. Plus, if we didn't go out tonight, I'm not sure of the next night I'm available to go out."

My heart sinks a little at his words. There's not going to be a second date. Or if there is, it's going to be a long time from now.

"This is Stephen Mann. He's my brother-in-law."

I shake Stephen's hand. I didn't know Killian had a sister.

"And that's Marvin and Benny. They both suck at poker."

Marvin throws popcorn at Killian. Killian runs over and pretends to tackle Marvin. It's strange, seeing Killian like this—relaxed and playful. I know he's called me a walking contradiction, but I'm beginning to see him the same way. He's serious and stern, one minute, and then playful and joking, the next.

"All right, settle, you two," Grant says. "It's time for you to lose some money." He pulls up another seat. "You can sit here," he says to me, holding on to the chair he just pulled up to the table.

"Thanks," I say, smiling, as I take a seat. I fold my hands in my lap to keep them from shaking.

Grant takes a seat on my left as Killian takes a seat on my right. All of the other men take their seats in the remaining chairs.

Marvin starts distributing chips to everyone in equal measure. When he gets to me, he asks, "You in?"

I glance to Killian, but he doesn't say anything. I notice his shoulders tense a little, but I think he would have said something if he didn't want me to play.

"Sure," I say.

"It's a hundred dollar minimum bet. Are you sure?" Marvin says.

I smile politely. "I'm sure."

"We will make Killian pay up when she loses," Grant jokes.

I want to tell Grant he's wrong, that I don't intend to lose, but I can't. I haven't played poker in years, and I'm a terrible liar. Father always used to say poker isn't about bluffing or telling the truth. It is about strategy and numbers. It's about knowing your odds. It's that simple.

Grant smiles at me. Marvin starts dealing out cards to everyone.

Killian leans over to whisper in my ear, "Do you know how to play Texas Hold 'em?"

"I know the basics. I'm sure I'll be fine."

I glance at my cards and wait for my turn. I quickly calculate my outs and odds. When it gets to me, I call. I have a thirty-five percent chance of winning, and the pot odds are thirty percent.

All the men call the initial hundred-dollar bet.

"What do you do, Kinsley?" Grant asks me.

I watch the initial flop. I get another nine to match my pair of nines. I want to smile, but I don't. I try to keep my emotions as neutral as possible as I begin counting my outs and odds again.

I answer Grant the only way I know how, "I'm a model."

"Oh, really?" Grant says, eyeing me. "I can see that. You definitely have the body for it."

Killian glares at Grant, but I can see it's just harmless fun. And, for whatever reason, I like Grant. He seems to know how to have a good time.

"She's more than that. She went to Yale," Killian says.

I'm surprised he is defending me.

I raise the bet on my turn, not by much though. It's just enough to only keep the serious players in the game. Benny folds on his next turn, but everyone else stays in.

"You're a pro player?" I ask Grant.

"Yep. I placed third in the World Series of Poker National Championship last year."

"Impressive," I say. I watch the next card played.

Another nine turns up, and I can't help but smile. I turn to Killian to pretend I'm smiling at him, but anybody that's paying me any attention would know why I'm smiling. Grant is the only one paying me much attention though, and his eyes are on my chest, not my face.

I glance at Killian and see his face has grown dark. His eyes look like they are going to shoot lasers right through Grant.

I place my hand on Killian's thigh. "Relax," I whisper to him before shocking both of us by kissing him on the cheek. It's the most brazen I have been. I gently squeeze his leg, and I feel his muscles relax, if only a little, as I massage his thigh.

I keep my hand there long after he has relaxed. I like feeling his strong body beneath my hand. When I chance a glance down, I see a hint of an erection growing beneath his jeans. I have more control than I realize.

I smile. If I move my hand just an inch, I could accidentally touch it and then pretend I didn't mean to do it.

"Kinsley, what are you going to do?" Grant wakes me from my dream.

I quickly remove my hand. "I call."

Grant calls before he says, "The trick to poker is paying attention. It's math. It's knowing your odds and how to read people."

I smile at Grant trying to give me advice. I already know his hand isn't worth shit. His face says it all, yet he still thinks he's won with, most likely, a pair of face cards. And looking around the table, he probably would have.

Marvin flips his cards, showing high king, followed by Stephen with a pair of tens. Then, Killian flips over a straight, to my surprise. But it's still not enough. Grant nods for me to flip my cards over.

"Four of a kind," I say to Grant.

His smile drops as he flips over two aces, giving him three of a kind.

"I win," I say shyly. "I'll try to use your advice for the next hand though."

Marvin pushes the chips to me while Killian chuckles softly next to me.

"Did your father teach you how to play poker, too?" he asks in my ear so only I can hear.

I shrug and blush, and he chuckles again.

We play for another hour or so until the only players remaining are Killian, me, and Grant. I stay out of the conversation to my relief as the boys talk about sports and cars. I glance over at Killian. He won't stay in the game for much longer though. He's down to his last chips.

"How did you two meet?" Stephen asks as he brings me another beer.

I taste it, but it doesn't taste as good as the one Killian ordered earlier.

I glance nervously at Killian. I'm not ready to share our story, but I suck at lying and don't want to lie to a member of his family.

"We met three years ago."

I choke on my beer when Killian says that. *God, I've got to stop doing that.* I turn to face him, trying to decide if he's lying or telling the truth, but Killian has the best poker face I have ever seen.

"I was giving a speech to a business class at Yale. While I was there, I paid a visit to an old friend." He doesn't look at me when he says the next words, "Eli Stratford. You remember him, Grant. He was Charlie's younger brother."

"Yeah, I remember Charlie. I didn't know Eli that well though. I didn't know you were friends," Grant says.

Killian shakes his head. "We weren't really, but like I said, I presented in front of a business class, and Eli was there. He introduced himself afterward, and I agreed to meet him for lunch.

"Anyway, we were at lunch, and the most beautiful woman I had seen came walking into the restaurant. I considered leaving Eli alone right there, so I could go after the woman, but to my surprise, she walked over to our table and kissed Eli on the lips. Then, she asked for the keys to his apartment, so she could study there instead of walking back to hers across campus. And she left. That woman was Kinsley. She recently moved back into town after graduating, and I asked her out. And here we are."

Killian still won't look at me. Grant puts his arm around me, and I force a smile on my face.

"Too bad the old man here snatched you up, but if you want to have a good time, you'll go out with me sometime," Grant says, winking.

I smile. "I don't know if I can go out with someone who loses to me in poker."

"I haven't lost yet—unlike Killian who is about to get slaughtered."

Grant begins dealing the cards again, drawing his attention away from me. My thoughts stay on Killian though, even as the cards are dealt. I don't remember that story. I don't remember that happening, and it's quite an extravagant lie just to keep Grant away from the truth—that we are basically having an arranged marriage.

I glance at my cards. I call on my turn. I'm giving half of my attention to what Killian just said and the other half to the game at hand.

After we have all called, Grant flops the first three cards.

I quickly count my outs and then calculate my odds—fifty-five percent. It's greater than the pot odds. I double the bet on my turn.

Why in the hell did Killian tell that story? How did he know I was dating Eli?

Another card is turned over. My odds increase to sixty percent.

I look at Killian. I notice a tiny bead of sweat forming on his face. His leg is shaking under the table. He increases the bet again. *He's lying.*

But just moments ago, the only sign was him avoiding my gaze. That was the truth. Suddenly, I remember. I remember seeing a strange, hot man having lunch with Eli. I remember going back to Eli's apartment and studying before waiting for him to walk me to my afternoon class, like he always did—except, that day, I never made it to class. When Eli got home from that lunch, we got in the worst fight we had ever been in. Eli seemed to think I was already engaged to another man. That it would never work out with us. He broke up with me that night. *Killian was the one that told him I was engaged. Killian broke us up.*

"All in," I say, pushing the chips into the middle of the table.

I can't stay here any longer. I don't care about winning or losing anymore. I don't care about flirting with Killian anymore. I just want to get out of here.

I see the shock on Killian's and Grant's faces, but they both push their chips in. Grant flips the last card, and then I flip my cards over, despite it being out of turn.

"Royal flush." I glance right and then left when they both flip over their cards—a full house and a straight. "I win."

I push my chair back and get up. I walk out without a word. I can't breathe as I run down the hallway. It feels claustrophobic, like the walls are closing around me. I won't survive in an elevator, so I run down the stairs of the hotel building instead. I need to be moving. I need to get away from Killian.

If it wasn't for him, I could still be with Eli. I could have chosen my own love, my own future. Instead, Killian convinced Eli to break up with me. Instead, he chose my future for me.

12

THE AIR OUTSIDE is warm and just as stifling as it was inside the hotel room. I begin the long walk back to my hotel—alone. I could call a car to pick me up, but I don't. I prefer to be alone.

I make it a few steps before I look up and see Killian standing on the sidewalk, waiting for me. *Damn it!*

The elevators must be faster than climbing down five flights of stairs in heels. I can't walk around him. I can't avoid him. So, I just walk to him.

"What just happened?" he asks.

"Nothing. We're done. I don't want to be friends. I definitely don't want to marry you. And I don't want your help. I just want to go back to being nothing."

I begin walking again, and Killian falls in step next to me. He doesn't say a word for an entire block. He doesn't touch me either. Despite how much I hate him right now, my body is begging for him.

"I'm sorry," he finally says. "I'm sorry I didn't tell you the truth."

I glare at him. "What is the truth?"

"The story I gave during the poker game is the truth. I was giving a presentation to a class at Yale. I knew Eli a little bit from my past, not enough to really have lunch with him, but then the opportunity came up, and I took it.

I knew from your father you were dating him. I just wanted to learn more about you, to see if you were happy with Eli. If you were, I wouldn't approach you. I wouldn't say anything to Eli about your father's arrangement with me. But if you weren't happy...well, I wasn't sure what I was going to do.

"When you came into that restaurant that day, you looked sad, withdrawn. Even when you kissed him, it wasn't a kiss of passion. I couldn't let you waste the only few years of freedom you had left on that douchebag. So, I told him the truth. Well, I told him you and I were already engaged, and no matter what he did, you would never marry him."

"He broke up with me that night because of you." My face is fuming bright red.

"I only did it to help you find someone who would make you happy. I thought, if you were away from him, you would find someone else."

"But I didn't! I didn't find someone else. You ruined the only real relationship I ever had. You are just as bad as my father. You tried to control my life!"

He eyes widen, and his mouth drops.

We both stop walking.

"That was never my intention. I just wanted you to be happy, and I know you weren't happy with Eli."

"How do you know if I was happy or not? What right did you have to decide anything for me?"

"I know because you never smiled, not once the whole time you were around him, and you have smiled over a hundred times since you met me. I know because your eyes didn't lust after Eli, like they lust after me." He tucks a stray hair behind my ear. "I know because you are an amazing woman who deserves to be worshipped by the man she is with, and all Eli did that entire time was complain about how clingy and annoying you were."

"I'm not clingy."

"I know. Eli's an idiot. You shouldn't have dated him."

"So are you."

"You're right. I'm an idiot, too. You should have dated someone else. You should have moved on after Eli."

I shake my head. "I couldn't...I couldn't date when I knew it would never go anywhere, when I knew it would always leave me heartbroken, when I knew I was always meant to be with you... except I didn't know who you were yet because you never told me."

"I'm sorry."

"I'm sorry, too. You shouldn't be forced to marry me to get a position in the company you clearly deserve."

Killian intensely stares at me, trying to understand what I'm saying, but I don't know what I'm saying. I just want him to know this situation is completely fucked up.

All I know is, I still want him.

I moisten my lips, begging for his lips to find mine. They do. His lips sink into mine as his hands go around my body. I moan against his lips.

I forget about being on a busy sidewalk on the strip. I forget about how mad at him I still am for lying to me. I forget about how angry I am at him for manipulating my life.

I just kiss and moan and beg.

Killian's kiss is aggressive and hungry. He wants me as much as I want him. He needs this.

I don't think about the fact that, in a few months, we could be walking down the aisle as man and wife, and having a one-night stand now could ruin it all. I don't care. I need him. I need to feel what it's like to have a man burying himself deep inside me as we both come.

We finished walking back to the hotel, kissing along the way, before I realize this is a bad idea. We can't walk into the hotel, kissing and holding hands. Everyone who works in the casino will see us and start rumors. Those rumors will get back to my grandfather, and he will assume we have decided to marry when that couldn't be further from the truth.

"Maybe we should go back to your place. I don't want any of the staff to see us together."

"This is my place." He releases my hand as soon as we get close to the entrance. "No one will suspect if we go up to our rooms together. Our rooms are right next door to each other."

"They are? You kept your room from the first night? Why do you live in a hotel room?"

"I feel more at home here. And having a hotel room here lets me be closer to work. I've had enough emergency calls I have had to tend to in the middle of the night that it's just easier to already be here."

I nod, understanding.

"Why do you live in a hotel when I know you have a home only a few minutes away?" he asks.

"I feel at home here. I've always felt at home in hotels. The mansion has never felt like home."

Killian smiles. "Your father used to say the same thing."

"Come on. This time, you take the stairs, and I'll take the elevator."

He laughs. "No, we will both take the elevator."

We walk into the casino, side by side, but we don't touch. Employees notice us and nod in our direction. This time though, I feel like they can see the truth. They know we are walking upstairs to go have sex. They all know. It will be the talk of the town tomorrow.

My hand shakes nervously at my side, and I try my best to smile at a bartender as she walks by, but it's weak.

"Relax. No one suspects a thing," Killian whispers into my ear.

"Don't do that," I hiss. "It just makes us look more suspicious to see you talking into my ear."

We make it to the elevator without drawing too much attention to ourselves. When the doors close, the tension between us is too much to remain frozen and not touching. Our bodies collide. Our arms wrap around each other as our lips touch in one of the best kisses of my life. I don't know if it's the tension that caused this kiss to be even better than the rest, or maybe it's the underlying anger I feel toward him. Whatever the reason, I don't want it to stop.

The elevator dings, indicating we are stopping, that the doors are going to open soon, that we have to stop. But we can't. We are desperate for each other, desperate to hold on to whatever this fleeting feeling is. I'm sure, as soon as we have sex, it will be gone, and we will go back to being mortal enemies. But, for now, it lasts.

The doors open, and Killian tears his lips from mine just in time for the woman standing there to only suspect that we were kissing, but not long enough to have proof. I notice her smile knowingly anyway as our heavy panting gives away what we were just doing. She's not an employee though. The woman who enters the elevator has no idea who we are.

It doesn't keep me from flushing a bright shade of pink though. I've never been caught making out with a man before, not even in high school or early college when Eli and I were dating. We never did anything so risky to chance being caught.

The elevator dings again on the top floor, the floor both Killian and I have rooms on. Killian motions with his hand for me to step out first. So, I do, pushing any thoughts of Eli out of my mind. Tonight isn't about him. I'll deal with those memories later.

Tonight is about need and desire. Tonight is about me finally becoming a woman who can sleep with a man without becoming attached. Tonight is about giving in to my own desires without thoughts of the consequences. Tonight is about me. It's about fucking.

I make my way to my hotel door and slip the key card in. I watch the red light flick to green. I push the handle down, opening the door. Killian's body is quickly pushing me inside as soon as the latch on the door releases.

I let out a small whimper when he pushes me inside. I wasn't expecting him to move so quickly.

He claims my lips with his in a brutal, carnal kiss. It's a kiss that can't be mistaken for anything but what it is—a desperate plea for me to give myself to him. Fuck, when he kisses me like that, giving so much of himself to me, I want nothing more than to give him everything.

I try to match the hunger of his kiss with my own, but my inexperienced tongue gets tangled in his. His tongue takes back control. This time, I let him do what he wants, and I enjoy the way he molds us together with just his tongue.

Killian breaks away from my lips as his hand finds my hair and releases the clip holding it up. His eyes follow my curls as they bounce down my back. His hand tangles into my hair as his lips find mine again, deepening the kiss.

I moan as he tugs softly on my locks.

I've never been controlled by a man before. Eli is really my only experience other than Brent—if that could even be called a sexual experience. And Eli was always soft, gentle, thoughtful. He didn't have an aggressive bone in his body, not like this man attacking me with his body.

Killian's hand finds my ass, and he lifts me. I wrap my legs around his waist, feeling his hard body beneath me. He carries me to the bedroom. I moan from the movement of my already drenched pussy rubbing against him with every step.

He drops me on the bed before his eyes admire my body. I bite my lip as I watch his eyes take in my black bra and panties beneath my dress. For the first time tonight, I feel happy I chose this skimpy dress.

His eyes stay on my body as he slowly and deliberately removes my high heels. It's one of the sexiest things I've ever seen, but I know it will soon be replaced when he removes his clothes. When my shoes are off, I stand and turn around. I lift my hair off my neck.

Killian knows what I'm asking without me having to say a word. His hand finds the zipper, and he slowly pulls it down. I feel his hot breath on my neck the whole time, each exhale sending shivers down my spine.

I drop my hair, and he slowly turns me around until I'm facing him. He cups my chin in his hand, and his thumb softly strokes my cheek.

"I need to hear you say it."

His words are cryptic, but I know what he's asking. I try to make my eyes as lust-filled as possible when I look at him. I know, no matter what I say, my words won't be enough for him, if my body isn't saying the same thing. And I'm not going to let him get away with just letting his lips and tongue taste me. I want more. I'm desperate for his cock to be inside me. I'm desperate to feel what a real release feels like from a man experienced in giving me what I want.

"I want you," I say.

He takes a deep breath before pushing our bodies together. "Not good enough." His eyes have grown intense with burning need.

I moan as his lips brush against my neck, sending more chills throughout my body.

"I need you."

He shakes his head against my neck. "Not good enough."

His hand presses against my soaked panties covering my pussy.

"Fuck," I let out.

His lips smile just a little against my neck. His lips move back to mine as he slips one finger into my panties. My breath catches in my throat at his slow, torturous touch.

I can't *not* have him. I can't let him walk away from this. I'll die if he doesn't take me.

His lips along with his finger finally pull away from me. I whimper at the loss of his touch. I grab ahold of his neck and shoulders, barely able to stand. My breathing is fast, and my heartbeat is erratic. I do my best to catch my breath before I speak, but I can't.

I look into his hungry whiskey-colored eyes and say the dirtiest, most truthful thing that has ever escaped my lips, "Fuck me, Killian. Take me, own me, control me. I can't survive another second without knowing how your cock feels inside me."

His head cocks slightly as he smiles brighter than I've ever seen. "It will be my pleasure."

As soon as the words leave his mouth, his whole body moves to another level. I didn't know another level of intensity could exist between two people. I was wrong.

My dress falls down my body as his shirt comes off. His pants fall quickly, and he steps out as he pushes me back onto the bed.

He kisses me now like I'm the only woman he ever wants to kiss, like I make him whole. And when he kisses me, I feel the same way. Not like I know I'm going to be left heartbroken after this. Our hands link together high over my head as his erection presses between my legs.

I feel my nipples growing hard beneath my bra, begging to be touched. He senses my need and releases my hands to unhook my bra. The cold air makes my nipples perk higher. He palms my breast with his hand as the ache grows in my swollen breasts. He finds my nipple and squeezes roughly.

"Fuck," I moan.

He smiles. "I think I like your dirty mouth."

"Fuck," I moan again. "Just don't stop."

I pant as he takes the next one in his hand and gives it the same attention he gave the first.

My pussy aches for attention as he presses harder against me. He senses that, too, and his hand releases one breast to sink down inside my panties. He finds my clit and rubs until I'm panting harder. I need him even more than before.

"Please," I beg.

His lips hover just above mine. "Please, what, princess?"

"Please, I need you inside me." My pussy aches harder, desperate to be filled.

He stands and pulls my panties off my body until I'm completely bare for him. He only takes a second to admire my body before picking up his discarded jeans, but it feels like his eyes soak me in for hours. I think, if I asked him, he could recall every curve, every freckle, and every imperfection of my skin. That's how well his eyes have taken in my body.

I watch as he pulls a condom out of his pocket. I try not to think why he would have one in his pocket in the first place, but my thoughts drift anyway. *Did he pick me up tonight with this intention? Or did he plan on picking up another random girl as soon as he dropped me off?*

The thoughts quickly float out of my head when he drops his boxers, and I watch his thick, hard cock spring free.

My breath catches at the sight. I have to touch it. I have to make him feel as good as he has made me feel.

"Touch it," he commands, reading my thoughts again.

I hesitantly reach my hand out to stroke him. He moans at my touch, giving me more confidence, and I tighten my grip around his straining erection. I move up and down, slow and steady.

"Fuck, princess," he moans.

I pick up speed, as his arousal somehow grows larger.

He suddenly grabs my wrist, and I stop the movement and look up at him with wide eyes.

"Enough," he says.

He rips the condom open with his mouth, an obviously practiced move. He easily slides it on, never taking his dangerous eyes off of mine. I sink back into the bed, climbing up further away from him. I feel my heartbeat race in anticipation of what is about to happen. I swallow hard, trying to push the nervous energy down, but it doesn't work. I can feel my heartbeat in my throat.

Killian climbs up the bed until he is on top of me. He kisses me hard and controlling as I feel him settle in between my legs again. I tremble slightly when he caresses my breast.

He looks up at me with troubled eyes. "Is this your first time, princess?"

"No," I whisper. But it might as well be. It's been three years. And even then, it only happened a handful of times, and none of them felt even a fraction as good as this has so far.

His eyes travel over my face, trying to understand the contradiction between my words and what my body is saying. He tucks a hair behind my ear, trying to calm my nerves. "I'm not going to hurt you, princess."

I nod, but I can't control my body. I can't keep it from reacting this way. When he realizes I'm not going to relax from just his words, he tries with his lips, with his tongue. His tongue sinks into my mouth, and I lose myself in his kiss.

His hand finds my clit again, and he works me into a frenzy of need. I moan as I grow closer. I'm so close to coming. My eyes open for just a second, and I see him giving me one final warning with his eyes before he sinks inside me.

"Fuck, Killian," I moan as he stretches me with his cock. I didn't even realize I could stretch that wide for him.

"You're beautiful, princess. Look at me," Killian says, taking me off the pain for a second.

When I do, I see the appreciation there. I moisten my lips moments before his lips join with mine again. I feel him sink further into me, but this time, my body welcomes the wince of pain because it knows it'll bring me closer to the pleasure about to ensue.

His hands lock back with mine, high over my head, as he gently rocks inside me. We both moan as he does. The pleasure begins to sweep over my body with each movement. His body moves slowly at first in a steady rhythm that my body easily matches.

His body quickly increases his rhythm, thrusting harder and faster. Each time his body presses into mine, another jolt of pleasure flows through every nerve ending in my body. Each thrust brings me closer and closer to exploding in ecstasy. Each thrust sweeps me further and further under his spell.

"Come for me," he says, his voice primal and raspy.

I realize he's panting just as hard as I am.

I moan as he thrusts again, bringing me so close.

"Come for me, princess," he says again.

This time, I do. I feel the warm waves of pleasure flow through me as I scream his name.

He comes right after me before collapsing on top of me. Our bodies stay pressed together for several minutes. In these few precious moments, our bodies are one.

And I know now that he will hurt me. As soon as he gets up and goes to clean himself off, he will rip me apart, taking a small part of me with him I can never get back. Because that was the best sex of my life. That's how sex is supposed to be. I just hope when he does finally leave, it only leaves a small hole in my heart instead of a gaping wound in his wake.

———

Heat creeps up my neck, waking me. I try to move, but I can't. Killian's body is heavy on top of mine. His stubble scratches against my chest when I try to move.

We fell asleep. I try to glance at a clock, but I don't find one. *How long have we been sleeping like this?* I try to move, and I find he is still buried inside me. Although he doesn't fill me quite the same way he did before.

This can't be happening. He was supposed to leave as soon as this was over. If anyone catches him leaving my room in the morning, we are going to be out of time to decide what we want to do. My grandfather will force us into getting married when that's clearly not what either of us wants. *So, why did Killian fall asleep on top of me then? If he doesn't want to be with me, why is he still here?*

"Killian," I whisper. I don't know why I'm whispering. Maybe it's because I'm ashamed of what we just did. I don't sleep with strange men—although Killian isn't a stranger anymore. I don't do this though. I'm a good girl. I don't sleep with someone on the first date—except I just did.

"Killian," I say louder.

He stirs slightly, but my voice isn't enough to wake him.

"Killian!" I say even louder.

His eyes open wide, and his body jerks off of mine. We both wince at the loss we feel as soon as his body leaves mine. I close my eyes and take a deep breath. I will not let the pain overtake rational thought. I will not.

"You need to go," I say without opening my eyes.

I feel his hand against my cheek, brushing my hair off my face. "If that's what you want," he says softly.

I keep my eyes closed, afraid I will cry if I open them. I refuse to be the woman who cries after sex. I will not let that happen. I will prove to him I can be just as heartless as him. I can sleep with a man without losing a bit of myself, without expecting more than one night.

"You need to go," I say again.

"Okay," he says.

I feel the bed shift as he stands from the bed. When I hear the bathroom door close, I open my eyes. I take another deep breath before getting up and walking to the closet. I slip on pajama pants and shirt. I grab a hair tie and quickly gather my hair in a bun on top of my head.

I glance at my phone. It's three in the morning. I sigh. I'm not going to get much sleep. I probably won't get any more sleep as soon as he leaves. But I need him gone before I do something stupid that will reveal I can't do this, just like he said I couldn't.

He comes back from the bathroom, but I don't glance at him as much as my body wants one last peek at his tight abs and impressive cock. I won't. I had my fun. Now, it's time to move on.

"I'll be in the living room," I say. I walk through the bedroom door and into the living room. I don't look back.

It only takes him a minute to get dressed. I glance up from my spot on the couch when he enters the living room. He's dressed. His hair is combed. He looks exactly like he did when he came to pick me up, completely unaffected by what just happened. He probably isn't affected. He does this once a quarter with different women all the time. I'm just his whore for the night.

Killian walks to me. He bends down and softly kisses me on the lips. "Sleep well, princess."

He walks to the door. I don't get up. I refuse to walk him to the door. That's what girlfriends do. That's what women in love do. I'm not in love, not even close.

My eyes follow him though. They follow him to the door. They watch as he pauses for just a second before he opens the door. His eyes meet mine. I swear they look sad, or maybe that's just my imagination. Probably just tired. I don't know. But then he opens the door, and he's gone.

I stay on the couch as one tear falls. It hurts, seeing him go.

Tonight was a mistake. I shouldn't have had sex with him... because I think I just fell a little for him. And if I fall for him, then that gives him the advantage. That means I will do whatever is in his best interest instead of what is in mine. I can't do that. I have to stay strong. I have to do what I need.

I should be angry with Killian. He lied to me. He took away another bit of my freedom. And I am. I am angry. I'm angry I didn't get to experience dating Eli for longer than I did. I'm angry I didn't date other men after Eli. I'm angry Killian is the only man who has ever made me feel loved...except it wasn't love. It was anger and passion. That's what made the sex so great. It wasn't real.

I wipe the fallen tear from my cheek, and then I grab the remote and turn on the TV. Tonight, for the first time, I don't think of my father and how much I miss him. Instead, I find a new hole in my heart, a hole that can only be filled by Killian. But it's a hole that will never be filled.

13

"Good afternoon, princess."

I freeze at the words. I was hoping I wouldn't see him today. Most of the executives don't work on the weekends. But, of course, that doesn't include Killian. Of course, he works on weekends. That's probably why he's so high up in the company at such a young age.

"What do you want?" I sound annoyed and angry. I'm both of those things right now. I didn't sleep a second after he left. I lift my coffee to my lips, trying to keep my aggravation and exhaustion at bay.

Killian raises his eyebrows. "Well, aren't you pleasant? Didn't sleep well?" He smirks.

My eyes shoot daggers in his direction, and he holds his hands up in defense, like I really was shooting something in his direction.

"What do you want?" I ask again, letting my anger I never got out last night bubble to the surface.

"I have a crisis I need your help with."

I roll my eyes and look back to the computer I finally figured out the password to. It was *princess*. I should have known.

Killian walks to me. "I'm serious. You are the only one who can help with this. I even have your grandfather's approval."

That has my attention, although I don't know why Killian would suddenly be helping me. Maybe he feels guilty for tricking me into presenting in front of half of the company when he knew they would destroy me with their questions. Maybe he feels guilty for the breakup between the only boyfriend I ever had and me.

"What is it?"

"Come on, and I'll show you."

He reaches his hand out to me, but I don't take it. I stand and follow him out of my father's office. I follow him out to the pool at the back of the casino. That's when I realize what he wants.

"No," I say.

"Come on, Kinsley. Our other model got sick at the last minute. It's you, or we will have to pay thousands of dollars to have them come back to reshoot next week. It will also mean the ads will be delayed. We need you."

Damn it! I hate his pleading expression and puppy-dog eyes. I can't say no to him.

"Maybe," I say, sighing.

He smiles. "I'll take that as a yes."

I shake my head, but he takes my hand and leads me over to where people are standing around, doing nothing.

"Here's your new model," Killian says, thrusting me into the center of the group.

The man in charge smiles when he sees me. "You're Kinsley Felton. You've modeled for *Seventeen*."

I smile. "That's me."

The man's eyes light up. It feels good to be known for my modeling career and not because I'm Robert Felton's daughter.

"I'm Brock Parry. I'm in charge of the shoot."

I smile, shaking his hand.

"But wait...will you do this shoot for so little money?"

I raise my eyes. He has no idea who I am. It makes me laugh.

"I'm Robert Felton's daughter, the owner of the casino. Don't worry about paying me. I'm doing this to help the company."

Brock smiles with a small flush on his cheeks. "Sorry. Let's get you back to wardrobe."

I follow him, but I feel Killian's eyes on me the entire time as I walk back to a guest room serving as a makeshift wardrobe room. I just hope, when I come back out, he isn't still here because I'm not sure how I'll be able to do this job with him here.

————

I don't know why I didn't expect to be mostly naked in the ad. Maybe because this is a classy casino, but I guess I should have expected this. I should have expected I would be wearing a scantily clad bathing suit. My hair is teased and curled in large waves. I'm wearing more makeup than a hooker. I look sexy, I realize, as I stare back at myself in the mirror.

I've worn bathing suits in hundreds of ads before, but I never looked sexy. I looked cute and pretty. Right now though, I look hot. I take in a deep breath as I wrap my robe back around me. I'm going to have to channel my inner Scarlett to do this.

It's what I've always wanted—to be treated just like every other model, to be looked at as a woman instead of a girl. Here's my chance. I'm not going to blow it.

I strut out of the room and into the warm Las Vegas sun. We are shooting in front of the new pool that will be opening next weekend, but despite the pool being closed, there are hundreds of people gathered around, giving their two cents on the direction of the shoot.

I find Brock and am disappointed when I see Killian standing next to him. Brock smiles when he sees me. He hugs me, like he has known me my whole life. I try my best to embrace him back.

"You look fantastic," Brock says.

I smile. "Thanks."

"So, Killian was telling me the look we are going for in the ad. We want sexy, hot, spicy. We want people to want to come to our hotel because they think it's swimming with people as hot as you."

I glance back at Killian, who is smiling brightly. I roll my eyes. He's enjoying this.

"I got it," I say.

"Great. We will start with some dry shots of you posing on the lounge chair, and then we will get you in the water for the film portion."

I nod. It doesn't sound too hard. I walk over to where the camera is set up, remove my robe, and hand it to one of the assistants who helped me pick out the red bikini. I feel everyone's eyes on me. It would make most people nervous or shy—having this many eyes on them all at once, staring at their body. But I don't feel like that. I like how my body looks.

I lie back on the lounge chair and put my arms above my head. My first reaction is to smile. And then I remember this isn't a *Seventeen* magazine shoot. I'm supposed to look like sex. I drop my smile as I arch my back while looking at the camera. The camera clicks, capturing the look.

"Great, Kinsley. Arch your back just a little more, and drop your eyes," Brock says.

I do.

"Perfect."

I let my hand fall to my neck as I've seen Scarlett do hundreds of times before. More clicks.

"Yes. Just like that!" he shouts.

I stifle a laugh. It's funny how much it sounds like we are shooting a porno sometimes.

I see Killian standing just behind the camera. His smile is gone, but his intense stare never leaves my body. So, I increase the seduction, wanting him to miss my body as much as I miss his. I want him to regret hurting me.

My hand falls lower until it grazes my breast.

"Keep it right there."

More clicks.

When Brock gets the shot, I let my hand slowly drop lower down my stomach until it's just grazing the inside of my thigh.

Killian bites his lip in response.

More clicks.

"Now, move to your stomach."

I do. More clicks.

"We got it!" he shouts.

I smile and stand. I'm immediately handed my robe that I wrap back around my body.

"That was perfect," Brock says.

He hands me a small index card with a couple of lines on it. That's when I realize the video ad will not be solo. I'll be shooting it with a man. I smile inside. It will give me a chance to see how affected Killian is.

"We will have you get in the water and get your hair wet. Your makeup is waterproof, so you should be fine there, but if we need to do any touch-ups, we will do it then. Then, we will have Cedric jump in and swim up to you. That will be the first shot, and then we will proceed with the rest of the scene after that. We will have cue cards with your lines on it if you forget. Any questions?"

I glance down at my index card one more time, but I already have the simple lines memorized. "Nope, I got it."

I walk over to the pool and hand Brock my robe before diving into the cool water. I shiver as the cool water prickles my skin, despite the warm weather. When I come up for air, I remember the pool was just filled yesterday. It hasn't had time to warm up. I flip my hair back, knowing that's how they will want it for the shoot. I feel Killian's eyes burning into me as I do, and I smile. He's definitely affected. Now, let's see how affected. I swim over to the shallow end where they want me so they can see my body from the waist up.

I glance down to the other end of the pool and see Cedric standing at the edge. I smile. He's tall, muscular, and tan. I definitely won't mind doing the shoot with him. I glance over and smirk at Killian's reaction. His deep frown is clear from across the pool. He either didn't know Cedric was going to be a part of the shoot, or he forgot. Either way, he doesn't look happy.

"Action!" Brock yells.

Cedric dives into the pool. I keep my eyes on him as he swims up to me. He grabs me by the waist, and I smile and giggle as his hands make his way up my body as he surfaces.

"Cut. That was great. We will move on as soon as we adjust the camera."

"I'm Cedric," the man says, running his hand through his long dark locks.

"I'm Kinsley."

"I think I'm going to enjoy this," he says.

I smile. "Me, too."

Brock walks over to us. "All right, now, we want you two to make out until we call cut. We will probably do it several times here, and then we will move to under the waterfall."

We both nod. Cedric puts his hands around my waist. I do the same to him. We both know better than to move our hands to each other's faces. It would ruin the shot.

"Action," Brock says.

I close my eyes as Cedric's lips touch mine. He doesn't tentatively kiss me, like he is just getting to know me. He kisses me hard and fast, like he has done this hundreds of times before. I kiss him back with the same intensity.

He's a good kisser, I think.

He tugs on my bottom lip, and I can't help it as a low moan escapes my lips. He smiles against me, tugging harder, moving our bodies closer together.

One of my hands travels up to the base of his neck, deepening the kiss. His hips press harder against mine until I feel his erection.

"Yes, just like that," I faintly hear Brock shout to us.

But I'm too lost in the kiss to hear Brock. Cedric kisses me harder until my tongue is sizzling.

"Cut!" Killian shouts.

That's when Cedric and I stop. Our breathing is heavy as I tremble slightly, but I don't move out from Cedric's arms.

He is smiling at me. "That was amazing."

I nod, unable to speak. When I glance back at the camera, ready for the next direction, I see Killian's face. His nostrils are flared, and his eyes are protruding out of me imploring me to stop as he bares his teeth at Cedric. He's pissed. I smile and wave at him before diving under the water and moving over to the waterfall. He's definitely affected by me and jealous as hell.

Cedric swims up behind me.

"So, how long have you been modeling?" I ask as we wait for them to move the camera to get the new angle.

"Two years. You?"

"Since I was twelve."

He smiles. "I could tell you were more experienced than most women I've modeled with."

I smile although no one has ever called me experienced. I'm the furthest from it. Sure, I've done hundreds of shoots, but only a few have ever been make-out scenes. Most have been just fun, cute poses.

"Action!" Brock shouts.

We both move under the waterfall. I don't know why people think this is sexy because it isn't. It's the furthest thing from it. I laugh as Cedric moves up closer together until we are kissing again. This time, there is nothing sexy about the kisses. As we kiss, we are both struggling for air beneath the water drowning us.

"Cut," Brock calls quickly.

We immediately move apart. We both cough up the water that was drowning us earlier.

"We are going to move back to the lounge chair," Brock says.

We swim to the edge and hop out. I'm still coughing up water as I do. I feel a towel being wrapped around me, and I glance between coughs to thank the person when I see whose arms are wrapped around me. It's Killian.

"Are you okay?" he asks.

Another cough of water spews out. "Yes, just swallowed some water on that last shot. It's nothing I've haven't experienced before."

"You don't need to do this."

I smile at him. "Yes, I do."

"I'm not talking about the shoot. You don't have to make out with some guy to get back at me for something that happened three years ago," he says seriously.

"I'm not. This is what you wanted." My voice drops. "You wanted me to fuck you and then forget about you. That's what I'm doing."

I walk away from Killian and do my best to dry myself off before I find Brock standing next to the lounge chair I was on before.

"Kinsley, I want you lying on your back on the chair, like you were before. Cedric, I want you lying on top of her. I want you to kiss and then stroke her hair. Then, I want you both to deliver your lines to the camera."

I smile, but inside, I'm terrified. I hate this kind of shoot. This is where it gets intimate, especially since we are both still drenched. I will be able to feel every inch of Cedric's body as he lies on top of me...just like I felt every inch of Killian's body last night.

I lie down on the lounger, and Cedric smiles as he lies on top of me.

"Well, this is awkward," he says when his wet body forms with mine.

"Don't act like you aren't enjoying it," I say, trying to sound relaxed.

He smiles. "You're right."

I feel his hard chest and abs pushing against me. I feel his hot breath on my neck, his erection throbbing against my core.

My heart is beating fast as Brock has us look intimately into each other's eyes. His are blue and bright, not dark and intense like I'm used to staring into. Cedric is a good-looking guy, but he's not Killian.

"You're beautiful," Cedric whispers into my ear.

My cheeks flush. I take a deep breath, but it's hard to get any air with Cedric's body pressed against mine. I feel everyone's eyes on us as Cedric tucks a strand of hair behind my ear. I'm too frozen to move or react. I have to get my act together, so I don't come off looking like a bored mannequin instead of a sexy model flirting with Cedric, like I'm supposed to be doing.

I smile at him. "You're pretty handsome yourself," I whisper in his ear.

I feel his erection harden beneath me.

"I'm more than just a model, you know. I just graduated from UNLV with a business degree. I'm planning on going to law school this fall. This is just a way to pay the bills."

I don't know why he is saying this, but he seems genuinely proud of what he has accomplished. It's no Harvard, but I am impressed.

"That's impressive," I say.

Cedric's eyes look lustful now as they drop to my chest and then come back to my eyes. "I don't usually do this. I don't usually ask models I work with out on dates. I don't like mixing business and pleasure. But you're not one of the typical models I work with, and I can't help myself. Will you go out with me?"

My eyes grow wide. I've never been asked out by another model. It's the cardinal rule you never break. I glance over behind the camera to see what Killian is doing. My heart still has hope we can work things out together. I'm still holding out a small bit of hope last night was more than a one-night stand. His body language earlier made it seem like he was jealous, but I'm not sure if jealousy is enough for him to want anything more to do with me.

When I spot him, I see him talking to the spunky makeup artist. He's laughing. She's flirting. He's flirting back. I'm nothing to him but a problem he needs to get rid of.

I turn my attention back to Cedric. He's handsome. He seems nice. He even has a future planned out beyond modeling. And I need to get over Killian.

Who knows? If this turns into something, Granddad might think I am capable of finding my own husband.

"Sure. I'm free tonight," I say.

Cedric's smile and erection grow in unison. His body presses closer to mine. "Tonight is perfect."

He lowers his lips to mine, which surprises me because Brock never told us to kiss. This kiss is real. It's not planned. It's tentative and gentle, just testing the waters in a way most first kisses do. When I kiss him back, wrapping my arms around his neck, I try to keep myself from comparing this kiss to Killian's. Cedric deepens the kiss.

His tongue easily slides into my mouth, like he has practiced this many times before. I don't care though. I feel his hand slide up and cup my breast, and I moan.

Shit, I moaned. I'm on camera, moaning, as a man I just met is feeling me up.

"Cut!" Killian shouts.

I look up and am shocked that he was the one yelling cut. He glares in our direction, but I don't know why. He walks over to us, as his face reddens and his jaw tenses.

His eyes travel to Cedric's and then mine. "This isn't a porno. Just kiss her, and then deliver your lines."

I gulp nervously as Cedric's body stays plastered to mine, but Cedric seems unaffected.

"Sorry, boss." Cedric looks back to me, winking as he does. "It's just hard not to get lost in a beautiful woman. I forgot I was doing a job."

"If you don't just do your job, you won't be getting paid, Cedric," Killian says.

Now, I'm glaring at Killian. That's taking it a little too far.

"Sorry. It won't happen again—at least, not until tonight," Cedric says, winking at me.

I giggle at Cedric. It wasn't the suavest of lines I've ever heard, but I don't care. I'm having fun, flirting with Cedric. I'm excited to see where he takes me to dinner tonight. That's two dates in two nights. I'm sure at this rate I can find a man my grandfather likes more than Killian. It was my father who was in love with Killian after all, not my grandfather. It might not be Cedric, but if I spend the next month dating, I'm sure I can do better.

I smile, happy to have a new plan. It's my own plan for my life. The modeling is fun, but it's not what I want my life to be.

"What does that mean?" Killian says.

"Kinsley agreed to go out with me tonight," Cedric says.

"Is that true?" Killian asks, looking at me.

My smile drops when I see a hint of sadness in his eyes. I don't know why he's sad. This is what he wanted—for me to live my own life.

"Yes," I say weakly.

Killian shakes his head. "Just finish the shoot. I'm not paying for overtime."

I watch as Killian walks away, but this time, he doesn't stop. He walks back into the hotel. He doesn't finish watching the shoot. And I have no idea why he reacted like a complete ass.

I turn my attention back to Cedric, back to the job at hand. And I do my best to erase any thoughts of Killian from my brain.

14

I HEAR the knock on my door. I glance down at the time on my phone —seven fifty-five. He's five minutes early. I finish applying my red lipstick before I head to the door. I check through the peephole first before I open the door. Cedric is standing there in a suit. I exhale, happy I wore appropriate clothing for once.

I am happy with the response he gives me. His eyes drop to the cutouts on each side of the black dress before dropping lower to take in my exposed legs. When his eyes find mine again, I see the appreciation there.

"You look even more beautiful, if that's possible."

"It's possible. You look beautiful yourself," I say, eyeing his tailored suit and toned chest peeking out from atop his slightly unbuttoned shirt. "I mean, you look handsome," I say, flushing a bright shade of pink already.

"Don't be."

He holds his arm out for me, and I take it.

We walk down the hallway and into the elevator in relative silence. It's when we get to the casino floor I realize Cedric doesn't know that I'm Kinsley Felton, daughter of Robert Felton. Maybe he won't notice the stares as we walk through the casino floor, arm in arm.

"Good evening, Kinsley," one of the bartenders says.

I nod my head in her direction, smiling. I try walking faster to get us out of here as soon as possible, but Cedric doesn't take the hint. Instead, he seems uneasy, as more and more employees begin staring at us. Some seem shocked to see me walking, hand in hand, with a man. Others smile knowingly. And others give me a friendly nod of recognition as we walk through the floor.

My nerves intensify when I see Killian sitting at the bar in the center of the casino floor. He's not alone; a dark haired young woman is sitting with him. She touches his arm and smiles. He grins back at her. I thought I was the only one he smiled at. I thought I was special. I'm not.

I tear my eyes from them as Cedric escorts me out the doors.

"Do you work here?" Cedric asks when we are outside.

"You could say that."

He stops us, as my answer didn't cure his curiosity.

"My name is Kinsley Felton. My father used to own the company. Everybody in there knows who I am because of it."

I run my hands through my long blond locks. I twist and twirl them as I wait for him to change how he acts around me, but he doesn't.

"That's cool." He shrugs. He begins walking again, but then he suddenly stops.

I curiously look at him. "Something wrong?"

"Wait...you don't work as one of the bartenders or something? I'm not sure I could handle dating someone who has men ogling them every night."

I laugh. "No, I'm not a bartender, but I am a model. What do you think men do when they see my ads or magazine covers?" I raise an eyebrow at him.

"Good point." He sighs before he softly kisses me on the lips. It's a sweet kiss. It doesn't send fireworks exploding throughout my body though.

He pulls away with a look of contentment on his face. "I guess I'll just have to be jealous then."

I smile against his lips. "I guess so."

"I do like jealous sex."

I twist away from him. "Me, too," I say. But I've never had jealous sex before, and even though we spent half the day making out while mostly naked, I'm not sure I'm ready to have sex with Cedric.

He quickly catches up to me and loops his arm back around me.

"Where are we going?" I ask.

We walk less than a block when Cedric stops. "Right here."

I smile without looking at the restaurant we are stopped in front of. I already know which one it is. It's one of my favorites. My father has taken me here hundreds of times.

"Is this okay?" he asks.

"It's perfect."

We take a seat in the beautiful restaurant. A piano player plays softly in the background, and red roses sit in the center of the table.

"Do you like red wine?" Cedric asks.

"Yes," I say.

I glance down at the wine list and find that my favorite is listed, the one Killian got me hooked on. I'm just about to suggest it, but Cedric interrupts me.

"I think we should share a bottle of the house cabernet. Is that okay with you?"

I sigh. I'm not going to get my favorite. But that's okay; I don't want to be thinking about Killian anyway. And drinking that wine will make me think of him. It will make me wonder if he has already convinced the woman he was with to go to his room with him— although I don't think Killian would have to do much convincing. I think most women he meets would willingly jump into bed with him. That means, if he's asked, she's already made her way to his bed.

"Sounds perfect," I say, trying not to think about Killian.

I watch Cedric order our wine. It felt nice that he asked my opinion before just ordering for me. I'm so used to Killian, who orders whatever he wants for us both.

"Where did you go to school?" Cedric asks.

"Yale."

His eyes widen. "Seriously?"

My smile drops from my face. "Yeah, I studied theater...although I don't think that's what I want to do. I don't technically have my degree yet, but they should be sending it soon. I missed finals, but my grades were high enough I didn't need to make them up."

"Why did you miss finals?"

I look down, not ready to hear his *I'm sorry* that is going to follow what I say next. "My father died the weekend before finals."

He reaches his hand across the table and grabs ahold of my hand in a comforting manner. "I'm sorry."

I smile weakly. "Thanks."

An awkward pause passes where I don't want to talk further about my father, but Cedric isn't sure if he can change the topic or not.

"I'm not really sure about what I want to do next with my life," I say. That's not completely true though. I don't know *exactly* what I want to do with my life. I know it doesn't involve marrying Killian. I know it doesn't involve modeling. "What do you want to do once you finish your law degree?"

"I want to start my own firm. I like corporate law. And then I want to settle down with a beautiful girl like you. Somewhere warm."

"Of course," I say, smiling.

"And I want to marry her. I want to have kids with her. I want my life to be her."

I blush. "I hope you find that someday."

His eyes stay transfixed on mine. "I'm getting close."

His eyes sparkle, and I quickly lose myself in them. It would be nice to be married to someone like Cedric. He seems nice. He seems like a gentleman. He seems like husband material, unlike Killian who is too focused on his work to ever give proper attention to a wife and family.

"Kinsley?" my grandfather says.

I turn and see my grandfather standing at the end of our table.

He has a stern look on his face. I see Killian standing behind him with a small smirk.

I try to pull my hand away from Cedric's, but he doesn't understand what's happening. He just tightens his grip as his thumb slowly moves over my palm.

"Hi, Granddad," I say.

"Who is this?" he asks, looking at Cedric.

"This is—" I start.

But, of course, Cedric, being a gentleman, jumps in immediately.

"I'm Cedric Allum. I'm her date for the evening—and, hopefully, if she will have me, for many dates after this."

I wince at his words, and Cedric looks at me in confusion.

"I'm not just a model," Cedric says in a rush, thinking that is the reason that my grandfather and I are so unhappy with what he just said. "I just do that on the side for some extra money, same as Kinsley. I just graduated with a business degree from UNLV. I got accepted into a law school in Chicago. I plan on being a lawyer, sir."

My grandfather is paying him no attention. Instead, he is looking at me. "I think you'd better end the date now, Kinsley."

I nod, unable to argue with him in such a public space. I don't look at Killian. And I don't look at Cedric as I begin to stand from my chair.

I take a deep breath before I do my best to look strong as I look at Cedric. "I'm sorry. You've been wonderful, but I think it's best if we stop this here."

"Why? I thought this was going well." He glances up at my grandfather. "If your grandfather and"—he looks at Killian—"your brother would like to join us, they are more than welcome. Then, they can get to know me a little better and feel more comfortable with us going out."

I chance a glance at Killian when Cedric calls him my brother. His smirk is gone. He's rubbing the back of his neck in annoyance instead of the fuming anger I was expecting. It seems he doesn't even see Cedric as worthy of a challenge.

"That won't be possible," Granddad says.

"Another time, then?" Cedric asks.

I smile weakly at his persistence, but he needs to learn when to give up.

That's when Killian steps forward. "I'm sorry, Cedric, but you need to go home and forget about Kinsley. Don't call her. Don't think about her. Don't try to reach out to her in any way. Plenty of other girls are out there who would be more suited to you."

I close my eyes to keep the sting out of them after what he just said.

"I think Kinsley is plenty suited to me," Cedric says.

"No, because Kinsley is *my* fiancée," Killian says.

Cedric gasps. Then, he looks to my left hand to find a ring that isn't there. His eyes narrow in my direction. "You're engaged?"

I twist my hair as I look at him. I don't know how to answer that. I'm not technically engaged. At least, I wasn't the last time I spoke with either of the men glowering over me, but it's too complicated to say I'm not engaged.

Cedric takes my lack of an answer as an answer. "She's all yours," he says as he throws his napkin down on the table before storming out.

I don't bother to follow him with my eyes when he leaves. I feel like crying. I feel like going home and spending the night taking a long warm bath, trying to forget what just happened. I feel like screaming at Killian and Granddad for what they just did.

"Come on, Kinsley. We have a table for us set up upstairs. We will have them add another chair. You'll eat with us," Granddad says. His voice is dripping with disappointment.

I nod, unable to say any words without losing it. I feel so embarrassed. I watch as my grandfather begins walking, but Killian hovers over me, waiting for me to follow my grandfather.

I take a second. "How could you?" A tear falls.

"You can't be with him. He's not a good guy."

"And you are?" I shake my head in frustration. "You can't tell me you want me to make my own decisions about my life and then make every decision for me! You can't tell him I'm your fiancée one minute but then tell me you don't want to marry me the next. You can't pick up a random stranger at a bar one minute and then say I can't go on a date myself. Talk about indecisive. What do you want, Killian? Other than the CEO position, what the fuck do you want?"

I close my eyes when I realize I just cursed in front of a table with children. I never curse. But Killian brings out the worst in me, the absolute worst.

"I want to marry you," are the words that leave his lips.

15

I HAVEN'T LOOKED at Killian since I sat down at the table opposite my grandfather. I can't. I don't believe what Killian said when we were alone downstairs. He didn't say anything else. It was just those five words.

"I want to marry you."

I don't believe them. I don't think I ever will until I see him down on bended knee. And even then, it won't be because that's what he really wants. It will be because that is the only way he can become CEO.

"What were you doing with that boy, Kinsley?" my grandfather asks.

Our waiter interrupts us, and my grandfather orders wine for the table. He asks Killian for his opinion but not mine.

When the waiter leaves, Granddad turns his attention back to me, waiting for my answer.

"He was nice. I met him at the modeling shoot earlier. I didn't realize I wasn't allowed to date while I waited for Killian to decide if he wants to marry me or not," I snark.

I feel Killian's eyes on me, but I still don't look at him. I'm too pissed to look at him. He did the same thing an hour earlier with a woman. *Why can't I?*

"You know the rules, young lady. The same rules still apply as when your father was alive. If you want to date, you run the guys by me. I will tell you whom you should or shouldn't date. You've made too many horrible decisions in the past to allow anything else. You shouldn't have been on a date with Cedric."

"I've made one horrible mistake. One," I say, glaring at my grandfather for bringing it up.

My eyes dart to Killian, but his searching eyes shooting back and forth between the two of us make it clear he doesn't know what we're talking about.

I move on. "What was wrong with Cedric? He seemed like a perfect gentleman if you asked me."

"Tell her, Killian."

Killian takes a deep breath. "Cedric is a scam artist. He only dates rich women and then scams them or steals money from them."

I turn to him. "And how exactly do you know this?"

"We do background checks on all our employees, including the models. There were some suspicious things when his returned. The suspicious information didn't touch my desk until after the shoot. Otherwise, I would never have let him do the shoot. He's a wanted felon in three states. We called the police. He was arrested as soon as he left the premises."

Fuck! How the hell am I supposed to make my own decisions in my life when I keep making the wrong ones?

The waiter pours us each a glass of wine, and I down my glass in one gulp. I can feel everyone's eyes on me as I do, but I don't care. The waiter pours me a second glass.

"This is why you can't make your own decisions without consulting Killian or me. You are too naïve, too easily taken advantage of, sweetheart. We are just trying to protect you."

I don't respond to Granddad's words, but I can't believe them. I didn't do anything, except go on a date with Cedric. I didn't make up my mind about him yet. If they had just given me time, they could have seen I would have turned Cedric down on my own.

"Are you ready to order?" the waiter asks.

My grandfather nods. "I'll have the sirloin, medium rare. Kinsley will have the same."

I don't hear Killian order. I'm too busy sulking. This is what my life will be like. Everything will always be decided by these two men. I will never get a choice in what I eat or drink. I will never get a choice in what I do. I will never get a choice in when I have children or what their names will be or what they do with their own lives. I will never get a say. I've never had a say.

I quickly sip on my wine, and before I know it, I've finished another glass. The waiter immediately fills it again.

"Regardless, I have some good news to share with you, Kinsley," Granddad says.

I'm not hearing him though. My head is spinning. I'm dizzy. I've felt this way once before, and I know what's going to happen next. I can't be here when it happens.

"Excuse me. I think I'm going to be sick," I say as I stand from the table.

I rush to find the restroom down on the first floor. I run, barely making it to a toilet stall before the contents from my stomach come back up.

God, I hate alcohol, I think as I heave into the disgusting public toilet.

A few seconds pass, and I hear the door swing open. *Great.*

Now, whoever has walked through that door will get to hear my embarrassment as I puke into the toilet.

I try to reach back to at least lock the stall door to keep the woman from seeing me, but I can't without moving away from the toilet, and my stomach isn't finished emptying yet.

That's when I feel his arms on me. Killian's holding back my hair as he slowly rubs my back.

"It's okay, princess."

I want to fight Killian off, but I'm too weak to do that. I vomit again and again, to my disgust. I can't believe he is in here, taking care of me like a real boyfriend would. But we aren't boyfriend and girlfriend. We aren't even friends. We are nothing.

When I finally finish, I feel like collapsing, but Killian holds me up.

"Come on, princess. Let's get you cleaned up."

Killian helps me stand and leads me to the sink. I watch as he turns on the warm water and puts a paper towel under the water before wiping my face.

He doesn't say anything. He just intently stares at me. There isn't disappointment on his face. There is just nothing. It's like he is doing a business transaction. That's what I am. I don't have to be stupid to know what my grandfather was about to say. He was going to tell me that Killian agreed to marry me. I'm not ready to hear those words from him. If he says them and I hear them, then it's over. I have nothing left to fight for. My destiny has already been decided, but I'm not ready to know what my future entails yet.

"I want to go home," I say.

He nods. "I sent your grandfather home. I told him I'd make sure you got home okay. I told him you would talk to him tomorrow."

"Thanks," I whisper.

I follow Killian out of the restroom. A woman, who was just about to enter, stares wildly at Killian. She's probably thinking we just hooked up in the restroom. I see Killian smirk at her, and my cheeks blush.

I make it out of the restaurant without stumbling, but Killian scoops me up.

"I can walk," I protest while hating and loving being in his arms. I hate the conflicting feelings.

"I know, princess, but you shouldn't have to."

I don't fight him. I just let him carry me into the casino. I let him carry me, despite the stares we get on the casino floor. I don't care. Let them think what they want about me. My life is over anyway.

To my surprise though, Killian doesn't take me to my room. He takes me to his. I don't protest. I'm too tired to do anything else. And we have some shit we need to work out anyway.

He lays me on his bed that is just like the one in mine. He leaves and quickly comes back with some water, aspirin, and the hotel's cookies. He hands them all to me. He doesn't have to speak to get me to take them. I know they will make me feel better.

"You shouldn't drink so much."

"No shit," I say before swallowing the pills.

He smiles. "You're cute when you curse."

"I learned from you." I sigh. "What do you want, Killian? Why am I here?"

He narrows his eyes at me. "Why did you agree to go out with him?"

I sigh. "Why not? I know what happened between us last night was just a one-time thing. And I just thought, if I could prove I am capable of finding a man on my own, one who is good for the company and good for me, then my grandfather would give me more time to be more involved in the decision. I just thought I could do better than you."

I study his face to see if my words hurt him, but they don't. "And you were out with that brunette at the bar anyway."

A small smile tugs at the corner of his lips. "That was my sister."

"Oh." I take a deep breath. "Why did you agree to marry me?"

"Because I want to be CEO. And I've realized this is the only way I will ever get what I want."

I sit up too fast, and the dizziness that ensues makes me grab my head. He grabs ahold of me and forces me to lie back in bed.

"I just want to go back to my own bed."

"No, not until we figure this out."

I sigh. "There is nothing to figure out. You want to marry me to get the CEO position, but you don't really want to be married to me. I don't want to marry you either. I'll tell my grandfather I don't care about the money or being connected to the Felton empire. You'll get everything you ever wanted."

"That won't work."

"It will. It was your plan after all. And you do no wrong, remember?"

"That's not true." His body moves closer to mine. "I do a lot of things wrong. I do a lot of things I shouldn't do."

I roll my eyes. "You've never done anything wrong in your life."

His lips crash with mine, burning into me full of hunger, of need. I feel my body giving in to the kiss, but I can't let it happen.

I push him away. "What was that?"

"It was me doing something I shouldn't."

"Why shouldn't you?"

"Because you can't fall for me," he says.

But when he kisses me again, I wonder if he is the one who can't fall for me.

I push him off of me. But his mouth finds my neck instead of my lips.

"I'm still mad at you," I say.

His mouth tugs at my earlobe. "I know."

"I'm still mad at you for making Eli break up with me."

I moan when he nips at the lobe.

"I know."

"I'm still mad at you for ruining my date with Cedric."

He tangles his hand in my hair, tugging my head back, so his lips have better access to my neck. "I know."

"I'm still mad—"

"I know." He moves his mouth back to my lips, shutting me up.

I'm about to make a terrible choice. As his tongue caresses mine, I know I'm going to end up fucking him again. His hands slide down the sides of my body, feeling my curves.

"Fuck, I want you, princess." His greedy eyes take in my body, but it's not good enough to see me in the sexy dress. He wants more.

His mouth kisses down my neck to the edge of the dress. His hands grab at the top, and when I don't protest, he rips the dress in half. It's the sexiest fucking thing I've ever seen.

His eyes now lust with a need to have my body. His hand grabs my breast without him asking, without him waiting to see if this is what I want. I've already told him with my parted lips, with my lust-filled eyes, with my heavy breathing. They all tell him how badly I want him, too.

"This is wrong," I say.

He takes my exposed nipple in his mouth. He twirls his tongue around the hard bud, making me forget why this is wrong as I moan his name. He grabs my other breast and twirls his thumb around it.

"Maybe," he says.

It makes me smile at him. He smiles back before disappearing between my legs. He pulls my panties down with his teeth, leaving me completely naked while he is still fully clothed. I grab at his shirt, and he gets the hint. He rips his shirt off. I watch as a few buttons fall to the sides. He stands and unzips his pants, removing them and his underwear.

He moves back on top of me, his lips hovering above mine. "I can't believe you let him kiss this," he says, running his thumb across my lips before devouring them with his own. "These lips are mine, not his." He kisses me again harder, marking me as his own, showing me how jealous he really was when I was kissing Cedric. "He doesn't have a right to these lips."

He bites on my bottom lip, tugging on it like Cedric did earlier, but when Killian does it, liquid pools between my legs.

When he releases it, I repeat his words, "These lips are yours."

He smiles at me. He moves down my chest and finds my breasts. He roughly grabs them, rougher than he has before. He takes one in his mouth, nipping hard at the nipple.

"He doesn't get to see these nipples. He doesn't get to taste their hard peaks or hear you moan his name as he drives you crazy."

I moan as his tongue drives me wild. "Just yours."

He moves lower, stopping between my legs. He takes my clit into his mouth, sucking ferociously, making it his. "He doesn't get the pleasure of watching you come."

I moan, "No, only you."

When he's done, he leans back and flips me over onto my stomach. He smacks my ass, hard. It stings, but it somehow also brings me pleasure.

"This ass? It's mine, not his."

"I'm yours, all yours," I moan.

He smacks me again before he pulls me onto all fours. I hear him rustle with the wrapper of a condom before I feel him pushing at my entrance.

"You remember that, princess, before you go on another date. You remember that, when you get back, I'm going to punish you like I'm going to punish you now. You don't deserve to come. You don't deserve to feel good. You deserve to be punished for not understanding that you're mine."

He thrusts inside me without warning. It hurts at first as he fills me. This time, instead of going slow, he moves fast, but this time, I accommodate him. It feels good, going faster.

"Fuck, Killian," I moan.

He slaps my ass again, and I cry out.

"Do you understand how jealous you made me?" He slaps me again as he thrusts inside.

"Yes," I moan.

"Will you do it again?" He crashes into me again.

"No, never," I moan as his balls crash into my clit.

"Why?"

He thrusts again, bringing me close, so close.

"Because I'm yours," I pant.

His hand reaches around, massaging my clit, as he crashes his body into me again.

"You can come, princess," he says as he massages my clit.

And I do. My body convulses as the waves wash through me. Killian follows right after, and we both collapse into a pile on the bed. His breath feels hot on my neck.

"You're mine, princess," he says before kissing me on the neck. "Your body, your soul, your mind, all mine."

Then, he gets off me to go clean himself off in the bathroom, leaving me spent on his bed.

A large smile is stuck on my face. Cedric was right. Jealous fucking is definitely the best.

I don't know what this means. *Does Killian like me more than he has been letting on?* I can feel my heart already falling for him. It's not just because the sex was the best thing I've ever felt. It's because he took care of me in a way no one ever has. He knew what I needed. He knew I needed him to feel jealous. He knew I needed him to own me. He knew I needed him.

———

I feel my time running out as I slip out of Killian's bed. He's still sound asleep, snoring, facedown on the bed.

Last night was amazing. By far, it was the best time I've ever had with a man. But it was just his way of trying to control me. He was manipulating me to do what he wanted. He doesn't care about me. And he sure doesn't love me.

I shake my head at myself. I can't believe he got me back in his damn bed. I used to be able to tell men no so easily. That woman is gone. At least around Killian.

I find my ripped dress on the floor. I can't put it back on. I go into the closet and find a T-shirt I doubt he will miss and slip it on over my head. I also find a pair of his workout shorts and slip those on. If anybody sees me, they will know for sure what happened last night, but it doesn't matter anymore. My time is running out.

I collect my ripped dress and purse off the floor.

Killian snores loudly, making me pause at his bedroom door to look at him. My heart aches as I look at him lying in bed. If I stayed for just a few more hours, I'm sure we would spend the morning together fucking and eating breakfast. It's what I want—to spend more time with Killian. But every moment I spend with him, the further I fall under his spell. I become more attracted to the idea of marrying him, of letting him run my father's company.

I can imagine it now. It would be a life of fucking, a life of butting heads, a life of me giving up my control. Our life together would be intense. I might even be able to love this man and have kids with this man.

The only problem is, he would never feel the same way about me. He would always resent the fact he was forced to marry me to get the job of his dreams. He would resent being forced to give up his life of banging different girls to come home to the same boring woman every night. He would resent his stolen life.

I can't do that to him. I can't do that to me. I don't know how to avoid that outcome without a fight though. And it's a fight I'm not sure I can win. But I have to try.

As much as I want to stay here and be kissed awake by this man, I can't, so I do the only thing I can do. I leave without a word, without a good-bye, without any explanation.

I make it back to my hotel room without anyone seeing me. It is four in the morning, so I wasn't expecting too many people to be roaming the halls, but this is Las Vegas. Anything and everything happens here.

I close the door to my hotel room and lean against it, taking a deep breath. I can't be around Killian anymore. I'll destroy both of our lives if I am.

I take the neck of the T-shirt I'm wearing and bring it up to cover my nose before taking a deep breath. I relax when I realize it smells like him. I take several more deep breaths before I make my way to my bed. I leave his shirt on and climb under the covers. I set my alarm for two hours from now. I drift back to sleep as I breathe in his manly scent, imagining his arms are wrapped around me instead of the shirt. The only decision I know is I'm done giving up control over my own life.

16

I KNOCK on Tony's office door a few hours before I'm supposed to meet my grandfather. I need to spend some time at the company—figuring out what life would be like here, what it would be like to run or even be a part of this company. Maybe then I might realize that this isn't really what I want. That would make it easier to walk away.

"Come in," Tony says from his desk.

I push the door open and sigh when I see the mess his office is in. If it's possible, I think it looks worse than it did the last time I was here. Now, there are empty plates of food rotting from what looks to be lunch from a previous day.

"Just wanted to see how you were doing," I say. But that's not true. I'm trying to figure out how I'm doing. I'm trying to figure out if I really belong here or if I'm just kidding myself.

"I'm doing all right. The real question is, how are you doing?"

I shrug as I walk into his office and take a seat across from him. "I've been better."

Tony gets up from behind his desk and takes a seat next to me. "Your father was one of the greatest men I ever knew. He was kind. He was fair." He chuckles. "He was incredibly strong. He didn't take any crap from anyone." He looks at me. "You're a lot like him."

I shake my head. "I'm not as strong as him. I'm not strong enough to carry on his legacy. I can't even convince people to do a simple expansion that is obviously needed. I can't even decide what drink to order or what food to eat. I can't even choose the right men to date."

I look up to see Tony smiling at me.

"I never said your father was perfect—or that you are either, sweetie. I just said you were both strong."

"I wish my father had told me what I was supposed to do—if he really wanted me to do what my grandfather wanted or if he wanted something else."

Tony sighs. "Now, that is something I can't answer for you. What I think matters most is what you want, what you think you were born to do. Whether that's finding a way to run the company yourself, marry Killian, or run off and have nothing to do with the company, the decision is yours."

My eyes widen at his words. "How did you know about Killian or about me possibly wanting to run the company?"

His words are warm as he says, "Oh, honey, the whole company knows you are supposed to marry Killian. Your grandfather isn't the best at keeping secrets. And you? You're easy to read. I know the only reason you are spending any time with an old man like me is to try to learn, to see if this is the path for you."

"Then, you know it's not really my choice, my future. It's my grandfather's. It's Killian's. It's not mine."

Tony frowns. "That's where you are wrong. It's yours. Your father always made sure of that."

"What do you mean?"

"It's not my place to say."

A knock interrupts us.

"Hey, Tony." A young man sticks his head into Tony's office. "Have you seen Killian?"

Tony shakes his head. "No, sorry. I think he's at a meeting at the Felton Red Waves. He won't be back until later this evening."

"Shit," the man says. "Is Lee around?"

I glance down at my phone. "I don't think he is going to be in for another hour."

"Shit," the man says again. "I need someone to sign these, approving the initial demolition, and I need it now. They already showed up. If I don't give them these forms, like, right now, they are going to leave. Then, who knows when the construction will start?"

"I'll sign them," I say without thinking.

The man looks at me in confusion. "Who are you?"

"I'm Kinsley Felton. I'll sign them. It's no big deal really," I say, although I don't have authority to sign anything. Grandfather won't care though. I already know he wants the expansion to happen, and so does Killian. It won't hurt anything for my signature to be on it instead of theirs.

The man looks to Tony, who nods his head and smiles.

The man still looks concerned, but he knows his ass is on the line if the project doesn't start today. He rushes the papers over to me and shows me where to sign. I sign and initial each spot, barely glancing at the papers. I should probably read them before signing, but this man is in an obvious rush. I don't want to give him a heart attack by waiting for me to read them. And it feels good to be making a decision for the company even if it is one that has already been agreed upon.

"Thanks," the man says, rushing back out of Tony's office.

When I turn back to Tony, his sly smile is plastered on his lips.

"What?"

He shakes his head as he tries to lose the smile, but he can't. "I think, with a little training, you would make an excellent CEO. You probably shouldn't start off in that position, but I think a few years under your belt would get you ready."

"You're crazy. All I did was sign some papers. I didn't do anything."

"You did more than just sign some papers. You convinced a man who has never met you that you were in charge. And don't think I didn't notice that, after you left last time, you didn't just change one small thing about my numbers. You completely redid everything to make it work. You saw trends no one else saw. That's impressive. You are obviously a natural when it comes to numbers and finance. We could use someone like you in this department."

I smile weakly. "Thanks." But I don't feel like I'm capable of doing anything.

Tony stands, returning back to his chair. "Killian is good-looking and charming, too, though. He wouldn't be a terrible choice either." He winks at me. "There is no wrong choice, as long as you are the one making the choice. Be a housewife. Be a model. Become CEO. Decide what you want and go after it."

I frown. I don't want him giving me dating advice, although the other advice I appreciate. I don't want anyone giving me dating advice. He doesn't understand what's going on in Killian's head.

"He doesn't care about me. He just wants to marry me to get the position."

Tony narrows his eyes. "I wouldn't be too sure about that. Word is, he just got promoted without marrying you. He might care more about you than you think."

But all I hear is that Killian got promoted to CEO. Last night, he knew the decision my grandfather had made. And Killian chose not to tell me my time was already up.

I no longer get a choice. At least not about becoming CEO.

"I need to go," I say.

Tony nods as I stand and leave without a goodbye.

———

I take my phone out to call my grandfather, to tell him to meet me earlier, it can't wait. I dial his number, but I get his voicemail. I end the call before I leave a message. That's when I notice the messages from Killian.

There are three text messages, asking why I left this morning without talking to him, telling me we need to talk, telling me what to do.

I also notice the seven missed calls and two voicemails from him.

I delete the voicemails without listening to them. I don't want to hear what Killian has to say. If he couldn't say it last night before fucking me, then I don't want to hear it now.

I pace back and forth thirty-five times in my father's office before I hear the familiar creak of the door being pushed open. My grandfather is standing in the doorway. He doesn't look happy to see me, but I don't give a shit.

I can't wait any longer, and the words fall from my mouth. "You made Killian CEO!" I shout at him.

He calmly walks in, setting a briefcase down on the desk. He doesn't say anything or even acknowledge me as he takes a seat behind my father's desk.

"You made Killian CEO," I say again, only slightly calmer.

He sighs in frustration. "Yes."

"I thought he had to marry me first. I thought it had to be agreed upon between the three of us."

"He did. He signed the papers yesterday afternoon, agreeing to marry you in six months. So, in good faith, I promoted him to CEO. He doesn't have the shares yet. That will happen after the wedding."

"What if I don't agree to the wedding?"

"You will. You don't have another choice. This is what is best for you."

"No, it's not. I don't want this. I don't want to be married to a man who doesn't love me. I don't want to marry someone just because you wished I were a grandson instead of your granddaughter. I won't do it."

"Kinsley, stop this. You will marry Killian. He's a good man. And I know he cares about you."

"You're wrong. He doesn't give a fuck about anything other than his work and finding his next good fuck."

His face turns red at my words. I take a deep breath, realizing what I just said to my grandfather. I've never cussed in front of him. I've never talked so crudely.

But, right now, he's not my grandfather. He's the enemy trying to control my life.

He calms his face before walking over to stand in front of me. He places both hands on either side of my shoulders. "This is what your father wanted, princess. He wanted you to marry Killian. He wanted you to support Killian in the role of running the company. He wanted you to have children to pass this company along to—just as my father did, just as I did to your father, just as your father is doing to you."

I feel a tear slip out of my eye. "But that's not what my father is doing. That's not what you are doing. I'm not getting the company with the same conditions as you got the company with or the same conditions as my father got. I'm being forced to marry someone, and only then do I get any say in the company. I'm not getting the same terms."

He smiles, like he thinks he's got me now, like he thinks he's won. "See? That's where you are wrong, Kinsley. You are getting the same terms as everyone else in the family. We all had marriages arranged by our parents. We all had marriages that were for the betterment of the company."

I frown as his words sink in. His words can't be true.

"That's not true. Mom and Dad met in college their junior year."

He shakes his head. "No, your mother was the daughter of the chairman of the Nevada Gaming Commission. We were having some trouble with getting our newest casino approved. Your father fixed the problem, proving his loyalty to the company and this family above everything else."

My mouth drops. I had no idea. I always thought my parents were in love. I always thought they cared about each other but maybe not. That might be why my father spent so many nights alone in his casinos instead of at home with my mother. That can't be true though. My mother was devastated when Dad died. She still is.

"You're lying."

He shakes his head. "Ask your mother."

I plan on it. "It doesn't change anything. I still won't marry Killian."

"You're stubborn, just like your father. He eventually caved though. You will, too." He glances at his watch. "You need to go home and get ready. I had a dress sent to your hotel room. I don't know why you stay here when you have a beautiful room at home." He sighs. "Be ready at eight tonight. That's when Killian will be picking you up."

I shake my head. "I'm not marrying him."

"Maybe not. But he at least deserves the respect of you telling him to his face."

I nod. "I'll go."

He's right. I need to put an end to whatever this is that's going on between Killian and me. I turn to leave, but his words stop me.

"There's one more thing you should know before you make a decision. If you refuse to marry Killian, the money is gone. I control the trust your father left you. You will have nothing but a theater degree to find you work. I'll call everyone and tell them never to hire you as a model again. You are doing this, or you are no longer my granddaughter. If you walk away from this, you are no longer a Felton."

Those are the words that will haunt me for the rest of the day. For the rest of my life.

"You are no longer a Felton."

I wish they were true. I wish I were never born a Felton.

I'd thought my future was entirely out of my control. I was wrong.

My grandfather just gave me control. I just don't like my choices.

17

I DON'T WEAR the cream-colored dress lying on my bed when I get back to my hotel room. It's a beautiful dress, one I'm sure my grandfather spared no expense to get for me. But I'm not wearing it. I don't know if it's because he chose it or if it's because it's an act of defiance to wear anything but that dress; possibly my last act of defiance. I don't know if it's because I can't stand to wear any color that resembles a wedding gown. I don't know if it's because I have a beautiful red dress I love and haven't had an occasion to wear it to. Whatever the reason, I chose red.

I stand in my hotel room in my deep red ballgown. I'm no closer to deciding if I'm going to say yes or no when Killian asks me. And I know he'll ask me. That's what tonight is about. That's why I'm wearing this pretty dress. That's why I've spent hours fixing my long blond hair. That's why I've spent hours covering my face in makeup.

Tonight is the night I decide the rest of my life. I just don't know what future that will be.

I hear the knock on the door. I glance at my phone. It's eight on the dot. Killian's on time tonight. I peek through the hole in the door and see him dressed in a tux. I take a deep breath, and then I open the door.

I watch him lick his lips as his eyes travel over my body. I hold my breath, trying to calm my beating heart, but it doesn't slow. His eyes catch mine, and it's not a look of lust peering back at me although a hint of that is still there. It's a look I've never seen come from his eyes, and I have no idea what it means.

For a second, I imagine this is how it feels when you are in love, and you know tonight is the night—the night your life will change forever, the night he will get down on a nervous knee and ask you to marry him.

If only I could find someone who would do this for real...

If only he were doing this for more than a promotion...

If only I were doing this for more than family loyalty...

He regroups himself and puts a fake smile on his lips. "I wasn't sure you would answer."

I return his fake smile. "I wasn't sure you would come."

"You didn't return my calls."

"I deleted the voicemails."

He sighs. "We have a lot to talk about."

I nod, but I don't say anything. I give him no indication of how I feel, of how I will answer when he asks—not that I even know myself.

He sighs again. "Let's go, princess."

We walk out of the hotel and casino without saying a word. I don't say a word until we make it out onto the street where I see a horse and carriage waiting for us.

I gasp when I see it. I wasn't expecting anything like it.

"I thought you deserved the full princess experience."

I smile as he helps me into the carriage before climbing in next to me. I really do feel like a princess in this thing. I'm not sure if that's a good thing or a bad thing though. I'm not sure I like being a princess. A princess, I've realized, has no control over her life. Her life is to her country, to her family. It's just like how I live my life for the company, for my family.

I wasn't expecting this. I wasn't expecting effort from a man who was just doing this because he had to. I was expecting dinner and a proposal. But I'm afraid he's put more effort into it than that.

The carriage takes us down the main strip and then turns off, moving us throughout the city. I have no idea where we are going. I'm not sure I care. I'm lost in this perfect moment.

Killian places his arm around my shoulders, and I lean my head against his chest.

"I'm sorry," he whispers.

"For what?" I breathe back.

"For lying to you. For breaking you and Eli up. For controlling any bit of your life. For ruining your date. For forcing you into a life you don't want. For everything."

"None of this is your fault." I suck in a deep breath. "You don't have to do this though. You already have the job. It's not going to be taken away just because you don't do this."

I pause, waiting for him to confirm or deny my statement. He does neither. He just looks at me with the same intensity he always does.

So, I continue, "We don't even know each other. I don't know how many siblings you have. I don't know your parents' names. I don't know your favorite color or food or band. I don't know where you grew up. I don't know why you are such a workaholic. I don't know why you never want to get married or have kids. I don't know if we are compatible together. I don't know anything about you, other than you are good in bed and intelligent enough to run the company."

His expression grows grave, but he doesn't say a word.

"I'm a huge Justin Bieber fan—like, huge. I've seen him in concert six times. My favorite movie is *The Notebook*. I've watched it at least a hundred times, and I still cry every single time. I have enough clothes and makeup to fill three regular-size rooms. I hate large houses. I'd prefer to live in hotel rooms for the rest of my life.

"It is always going to take me longer than it should to make my mind up about what I want to order and even longer to make up my mind about anything else. And I'm only occasionally going to be okay with you making those decisions for me although you'll never really know when I want you to decide for me or when I want to make my own decisions.

"I'm never going to be okay with just being a housewife. I'm always going to want to find a way to fight my way into a leadership position at the company. I'm always going to want the fairy tale. I'll always want to be desperately in love and have kids," I say.

His hand reaches up to my lips, squeezing them together, silencing me. "It doesn't matter," he says, never taking his eyes off mine. He slowly releases my lips.

"It does. Trust me, you don't want to be stuck listening to Justin Bieber for the rest of your life when you prefer Justin Timberlake."

He chuckles. "I don't really like either."

"What? You don't like JT?"

"No," he says, like I'm crazy.

I shake my head. "See? You can't do this. Your life would be filled with the music of Justins and little kids running around and indecisiveness." I tuck my hair behind my ear. "It's not what you want." But I'm not sure who I'm convincing with that statement.

As I stare into his eyes, I want to know everything about him. I want to listen to whatever crappy music he enjoys. I want to meet his parents and siblings. I want to argue with him about how long it takes me to order. I just don't want to marry him.

The carriage stops in front of Crystal Waterfalls, my favorite casino. My eyes are wide as I stare at him. He climbs out before holding his hand out to me. I take it, and he helps me out.

Killian doesn't let go of my hand as we walk into the building that, to my surprise, is empty. I don't see a soul walking around. I blink rapidly, thinking what I'm seeing is a dream. It's not. The casino is a ghost town.

I see a trail of rose petals on the floor. It starts next to the river that goes through the center of the hotel and casino. I let go of Killian's hand as I make my way over to the edge of the river. I let my hand dip into the cold water, like I have done hundreds of times before. Petals are floating on top of the water.

I slowly follow the trail of rose petals as I hear Killian walking behind me, but he doesn't try to walk next to me. He lets me discover everything by myself.

The rose petals follow the river. I follow them through the main casino floor, going past all the flashing lights of the slot machines, past the empty card tables, past the shops and restaurants. I follow them until they get to the door. It's the door to my favorite place in the world.

I hesitate at the door, trying to calm my beating heart. This is it. I push the door open, and at the same time, I suck in a breath.

It's beautiful, even more beautiful than usual. Lights are strung over every tree. And the smell from all of the roses and fresh flowers in the garden overwhelm me, as they always do whenever I step into the hotel's garden. The waterfall rushes water over its crest just as calmly as it always does.

But what has taken my breath away are the rose petals and candles covering the floor. It looks like tiny shining stars on the floor of the garden.

I slowly turn back to the door. Killian is standing in the doorway, looking at me with a smile on his face. His head cocks slowly to the side as I smile back at him.

It's a fairy tale in here. It's just not real.

I feel my body tremble as he walks silently to me until he is standing just inches from my body. I hear music start up in the distance. I glance away from Killian and see a violinist playing. I turn back to Killian.

"I would have had her play Justin Bieber, if I had known."

His words make me smile a little brighter, but my body is still trembling.

I watch his tongue run over his lip. I want his tongue on my lip.

"My favorite movie is *The Hangover*. It makes me laugh every fucking time. I have a surprisingly little amount of clothing. I love playing poker and blackjack, even when I'm getting beaten by you. My parents both live in Las Vegas. I've lived here my entire life. I have one younger sister close to your age, one older sister, a brother-in-law —whom you already met—and a three-year-old nephew whom I would do anything for. I'm a workaholic. I'm stubborn. I'm control-ling. I hate waiting for decisions. I've never wanted to get married. I've never wanted kids. I don't have a favorite artist, but I've been listening to the song 'Let Her Go' by Passenger on repeat lately."

I swallow hard. He's not going to propose. My head drops slightly in disappointment. This is good though. He needs to happy. At least one of us should be. I can give him that.

My eyes widen though when I watch him drop to one knee as he holds my hand.

"Princess, I know we might not know everything there is to know about each other. I know we, on paper, are all wrong for each other. I know you think the only reason I'm down on one knee right now is because of the loyalty I have for your father.

"You're wrong. I'm down on one knee right now because you are the strongest woman I have ever met. You are determined, honest, beautiful, and, yes, a little naive. You are every bit as strong as your father was. I might not make the perfect husband. In fact, I know I won't. But I want to spend the rest of my life falling in love with you."

He pulls a box out of his pocket. He pops it open, revealing a gorgeous princess cut diamond. "Princess, will you marry me?"

I bite my lip as I look into his intense eyes. I have no idea what to say.

Yes.

No.

I don't know.

They all go through my head. And then they all zoom out again. None of them is the right answer. None of them will make either of us happy. None of them will bring an end to this story.

I finally open my mouth to say the only word that feels right leaving my lips, "Maybe."

A slow smile tugs at his lips as he shakes his head at me. "That's not going to work. I can't take that as a yes. I need to hear you say it."

I take a slow deep breath as I tuck a loose strand of hair behind my ear. I open my mouth to tell him my answer when our phones simultaneously go off. I pull my phone out from my clutch.

Mother, the screen reads.

I see Killian reaching into his pocket. He runs his hand through his hair.

We both press accept at the same time. We each lift the phone to our ears at the same time. We both say, "Hello?" at the same time.

We both feel the pain at the same time.

18

"I'LL CALL a car to take us," Killian says immediately, dropping his question.

Now that there are more pressing issues to deal with, it doesn't matter if I say yes or no. His perfect proposal is ruined. Maybe that's a good thing because I'm not sure I had the strength to tell him no, even when it's what is best for both of us.

I watch as Killian talks on the phone as he paces back and forth in the beautiful garden. I...I don't move. I don't know how to feel. It doesn't feel as bad as the last time I got a call like this. It doesn't hurt nearly as much, but it still hurts. Maybe because Granddad is just in the hospital and not dead. Maybe it's because my father was my everything. Maybe it's because, this time, I might have a chance to say goodbye, if that is what this comes to.

I watch as Killian quickly makes his way around the room, blowing out all the candles. I don't move though. I can't. I feel him grab ahold of my hand, but I still don't move. I'm not even sure if I'm breathing or if my heart is still beating.

"Kinsley, we need to go out front. The car should be here any minute."

I still don't move. Killian puts his arm around my shoulders and guides me forward. I move but only because his arm is around me. It takes a long time to make our way through the casino and back out onto the strip. Neither of us speaks as we move. We just move as one unit.

When Killian pushes the doors open to the vibrant lights of the busy strip, I move. I don't know if it's the lights or what that jolts me back to reality. Whatever it is, I'm thankful.

I see the blacked-out Cadillac Escalade parked in front of the casino. I grab Killian's hand. "Come on," I say as I run to the car. Killian runs with me.

I pull the door open and dive into the car as quickly as possible. Killian has already run around to the other side and is jumping in. I close the door and hear a small tear of my dress from getting it caught in the door. I pick up the torn fabric and run it back and forth between my fingers. The fairy tale is over. I glance to my left where Killian sits. This is over.

It hurts to know it's true, but it is. This will wake both of us up. It will make both of us want to live a full life—a life we choose, full of happiness and mistakes, a life we live for us.

Killian closes his eyes when he sees it in my eyes. This is over. He knows it as well as I do.

I tell the driver which hospital Granddad's at, and then we are driving away from the casino, away from my life, away from the fairy tale, and back to reality.

———

"Mom," I say to the blond woman slumped over in a waiting room chair.

Her hair is a mess. It's ratted and dirty. I don't know when she showered last. She's wearing an old T-shirt of Dad's and pink pajama pants. She at least had enough sense to put on tennis shoes.

"Mom," I say again as I grab her shoulders while I squat in my dress in front of her.

She moans but doesn't look up at me. I grab her cheeks, lifting her head. The smell of alcohol is intense on her breath. I have to look away from her to take a deep breath.

Shit, why did she have to do this today?

I have no idea how to deal with her while she's drunk. Dad was always the one who dealt with her when she was drunk. I never had to. Now that she's a raging alcoholic every other night, I don't know what to do. I feel guilty for not taking better care of her, for not staying at home and being there for her. But I thought it was for the best. I thought her therapist and AA sponsor would handle her. I thought she would be better by now.

We never got along, even before it happened, even before I destroyed the family reputation. We never got along when she was sober. We have never gotten along.

"Here," Killian says.

I look over my shoulder and take the coffee out of his hand.

"Have her drink it. It will help."

"Mom." I place the cup in her hand. I wait until she has a good grip on the cup before I remove my hand. "Drink this."

She does. I sit in the chair next to her and take a deep breath for the first time since she called me. How she managed that call, I don't know. I don't know how she did it in the state she is in.

I look up and mouth, *Thanks.*

Killian nods his head as a nurse runs up to us. I stand, afraid she is here to tell us bad news.

"Are you relatives of Lee Felton?"

Killian and I both nod.

The woman sighs. "Good, I need someone to fill out the insurance forms."

My eyes grow wide. I can't deal with this shit, not right now. I need to take care of my mother. I need to see my grandfather. I don't need to be worried about figuring out what insurance he has.

"I'll do it," Killian says, to my surprise. He leans over and softly kisses me on the cheek before he begins following the nurse.

"Wait. How is he doing?" I ask the nurse.

"He's still in surgery. But I'll have someone come to get you as soon as the surgery is over."

I nod and then sit back in the chair next to my mom. I don't know if Killian will be able to fill out the forms. But I have faith he will find a way to keep the nurse away for a little while at least.

I glance over at my mom, who is now sitting up a little higher in her chair. I watch as she runs her hand through her long locks and then sips on her coffee. It seems to be helping.

I shake my head, disgusted that she is drunk. I never imagined she would fall to this level. She seems so lost without my dad. But I know that's not true. She never really loved my dad. She only married him for the money, for the house, to pass on wealth to me. I realize now, looking back on their relationship, they were never happy together. They never loved each other. They never chose each other.

"I'm not drunk," my mother says, glaring at me.

"I never said you were."

She smiles slyly. "You're disgusted. That's what you thought. I'm not drunk. I've only had two drinks."

"Then, why do you look like complete shit? I know it's not because you gave two shits about my father. And you sure as hell don't care about what happens to Granddad."

"Wow, someone has finally grown a pair." She takes a sip of her coffee before staring off into space.

I think the conversation is over, that this is all I'm going to get from her. She's drunk. There is no other word to describe her state.

"I loved your father very much, more than even he knew."

"You don't need to lie to me. Granddad told me. He told me the truth—the only reason you got married was because it benefited the company and your pocketbook."

Her eyes meet mine, but I don't expect to see the pain in them.

"You have no idea what you are talking about. I loved your father very much. Yes, our marriage was arranged, but it was arranged because I loved him, and it was the only way to get your father to notice me instead of being stuck in his career. The opportunity arose, and I took it."

She takes a deep breath. "Don't you dare accuse me of not loving your father. I gave up everything for that man. I never wanted children. Did he tell you that? I never, ever wanted fucking children. But I had one for him. He wanted children, someone to pass on his precious company to. So, I had one.

"I wanted to move out of this godforsaken place. I wanted to move somewhere with a beach, but I never did. I stayed with your father, even when he stayed late, night after night at hotel after hotel blaming it on work. I knew what he was doing. I loved him, even when he didn't love me back."

Tears are streaming down her face. "I loved him, even when he loved other women." A sob escapes, and she takes a minute to just let it out of her whole body.

"Don't you dare accuse me of not loving that man. I loved him desperately and without asking for love in return. It tears me apart to think that one of the only remaining links I have left to that love might be dying on the operating table." She glares at me. "And the other is about to make the biggest mistake of her life."

I take a deep breath, trying to take it all in, but it's a lot to take in. She accused my father of not loving her, of cheating on her. I don't want to think about it. I've always loved my father. I don't want to know if what she said is true. I can't know.

"What do you mean, I'm about to make the biggest mistake of my life? I thought I already did that five years ago."

She laughs. "What you did wasn't a mistake. I know I told you time after time it was. I know I blamed you for my failed marriage. I blamed you because it was easier to blame you than myself. It wasn't your fault. It was mine. I should never have agreed to marry your father. It was the worst mistake of my life. I ruined my life forever when I said, 'I do.' I can't get back the last twenty-five years. They are gone. I don't even know if I can figure out how to live again for another twenty-five years."

She stands from her chair, surprisingly steady on her feet. "Don't make my mistake. Don't marry that boy. I'd pull the trigger before I made that decision again."

My mother scares me with her words. I've never heard her talk like this.

I watch her walk toward the restroom, and then I stand and follow her. I'm afraid to leave her alone after she basically told me I should kill myself rather than marry Killian.

I stand outside the restroom as I text Scarlett. I ask her to meet us at the hospital. I tell her I'm worried about my mother's mental state and I need someone to stay with her twenty-four/seven for a while. I know I will owe Scarlett big time for doing this for me, but I don't care. It will be worth it. There is no way in hell I can spend the next few days watching my mother.

I'm not sure I believe a word out of my mother's mouth. I never have. Our relationship is too far gone to be repaired.

When Scarlett texts she will be here in the next half hour, I sigh in relief. I just have to watch my mother for a half hour. Then, I can move on to more important things. Then, I can go back to praying like hell that my grandfather lives.

19

I FEEL a hand on my shoulder.

"I brought you some coffee and breakfast."

I rub my eyes before glancing up at Killian. I take the coffee and breakfast sandwich he brought me before I glance back to my grandfather's hospital bed. He made it through the open-heart surgery, but he still hasn't opened his eyes yet.

I unwrap the sandwich and find a bacon and egg sandwich. I take a bite, letting the greasy goodness dissolve in my mouth. I glance at the clock on my phone. It's seven a.m. We've been here all night.

"You should go home, Killian. You need to get some rest. You've been a great help, but there is nothing else you can do. We have to wait until he wakes up."

He shakes his head. "I'm not going anywhere."

I sigh and take another bite of my food.

Killian has been amazing. He was able to fill out the insurance information without any help. He helped get my mother into Scarlett's car last night. He kept me fed all night. He found some clothes from the gift shop so I could change out of the ballgown I had been wearing. He found me a blanket and pillow, so I could get some sleep. He's been by my side the entire night—taking care of me, holding my hand, doing anything I needed without ever asking what I needed. He just knew. He knew better than I did.

I don't ask him again to leave. In fact, I like having him here.

Killian sits down next to me and unwraps his own sandwich. We eat in silence. Both of our eyes stayed glued on my grandfather, looking for any signs of movement or for any signs he is still in there.

When I'm done eating, I toss my wrapper into the trash can beside the bed. That's when I realize what will make Killian leave. I realize what will make him go back to bed or to work or to wherever he feels he belongs instead of wasting his time in a hospital room.

I slowly turn to face Killian. I don't look sad. I don't look happy. I don't look like anything. "I have an answer for you."

I watch as his eyes fill with regret and pain, a face I wasn't expecting.

"I don't want to hear it, not until after your grandfather wakes up."

"My answer isn't going to change though. Even after he wakes up, I'm still going to have the same answer for you."

"Maybe, maybe not. Either way, I can't hear it until after he wakes up."

I sigh. "Okay." I don't feel okay though.

I need to stop pretending Killian is my future. I need to stop relying on him. I need to stop relying on anyone but myself. I need to be able to make a decision about my life and then deal with the consequences, no matter how awful they are.

I turn back to my grandfather. His eyes open. They open wide.

"Granddad," I sigh as I stand. I embrace his body in a hug.

"Hi, princess," he breathes into my ear as his arm comes around me.

When he releases me, we both turn and stare at Killian.

Terror flashes over Killian's face as he realizes, at any second, I will give him my answer. But he shouldn't seem so afraid. He'll want to hear my answer. My answer will set him free.

"I'll let the nurses know he's awake," Killian says, leaving the room.

I laugh softly at his reaction.

I wait until the nurses and doctors check Granddad over. I wait until after they tell me he should make a full recovery in a few days. A week, they guessed. Then, he will have to frequently meet with a cardiologist for a while, but he seems to be out of the woods for now. I wait until Killian leaves to call everyone at the office to let them know Granddad is okay. I wait until Granddad sits up and seems comfortable. I wait until he is alone. I wait until I'll explode if I wait any longer.

"I'm not going to marry him. I refuse. I'm not going to let you or Dad or Mom or anyone else choose for me anymore. I've made mistakes in my past, yes. I will always regret those mistakes, but I haven't been living since I let you guys control me. Since Dad's death, I've tried to make my own decisions. They haven't always been the best, but I've made them for me."

I pause, giving him a chance to yell at me or tell me I'm wrong.

He doesn't, so I continue, "I can find my own husband on my own time. I don't need your help. I don't need the money either. I might have a useless degree I don't care about, thanks to you, but I'm smart. I can go back and get my MBA. I can go back and get any degree I want. I can make something of myself on my own. I don't care if I have to live in a box and eat cereal for years until I have enough money to buy a place. But it will be *my* place. It will be *my* money."

I take a deep breath. "I refuse to turn into my mother. I refuse to be that miserable. I won't marry him," I say, collapsing into a chair. Standing up to Granddad took everything out of me.

I look at my grandfather who has yet to say a word. Instead, he is just sitting there with a serious look on his face. It probably isn't fair to him to spring all of this on him, only hours after he woke up from open-heart surgery, but I don't care. I can't live without making my own decisions. I can't keep living like a princess. I have to find my own way in life.

He pats the side of the bed, and I slowly, cautiously get out of my chair and sit on the edge of his bed.

"You're just like your father."

I stare at him in confusion.

I loved my father. He was an amazing man, but I'm nothing like him. He was strong where I'm weak. He was decisive where I'm indecisive. He was a workaholic where I'm lost.

I shake my head. "I'm not."

A smile tugs at Granddad's lips. "You are. You won't listen to anyone. You choose your own path. And you defy my every decision, just like him."

"I never—"

He puts his hand up, stopping me from arguing with him. "I always thought you would fight me till the very end on my decision for you to marry Killian. I don't think I ever thought you would follow my command. Maybe, if your father were still alive, you would have listened better to him, but I doubt it. Somehow, I think we would have ended up here, both at odds and neither of us wanting to give in."

My head drops. He's not going to back down. I'm going to have to find my way on my own with no money.

"Lucky for you, a heart attack changes an old man like me."

My face lifts as I try to decide if he is serious or not.

His face looks sad. "I didn't listen to your father when he pleaded with me to let him choose his own wife. I thought I knew better." He rubs his neck. "I'm not sure if the company benefited greatly from their union. I know he was never happy in his marriage."

He sighs. "I can't change your dad's fate, but I can give you a chance. I know you have been trying to prove you are worthy of running the company."

I nod.

"You've failed horribly."

I frown but don't deny it. It's true. I'm not the right person to run the company.

"I am willing to give you a chance though."

My eyes brighten just a little.

"Since I promoted Killian to CEO, there is a spot open in the company. We will need a new VP of Operations. I've been looking around, but I haven't found anyone worthwhile yet. Tony obviously isn't a good choice."

I nod, willing him to say the words I want him to voice.

"I'll give you the job."

My hands go around him, tightly holding him, before he even has a chance to say the rest. He pushes me back up after I've finished smothering him.

"Now, the job comes with some conditions. You will attend business classes."

I nod. I already planned on doing that.

"You will run every decision by either Killian or me."

I nod, not liking that as much, but I'll accept it—for now.

"Lastly, this is a trial run. If you last a year, it can be a permanent position, but Killian or I can fire you for any reason at any time."

I take a deep breath and nod. His terms seem fair, considering I have never run a company like this before.

"If you last a year, I'll give you all of my equity."

I raise an eyebrow at him. "That would be…"

He nods. "You would have controlling power over the company. You would have fifty-one percent. Killian will only have forty-nine."

I take a deep breath, trying to calm my nerves. I can't believe what he is offering me. I don't understand what changed since the heart attack, but whatever it is, I'll take it.

"Do we have an agreement?"

I smile. "Yes."

I extend my hand, and we shake on it.

"Now that, that is taken care of, what is that boy still doing here?"

"What do you mean?"

"I figured, since you aren't wearing a ring and you finally got the balls to tell me you aren't marrying him, no matter what, it meant you told him no."

I nervously twist my strands of hair in front of my body.

"Kinsley?"

"I haven't answered him yet. I tried to earlier, but he wouldn't let me."

"Then, answer me this. How do you feel about that boy?"

"What do you mean?"

He rolls his eyes at me. "Do you love him? And don't you dare lie to me. I've been through enough these last few days. You wouldn't want to give me another heart attack because you lied to me."

I shake my head at his dramatics. I don't know how to answer him because I'm not sure how I feel.

"Maybe. I don't know," I say, getting up from the bed and pacing the room.

He doesn't rush me or ask me any further questions. He just watches me pace and encourages me with his patience to tell him.

"He makes me feel warm when he's around me. I ache when he's gone. He challenges me. He frustrates me."

I walk to the other side of the room.

"He charming, intelligent, strong. He's taken care of me more than he should."

I pace again.

"He was willing to marry me for no other reason than because he felt he made a promise to my father."

I pace again.

"He's decisive and opinionated and so controlling that it pisses me off."

I pace.

"He's serious. He hardly ever laughs. It's annoying really."

I pace.

"He sucks at blackjack and poker. He sucks at all card games."

I stop.

"You love him," he says.

I shrug as tears well in my eyes. "It doesn't matter if I love him. It only matters if he loves me."

And I already know the answer. He doesn't.

Granddad holds his arms out to me. I walk over to his bedside and curl up like a child would in her mother's lap. I let the tears fall as he gently rubs my back until no more tears can fall.

"I'm going to tell you a story I promised I never would."

I hiccup.

He smiles and kisses the top of my head. "It was three years ago. Your father had fallen ill."

I sit up before turning to look at him. "What do you mean, my father was ill?"

He sighs. "You were in school. It was stage one colon cancer."

"What?"

"Calm down. They were able to easily cure it because they'd caught it so early. We didn't want to worry you since there was nothing to worry about. He wouldn't have died from the cancer."

I nod although it doesn't make me feel any better they kept secrets from me.

"Anyway, the cancer scare was enough for your father to rethink his life plans. He loved his work. He loved running the company. It's all he'd ever dreamed about, but it made him realize he wanted more. He wanted to retire, to travel, to find out what living was like, outside of the daily grind of work."

I nod.

"At the time, Killian was aware of what we wanted him to do. He had worked for a few months in the VP position and was doing better than any of us had expected." He pauses. "So, your dad offered him the CEO position with no strings attached."

"You mean, he could have had the position without marrying me?"

He nods. "Yes. He told Killian to think about it, but he wanted an answer soon. Killian went to see you shortly after that."

"I remember. He broke Eli and me up just to spite us, just because he could."

"Is that what he told you?"

"He didn't have to. I understood."

Granddad shakes his head. "He needed to see you. He realized he would be making a decision not only for himself, but also for you, too. He saw how unhappy you were with Eli. Well, I don't really know what else he saw when he went to see you. All I know is, when he came back, he told your father he wasn't ready to take the CEO job yet. He said he wanted to keep the condition that he would have to marry you in order to get it."

I suck in a breath. That can't be true. He wouldn't have come up with a plan so that we wouldn't have to marry—except that he did... to give me a choice about my future.

"Your father realized shortly afterward that he wasn't ready to retire yet. And they never spoke of it again."

"Why would he do that?"

"Oh, sweetie. Isn't it obvious?"

I think for a minute before nodding because it is obvious. There is only one explanation for it.

20

"You're still here," I say when I exit my grandfather's hospital room.

Killian is sitting in a plastic chair in the waiting room. He's still wearing a tux. He must not have found any gift shop clothes that fit him.

"I told you I would stay," he says, standing and putting his phone back into his pocket. "How's he doing?" He nods toward my grandfather's room.

"Granddad is doing well. He's a pretty tough old man...although his heart might have just grown a little softer."

Killian raises his eyebrows but doesn't ask about it, and I don't say anything else about my grandfather.

Instead, I walk to Killian until my lips are just a breath from his, until my body is trembling again, just like it was the last time our bodies were this close to each other. I close my eyes and try to calm my body, but it doesn't work. I open them again and am faced with his intense dark eyes transfixed on mine.

"Ask me," I breathe onto his lips.

I watch him suck in a breath, but he doesn't say anything.

"Ask me," I say again.

"Princess, will you marry me?"

He doesn't get down on one knee. He doesn't pull the ring box still tucked in his pocket back out. He's already decided he knows the answer.

I smile because he's mostly right. "No," I say.

His eyes close, immediately blocking me off. His breathing returns. His head drops.

"Now, answer a question for me."

He takes a deep breath before opening his eyes. "Yes, princess?"

"You have to promise to be completely honest."

"I will," he says.

My heart is racing much too fast. My shaking has increased instead of slowed. My eyes try to close, but I force them to stay open, to stay on him to read his reaction.

I let one more beat of my heartbeat before I ask, "Do you love me?"

A smug grin forms on his face as he takes a couple of seconds longer to answer me than I anticipated. I was wrong. Him deciding to marry me, no matter what, didn't mean what I thought it did. It's part of some other master plan that I don't know about.

"Maybe," he says the word as innocently as I have countless times to him before. His smug smile grows larger.

I can't help the smile that forms on my lips. "I'll take that as a yes."

I launch my lips onto his. It's been too long since I tasted him, too long since he wrapped his arms around me, like he is doing now, too long since I felt truly loved by someone since my father died.

The kiss is more than a kiss. It's a declaration of love, a promise of what could be. It's a chance, a chance to be together because of our choices and no one else's.

He tries to break away from the kiss when my hands start tugging at the hem of his shirt. "Princess, I love your enthusiasm, but we can't do that here. People are watching."

I smile larger though as I grab ahold of his hand and pull him down the hallway. An old episode of *Friends* pops into my head as we make our way through the hospital.

I pass a dark looking room. No nurses are hovering around. I peek through the cracked door. It's empty.

I tug on Killian's arm, and he follows me into the room. I shut the door behind us, and my lips attack his again as my hand pulls at the hem of his shirt. It's then I realize I don't need his shirt off. It's his pants I should be working on.

I grab at the button. It unbuttons quickly, and then I'm unzipping his pants.

He smiles against my lips. "God, if I had known what kind of crazy woman you would turn into when I told you maybe I loved you, I would have told you sooner."

"Shut up, and help me get these pants off of you."

He laughs but complies, and his pants fall to the floor. He grabs my ass and pushes me against the wall.

I moan as his lips touch my neck, and his hand finds my breast.

"This is going to be quick," he says into my neck.

I nod. "Yes, quick," I say. I'm barely able to speak.

I feel him smiling again as he reaches his hand into the front of my pants, cupping my pussy.

"Fuck, Killian!" I scream.

He clamps his hand over my mouth, silencing me. "You can't scream. You can't moan. You have to be silent."

I nod my head, agreeing.

He tugs my pants down, and I feel them fall to the floor.

He rubs his hard cock at my entrance. "God, you're so wet already, baby."

"Please, I need you now," I whisper.

He rubs his cock one more time over my clit before he lifts my legs and thrusts inside me in one motion. I bite my lip to keep from screaming out his name. When I look at him, I can tell he is doing the same. He doesn't hesitate though. He thrusts quickly in and out of me.

God, I want to moan. I want to scream. I want to have him fuck me like this over and over again.

But something does escape his lips when his cock is buried deep inside me with his beautiful eyes locked on mine. "I love you, princess."

He thrusts again, keeping me from responding the way I want to. He thrusts again, building us closer.

"I love you, too," I moan a little louder than I should.

It's then that I realize I forgot one little part of that *Friends* episode. They get caught.

The door opens, and the lights flash on. I glance up, and we both laugh as a young nurse stares at Killian's bare ass. We both laugh as she closes the door and runs away in embarrassment.

Killian starts thrusting again.

"What are you doing?"

He shrugs. "Might as well finish."

———

I try to catch my breath as I pull my pants back up. I watch as Killian buttons his pants. The nurse has yet to come back, but that's probably because she has called security by now.

Killian doesn't seem to care about getting thrown out though. He walks to me, putting his hands on my waist. "I love you, Kinsley," he says before softly kissing me on the lips. "I know you're not ready to marry me yet. And that's okay. But can we at least date?"

I laugh. "Maybe."

"Yes," he says sternly, making me laugh again.

"Yes," I say.

He lifts me and spins me around as he kisses me again.

But the spin is ended abruptly. I look to the door, thinking maybe the nurse has come back, but no one's there.

"What is it?" I ask.

"Why aren't you marrying me? I thought that was the only way you could be a part of the company."

I smile. "I told Granddad I didn't care about being a part of the company. I told him I didn't care about the money. I told him I refused to marry such an arrogant ass."

He frowns, making me smile larger.

"I told him I was tired of living my life for other people. I told him I'll be making all the decisions in my life now."

He hugs me again. "That's great. I'm so proud of you, princess." He lets me go. "What are you going to do now?"

"Other than be your girlfriend?"

He nods.

"I'm going to be your new VP of Operations."

He grabs me and lifts me, spinning me around again.

We kiss. We laugh. We fall further in love.

When he puts me down, I know I have made the right decision.

The door swings open again, startling us. Two men in black suits walk through the door. They are not security guards.

"Are you Kinsley Felton?" the man says.

"Yes," I whisper.

Killian wraps his arms around me tighter.

The man walks toward us. He grabs ahold of my arm. "Kinsley Felton, you are under arrest."

I expect him to say, for having sex in a spare hospital bed. But that doesn't make sense.

He finishes his sentence, "For money laundering and fraud."

I stare at him, wide-eyed. I have no idea what he is talking about.

Killian is still holding on to my waist, refusing to let me go.

"I'm going to have to ask you to let her go."

Killian does reluctantly, and the man puts the cuffs on me. The man begins walking me out of the room. I hear Killian running next to us.

"Excellent job, Agent Byrne," the man who has me in cuffs says.

I turn to my right to face the direction where the man is talking, but I have no idea who he is talking to. All I see is Killian. Killian *Browne*.

Killian's eyes grow heavy, sad, as he looks from me and then to the man who has me in cuffs. "Thank you, Agent Phillips," Killian says weakly.

My mouth drops. Killian isn't Killian. He's not a CEO. He's a cop or with the FBI or CIA or whatever the hell agents work with.

I force myself to keep my eyes off of Killian or whatever the hell his name is as the man leads me out of the hospital and into the back of a blacked-out Suburban.

I was wrong. I'm always wrong. Killian doesn't love me. He doesn't care about being a CEO. He was just doing his job.

I try to push Killian out of my head. I try to focus on whatever I'm facing as the car speeds off, leaving the hospital behind. I can't help it though. I glance back at him. Killian's standing on the street, staring at me with an intense stare on his face.

I hate him, I think.

But I don't. The lingering love is still there. I still feel his warm cum pooling between my thighs. I still feel his love even if it didn't exist.

I turn away from him.

Any normal woman would be afraid. Being arrested is most people's worst nightmare. It should be mine, except this isn't the first time I've made a mistake. It feels just like the last time. The pain from being betrayed by a man I thought loved me is the same.

The only difference is, last time I knew what the mistake was. But, this time, I have no clue.

The End

Keep reading for Maybe Never...

MAYBE NEVER

1

KINSLEY

I PACE back and forth in the holding cell, unable to sit patiently like the rest of my cellmates. One woman lies back on one of the benches, seemingly asleep, while another sits across from her, picking the nail polish off her fingers.

Not me though. I can't sit. Not when I have no idea why I'm here. So, instead, I pace back and forth in the small cell, hoping that, soon, someone will come to tell me what the hell is going on. I also have to pee, which is keeping me from sitting down, but I'm not going to go in the toilet in the corner of the room—at least not until I can't hold it any longer.

I think back to the last time I was here. It was the same jail and the same holding cell with the same disgusting yellow walls. Last time, I was calmer, much calmer, because I had accepted that I deserved to be in prison. I had confessed.

I stop pacing when the woman lying on the bench snores, startling me. I don't know why I'm back in jail now. *What did I do?* The agent mentioned something about fraud and money laundering. I didn't do either of those things. It must be a mistake.

And Killian...

I can barely even let my heart go there. One day—actually, less than a day, more like one hour, was all I got with Killian. It's all the time I got to think about a possible future with him.

I thought I loved him.

I thought he was the one for me.

I was wrong.

Killian isn't Killian. Killian is a liar. I chose wrong, again.

I glance at the clock barely visible outside the holding cell. It's past midnight. They won't question me tonight. I won't be arraigned tonight. They won't do anything with me tonight. I'm stuck here, in this cold room, with two strange women.

I take a seat on the only remaining bench in the room and rest my head against the wall. I cross my arms over my chest and rub my hands over them, trying to warm up, but I'm still shivering. I push the urge to pee, along with thoughts of why I'm in here, out of my head. I push Killian out of my head until the only thing that remains is last time.

This feels just like last time when I had fallen for a man who wasn't what he seemed. Now, I fell again for the wrong man. Even though my father and grandfather had handpicked him, they picked wrong. Maybe there isn't a man out there for me.

I should have learned my lesson the first time. Instead, I'm back in this cell again, and this time, I don't know when I'll be getting out.

2

KINSLEY

FIVE YEARS EARLIER

THE BELL RINGS, and I walk from my English class to my locker. I feel the excitement floating off the students and teachers all around me, as everyone is happy to be ending another school year. Everyone is excited, except me.

I walk slowly through the hallway, hoping to get one last glimpse of the man I'm crazy about. One last glance of the man whom I will probably never see again. That's not true. I'll occasionally see him at family functions that involve close family friends, just like I always have. But it won't be the same as seeing him every day in the hallway, at lunch, or on the football field every fall.

The man I'm in love with is graduating today and is going to UCLA in the fall while I'll be stuck here, in Las Vegas, for another year. I could follow him to UCLA when I graduate, but there's a high chance that, by then, he'll already have a girlfriend and have forgotten all about me.

I stop at my locker, pausing for far longer than it takes for me to get my backpack out so I can look for him. His locker is just across the hallway from mine, but he never comes.

In frustration, I slam my locker door closed and begin the long walk to my car. I continue to walk slowly, hoping to see him if I stall long enough. I don't though. I don't seem him anywhere.

I get to my white Lexus faster than I had hoped. I open the door and slam it in frustration because I didn't see him. I didn't get to say good-bye one last time. I don't get to hear his voice one final time. He didn't care enough to find me.

I shake my head as I start up the engine. *Why should he care about coming to see me?* I'm nobody to him. Just a lowly sophomore who has been friends with his family since forever. Just a stupid girl who has a silly crush on him, just like every other girl in the school whom he doesn't care about. And he sure as hell doesn't love me.

I'm tired of being that girl though—the girl who is a goody-two-shoes, who gets good grades, and who follows the social hierarchy. I want to go after the bad boy who everyone wants but is too afraid to go after.

I'm going after the man I love. I'm going after the bad boy. I'm going after Tristan Slade.

I grab the door handle to go find him, but a tap at my window startles me, and I stop short. I turn to see who it is, assuming it's Eli since he asked me out earlier this week, and I have yet to give him an answer. I couldn't, not when there was still a chance that Tristan might want to date me.

I should say yes though. Eli is a good person, attractive, and smart. My family has known his family for years as well. I should say yes to him.

It's not Eli at my window though. It's Tristan. And he has a wicked grin on his face as he flips his long brown hair out of his eyes. I roll down my window as my breath quickens, like it always does every time he comes near me.

I open my mouth to ask what he's doing here, but no words come out. I feel my face burn in embarrassment.

He smiles bigger. "You didn't think I'd leave without telling my favorite girl good-bye, did ya?"

I smile and take a deep breath. "No."

Tristan leans into the car, giving me a quick hug and peck on the cheek. My body immediately relaxes. That was all I wanted—a chance to feel just for a moment that he cares about me even if he only thinks about me as an annoying little sister.

He pulls his head back out of the window, and I think he's going to go. I'm surprised his entourage hasn't found him yet to drag him back to wherever the latest party is. He pauses for a second as he stands outside my car, looking at me.

"You want to go to a party with me tonight?"

I raise my eyebrows at him. He didn't really say that. He didn't just ask me out. It must be an illusion. So, I just smile innocently at him and pretend normal words just came out of his mouth instead of the ludicrous words I heard.

He reaches his hand into the car until he's touching my cheek. "Kinsley, are you okay?"

I swallow down the lump that has made its way up my throat. "Yes."

"Your cheeks just look even redder than usual."

He removes his hand from my cheek, and my hand replaces it. My cheek does feel warmer than usual, probably because it liked the way his hand caressed it.

"So, I'll pick you up at seven then, Kins?"

I nod although I'm not sure what I'm nodding to. He smiles and winks at me before he walks away, leaving me alone in my car. Leaving me alone to realize that Tristan Slade just asked me out.

———

I've changed a hundred times since I got home from school. I don't know what to wear. Tristan never said what party we were going to, although I can guess. Only a handful of people would be lucky enough to host a party Tristan Slade would attend. Vanessa, Cade, or Samantha are at the top of my list.

I hear the doorbell ring downstairs, and every nerve in my body ignites with anxiety. It's just after seven. It's him. I know it without glancing out the window to see if his black Mustang convertible is here. I know.

I grab my red jacket and slip it on over my white crop top I've paired with a short black skirt and heels. I zip up the jacket so my father won't be able to see my bare stomach before I go out.

I haven't gone out on a date before, and although I've modeled similar outfits in magazines, I have no idea how he would respond to me wearing something like this on a date. And I'm not going to press my luck and embarrass myself by having my father force me to change my clothes when he sees a boy is coming to pick me up—especially a boy like Tristan. Even though my father has known him since we were both toddlers, it doesn't mean my father likes or trusts him.

I walk down the stairs and find Tristan standing in the entryway, smiling at me. I pause as my heart skips at his smile before I check out the rest of his body. He's wearing jeans, a dark shirt, and a leather jacket, despite the warm weather outside.

"You look beautiful. You ready to go?"

I hold up a finger, indicating I need one second. I skip past Tristan to let my father know I'm going out. I check his office, but he isn't in there. He never is. I try the kitchen next and find him making himself a peanut butter sandwich—the only thing he knows how to make for himself.

He looks me up and down. "Going somewhere?"

"Just out to some graduation parties."

He smiles and nods. "With a Mr. Tristan Slade."

My eyes widen. "How did you…"

He shakes his head and puts the top piece of bread onto his sandwich. "I was at his father's house the other week. The topic of you two together got brought up."

My mouth drops. *They were talking about the two of us? Is Tristan only going out with me because of my father and his father's relationship?*

"You're okay with me going out tonight?" I ask.

My father walks over and softly kisses me on the forehead. "You look beautiful, princess. Of course I'm okay with you going out tonight, even if I'm not thrilled with the idea of you dating yet."

I smile brightly at him. "I'll be back by curfew." I turn to leave.

"Stay out as long as you want."

I turn back to see my father casually walking back to his sandwich. "You deserve to have a bit of fun for once in your life. Just don't tell your mother." He winks at me.

I take a deep breath, feeling better about tonight now I know it can last as long as I want, which is forever if I get my way.

I turn to walk back to Tristan, but I still hear my father's words as I leave.

"I'm sorry, princess."

I pause for just a second at his words. *Why would he say he's sorry when he just said I could go out?* I turn back to ask him, but he's gone, and Tristan is waiting.

I find Tristan still standing in the entryway.

"Ready," I say, unzipping my jacket a little as I approach him.

He smiles at me and grabs ahold of my hand when I get close. I freeze at his sudden touch. We've touched before, but we've never held hands, not like this. This touch, I love.

We walk to his car, hand in hand. He only lets go after he has opened the door, and I have to climb in. I unzip my jacket and take it off as he climbs into the driver's side. He starts the car and backs it down the driveway.

Grab my hand, I think.

I rest my hand on my thigh for easy access, but he doesn't grab it. And I'm not bold enough to grab his—at least not yet, but maybe by the end of the night.

"Where are we going?" I ask in a shaky voice.

"Vanessa Waters' party. We just need to make a quick stop first to pick something up."

I nod, not surprised by his choice of party. I don't ask where we are going first though because I assume it's to pick up alcohol or something for the party. I just hope it's not to pick up another girl.

"How does it feel to be done with school?" I ask, trying to keep my mind off the fact we could be on our way to pick up another girl.

"It feels awesome as fuck." He winks at me.

I tuck my curly, long blonde hair behind my ear. I don't know what else to say to Tristan. I don't know what else to do. This is going to be a long night if I don't think of more to say—and soon.

So, I say the only other thing that's on my mind, "My father said he talked to your dad this past week about us. Do you know what that was about?"

Tristan keeps his eyes on the road. "No, I don't talk to my father much."

I look down at my hands in my lap. "You didn't ask me out because one of our fathers asked you to. Did you?"

He glances my way now with a deep frown on his face. It is quickly replaced with a smile as he grabs my hand and pulls it to his lips, softly kissing the back of my hand.

"You're here because I like you."

My heart flutters at the thought. *Tristan likes me.*

———

Tristan holds my hand as we walk down the strip toward the Felton Grand.

When he parked just off the strip, I curiously looked at him, but I didn't have the courage to ask him why we were here. I don't know what we are doing here, and I'm more nervous than ever Tristan is only going out with me because of my father or his.

"What are we doing here?" I finally get the courage to ask as we enter the casino my father owns.

He smiles at me just as confidently as before. "I have to pick up a package, and then we will head over to the party."

I take a deep breath as we walk onto the casino floor. I'm going to be noticed by someone here. I spend almost every day after school here with my father. Everyone knows who I am. I don't want them to notice. I don't want to feel embarrassed because I am here with a guy.

"What kind of package?" I ask.

His eyes scan the floor, looking for whomever we are meeting. And then his eyes see my worried face, and his smile turns to a frown. "What's wrong, Kinsley?"

"I-I don't want anyone to know we are here." I tug on my long curls, twirling them in my hand, to try to keep my nerves at bay. I let my eyes just barely meet his. "I don't understand what we are doing here. I just want to go to the party."

Tristan's frown relaxes. He tightens his grip on my hand and walks me back to the lobby. I follow, glad to leave the casino floor without being spotted and questioned, but I now feel like a scared little girl. That's not how I want to seem to him.

He lets go of my hand. "I'll be right back," he says, distracted by his mission, until he sees my face.

Whatever he sees makes him pause before walking the foot back to me. He tucks a loose strand of hair behind my ear before leaning toward me.

I watch his lips lower, and smile, expecting to feel a kiss on my cheek. Instead, his lips land on my lips. I suck in a breath when I feel his moist lips touch mine. He quickly slips his tongue into my mouth and tangles his hand in my hair, not settling on just a quick peck on the lips.

I've had only one other kiss on the lips. I was twelve, and the boy kissed me on a dare. It was nothing like this. This is a real kiss. This is what being kissed by Tristan Slade feels like. It feels magical, feeling his lips on mine. I feel important. I feel special. And, for the first time, I feel *wanted*.

When his lips leave mine, a smile curls on my lips. I don't open my eyes, but I can feel him grinning at my smile.

"I'll be right back," he says.

I nod and keep my eyes closed. I let my whole body take in every feeling from that kiss and lock it away in my memory forever. I don't want to forget it. Not even after I go on more dates and date more men. Not after I'm married with kids. Not when I'm ninety. I don't want to ever forget how I feel right now because I can't imagine anything feeling better.

I open my eyes when I'm sure the memory is forever ingrained in my head. I don't let my mind drift back to whatever silly reason we are here instead of already at Vanessa's party right now. All I can think about is that Tristan likes me.

I keep my eyes glued on the hallway that leads to the casino floor as it tempts me to go find him. My previous worries of being spotted by someone who knows me left the moment his lips touched mine. Now, all I care about is being close to him.

I take a couple of steps forward, unable to wait any longer in the lobby where he left me, when I see him rounding the corner. It doesn't keep me from moving closer to him though. I stop when I'm a foot away from him, realizing I don't know what to do. I want to kiss him again, but a second kiss now would be too soon after the first. I want to hold his hand again.

I can do that, I think.

Then, I see the small black bag in his hand. My eyelids blink rapidly as I try to understand what I'm seeing, but I don't understand what is in the bag. It's not alcohol. It almost looks like it could be...

Tristan tucks the bag into his jacket pocket when he notices my stare, and he quickly takes my hand back in his. My thoughts of what could be in the bag drift away. I longingly look up at him, but he just smiles at me. I guess I won't be getting my second kiss after all.

———

The music is loud and overwhelming as we enter Vanessa's parents' house. I lose Tristan's hand as we enter the house, immediately making me feel cold and empty. He keeps walking toward a group of seniors in the living room while I stand frozen in the entryway crowded with people. Everyone has a red Solo cup in their hand and a smile on their face. Everyone is happy to be at the last party of the year and to have a break from school for the summer.

I haven't been to many parties like this—not that I haven't been invited because I have. I have just always been the good girl, the rule-follower. I never felt the need to go to parties with underage drinking and who-knows-what going on upstairs, but all it took was Tristan asking me out, and now here I am.

I walk into the living room where Tristan is, but I feel a hand on my shoulder immediately bringing me to a halt. The hand isn't Tristan's. I know that because I can see him across the room, laughing at something Vanessa said. She's whom he should be with, not me. She's beautiful, confident, and a bit of a rebel, just like him. She's nothing like me.

I turn to see whose hand is on my shoulder, and I find Eli standing there, smiling brightly at me.

"I didn't know you would be at this party."

I force my lips to return his smile. "I didn't know I would be here either."

"Let me get you a drink," he says.

"No need," Tristan says, thrusting a red cup of beer into my hand.

I smile at him and take the cup. "I'll see you later," I say to Eli.

Tristan guides me away from Eli. He stops and raises his eyebrow at me. "You and Eli?"

"No," I say quickly.

"Good," he says, wrapping his arm around my waist like he owns me.

I take a sip of the beer. It's warm and disgusting, but I force the liquid down my throat anyway. And then I take another sip and another.

Tristan guides me outside to the back of the house where there is a DJ and a makeshift dance floor set up next to the pool. Several people are already in the pool in various stages of dress—fully clothed or just underwear. And I saw one guy who was either naked or wearing nude-colored underwear.

"Want to dance?"

"I'd love to." I feel my face light up brightly.

I watch as Tristan downs his beer, and I do the same. He takes my cup from me and tosses our cups on the floor. He then takes my hand and moves me onto the crowded dance floor.

We begin dancing effortlessly to the music. We're not touching, despite how badly I want to touch him, but then, as if God were answering my prayers, I'm bumped forward into Tristan's arms. I giggle up at him, embarrassed that my hands are now pressed against his firm chest. He doesn't seem to mind though. Instead, he twirls me around so my back is pressed against his chest and my ass is pressed firmly against him. His arms wrap tightly around me, and we begin dancing again.

How could this get any better?

That's when I feel his hot breath against my ear.

"You're a good dancer."

I feel my cheeks flush. "You, too."

His lips touch a place I've never been touched before—my neck. I never imagined that place would feel so good, and it causes me to moan at the unexpected pleasure. My soft moan only encourages him further.

I glance around the dance floor as his kisses travel lower to my shoulder. I'm worried someone is going to see us, but no one is watching.

He spins me back around, still holding me in his arms, and his typical wicked grin is on his face. This time, when he leans in, I expect him to kiss me on the lips, not the cheek. I meet him halfway until our lips are pressed together.

I surprise myself by slipping my tongue into his mouth before he has the chance to do it to me. My hands automatically go around his neck as I lose myself in the kiss. His hands find my hips, holding me tightly against him, until I think I can feel his erection growing against me—an erection I am causing with my kiss.

When he pulls away, just an inch from my lips, I'm panting hard. The kiss has stolen most of my breath from me.

He glances up at the house and then back at me. "Let's go."

I narrow my eyes. *Go? We just got here.*

Tristan grabs my hand, and then he's guiding me through the crowd of people and back into the house. I follow because I want to be with him, but I feel like I did something wrong if he already wants to go.

We walk back through the living room, and several guys he was talking to earlier wink at him as we walk by. I just smile at them, like I know what they are doing, but I don't. I don't know why they winked at Tristan.

We walk back to the entryway, and I expect him to lead us out of the house. He doesn't. Instead, he leads me up the stairs of the house, up to where there are fewer people.

We pass closed door after closed door until he sees a door cracked open. Tristan peeks his head in and gives one look to someone inside the room. A young boy, who I'm guessing is closer to my age than Tristan's, scurries out with who I assume is his date behind him.

Tristan leads me into the room and immediately makes his intentions clear. He slams the door behind us and presses my back against it. His lips attack mine in a kiss that is more carnal and passionate than any kiss I've had before.

I smile and kiss him back. I was wrong. This kiss is better than the first kiss he gave me in the lobby of my father's casino. This is the kiss I need to remember.

This kiss doesn't stop though. It continues right into the next and then the next.

His hands travel over my stomach and to the bottom of my shirt. I suck in a breath but don't stop him as his hand slides under my shirt. I break from his lips when his hand fondles my breast. It's too much pleasure to feel both his kiss and his touch at the same time.

He doesn't allow me much of a break before his lips find mine again. My brain tries to take in everything, all of the senses flowing through my body, but it's too much.

I push him back, needing a breather, as I realize what he brought me up here to do. *Sex.* He brought me here to have sex.

Can I really go from having my first real kiss to having sex all in the same night?

Tristan's not a stranger. I've known him my entire life. He's got a bad-boy reputation of sleeping with girls and then leaving them. He wouldn't do that to me though. I mean more to him than that.

I look at his lust-filled eyes locked on my breasts, and I know my answer. Yes, I will sleep with him. He won't hurt me. And I want him just as much as he wants me.

I seductively remove my shirt. I don't take my eyes off him as he takes a step back so he can take me in. His eyes grow with lust at seeing my bare skin. I watch him take his jacket off, followed by his shirt, exposing his muscles and tattoos I didn't know he had.

I walk closer to him and begin shimmying out of my skirt until I'm standing in just my underwear in front of Tristan, who is still wearing his jeans. I walk until I'm just in front of him and grab ahold of his jeans. He curiously looks down at me but doesn't say anything.

I slowly undo the button on his jeans, followed by the zipper. And then I slide his jeans down until they are around his ankles. To my surprise, he isn't wearing any underwear, and I can't keep the gasp from escaping my lips at the sight of him, at my first sight of a naked man.

He grins at my response. He takes my hand and guides me to it until I'm firmly grasping his cock in my hand. I stroke it once and watch as he moans at my touch. His hand stays on mine as he guides my hand up and down showing me what to do and how he likes it.

I must begin to be doing it right, because after a few more strokes he removes his hand from mine and moans loudly as I continue stroking. His hand goes to the back of my head pushing it down to his cock.

"Open your mouth," he says.

I do, and he pushes his cock inside. It's a strange feeling having him inside my mouth, and now I'm even more clueless as to what to do than I was before. I don't have to do much though as he pumps his cock in and out of my mouth. I gag once, but when I hear how loudly he moans with each thrust, I don't care he is making me gag. I want him to enjoy this.

He thrusts again, and then he moans, "Kinsley," as salty cum fills my mouth.

I swallow, wipe my mouth, and stand to see him grinning wildly at me.

He tucks my hair behind my ear and firmly kisses me on the cheek. I smile at him, but I'm not done with him yet. I want more. I want everything.

I move to the bed and lie down. "Come here," I say, patting the bed with lust in my eyes, trying to show him I want more without saying it.

He smiles at me and begins walking to the side of the bed. The door to the bedroom flies open before he gets to me. I grab the throw blanket on the edge of the bed and use it to cover myself as best as I can. When I glance at the door, I see Eli standing in the doorway, wide-eyed.

Eli glances at a naked Tristan, and his face turns furious. "Get out," Eli says to Tristan.

Tristan walks over to his jeans and casually slips them on, like he's not in a rush at all. He grabs his T-shirt from the floor.

"Tristan..." I say from the bed.

He turns to face me with a smile on his face. "The moment has passed, Kinsley. I'll let you get dressed and meet you downstairs."

I nod at his reassuring words. I won't be sleeping with Tristan tonight—well, at least, not right now—but I do plan on sleeping with him.

I watch as Tristan walks past Eli. The men glare at each other, and then Eli shuts the door, leaving me alone in the bedroom with nothing but my disappointment to give me comfort.

I quickly get up and get dressed. I put the blanket back on the bed as it was so the room doesn't look like it was disturbed. Although, after a night like tonight, I'm sure the whole house will look disturbed.

I'm just about to leave when I spot Tristan's jacket lying on the floor. I pick it up and put it on. I take a deep breath of the sleeve, trying to get any scent of the man I'm in love with. A man I've been in love with since I was twelve—or maybe earlier, if I'm honest with myself.

I walk out the door to a waiting Eli. I frown at him as I walk past. He grabs my arm, trying to stop me.

"Why did you do that?" I snarl at him.

"He's not good enough for you."

I roll my eyes and keep walking. "You don't get to make that decision."

I know Eli is following me as I make my way downstairs, but I don't care. All I need to do is find Tristan again. Once I'm back in his arms, everything will be right again.

I grab another beer as I make my way through the house. I need more alcohol in my system after one of the best nights of my life was interrupted by a man I don't care about. I drink my beer as I search the main floor of the house for Tristan.

After walking the entire main floor, I haven't spotted him, but I have finished my beer. I place the empty cup on the counter in the kitchen and head back to the living room to get another beer. I search for Tristan the entire time, but I still don't find him.

"He's outside," Eli says from behind me.

I turn slowly and narrow my eyes, not understanding why he would help me find Tristan when he just interrupted us.

"Thank you," I say anyway.

I grab another beer and begin walking toward the back door that leads outside to find him. The walk turns into a run as I can't wait to find him, but it takes me longer than I want to get to him due to the number of people I have to push through.

I finally get to the back door, and I slowly walk out to the warm summer air. I walk past the dance floor where Tristan and I were dancing earlier, but I don't spot him.

High-pitched squeals get my attention though, even over the booming music. I turn to see what the squealing is about when I see Vanessa in the pool with several of her girlfriends. Tristan throws her before swimming after her. I watch as he surfaces again, grabs ahold of Vanessa, and kisses her on the lips.

I drop my beer at the sight of him kissing another girl so quickly after me.

Tristan's eyes meet mine for just a second, and for just a moment, I see an ounce of worry there. He lets go of Vanessa, and to my surprise, he begins swimming toward me, like there is anything he could say to make this better.

He *used* me. He got what he wanted from me, and now, he is moving on.

I turn to go back into the house just as the tears fall, but I won't let him see that. He doesn't get to know that he hurt me, but he knows he did. That's why I hear him calling my name. Even as I run back into the house, I can still hear my name being repeated over and over.

Only once I'm back in the living room does his voice disappear, and it becomes replaced by my sobs. I spot Eli walking toward me, but I'm not ready to face him. Not yet. Not when he was right, and I was wrong.

I should have chosen Eli instead of Tristan. Eli is light while Tristan is dark, and I chose the darkness, thinking I could find the light in him. I couldn't though. He betrayed me the first chance he got.

I keep walking, needing to get out of the house. I need to go home. I make it to the entryway when I begin to hear sirens in the distance, growing louder with each second.

Shortly after, someone yells, "Cops!"

All at once, the house turns to panic as underage high schoolers begin pushing their way to get out of the house before the police arrive. I'm pushed out of the house in the process, but I don't have time to call for a ride like I was planning. I can't run. Not in my heels. I wouldn't make it far enough to escape being picked up by the cops for underage drinking.

I feel around in Tristan's pocket, hoping his car keys are there. I feel the bag he picked up at my father's casino. I try the other pocket and smile slyly when I find the keys, giving me just enough relief from the tears staining my face.

I move as fast as I can toward his car parked on the street. I climb in and start the engine, not feeling at all guilty that I'm taking his car while he'll be stuck to deal with questions from the cops about his drinking. I don't care. He deserves much worse after what he just did to me.

I start the car and step on the gas. The wheels squeal as I turn the corner, making it off the street just as I see the lights of cop cars turning onto the street where the party is going on. I smile, wiping the tears that are almost gone from my eyes.

I won't cry over that jackass. I glance down and realize I'm still wearing the asshole's jacket. I immediately take it off while keeping an eye on the road and speeding toward my house. I throw the jacket onto the passenger side. That's when I see it—the damn little black bag he picked up in the casino.

Now that I no longer lust for Tristan to distract me, I feel my curiosity grow until I can't wait any longer to find out what is in the bag. I grab the bag and fumble with the opening, but the string doesn't budge.

"Ah, come on," I curse at the bag that doesn't open.

I try again, pulling harder on the string until the bag pops open. White powder falls from the bag and onto my lap.

"What the hell?"

I try to dust myself off, but it's no use. I'm covered in white powder.

My mind finally makes the connection.

It's cocaine.

That's what Tristan was doing at the casino—buying drugs.

He's not who I thought he was. Not at all.

Tristan's a horrible, vile man who is nothing more than a druggie.

I throw the bag of drugs into the front seat and watch more powder fall onto the seat. My dream since I was twelve is gone. Shattered into dust, just like the dust of the cocaine scattered around his car.

I drive faster as my anger overtakes me. I can't believe I was so stupid. I can't believe I made such a ridiculous mistake going after Tristan. *Stupid, stupid!* I hit my hand against the wheel.

I round a corner, passing the busy section of downtown, when everything begins moving in slow motion. A child takes a step off the curb onto the street in front of me. I slam on the brakes, but my movement is too slow, slower than it should be. I turn the wheel, but the wheel moves even slower than the brakes.

I hear a woman scream.

I see the car miss the boy by no more than an inch.

Then, the car crashes into a light pole.

I feel my body jerk forward but am stopped abruptly as the airbag hits me.

Then, suddenly, everything moves fast. Much too fast. Sirens sound and approach quickly. I climb out of the car without a scratch on me. But it's not me I'm concerned with anymore. I glance across the street to the woman tightly holding her child with tears streaming down her face.

I could have killed her child. I could have taken away everything precious to her. And all because I made one bad decision after the next. A cop car approaches cautiously and stops just a few feet from where I'm standing.

He climbs quickly out of the car and runs over to me. "Is everyone okay? What happened?" he asks with a calm yet commanding voice.

I glance at the car and then back to the policeman. The car is filled with drugs. I've been drinking while underage and probably had more than the legal limit. I drove a car no one gave me permission to drive. I almost killed a child.

I'm going to jail. That much, I'm sure of. And I don't know when I'll be getting out.

I glance at the child who is visibly shaking in his mother's arms.

"You need to check on that child. You need to make sure he is okay," I say, gathering my courage, as I stare at the precious boy who, by some miracle, was spared. It had nothing to do with my ability to control a vehicle and everything to do with a miraculous event. "And then you need to arrest me."

3

KILLIAN

KINSLEY'S FACE when Agent Phillips called me Agent Byrne will forever be ingrained in my memory. Her gasp will forever be burned into my ears. The way her mouth fell open at his words before quickly turning into a grimace will haunt my dreams. Her beautiful bright eyes full of hope moments before turned to dark orbs that immediately shut me out of her life and her heart. It was a look I never wanted to see on her face.

I watched as Kinsley was placed in the back of one of our SUVs and driven away. The pain I felt at seeing her headed toward a jail cell hurt worse than I could've imagined. I never wanted this.

I turn to Agent Hayes, who is walking toward the second SUV. "This wasn't supposed to happen. Kinsley wasn't supposed to be arrested."

Agent Hayes stops and looks at me. "We have evidence she was colluding with her father and grandfather."

"What? You know that's not true. You know there is no way in hell that woman had anything to do with her family's criminal behaviors. They won't even let her run any part of the company. They won't let her decide what food to put into her mouth without questioning her first. She isn't involved in this."

Agent Hayes shakes his head. "You've gotten too close to the girl. Too close to make a reasonable judgment about her."

I run my hand through my hair in frustration. "My feelings for her have nothing to do with this. She's innocent."

He frowns at me and climbs into the driver's seat. I climb into the passenger seat next to him, and he quickly begins driving.

"She might be naive, but that doesn't make her innocent," he says.

"Why did you guys move in tonight? You were supposed to give me more time to gain his trust, so I could find out if they were hiding anything more."

"You're delusional. You've been undercover for too long. There was nothing left to find. The decision was made to move in before Lee Felton died, just like his son. Otherwise, we would have had no one left to prosecute, other than the granddaughter."

"You shouldn't be prosecuting her."

"That's not for you to decide."

I take a deep breath, trying to remain calm. No one will listen to me if I flip out, even though I'm the one who's been undercover for five years. I'm the one who should be making the decisions, not them, but I've made one too many mistakes in my past to be trusted.

"Offer her a plea deal then," I say.

"What?" Hayes glances from the road to me as we stop at a red light.

"Offer her a deal. Kinsley walks if she testifies against her grandfather."

He scrunches his nose. "But we don't need her to testify against her grandfather. We have enough evidence to convict him."

"Maybe, but he will have the best legal team money can buy. We need to be sure."

He looks back to the road and drives again as the light turns green. "I will see what I can do."

I take another deep breath, trying to relax, but it's impossible when I know Kinsley is on her way to a jail cell. A cell she will be stuck in for at least tonight, possibly much longer. A deal would at least give her a chance at freedom.

"You must be excited about getting a break now that your under-cover stint is over. As soon as the trials are over, you will be able to go home for a while or go on a vacation."

I nod, but I'm not excited. I don't know where my home is anymore. I don't want to leave Las Vegas, not now that I've met the girl who has haunted my dreams for five years. I thought she was a naive, scared little girl. I thought she was weak and not able to make a decision for herself. I was wrong.

I've been a part of countless arrests. Every single person I've arrested or seen arrested had fear in their eyes when it happened. Every. Single. One.

Not Kinsley though. She faced being arrested head-on without a drop of fear on her face.

She stood up to her grandfather, a man I know to be a criminal.

She survived her father's death without losing any more of herself.

I was wrong about Kinsley. She's not just a princess. She's also a survivor. And possibly even a warrior.

But as much as I'm afraid I've fallen for her, I can't be her future. I can't be with her and still be with the FBI. As soon as she finds out the truth, she will hate me anyway. My future is with the FBI while her future...well, her future is with anything but me.

4

KINSLEY

THE DOOR to the holding cell opens, jarring me awake. I look around and find a third woman sitting in the holding cell with us. I rub my neck that is sore from sleeping against the hard, cold wall all night.

"Kinsley Felton," the officer says.

I stand and feel my knees crack from sitting all night.

"Come with me, please," he says.

The man leads me out of the room and into another room just down the hall. A room for questioning. The same room I was in last time.

He indicates for me to take a seat in the metal chair at the table. I sit down and wait for the door to open again. I pick at the rust on the metal table, just like I did last time, while I wait in the dark gray-colored room. I don't have to wait long.

My lawyer walks through the door, followed by FBI agents.

Our family lawyer, Mr. Greene, takes a seat next to me. "Don't worry, Ms. Felton. They have nothing to hold you on. I'll be able to get you out of here today."

I nod, and then my eyes widen at the men sitting across from me. Both men are from the poker game—Grant and Stephen. Grant still looks as cocky as ever, sitting across from me. The only difference is, his blond hair has recently been buzzed short. Stephen looks exactly the same—tall with buzzed short black hair.

"We meet again, Ms. Felton," Grant says.

I frown at him. "Except we weren't properly introduced last time we met." I turn to Stephen. "I'm guessing you aren't Killian's brother-in-law." I turn to Grant. "And I'm guessing you aren't a world champ at poker."

He smiles at me. "I guess not. I'm Agent Hayes, and this is Agent Liddell."

I don't smile at them. I glance at the door behind them, waiting to see if Killian will be walking through the door.

"He won't be coming," Agent Hayes says, reading my thoughts.

I frown at him but don't say anything further.

"So, here is the deal, Kinsley. We have physical evidence that could put you in jail for ten to fifteen years on fraud and money laundering charges. Your signature is all over all sorts of documents, proving you were involved in your grandfather's and father's legal troubles," Agent Hayes says.

I narrow my eyes. "What do you mean? My father and grandfather weren't doing anything illegal."

My lawyer places his hand on my arm, reminding me to let him do the talking. But I can't, not when my family is at stake.

"We've arrested your grandfather. He would be sitting in a jail cell right now if it wasn't for his need for medical attention. And your father would have been in a cell as well," Agent Hayes says.

I gasp at his words.

He continues speaking, "We have been investigating your whole family for the past five years. Your family has come into lots of money, more money than possible based on the income of your company.

"We've had undercover agents planted in the company. Agent Byrne was able to infiltrate your family to the fullest extent. We have evidence to convict your grandfather on many high-felony charges, including money laundering and fraud. He's looking at twenty-five-plus years," Agent Hayes says.

That can't be true. My family would never do anything illegal. We have always earned our money justly. Granddad is a stern man, and he would never do something like this. And I know my father wouldn't have.

The FBI is wrong, all wrong.

"But I wouldn't worry about your grandfather right now. I would worry about your own future. Ten-plus years. Based on your past transgressions, we might even get you on more," Agent Hayes says.

I glare at the man sitting across from me.

"You can't bring that up. It was buried five years ago."

Agent Hayes smiles. "Everything can be brought back up. Now, we can make this all go away for you. We can make it so you walk free today and never have to come back here."

"How?"

"All you have to do is agree to testify against your grandfather," Agent Hayes says.

"No," I say automatically. "I won't hurt my family."

He turns to my attorney.

"No. You don't have anything to charge Ms. Felton with, except some forged signatures that can be easily proven not to be hers. She is not taking a plea deal," Mr. Greene says.

"Then, we will bring the charges against her and go to trial," Agent Hayes says.

Mr. Greene leans over and whispers in my ear, "Do you know of anything that could incriminate your grandfather?"

"No," I whisper back.

He nods and turns back to the men. "What would you want my client to testify about?"

"We have reason to believe she knew of the actions of her father and grandfather, and while she didn't necessarily partake in the criminal activity, she knew exactly what was happening. We need her to testify to meetings she attended that occurred between her father and grandfather," Agent Liddell says.

"No," I say again.

"Think about it," Agent Liddell says, looking at my lawyer instead of me.

My lawyer whispers in my ear again, "Right now, I know I can get you out on bail. I wouldn't take the plea. But it is something to consider if the evidence is as strongly against you as they claim."

I nod but don't accept that. I don't accept that I might need to take a plea when, this time, I did nothing wrong. And I'd rather go to jail and think of it as penance for my past transgressions than say anything against my family.

"Is that all?" I ask.

"In a hurry to get back to your cell?" Agent Hayes asks.

"It's better than being in here."

"Your arraignment is scheduled to start in an hour. In the meantime, think about taking the plea. I'd hate to see a pretty woman like you end up spending the best years of your life in prison," Agent Hayes says.

Everyone stands, and an officer leads me back to the holding cell but not before I get one last glare in at the agents.

I walk down the hallway leading back to the holding cell, the entire time scanning the area for Killian. He's the reason I'm here. Whatever he found, that's why I'm here, and it's why my grandfather is handcuffed to his bed.

And, as soon as I get out of here, I plan on finding Killian. I plan on finding out the truth.

5

KINSLEY

"Here are the conditions of your bond. Read it carefully, and then sign here," the officer says, pointing to the bottom of the paper.

I take the pen and sign my signature without reading it. The same signature is supposedly all over several criminal papers. It's the reason I was locked up for almost twenty-four hours in the first place. It's the reason I could go to jail for ten years.

I slide the paper back to the officer, trying not to think about it when there are so many things I don't know or understand. Things I don't believe to be true. I don't believe my grandfather or my father would have done anything illegal, especially when it came to the well-being of their company.

"Here are your belongings." The officer slides over my phone, ID, and lip gloss—the only things I had on me when I was arrested.

I take them and put them in the pocket of my sweatpants. I tuck my long blonde hair behind my ear. It feels tangled and greasy from not showering.

"You're free to leave then."

I turn from the officer and walk out the door of the jail. I take a deep breath to keep the tears at bay as I walk out into the warm Las Vegas air.

"Oh my God! Are you okay?" Scarlett says, running toward me.

She immediately wraps her arms around me, like I've been off at war for a few years instead of just sitting in a holding cell for one night.

"I'm fine, Scar."

She releases me and begins looking me up and down. She inspects every inch of me, but I don't know what she expects to find. I'm not bleeding or permanently scarred. I didn't get any tattoos or join a gang.

"I'm fine," I repeat.

She suspiciously eyes me, like she doesn't believe me. "You should get a doctor appointment just in case."

I roll my eyes at her and start walking toward the car she drove to pick me up. "I'm fine."

"You don't know that for sure. You could have caught hepatitis or something while you were in there."

"Scar," I whine, "I'm fine."

I give her a stern look before I quickly walk the rest of the way to the car. Scarlett scurries behind me in her heels. Each step of her heels makes a loud clicking on the concrete making me jumpy. You never know when a strange man is coming to put me in handcuffs again.

I open the door to her red Mercedes two-door coup, feeling exhausted and tired. I just need to go home and sleep. Everything will make sense after a good night's sleep. Even though it's two or maybe three in the afternoon, it feels like two or three in the morning to me; that's how exhausted I am. I just need to sleep for twenty hours straight, and then I'll wake up and realize this was all a dream.

I move to slide into the passenger seat, but something makes me stop. I don't know why I look behind me, but I do. I think I'll always look behind me, keeping one eye open when I sleep because anyone could betray me at any time.

When I look up, I realize why I had the feeling as I see Killian standing just outside the jail building. He intensely looks at me, like he always does. His dark brown hair looks a little unkempt on top of his head, and it's obvious he hasn't shaved since the last time I saw him. He's dressed in a suit, much the same as he has been almost every day I've spent with him. Every day, except for the one day he took me on a date, but it wasn't really a date. It was just a way for the other agents to try to get information from me. It was just a hoax.

I feel my anger bubbling inside me, I slam the door, and my feet begin moving toward him before I even have a chance to think about what I'm doing.

"Kins?" Scarlett asks hesitantly.

"I'll be right back," I say as I continue to walk toward Killian.

He keeps his overpowering eyes on me, his face not showing me any emotion or giving anything away as I walk to him. When I get close, he indicates for me to follow and then begins walking away from the building. We walk two blocks before he ducks into an alleyway and stops, turning to face me.

"You okay?" he asks.

I roll my eyes. "I'm fine." I'm annoyed that everyone keeps asking me that. "Why are we here?"

"We couldn't have this conversation in front of the jail. Too many cameras and witnesses." He pauses. "I'm not supposed to speak to you. It's not good for the case."

"I see. Then, why are you?" I raise my eyebrows.

He innocently looks at me. "Because I couldn't stay away."

I open my mouth to speak, but Killian's lips crash with mine, and I stumble backward in shock. He easily catches me in his arms, as if he was expecting my reaction. His lips are brutal against mine, demanding more from me. Even though our last kiss was just last night, it feels like we haven't kissed in years. The kiss feels like home, something I'm desperate for after spending a night in jail.

Those feelings quickly go away though as thoughts of last night creep back into my head. I try to lose myself in the kiss again and pretend there is nothing wrong. That he wasn't the reason I just spent a night in jail even though I had done nothing wrong. I want to love him, but instead, I hate him.

I try to push Killian back to get him to release my lips so I can show him I hate him, and I no longer care about him. He doesn't budge though. He kisses me harder, making it even harder to resist. Every kiss brings me closer to giving in to him and forgetting my hatred. So, instead, I decide to attack back with my own defiant and brutal kisses. I bite and nip and pull at his lips as my hands claw at his back.

He doesn't fight me. He lets me take my anger out on him, as if he thinks he deserves the pain I'm inflicting. He does. He deserves worse after lying to me and my family. He deserves a whole lot worse.

I bite down hard this time, hard enough to draw blood and for him to let go of me. He touches his fingers to his lips and then removes his hand, looking at the blood. His eyes then look to me, and I see the lust still in his eyes. He still wants me, but he doesn't love me. He doesn't care about me. If he did, he would have told me what was going on before he had me arrested. He wouldn't have let me get so invested in him when he wasn't being truthful. He was using me.

"What was that?" I ask.

"It was a kiss. It was—"

"Stop. I don't want to hear it. We are over. It doesn't matter what it was."

Killian sucks in a breath but doesn't argue with me.

"Why have you been investigating my family?"

He blankly looks at me but doesn't say anything.

"What did you find?"

Again, he stands stoic and doesn't answer.

"Why did you propose to me? Why did you try to become CEO? Why was I in jail? Why? Just...why?"

He doesn't answer me or show any reaction to my questions.

"My family did nothing wrong. Not my grandfather. Not me. And especially not my father." I don't know why I feel the need to defend my father now that he's dead, but I do. I think I feel even stronger about fighting for him because I loved him more than anyone, and he's not here to defend himself. I won't let his memory become tarnished.

"How long have you been investigating? The full five years you have been working for the Felton Corporation?"

He doesn't answer me, but there is one question that he might answer—one question he owes me.

"What is your name? Your real name?"

I wait for Killian to answer, to say anything about what happened.

He doesn't. He just looks longingly at me.

I shake my head as I begin pacing back and forth in the small alleyway. It must have rained last night because I notice a small puddle of water as I walk through it.

"You owe me your name, don't you think? We slept together. You proposed to me. Don't you think you owe me your name?"

His eyes soften and sadden at my words. I've affected him but not enough for him to talk to me or tell me anything.

"If you're not going to talk to me, then why am I here?"

Killian isn't going to tell me anything. I really wasn't anything to him. Just someone he could sleep with to make his time undercover more enjoyable.

He moves his hand to touch me, but I brush it away. He doesn't get to touch me again if he's not going to talk to me.

"I came to say good-bye. I won't come to speak to you again—at least, not outside of a courtroom or FBI building."

He hesitates, and I feel tears welling in my eyes at the thought that I might never see him again. Even now that I know the truth, it doesn't stop me from getting emotional at the thought I might never see him again outside of a courtroom or interrogation room. It won't be like this again.

"And I came to say I'm sorry. I never meant to hurt you or to let you get so emotionally invested. I was just trying to do my job. I never wanted this. You understand why we can't be together? Why we have to say good-bye now?"

I nod. "I understand that you never cared about me and were only doing your fucking job!" Anger escapes my mouth with my words. I was trying to hide it because as long as I was hiding it, he wouldn't know how much he truly hurt me.

He winces, feeling hurt by my words.

I close my eyes, trying to calm myself before I speak again. When I open my eyes, I say the only words I have left to say, and I say them without any emotion, despite the pain I feel inside, "Good-bye, Killian."

"Good-bye, princess." He opens his mouth to say more, but then he stops himself. He turns to walk away, but then he stops and walks back to me, like he's changed his mind again. "Take the deal they are offering you. You don't deserve to go to jail. I don't want to have to testify against you. If this goes to trial, you will go to jail. Take the deal."

"You're incredible. You don't tell me anything. You lie to me the entire time I've been with you, and then you tell me to give up everything I've ever known. You're just trying to get me to testify against my grandfather. I won't do it."

"You have to trust me on this. They will nail you. They have the evidence they need, and your grandfather will go to jail, no matter if you testify or not. So, take the deal. There is no reason to sacrifice yourself just to be loyal to a family who has never been loyal to you."

I shake my head. "No."

He grabs my shoulders. "Please, just listen to me."

"Why should I? You won't answer any of my questions. Not one single question. I don't even know who you are."

His eyes look sad. He removes his hands from my shoulders and runs one hand through his hair in frustration. "That's what I thought."

I look at him for one second longer. Just long enough to remember everything. His intense brown eyes. His lips that hardly ever smile. The rough stubble of his five o'clock shadow and every muscle flexing against his suit jacket.

And then I walk away without saying another word. I begin walking back down the street to find Scarlett when I feel his hand on my shoulder.

"Wait."

I turn and look at him. He pants, catching his breath.

"My name is Liam Killian Byrne, but everyone calls me Killian."

His eyes tell me he's being honest. He's not bluffing. I studied him long enough at the poker table to know when he was lying or telling the truth, but I don't thank him for offering me that one piece of honesty. Instead, I turn away from him and continue to walk to Scarlett's Mercedes. He might have told me his real name, but that's not enough for him to earn my forgiveness. I won't ever forgive him if my grandfather goes to jail and my father's company is lost in scandal.

"You okay?" Scarlett asks as I open the car door and slide in.

"I'm fine," I say for what seems like the millionth time.

Scarlett hesitantly steps on the gas.

I'm not fine though. I just said good-bye to a man my heart is still beating for. I said good-bye to a man I still love, despite everything.

I shake my head. I chose Tristan, and it was the worst mistake of my life. I chose Eli, but he couldn't stand up to my family's scrutiny. My father chose Killian, and now he's going to tear our family apart.

I don't know how to choose my future. And I don't trust my family to choose either. I don't even know what my choices are. All I know is, I have to keep my grandfather from spending the rest of his life in jail. And I have to keep the Felton Corporation from being torn apart by the FBI. I will have to spend the rest of my life alone. I can't face the possibility of choosing wrong again.

6

KILLIAN

I WALK BACK into the FBI building across the street from the jail we were holding Kinsley in. I'm surprised to be welcomed with hooting and hollering when I walk inside.

Several people shake my hand and congratulate me as I walk through the lobby. The building is full of people whom I hardly know and have barely worked with at all in the last five years, but they feel the need to congratulate me.

I continue walking through until I reach the door that says *Agent Bisson* on the door, my boss's office. I knock before entering and find him sitting behind his desk. When he sees me, he stands and walks over to me with a smile on his face.

"Excellent work," Agent Bisson says.

I nod and attempt to move my lips up into a smile, but instead, they stubbornly remain pursed.

"You've more than earned the promotion coming your way."

"What?"

"You'll be promoted to senior agent after this is all over. You've more than earned it."

"Thank you, sir."

I'm not sure what to think. I've worked for five years to get this promotion. My father will be more than proud. It's always what he wanted out of a son, but when my boss told me I was getting a promotion, I felt nothing.

That's not a normal response to a promotion. I should feel excited or happy or proud, not indifferent.

I hear him talking about what my promotion will entail, but I don't really hear him. I'm lost in my own world and thoughts again. Lost in Kinsley and what should have been.

I should have gotten more time with her. More time to earn her trust and make her fall for me. I've fallen for her. I fell for her almost three years ago when I broke up her relationship with Eli, but it wasn't until I met her, not until I had her, that I realized how hard I had fallen.

I thought I had time. Time to allow her to fall just as hard for me. So hard that, when I told her the truth, it wouldn't matter because she'd know I loved her. I thought we could make it work and she would never be arrested. Now, I'll never know.

"You've more than made up for your past indiscretions, Agent Byrne."

"Thank you, sir."

"You going home over your four weeks off after the trials are over?"

"Yes, sir."

"Good, I wish we could give you longer than four weeks. You deserve longer after five-plus years, but it's all I can give you right now. We have too many open cases and not enough undercover agents."

I nod somberly.

"Cheer up, son. You're a hero around here right now, and you'll be able to leave on break soon. If their lawyers are smart, they will negotiate a deal when they see the evidence you collected against them. With any luck, it won't go to trial, and you will get to take your break in a matter of weeks. If not, you should be able to go in a few months once your testimony is done."

I nod, unable to speak about the fact that I know Kinsley won't take the plea deal as much as I want her to. She won't betray her family. She won't leave and take the easy route as much as I want her to. And her grandfather is a stubborn man. He won't go to jail either without a fight.

"Is that all, sir?"

"Yes, and don't forget to set up a meeting with the prosecutor tomorrow to begin preparing for trial, just in case."

"I will, sir."

I walk back out of his office and head to the main floor, the whole time thinking of Kinsley instead of what I'm going to do next. All this time, I've been living in a hotel room at the Felton Grand. I'll have to find an apartment now because I can't see her again.

"Stop it," Agent Hayes says to me.

I glance up at him, not understanding.

"Stop thinking about her. You can't have her. It would ruin your career and the case. You have to stay away from her."

"I don't know what you are talking about."

"Sure you do. I saw you with her outside the jail. I read your reports that were biased toward her. Stay away from her, or you'll end up in a jail cell yourself."

I glare at him but don't argue. He's right. I can't have it both ways. I'm either loyal to the FBI or her.

"I have a report to write."

"Good, see that you write it without telling the whole FBI that you love her. Here's your ID and FBI badge."

I roll my eyes at him and take them from him. Choosing the FBI means I'll be returning to a life I haven't known in five years. While I was undercover, I got to pretend I was someone else and could put the past behind me. Now, I have to face my life head-on. A life I never wanted to return to, filled with more pain than I can bear. A life that is no longer who I am.

7

KINSLEY

SCARLETT PULLS into the driveway of the house I grew up in. I've been living in a hotel room at the Felton Grand, but I can't go back there. It would remind me too much of Killian, and I can't handle thinking about him.

I get out of the car without talking to Scarlett. I haven't spoken to her since I got in the Mercedes, despite her incessant trying. I just couldn't.

I throw the front door open without testing the lock first. It's almost always unlocked. I run up the stairs two at a time and run down the hallway to my childhood bedroom. I run to my bed and collapse on it just as the tears begin burning in my eyes.

I hear Scarlett come in, but I still don't say anything to her. I'm not sure what she is going to do, but then I feel her wrap her arms around me as she lies next to me on the bed. She doesn't say anything further, and she doesn't try to question what happened or why I'm crying.

I let everything out. I let the fear out I felt while I was sitting in the holding cell. I let the worry out at realizing my grandfather and father could have done something illegal. I let the pain out Killian caused me. I let it all go.

And, when it's all out almost an hour later, I finally speak, "I still love him."

"I know," Scarlett says.

"I can't go to jail."

"You won't. You did nothing wrong."

"Granddad can't go to jail either."

Scarlett doesn't respond. Instead, the room is eerily silent.

"Scar?" I say, sitting up.

She stares down at my comforter.

"Granddad can't go to jail. They can't ruin my father's memory."

Scarlett hesitantly looks up at me. "But what if he did something? What if he did lie and cheat and smuggle money or whatever they are charging him with? What if he deserves to go to jail? What if your father helped him?"

I stand from the bed. "He didn't do anything. Neither of them did!"

Scarlett gets up. "But what if they did? The FBI wouldn't have arrested your grandfather if he didn't do something wrong."

"They arrested *me*, and *I* didn't do anything wrong."

Scarlett doesn't say anything, but she looks guilty, like what she wants to say next is going to hurt. She opens her mouth to say the words anyway, "But you did do something wrong, Kins, or they wouldn't have arrested you. Even if you didn't mean to. Even if you were just doing whatever your father or grandfather had asked of you, you did something. You were just too naive to know what you were doing."

"Get out!"

Scarlett looks at me in shock.

I walk over to my bedroom door and open it, indicating for her to get out. I'm not going to listen to her blame my father or Granddad or me for what's happened.

"Get out," I say firmly.

She sighs and picks her purse up off the floor where she must have dropped it before climbing onto my bed.

"Call me when you realize I'm right."

I don't say anything, even though I think of several comebacks I would like to say to her. We've been friends too long, and I know, deep down, she is just saying what she believes to be true. I just can't believe her words.

I walk back to my bed, planning on sleeping the rest of the day away. I try to sleep—God knows I need it—but I end up tossing and turning.

Killian. I want to call him and see him, but I can't. Killian is gone, replaced by Liam. That's his name. Liam. Killian doesn't exist. Just like everything that happened between wasn't real.

I take out my phone while I wait for my pancakes. I type in his name—*Liam Killian Byrne*. Nothing comes up though. Not a Facebook page. Or Twitter. Not a mention of a school he attended—just nothing.

I sigh in frustration and put my phone back in my pocket. I close my eyes trying to fall asleep again. Maybe this nightmare would end if I slept.

After trying for three hours to fall asleep, I get out of bed and make my way downstairs. My mother is passed out on the couch with a fifth of tequila gripped in her hand.

I exhale. I can't deal with her right now. Tomorrow I'll take her to rehab. Tomorrow I'll find a solution to everything. Today I just need to find a way to keep breathing.

I continue walking on until I find myself in front of my grandfather's bedroom and push the door open.

The smell of his cigars immediately overwhelms me as I step inside. The furniture in the room is all dark oak. The comforter is shades of red. On each wall is all of my grandfather's accomplishments — a picture of every casino and hotel. I glance at his nightstand where there is a picture of his family. I must be no more than five in the picture. It was the last picture my grandmother was in. Lying next to it is a business book and his reading glasses.

I pick up the book. It's a book on leadership. I take the book onto the couch in the living room and open the book to the first page to begin reading.

Scarlett's wrong. Killian's wrong. The FBI's wrong. Granddad is a good man who loved the company. He would never have done anything to endanger it.

———

"What are you doing?" my mother asks when we are halfway to the rehab center.

"Getting you help."

"I'm not the one who needs help," she spits at me, referencing my current predicament with the law.

It is only a matter of time before she brings up the last time again.

At hearing my mother's words, I purse my lips but don't allow my anger to overtake me. I won't allow her to get to me like last time. But the memories of last time, the memories of five years ago, still ring in my ear.

The drive home from jail is long and silent. My father sits in the driver's seat, next to my grandfather. Neither of them has said a word to me since they picked me up, but from their expressions, I know they are disappointed in me, worse than disappointed in me. As soon as I walk through the door to our house, I will be lectured. I try to prepare myself for it as I sit in the back seat of the car, but I know I will deserve it or worse, and there is no way to prepare for it.

We pull up to our house. My father parks his Audi in the driveway, but none of us move to get out. None of us want to deal with what we all know must happen once we get inside.

We have to deal with the reality that I might go to prison. That the Felton Corporation is now under investigation for selling drugs since the man who gave Tristan the drugs was an employee. Since I was found with the drugs, that makes two people linked to the Felton Corporation.

The family of the boy I almost hit is suing. Once they found out how much money our family had, they decided to sue for emotional damages I caused the boy and mother.

Tristan's family is pressing charges against me for stealing and damaging his car.

There has been a wave of cancellations of events and bookings in our casinos and hotels after our family was portrayed as druggies and our hotels as drug rings. We are at risk of losing everything my family has worked for because of me.

Granddad is the one who finally decides it's time. He opens the door and climbs out. So, my father and I do the same. Still, no one says a word as we walk into the house.

That silence ends though as soon as my mother sees me.

"You fucking little shit," my mother says, striking me hard on the cheek while holding a bottle in her other hand.

It burns where she hit me, but the embarrassment and pain of being slapped by my mother at sixteen hurt worse than the physical pain. My father moves to stop my mother from doing it again, but out of the corner of my eye, I watch Granddad stop him. My mother slaps me again, but this time, I expected it, which somehow lessens the pain.

My mother raises her hand a third time.

"Enough," Granddad says.

My mother stops mid-air, and instead, she lifts the bottle of amber liquor to her lips, swallowing large gulps. "You stupid fucking child! You've fucking ruined everything!"

My mother storms over to my father, and as she walks by me, I smell the alcohol seeping out of her pores. She's had more than she should have, more than anyone should have.

"This is your fault," she says. Her face is red. "We should never have had her. I told you! I told you she would destroy the family!"

At my mother's cruel words, I feel tears falling, but she's right.

"Kinsley hasn't destroyed the family. She has merely provided a setback, but we will get through this, just like every other crisis our family has faced," my father says.

"Don't bullshit her! She has destroyed the family. We will recover—we always do—but Kinsley has effectively destroyed the image of the family and company. And, no matter what we do, the shame of public opinion will never go away. The question now is, what do we do with her? I say, throw her out on the streets. Disown her. Let her go to prison to pay for her crimes," my mother says.

"No, that won't do. It would make the family look worse. Boarding school perhaps?" Granddad says.

"Rehab?" my father suggests.

I feel more tears burn as my father suggests rehab. I never told him the drugs weren't mine. I never turned in Tristan. I just...couldn't. Not when I was so stupid to do what I did. Not when I almost killed someone for my stupid mistake.

"I'll do whatever you say. Whatever you want," I say.

The room falls silent.

"What do you mean?" Granddad asks.

"I made a mistake, a horrible mistake I will never forgive myself for. I make horrible decisions. I chose a horrible person to date... I won't do it again."

Granddad smiles at me. "Excellent. Then, it's settled. You will speak to me or your father from now on before making any decisions, no matter how trivial. Do you understand?"

"Yes."

"And when the time comes, your father and I will choose the man you marry."

I nod.

"Good. Now, go to your room, and don't come out until dinner."

I nod and head off to my room, feeling better, knowing I will never make this horrible of a mistake again. I will never hurt my family or anyone else ever again. I will never choose whom I will date or fall in love with again.

My mother didn't drink again after that day. Father and Granddad got her help and convinced her, if she continued to drink, it would just further ruin the reputation of the family. She didn't drink again until my father's death.

Now, I have to put a stop to it. Not because she will destroy the family. Her drinking is the least of the family's worries at the moment, but because, deep down, I still love her. I don't want her to drink away her life any further.

I remember my promise. That I would never date or choose who I fell in love with again. I'd let my family do that. My family chose

Killian though, and he turned out wrong, but I chose him, too. We both chose wrong. They all end up like this—with a broken heart and family.

I park the car in front of the rehab center, the same one she went to last time.

"Go inside," I say calmly to my mother.

She laughs. "I'm not going inside. I'm not the one in trouble. I'm not the one who has done something stupid again and given up my freedom."

"No, you're right. I'm the bad apple in the family. But I'm not the only bad apple. It seems I come from a family of bad apples."

My mother moves to grab me, but I'm already prepared. I grab her arms, and in her drunken stupor, she is too weak to hurt me.

"Go inside, mother. Get clean. You won't get any money if we are all in jail unless you get clean."

That makes her pause for just a second. I shake my head. She didn't love my father like she told me. She loved his money.

"Go," I say again.

This time, she gets out of the car. I get out, too, as much as I don't want to, and I help her walk inside. I help her check herself in. And then I leave her to be taken care of by the rehab center. If only fixing the rest of my family's problems were so simple.

8

KILLIAN

I UNPACK the last of my boxes in my new apartment. I started at six a.m. and didn't have many boxes since I'd been living out of a hotel room for five years, so it's just thirty minutes later when I finish. The apartment is small compared to the luxurious hotel room I was staying in, but it will do for now.

I won't have the apartment for long anyway. Once the trials are over, I'll be on break for a few weeks where I can go home or go on vacation. And then I'll get a new assignment, which could be anywhere in the country.

So, this apartment will do. It's modern and fully furnished, and it does month-to-month leases. That's all that matters.

I grab a bottle of water from the fridge and chug it. I have time to work out before my meeting with the prosecutor this morning. I think about heading to the exercise room at the main building in the apartment complex, but I don't think working out indoors will be enough to distract me.

So, instead, I grab my headphones and connect them to my phone. I turn on Spotify and pick the first playlist, which is Today's Hits. Then, I crank the music as loud as I can. I don't bother warming up. I run at full speed as soon as I make it out of my apartment building. I don't know the area well enough to know where I should run, so I just run through a neighborhood while focusing on my breathing and the music.

I breathe in and out to the beats of Adele, followed by The Weeknd and then Beyoncé. My speed matches the song that is playing, which means I run faster or slower, depending on the beat and not how my body feels. I listen to the lyrics, really concentrating on each word to keep every other thought out of my mind.

It works until Justin Bieber comes on, singing about how sorry he is to some girl, and I lose the rhythm of my breathing and running. I quickly lose my breath until I can't breathe or run. All I can do is listen to the lyrics of the song and think about how much Kinsley loves Justin Bieber. I might not be a fan of his music, but I will never be able to hear his songs again without thinking about her.

I walk back to my apartment, replaying the song over and over again in my head and picturing how I could say sorry to her. *How can I make it up to her?*

I can't though, and even if I could, I could never say sorry enough to make it up to her. Because *sorry* isn't enough after you've destroyed someone's family.

When I make it back to my apartment, I shower and change into a suit. The same suit I would wear when I went to work at the Felton Corporation. It feels weird to put it on and not go into work there. Instead, I'll be going to the FBI office.

I grab my laptop I used last night to finish my last report on the Felton case. I made sure it contained no feelings of empathy for the Felton family. I place the laptop in my briefcase and then head out to my Chevy Malibu rental car.

The drive to the FBI office building seems long. I'm used to just walking downstairs to my office at the Felton Corporation. I find a parking spot on the street and then make my way through the dry heat and into the building. People smile at me, but I don't return the pleasantries as I make my way through the building to the law offices where the prosecutor wants to meet. I don't understand the point in fake smiling when you don't feel like smiling. Although, with that attitude, I might never smile again because I'm not sure I'll ever be happy again.

I make it to the door of the prosecutor's office. The door is closed, but I don't bother knocking. It's one thing the FBI has taught me—to own my power as an agent. And walking into someone's office is a great way to show people I have power while also catching them off guard. I can see people in their real state instead of the fake demeanor they most often offer me.

The man behind the desk isn't fazed though as I walk into his office, unannounced. Working in an FBI building like this, full of agents who probably walk in on him all the time, probably did that to him.

He looks up at me but doesn't smile. I like this man already.

"Agent Byrne, I presume?"

"Yes." I extend my hand to him.

He takes it, and we shake.

"I'm Roy Fowler, the head prosecutor. Have a seat." Roy motions for me to take a seat opposite him.

"I've spent the last few months reading through all of your reports. Excellent job. This will be an easy open-and-shut case if you ask me. Honestly, I shouldn't even offer Ms. Felton a deal because it's such an airtight case, but we did offer her a deal already. I could rescind it..."

"No!"

He looks at me with a confused expression, and I shut my mouth, realizing I can't stand up for her anymore, not here.

"I was saying I could rescind the deal, but I'm not going to. I don't think she was the ringleader in this. I think she was just doing what her family told her to, and she didn't even realize she was breaking the law.

"I've thought long and hard about Mr. Felton, and based on his age, I'm planning on offering him a deal for ten years. He'll easily get out in five to seven. The most important thing is for him to step down from running the company to ensure the company is now run legally."

I take a deep breath, realizing he isn't going to send Kinsley to jail. The offer he is going to make to her grandfather is more than fair. "I think that's fair."

He nods. "If they are smart, they will take the pleas, and this will be over this week, but if they decide to go to trial, I want you to be ready to testify. We could go to trial against Ms. Felton as soon as next week if she doesn't take the deal by tomorrow. Her acceptance of the deal or conviction, if it comes to that, will put the pressure we need on Mr. Felton. Either way, I don't think he will go to trial if she agrees to testify against him or ends up in jail herself."

I suck in a breath. It takes everything inside of me not to defend Kinsley.

"Anyway, here is a list of questions I will be asking you when you testify as well as some questions the defense might ask you about Ms. Felton. I want you to spend the morning going through them on your own. Then, this afternoon, I will have time to better prep you on your answers to ensure they are clear and concise."

I look down at the long list of detailed questions about Kinsley I don't want to answer, especially in front of a jury. "I understand."

I take the papers and leave the room, hating the fact that the rest of the day is going to be spent thinking about how I'd answer questions that could put Kinsley behind bars for at least ten years. I hope she's smart enough not to let it come to that.

I shake my head. It's not that she isn't smart enough. It's that she cares about her family too much. I have to find some way to convince her to take the deal before I am forced to send her to jail.

9

KINSLEY

Ten years.

That is the minimum prison sentence I face.

Ten years. Or longer.

I would be in my thirties when I got out of jail. All of my twenties would be wasted. I would have no chance of finding a career. No chance at finding out who I am while I'm young. No chance of falling in love before I'm thirty.

My lawyer said I could take a plea deal if I wanted. Testify against my grandfather, and I would be free.

I said no.

My lawyer agreed that not taking the plea deal was the best. But my lawyer also represents my grandfather. He's not looking out for what's best for me. He's looking out for what's best for Granddad.

But I won't take the plea deal to save myself. I have nothing to testify against Granddad anyway. And I don't think Granddad did anything wrong.

I may not trust my lawyer, but I do believe he can keep me out of jail. He's the best. We are paying him a ridiculous amount of money to defend us against something we shouldn't even be fighting. He will keep us out of jail.

A signature is the only evidence the FBI has against me anyway. My signature. One stroke of a pen.

My lawyer says it can easily be proven my signature was forged. That the entire documents are fake. I believe him. But it doesn't keep my stomach from tightening in knots as I drive away from my lawyer's office.

I catch movement out of the corner of my eye that draws my eye away from the road to the building next to me. A man in a sharp suit with an intense scowl on his face exits the building.

Killian.

He glances up, and our eyes meet. The pain from our last meeting comes flooding back. Pain. Anger. Hurt. Need. They all mix together until I have no idea which feeling is strongest.

Just the sight of him has my body twisted and aching. I didn't want to see him again, especially not so soon when I haven't persuaded my heart to let him go yet. But here he is, and I feel my heart begging me to pull the car over and run into his arms. Need grows in my belly, the need to kiss his lips again and take him back to my house so I can ride him until he satisfies my lust. I also feel the need to turn my car and run him over for what he has done to my family. I just don't know which of the three feelings is strongest— love, lust, or anger.

I don't get to decide which feeling is strongest. Fate and Killian decide for me. Killian breaks eye contact as he turns away from me. I glance back to the street, and the light is now green. So, I drive away from Killian. I say a second good-bye, keeping the tears buried deep inside. I don't know if I can bear to say good-bye again.

I have to find out the truth, and the only man I can find out the truth from is my grandfather. I have a million more questions that need to be answered. The only person who will be able to answer them is my grandfather. So that's where I'll go—to get the answers to the only questions that matter.

———

Granddad's hospital room looks the same as the last time I was here. There is just one marked difference. One of his arms is handcuffed to the bedrail. He can't even get out of bed on his own, but the officer decided to handcuff him anyway.

I run over to his side.

"Granddad," I say hesitantly as he lies in bed, seemingly asleep. I should let him rest if he is sleeping, but this can't wait. I need to know. I need to know as much as I can.

His eyes slowly open, and then he smiles when he sees it's me and not a nurse or doctor or police officer.

"Kinsley, I'm so glad you came. I heard they released you last night, but I wasn't sure if you would want to see me."

I take his frail hand in mine. "Of course I want to see you. You're my grandfather. I love you. You're the only family I have left."

He raises an eyebrow.

"I don't count Mother. I dropped her off in rehab this morning anyway. She needs to get better."

He pats my hand. "I'm glad you did that. She needs help."

"What about you? How are you doing?"

Granddad shrugs. "I've been better."

"They told me you are getting out of here tomorrow morning."

He nods but doesn't say anything more. He's not going to talk to me. He's not going to tell me what the hell we were both arrested for without me asking.

"What is going on? What happened? Why were we both arrested?"

He looks out the window of his hospital room without answering me. I give him a second to gather his thoughts, but I soon realize that is not what he is doing. He's avoiding me, not answering me, which surprises me. I thought, once I asked, he would answer, just like always, but I guess being faced with spending the rest of your life in jail changes a man.

"Granddad, did you and Dad do what they say you did? Did you lie and cheat to grow the company? Did you commit fraud and money laundering to build the company?"

Granddad's head whips to look at me. His face is red, and his nostrils are flared. "Hell no, we didn't do any of those things! I can't believe you would even ask me such a thing. You think your own grandfather would commit a crime? Your own father?"

"No," I say firmly. "I don't *want* to believe what the FBI says is true. I *don't* believe what they say is true. I just need to hear you tell me the truth. I need to know why I'm facing charges of crimes I didn't commit, why you are facing charges if you didn't commit the crimes either."

He takes a deep breath, and his face softens, the shade of red turning to pale pink. I hand him a cup of water from the bedside table, and he slowly sips it. His face returns to a normal shade instead of the burning fire that swept across his face moments ago.

"Why?" I ask again when he seems calmer. "Even our lawyer suspects you and Dad did this. What proof does the FBI have?"

"Five years ago, when you were arrested, and they found the drugs had come from one of our casinos, the FBI began investigating the company. They thought the company might be tied to a drug ring or something. It wasn't, but it made them very suspicious, suspicious enough to plant undercover agents in the company, except we didn't know that. We thought, when the FBI stopped talking to us about a year after your incident was over, they had found us innocent.

"Killian, the FBI agent they planted, never found anything. After five years, he never found anything, but the FBI couldn't give up after spending five years investigating us. Killian framed us because his superiors told him to. Killian had to prove himself to the FBI after he made a mistake that should have put him in jail."

"What mistake?"

"It doesn't matter. What matters is, you stay away from him. He's the enemy, not me. He's the criminal."

I nod. I believe the man sitting in front of me over the man who has lied to me.

"Good."

I watch my grandfather's movements the whole time he is talking, trying to decide if he is telling the truth or not. I don't know if he is telling the truth, but I feel like he is. I feel like he has to be, not because I believe my grandfather to be a good man, but because I know my father was a good man. My father wouldn't have committed a crime, and there is no way my grandfather could have done something like this without my father knowing.

"Don't worry about the company, Granddad. I just want you to focus on getting better and staying out of jail."

Granddad frowns, and I know he is going to protest.

"I still don't think you are strong enough or capable of running the company—"

I narrow my eyes at him. "You don't exactly have a choice. Killian was a terrible choice. You chose to give half of the company to the one man who had been working against you. Tony is a worse choice. There is no one else in a high enough position who can run it. At this point, it's me or nobody. I can do this. The mistakes I made were nothing compared to the mistakes others in this family have made."

Granddad winces as he reaches over to the bedside table and grabs a piece of paper. "I was going to say that, despite my reservations, you're right. I don't have a choice."

He hands me the piece of paper he had typed up, and I quickly read it. He is giving me temporary power over the company until he is healed and his trial is over.

"Thank you. I'll do you proud."

He smiles. "You will because you'll do everything I say."

I shake my head. "No, I won't. I'll do what is best for the company, no matter what that is. I'm not sure I have the best judgment in the world, but now, I know that it can't be any worse than yours. If I sign this, I want full authority over my life and the company. I want your trust. I don't want to be your puppet."

He thinks for a second and then smiles. "I was hoping you would say that."

He hands me a pen, and I hesitate over the papers.

Can one signature change your life? One signature, whether mine or not, sent me to jail. I'm about to find out for the second time if one signature changes everything.

10

KINSLEY

I PULL the car into the driveway of my family home. A home I feel both closer to and further away from. Closer because I feel like I have to rely more on my family in order to get through these next few months. And further away because I'm afraid the walls of this household secrets I'm not ready to face.

I turn off the car and walk over to the passenger door. I open it for Granddad and help him out of the car.

"Thanks, princess," he says.

I smile at him, not correcting him, just allowing him to use the name that only my father ever really called me.

And Killian...

Now, neither of those men will ever call me that again because both are out of my life.

"Just take it slow. No need to rush inside."

"I know I'm safe as long as you are by my side," he says.

I smile and nod at him as we walk slowly inside. I hope that is true. I hope I can stand by his side through everything coming our way.

I help him inside and to his bedroom and into bed. I glance at the clock. I need to get to the casino. I scheduled some meetings for this afternoon to ensure everything has been running smoothly since his heart attack.

"I need to get going, but the nurse should be here soon, and I'll notify the staff to look in on you. Do you need anything before I go?"

"Where are you going?"

"To check on how things are going at the casinos."

He carefully eyes me. "Don't change anything without consulting me first."

I just smile. I don't argue with him. What he doesn't know won't hurt him.

"I have to go," I say before softly kissing him on the cheek.

I quickly run upstairs to change into something more appropriate for business. I slip on a business suit and heels, and then I run out the door to my car.

I am at the casino in a half hour.

When I walk up to the casino, I'm surprised by the crowd gathered outside. I watch as people pull out their phones when they see me walking into the casino. I try to smile brightly as they take my picture, seeming unfazed by the scandal swarming around my family.

I wave to the crowd at the door and then walk inside. I'm surprised to see the inside is just as crowded as the outside. I guess I expected no one would want to gamble or stay at a casino filled with scandal. Instead, it seems we have tripled our crowds overnight. I guess what they say is true; any press is good press.

I head straight to my father's office and close the door behind me. I walk over to the desk that is now covered in notes and papers people have dropped off, but no one has received because no one has been here. My father is gone. And now my grandfather. And Killian. That leaves me.

I quickly sort through the papers into things that need to be dealt with urgently and things that are less important.

Then, I dial Tony's number.

"Hello?" Tony says in confusion.

"Tony, it's Kinsley. Can you get everyone gathered in the meeting room in twenty minutes? I need to make sure everything is being handled since my grandfather and I were arrested."

"Sure, Ms. Kinsley."

"Thanks, Tony." I hang up the phone.

The last time I'd tried to run a meeting, it went horribly, horribly wrong. I don't even know what to say now, other than to make sure everyone is doing their job, especially since everyone who was anywhere near the CEO position is gone.

I gather every drop of strength I have as I stand, and I begin walking to the meeting room.

I have to walk past Killian's office on the way. I pause at the door that still says *Killian Browne* on the outside. The door is shut though, so I can't see inside. I don't know what I expect to see. He's not in there. And he never wanted me. He was just doing whatever the FBI had told him. He was getting my father and Granddad to trust him so he could find out whatever he thought they were hiding. That's it. Nothing more.

I have to think of Killian as nothing but a man who worked for the FBI. Just a man my family tried to get me to marry. Nothing between us was real, but it doesn't stop me from hoping he is somehow still in the office, just like he was the day I walked in with Tony.

I force myself to walk past his office to the meeting room where Tony is waiting for me at the door. He smiles at me but doesn't say anything about the charges or situation I'm in. He just looks at me with a confident smile I match on my face.

"You ready?" he asks.

I take a deep breath, trying to channel every part of my father's strength inside me. "Yes."

Tony opens the door for me, and I confidently walk inside because I know I'm capable. I'm my father's daughter. I can do this.

Then, I glance around the room at the ten executives seated at the table, and I feel my anxiety creeping back in. I take a seat at the end of the long table.

But then Tony walks in with the same smile on his face, and I relax.

I can do this, I repeat over and over in my head.

"I called this meeting to..." I lose my train of thought as I feel everyone staring at me.

"You can do this," I feel my father telling me.

I take a deep breath and start again. This time, I look up at the men and women gathered around the table, and I feel calmer than I ever have.

"I called this meeting to discuss how things have been going since my grandfather had a heart attack and the sudden news that followed. I would like to hear from all of you about how things have been going and what ideas you have to keep the company moving forward during this difficult time for my family and the company."

I glance around the table, but nobody speaks. I don't back down until I have met everyone's eyes.

Finally, one gentleman sitting to my right speaks up, "As you can see from when you entered the casino, the number of customers has increased almost threefold, which sounds great. However, we were not prepared for such an increase in customers. We don't have the staff to handle such a large number of people, and we have had several employees simply not show up to work. As a result, we have had to turn customers away."

I nod. "Has this been the same experience across all of our hotels and casinos nationwide?"

"Yes," a woman to my left says.

"Any ideas on how to solve this problem?" I ask the group.

"We have been asking our employees to do overtime to make up for those who haven't been showing up. It's the same strategy we have used in the past when employees haven't shown up, but we can't ask them to do that forever."

I nod although I didn't realize we had a problem with employees not showing up to work. "What about hiring new employees so we can fill our hotels and casinos to capacity?"

"That would work in the short-term, but when the decrease in customers returns to our old rate, we would have to lay off lots of employees."

I shake my head. "No, we won't. We can hire the same amount of employees that we will need for the expansion of the hotel, so they can stay on. Test raising our rates during this period and see if demand decreases or stays steady to help pay for the increase in employees. Let's get a marketing and PR team together to capitalize on the current situation and spin it to our favor, so the world is behind us." I can't believe the words that are coming out of my mouth, but there they are. Each word that falls from my lips makes me feel more and more confident.

"Are you sure the numbers will work? Will we make enough profit? We can't afford to be in the negative at a time like this," the woman next to me says.

I think back to the numbers that were lying on my father's desk. I quickly calculate the risk and reward associated with the plan.

I smile. "It will work."

"What makes you so sure?"

"I just ran the numbers in my head. Even if the numbers fell off, going back to our normal rate—which wouldn't happen because we are going to increase our marketing to capitalize on the situation— we would still be in the positive. So, make it happen."

Those around the table stare back at me with obvious confusion on their faces.

"What?" I ask, looking around the table. I touch my face, afraid I have something on it since everyone is looking at me so weirdly.

"Who is in charge now that Mr. Felton is incapacitated? Or will he be working from his home for now?" the woman next to me asks.

"I'm in charge."

"You?" she asks.

"Yes. So, when I say implement the plan I just told you, you need to do it."

I look around the table at everyone's stunned expressions.

"Is this a permanent position for you or just until your grandfather chooses a new replacement?"

I glare at the man who just asked. "It's permanent." I don't want them thinking they can just walk all over me until my grandfather chooses a replacement.

"But will you be able to run the company with the charges against you?"

I turn my glare to the woman who just asked me that. "I have full faith the charges against me, as well as the charges against my grandfather, will be dropped soon. There is no merit to the charges."

"But what if—"

I glare at the woman. "If, nothing. I will not be discussing the charges against me or my grandfather any further. It isn't a concern for the company. We always have what is best for the company at heart. That isn't going to change, no matter what happens.

"Now, do any of you have further questions about the company or what our focus should be in the upcoming months?"

I look around the room as everyone shakes their head.

"Good. If anyone has any questions, please contact me or Tony. He will be my assistant and will get any questions you have to me. Understood?"

I smile as I look around the room, and everyone nods.

I can do this, I think. *I can run a company*. I just need a little confidence and a little more practice. *I can do this*.

11

KILLIAN

A SENSE of calm washes over me as I walk into the Felton Grand casino. I shouldn't feel this way, walking into a place I'm helping to destroy. I shouldn't feel like I'm walking into my home.

I walk through the casino to the door that says *Employees Only*. I swipe my employee card, and it still works. I open the door.

I shouldn't be here.

I shouldn't be doing this.

Kinsley might not even be here, but I have to see her. I have to try one more time.

I walk down the hallway to Robert's office. I grab the door handle, but it's locked. I knock, but no one answers, and from what I can tell, it's dark inside. I walk past my old office that still looks the same. I could go in and pretend this is still my life. That I get to feel important and useful, helping to build a company, instead of feeling like a fraud FBI agent. I rest my hand on the handle of my office door, ready to go inside, when I hear the door to the meeting room open.

I watch as several of the other execs file out of the room. I nod at them as they walk by with shocked, wide-eyed expressions on each of their faces. I wait until the last one has passed, and that's when I see her.

Kinsley closes the door behind her as she takes a deep breath with a large smile on her face. I can't help but smile at her, too. Whatever happened in there happened because she finally found herself. She found the piece of confidence that was dampened years ago. She looks beautiful and strong, standing there in her business suit.

Kinsley tucks a strand of her long blonde hair behind her ear as she looks up and straight into my eyes. She freezes when she sees me, not sure what to do, and then she narrows her eyes at me, like she's not sure if I am really here.

She begins walking down the hallway, her eyes now looking at the floor instead of me, but I can't keep mine off of her. Despite staring down, she struts down the hallway like she owns the place. When she gets to me, I plan on stopping her and dragging her inside my office, but she stops and looks at me, and I freeze. I try to read her face, but I can't.

She raises her eyebrows at me.

"We need to talk," I say.

She doesn't hesitate like she usually does. She doesn't say maybe. "No."

And then she's walking again, and I have to resort to my original plan.

"It wasn't a question." I pull her into my old office and quickly shut the door behind me.

She glares at me, but it looks more cute than menacing. "I want your employee access card back." She holds out her hand waiting for me to give her the card.

I shake my head and get straight to the point. "Take the plea deal."

"If that's why you came here, then you are wasting your time and mine. I have a lot of work to do. After we found out that the man we'd thought could run the company is a lying scumbag, a lot of work has been left to me to do." She folds her arms across her chest.

I smile. She deserves to run the company. But it will ruin her. Her legally running the company will make her look guilty. She will end up in prison.

The smile drops from my lips. "You're running the company now?"

"Yes, I'm running the company." She scowls at me. "I'm a fast learner. I can do this."

I run my hand through my hair, frustrated that I keep screwing this up, but I can't tell her the truth. "I know you can run the company. That's not what I'm worried about."

I begin pacing the room, trying to think of what I can tell her that will change her mind. When I turn back, all I see is her getting more and more annoyed with me.

"What do you know?" I ask, hoping she will say enough so I can tell her the truth. If I can tell her everything, then she might listen to me.

But she stares back at me with a blank expression. She cocks her head to one side. "What do I know about what?"

I shake my head. This is a bad idea. I turn to pace again, but she reaches her hand out and touches my arm. I freeze at her touch as it electrifies my body. I don't know what it is about her that affects me like this. There is nothing sexual about her touch. It's not even that comforting. I'm not even sure she realizes she is touching my arm.

"Take the plea. If not for you, do it for *me*."

She scrunches her nose. "I'm not going to help you lock Granddad away."

"You won't. You don't know anything that could worsen his case. Just don't make me testify against you. Don't make me hurt you, princess."

She lets go of my arm. "You can't hurt me, *Liam*. I didn't do anything wrong."

I hate hearing the name *Liam* coming out of her mouth. "I can hurt you though. I could send you to jail with my testimony."

"It would be a lie."

I shake my head. "It wouldn't be."

"Then, tell me what you saw. What evidence do you think you have against me? Tell me what you think I did?"

"I don't think you did anything, but with what I saw, the FBI will

249

make the jury believe you knew what you were doing." I can't tell her more though. "You just have to trust me."

"I can't, Liam, not after you lied to me."

"Take the plea deal. Choose your own freedom."

"Tell me the truth, and maybe I will."

I eye her suspiciously, trying to decide if she would change her mind if I told her. I've studied everything about this girl for five years, from afar and up close. She's too loyal to her family, no matter the cost.

"You won't. Even if I told you the truth."

"Maybe, maybe not. It depends on what the truth is."

"You won't."

"Try me. Let me make up my own mind." She steps forward in a challenging manner until her body presses against mine.

I try not to show her how much her body affects me, but it's a useless endeavor. My eyes fill with need, and my body aches for her, to kiss her and own her body until she forgets why she hates me.

"Trust me," I say.

"I can't."

I close my eyes in defeat. I hear her phone buzzing in her pocket and watch as she pulls it out and glances at her screen.

"It's my lawyer," she says.

"Take it." I nod toward her phone. I lean forward and softly kiss her on the cheek because I need to touch her skin. And then I walk toward the door.

I know this is the last time we will be in the same room without her hating me. She thinks she hates me now, but she doesn't know what hating me really feels like. After I testify against her and her grandfather, she will detest me.

"My name's not Liam. I haven't been Liam since I was seven. I'm Killian. I didn't lie about that."

Kinsley smiles at me, and it's a memory I will take with me forever, a last piece of happiness she gave to me. And then I leave her to find out how long she has left before her life changes forever.

12

KINSLEY

KILLIAN CAME to see me again. Each time I see him, it gets harder and harder to tell him good-bye. Each time, it gets harder and harder to tell him no when his body is asking for more.

I walk over to my closet and pull out the pastel-pink jacket I've chosen to wear with my khaki dress pants. My lawyer said appearance is important in court. I'm supposed to look professional but not too professional. Pretty but not too pretty. He said the most important was to look young and naive, not like a sharp businesswoman.

That's not hard for me. Young, naive, and pretty is what everyone thinks of me on a normal day.

I slip the jacket on and take a deep breath, trying to calm myself, but it's no use. Granddad still isn't well enough to leave the house. My mother is still in rehab. Scarlett and I haven't made up yet. I have no one to go to court with. No one to lean on for support. I'm on my own.

I grab my purse and head downstairs.

"Would you like any breakfast?" Paige asks when I walk past the kitchen.

I stop, and my stomach growls. She smiles at me.

"I don't know," I say because I have no idea if I could stomach any food right now.

"I'll make you a smoothie so you can sip it on your way."

"Thanks."

The doorbell rings, and I stare at her in confusion. "Are we expecting anyone?"

She shakes her head and then goes to gather ingredients to make the smoothie. I sigh and walk to the door. I don't want to deal with anybody today. I just want to go to court and then climb back into bed and cry.

I open the door, and my mouth falls open.

"Hi, Kins," Scarlett says hesitantly.

"Hi," I breathe back.

"I, uh...I came here...I mean, I just thought..."

I take in Scarlett's appearance of heels, a black skirt, and a white blouse. I smile.

"Thank you," I say.

She smiles back at me, and that's all it takes to make up. We don't need any other words. We don't need to say we are sorry.

Scarlett wraps her arms around me, and I can finally breathe. It's exactly what I needed. Someone to support me today. To know someone will be sitting on my side of the courtroom with me. When she lets go, she grabs my hand instead.

"We've got this," she says.

I nod, unable to speak. *We've got this.*

"You ready to go?"

I nod again.

"Smoothies for two," Paige says from behind me. She hands Scarlett and me each a strawberry-banana smoothie. "Best of luck, sweetheart."

"She doesn't need luck. We've got this," Scarlett says, winking at me.

I smile as we walk to her car. I climb in the passenger seat, feeling good I don't have to drive myself.

"How's your grandfather doing?"

"He's recovering well. A therapy team comes twice a day to help him get stronger."

"That's good," she says, backing the car out of the driveway.

"Company doing well?"

"Yeah, it's doing better than ever actually."

She smiles. "There is no such thing as bad press."

I smile, too. "That's what I thought."

She hesitates before asking me the last question, the one she's dying to ask if I know Scarlett at all, "And Killian?"

I twirl my hair around my fingers. "It's over. He's going to testify against me today. I think, after hearing that, any lingering feelings I have for him will disappear."

"It's okay if they don't."

"No, it's not. I need to move on."

She nods.

"Do you want to talk about—"

"No." If I think about where we are driving, about what I'm going to have to do today, I'll lose any bit of strength I have worked so hard to get. I need to save it all for the courtroom.

"I went on an audition," Scarlett says, trying to distract me.

"Yeah? For what?"

"A horror film."

I raise my eyebrow. "Horror? Really? How did it go?"

She laughs. "It was horrible. Evidently, I make a terrible scared face. And they said I was too pretty for horror anyway."

I laugh a little, too. "I can't imagine you covered in blood. You should try romance or comedy or suspense."

"Yeah, I don't think I could handle being covered in blood." Scarlett pulls into a parking spot outside the courthouse.

She turns off the ignition, but neither of us moves or looks at each other. We just breathe. In and out. Our breaths unsteady and weak.

Scarlett breaks first. "Ready?"

I look out the window at the looming building that looks fifty-plus years old. I look at the blue sky. The weather today is beautiful and perfect.

I didn't do anything wrong. Granddad didn't do anything wrong. Dad didn't do anything wrong. Justice always wins.

"Yeah, we've got this," I say, grabbing Scarlett's hand.

I've got this.

———

"Let's go in," my lawyer, Mr. Greene, says.

I follow him, and Scarlett holds my hand. We walk into the courtroom that is more crowded than I expected.

"Who are all these people?" Scarlett whispers to me.

I shrug. "I don't have a clue."

As I look around, I realize who the people are—reporters, agents, and others who are just curious about a high-profile case. None of them are friends or family though. Even though I don't really see any of their faces, I know none of them are on my side.

I follow my lawyer up to the table at the front, a table I never imagined I would ever have to sit behind. Scarlett squeezes me again to try to comfort me, but it doesn't help. I can see the worried look on her face.

"I'll be sitting right behind you."

"Thanks, Scar."

She smiles, and then true to her word, she takes a seat at the bench behind me.

My lawyer pulls a chair out for me, like we are sitting down for dinner at a nice restaurant, not like he'll be defending me in court. I take a seat, and he sits next to me. Then, he begins pulling out papers from his briefcase while I sit nervously.

I feel the sweat building under my shirt. I nervously tap my foot under the table. And then I swing my leg. And then I tap again. I switch back and forth, trying anything to calm myself, but it's useless.

Mr. Greene leans over to me. "It's normal to feel nervous and scared. You shouldn't be here after all, but just make sure you don't look guilty. Just be as natural as you can."

I nod.

"All rise," a woman says.

I stand next to my lawyer as everyone else in the room also stands. I watch as a judge and jury file into the room, and then we all take our seats.

I see the judge's lips moving, but I don't hear the words. I'm too busy tapping my foot again to listen. I watch the prosecutor stand. He's older. His hair is graying, and he has wrinkles around his eyes.

He begins speaking about why we are here. That, by the end, he is going to prove my guilt. He doesn't speak to me. He talks to the jury while occasionally motioning to me. It makes it easier for me to pretend like I'm not here.

I try to picture myself sitting on the beach. When that doesn't work, I imagine myself hiking in the mountains. Image after image goes through my head when the prosecutor speaks and then when my lawyer speaks. Their words don't matter. I don't have to respond to them. I won't have to testify until next week—if at all, depending on how today goes. So, I just try to forget I'm here. It's all I can do.

"Agent Byrne will take the stand now."

When I hear Killian's name, I can't help but listen. I keep my eyes forward though as Killian makes his way into the courtroom. I don't look at him until I watch him climb up into the witness box next to the judge. He only glances at me for a second, but it's enough. Enough to calm me and excite me at the same time, and then his eyes go right back to the prosecutor.

"Can you explain your relationship with Ms. Felton?"

Killian looks to the jury. "I was an undercover agent for five years at the Felton Corporation, the company her family owns and operates. I also spent time getting romantically close to Ms. Felton in order to gain her trust."

"And what was Ms. Felton's relationship with her father and grandfather?"

"She was close to them."

"Close enough that they didn't have any secrets between them?"

Killian nods. "I would guess not, but I can't be sure of that."

The prosecutor nods and walks back to his desk. He picks up a piece of paper in a plastic cover. "I would like to submit the first piece of evidence."

He places the piece of paper in front of Killian. "Can you describe for the jury what this is?"

"It's a document, a contract of sorts between the Felton Corporation and their investors, stating how much money the Felton Corporation earned during a specific time period. It's a lie the Felton Corporation presented to their investors to get them to invest more."

"Whose signatures are at the bottom?"

"Robert Felton, Lee Felton, Kinsley Felton, and mine."

He nods and then passes the paper to the jury for them to inspect and then over to our table where I glance at the evidence for the first time. I look at the paper. I look at my signature at the bottom, and that's when it all comes flooding back.

I remember my father brought me in almost three years ago over my summer break. I remember signing a bunch of papers about my inheritance. It was in a room full of executives and employees watching me sign. The company was in the middle of discussing a merger, and my father couldn't take a break from the meetings. I'm sure Killian was there. He watched me sign this paper. That's what he is testifying to. That's why he thinks I will go to jail. But they are wrong. All wrong. This paper doesn't say anything about what they are suggesting. And if it did, the numbers on it must have been a mistake. We wouldn't have purposely misled anyone about our company.

The paper is taken back out of my hands quickly. Too quickly for me to really read it. All I know is, I signed it without a second thought. I used to sign everything placed in front of me without a second thought.

I watch as the prosecutor walks the paper back to Killian. "Can you confirm for everyone how you know this isn't a forgery and the signature at the bottom belongs to Kinsley Felton?"

I suck in a breath and wait for Killian to confirm what I already know—that I did sign the paper. If that paper does, in fact, seem criminal, even if it was a mistake, they could still convict me unless we find a way to prove it was a mistake. It wasn't intentionally done. They only have one piece of paper. One signature. Not a trail of documents. That's not enough to show proof of money laundering or fraud.

Killian looks at the piece of paper, and then he looks up at me. I think he's preparing me for the words that will come out of his mouth, the words that will convict me.

Then, he opens his mouth. "I can't confirm this signature is Kinsley Felton's."

The prosecutor raises his eyebrow at Killian, obviously not expecting that answer. "Are you sure you didn't witness Kinsley Felton signing this piece of paper?"

"I didn't see her sign anything."

The prosecutor walks back to his table and shuffles through some papers. When he finds what he is looking for, he says, "Your report, dated three years ago, clearly states you witnessed Kinsley Felton sign this paper. Are you telling me this report is wrong?"

"Yes. I witnessed Kinsley Felton sign something, but I wasn't sure what. At the time, I assumed it was this paper. No, I *hoped* it was because I was tired of my assignment after being undercover for three years, and I wanted evidence to release me from my duty. After thinking about it now, I realize she was signing a birthday card for her mother. As you can see from the date on the report, her mother's birthday was the next day. I believe her father or grandfather then forged her signature onto this document. I believe they couldn't convince her to go along with their criminal activities, but they wanted the company to stay in the family, so they forged her signature."

"Agent Byrne, I would like to remind you that you are under oath. Whatever you say must be the truth, or you could go to jail if what you've said is proven to be false."

"I understand."

The prosecutor glares as Killian, but he remains calm and composed. I don't understand why he is lying for me, why he is protecting me.

"Then, I would like to call for a recess," the prosecutor says.

My lawyer stands up. "Your honor, I would like to call for the charges to be dismissed against my client. The prosecutor has no evidence against my client other than a forged signature. They don't have any other evidence or witnesses to call."

The judge turns his attention to the prosecutor. "Is that true?"

"Yes, your honor, but we would like more time to reexamine our evidence. We still believe Kinsley Felton is guilty."

"For the time being, if you are not prepared to continue now with this trial, then I have no choice but to dismiss the charges against Kinsley Felton. Ms. Felton, you are free to go."

13

KINSLEY

I HAVE no idea what just happened, but the room seems to be spinning with chaos. I turn to face Scarlett, who is smiling brightly at me. I watch as Killian steps down from the stand and is immediately scolded by the prosecution. Killian doesn't glance my way. He just walks straight down the aisle and out of the courtroom.

I begin walking down the aisle as well. I don't bother speaking to my lawyer. Scarlett tries to get my attention, but I motion that I'll be right back, and she looks at me with a knowing face.

I make it through the crowded courtroom and out into the hallway, but I don't see Killian. Instead, cameras and microphones are thrust into my face as reporters ask about how I feel now that the charges have been dismissed.

"Good," I say with a blank stare as I look out past them for Killian.

I see a group of men wearing all black suits, and I begin walking in that direction. When I walk closer, I see Killian standing next to one of them while another man is speaking harshly to him. I hide around the corner so I can hear the conversation but not be seen.

"You can forget about that promotion. In fact, expect a demotion coming your way. You're lucky I'm not firing your ass right now."

"Yes, sir," Killian says flatly.

"And if I do find clear evidence that you were flat-out lying on the stand, I will fire you and send your ass to jail. Do you hear me?"

"Yes, sir. I wasn't lying. I realized my report was wrong. After thinking about it more and getting to know the Felton family, I realized there was no way her father would allow her to sign any documents for the company. I thought back and remembered the birthday card sitting on the table."

"I don't want to hear it. Just get out of my sight and get your shit together before Lee Felton's trial."

"Yes, sir."

I watch Killian walk past me without looking at me, and I follow him. We walk past the metal detectors. We walk out the front door and down the front steps with me trailing a few feet behind him. He walks to the driver's seat of his car while I climb into the passenger seat.

"What are you doing?" Killian asks.

"I should ask you the same question."

"Get out of the car, princess." Killian grips the wheel but doesn't move to look at me.

I can't read him, and it's killing me. I have to know why the hell he risked his job for me. *Why did he lie on the stand for me?*

"No, not until you tell me why you lied."

Killian looks at me now with his dangerous, dark eyes that are hiding more than I even knew was possible to hide. He doesn't answer me. He backs the car out of the parking spot without a word or glance in my direction. As he turns onto the street, and I realize I need to text Scarlett.

Me: Got a ride home with Killian. Thanks for coming with me today.

Scarlett: No problem. Glad the truth came out. Be careful.

Me: I will.

Scarlett: Call me later.

Now that I've done the responsible thing, I can turn my attention to Killian and get him to speak to me.

"Where are you taking me?" I look around, trying to find any clue as to where Killian is driving us.

"I'm not taking you anywhere. I'm driving home. You are stealing a ride."

I frown. After what he just did for me, I thought it meant something. I thought he would open up to me and finally tell me the truth.

Killian doesn't though. He is cold as ice.

I don't try to get him to speak to me again. I just stare out the window at the buildings that pass by as Killian drives. We don't turn the radio on. We don't look at each other. We both just exist, lost in our own thoughts.

I try to figure out what just happened. Why I'm not still sitting in the courtroom, sweating and worried that I could go to jail for something that was nothing more than a mistake, and the only thing I can come up with is...

"You love me."

Killian looks at me, and I can see it in his eyes even if he can't admit it to himself.

"You love me. That's why you couldn't testify against me. That's why you risked everything to save me. You risked your job. You gave up a promotion. You risked going to jail yourself. All for me. The only explanation is that you love me."

I watch him swallow hard before his eyes drift from me back to the road, but I'm not going to take his silence any longer. I grab his head and force him to look at me, even though we are driving on a busy Las Vegas road. I'm willing to take the risk because I can't wait another second to know.

"You fell in love with me even though you weren't supposed to. You fell for the supposed criminal. Admit it. You. Love. Me."

I bite my lip, waiting for his answer that still hasn't fallen from his lips. Maybe I was wrong. Maybe I just want him to love me so badly that I see anything he does as an admittance of his love.

"You're wrong," Killian finally says as he pulls into a parking spot. He turns off the ignition.

My eyes widen at his words. It hurts more than I want to admit because, despite everything, I still know how I feel about this man. I know, because the second he protected me, the hatred I thought I felt disappeared. The hate was just part of the love I feel for him.

"I didn't lie on the stand because I love you."

I drop my eyes to my lap as I pull on the hem of my jacket. *How can I be so stupid and fall for the wrong man time and time again? I'm so incredibly stupid.*

"I lied because you are innocent, and all my testimony would have done is send an innocent woman to jail for something you weren't involved in. I told the FBI that earlier. I told them not to arrest you. They did anyway. I wasn't going to let an innocent woman go to jail."

I still can't look at him. I'm too afraid I'll cry because, as nice as his words sound, they aren't what I need to hear. "Thank you. Thank you for lying for me."

I hear him unbuckle his seat belt, and I do the same. I'll have to call a driver to come pick me up and take me back to my house.

I feel his hand on my cheek as he gently turns my face to him until he can see my eyes and the tears all but pouring down my face.

"You were also right. Even if I thought you were guilty, I would have still lied on that stand today because I love you."

His words are all it takes for the tears to pour out of my eyes, but now, they are happy tears instead of the painful ones falling before. His thumb wipes the tears from my face, and I hold his hand to my cheek for just a second longer, loving the comforting feeling it brings me.

"I love you, even though I shouldn't," he says.

I smile at him, and then I grab the nape of his neck and pull him to me, so our foreheads are touching as our eyes close. I need a moment of calm intimacy before the storm hits. With our foreheads pressed together, I can breathe in the same air that he does, and it's just what we both need. Our breathing syncs together and calms our bodies, finally relaxing, despite everything going on. We open our eyes at the same time, and the eyes looking back at me aren't filled with fear. They are filled with hope and love, matching how I feel. It's just one moment that connects us and promises a future that, seconds earlier, didn't exist.

We break at the same time, needing to further the connection to something more. Our lips collide in a heated kiss.

It is better than any I've had before. Because this kiss is with a man I love and who truly loves me back. This kiss is with a man who sacrificed his job for me. It's a make-up kiss, an I-love-you kiss, and a promise-of-a-future kiss; all rolled into one.

This kiss is what all kisses should be. Perfect.

14

KILLIAN

Kinsley's lips touch mine, and I lose it. I lose all my control I've been working so hard to keep in check these last few days because we can't do this, except we are and it's everything I remembered it to be.

I tangle my hand in her long hair I never thought I'd touch again as her tongue battles mine, begging me for more than I can give her while in the front seat of the car, but I don't want to break my lips away from hers to move inside my apartment. Not now that I'm kissing her again.

I'm too afraid that, if I stop, one of us will come to our senses. I will remember I'm risking my entire life to be with her. Everything I've worked hard for during the past ten years will be over if I choose her. And I'm afraid, if she stops to think for a second, she will realize that, deep down, she still hates me because, although I didn't testify against her, I will testify against her grandfather.

So, instead of letting her go, I pull her across the center console of the car and onto my lap. She squeals against my lips, but I don't let her go. I can't.

"God, I can't believe I'm kissing you," I say between kisses against her lips.

Kinsley tries to speak, but I prevent her with my lips until she is pulling away from me so she can speak.

I relent and lift her hair off her neck so I can kiss her exposed neck as she speaks. I feel her voice vibrate against my lips as I kiss her neck.

"I can't believe I fell for the one man I swore I wouldn't fall for." Her words turn into more of a purr as I send chills all over her body with just my lips against her neck.

I grin, seeing how much I affect her. I've always been good at turning women on, but it's different with Kinsley. When I kiss her, it doesn't just turn her on. She comes alive at my kisses, and it brings me to life in a way I haven't felt in years, a way I didn't think was possible after what I'd dealt with in my past.

I move my kisses from her neck to her earlobe. I gently nip at it and watch as she squirms in my lap, which only makes me grin wider. I love seeing her like this, relaxed and carefree, but I love seeing her naked and spread out on a bed for me more.

I grab the handle of the door and push it open before I climb out of the car with Kinsley still in my arms. She laughs as we climb out and wraps her arms around my neck, trusting me completely. She leans back down to kiss me as I shut the door with my foot.

I stop her and rub my hand down her cheek. "You still trust me, don't you? Despite everything I've done to you? Every lie that has fallen from my lips? Do you still trust me?"

I look into her gorgeous, innocent eyes. "Yes"—she smiles—"I still trust you. I must be a fool, but I do."

I smile, more in awe of her than before as I begin walking with her in my arms. "Not a fool. Just strong."

Kinsley bashfully shakes her head as her cheeks blush a light shade of pink. "I'm not strong."

"It takes a strong person to forgive and trust someone after they lied to you."

"Or a foolish one."

"Or someone who has a beautiful soul and is able to see the best in people, even when they can't see it themselves."

"I've made a lot of mistakes. Maybe that's why it makes it easier for me to forgive."

"I've made a lot of mistakes, too, but I still can't get past the forgiving myself part."

Kinsley nods, and then I'm done talking as the sun glistens off her still moist lips. I softly kiss her. I'm trying not to push things too far until we make it into my apartment, but it's no use. We can't do slow, not after it's been this long since we've been with each other.

So, instead, I force my legs to move faster so we can get to the apartment sooner, but it's not soon enough for her. Her hands reach inside my jacket, trying to push it off my body. Her hand goes to my tie, loosening it, and then she pulls it off my head and drops it onto the sandy, dry ground I am walking on.

Since she can't get my jacket off, her jacket goes next, falling to the ground, making a small dust cloud as it lands. I get her to the door of my apartment before we lose any more clothing. I couldn't stand it if anyone got to see her body but me. I couldn't fucking stand it.

I unlock the door and push inside the apartment that suddenly feels brighter and more like home from just having her in here. I walk past the kitchen and turn right before remembering my bedroom is the other way, so I turn back around.

She laughs at my inability to make my way around in my own apartment.

"I just moved in," I say, trying to explain my actions.

She moves her lips to my ear. "Or maybe I just affect you so much that you can't think." She moves her tongue around the edge of my ear.

Yep, I can't think straight when she does that. She stops and looks at me, aware that all my thoughts, other than her, have just left my brain. She smiles, satisfied with her work.

I push the door open to my bedroom that has nothing other than a king-size bed in it. It's about all that would fit in the bedroom, and I fall onto it with her in my arms. When we hit the mattress, I feel all of my worries fall away.

Kinsley doesn't waste any time as she grabs at my jacket again, wanting it off, and I'm happy to oblige. I hate wearing suits in the Las Vegas heat, and no matter how many times I wear them, I will never get used to how warm they are to wear here. I toss my jacket onto the floor, followed by my shirt.

Her eyes travel over my abs and chest, appreciating the hard work I've put in at the gym. She runs her hand over my body and then pulls at my pants. I stand and pull them off along with my underwear. I pull a condom out of my pants pocket before I toss them to the floor. I toss the condom on the bed for later. Her eyes darken in appreciation of my hard cock straining to be inside her. I can't wait to have her, but somehow, I'm undressed, and she's almost fully clothed.

She begins unbuttoning her blouse, and it gives me an idea. I grab her hand and help her stand while she curiously looks at me. I take a seat on the edge of the bed where she just was, so I'm now sitting, and she's standing.

"Undress for me."

Her eyes widen a little as she looks at me, and then she bashfully wraps her arms around me. She shakes her head. "No. I'm not wearing anything sexy. My bra and underwear are just boring and simple. It's not pretty lingerie. I just want you."

"All the more reason to strip slowly for me so I can enjoy your body, not your lingerie."

I don't know why I'm so persistent with this. Perhaps it's because I think she needs to feel confident when she sleeps with me again. It needs to feel like her decision, not mine, and I want her to realize she is strong and beautiful, no matter what is going on around her.

She takes a deep breath and then starts undoing the buttons on her shirt again.

"Look at me," I say when her eyes focus on her shirt and not on me. I can never get enough of her blue eyes that twinkle when I look into them. They are almost as incredible as her lips that are somehow always a bright shade of red.

She continues unbuttoning her shirt. When she reaches the last button, she slowly shrugs the shirt off, inch by inch, exposing more and more skin, until her plain nude bra makes her flawless skin that much more impressive.

Kinsley lets her hands travel over her body, touching every curve, until her hand reaches her pants, and I can't believe she doesn't do this with men every night because she definitely knows how to seduce a man.

My cock throbs between my legs to the point I'm not sure why I asked her to strip because I'm not sure I can wait. I move just an inch toward her, but she puts one finger up and shakes it back and forth.

"Nope. Not yet," she says.

I bite down on my fist to keep from growling in frustration like I want to.

Instead of giggling at me, like I expect her to, she turns up the seduction. She runs her tongue across her lip as she slowly, torturously unbuttons her pants. And then she slowly shimmies them down her body until all that is left is her nude thong and bra.

She slowly reaches around her back and undoes the bra letting it fall to the floor. My cock hardens for her, needing her now and unable to wait.

"I can't wait." I jump off the bed and grab her, bringing her to bed with me.

"So impatient." She runs her hand down the rough stubble on my cheek.

"I'm plenty patient. I waited three years after I saw you to have you the first time, and after waiting that long, I don't want to wait ever again."

Kinsley smiles, but her lips fall into a moan as I brush my thumb over her hardened nipple. True to my word about not being able to wait, I take her other nipple into my mouth, and am rewarded by an even louder moan. I use my tongue to drive her wild as it flicks and swirls and massages her nipple. Her hands claw at my head, firmly holding it to her breast and then trying to push me away when the sensations are too much. I suck again, and then she's pushing me onto my back before falling on top of me.

I smile and release her breast, loving the view of her on top of me. She sits up, and my view of her body increases.

I can't stop looking at her. "You're beautiful."

She tucks her strands of hair behind her ear in her adorable way, but her eyes stay intense and lust-filled as she stares down at me. I reach between her legs, pulling her thong aside so I can feel her drenched pussy.

"So wet, princess."

"Yes," she moans. "I can't wait either."

Hearing her say that pushes me to my brink of control. I grab her thong and rip it in two. I quickly slip the condom on that I had tossed on the bed, and then Kinsley is climbing on top of my cock.

"Fuck, princess," I say as she sinks her tight pussy on top of me.

I grab her hips, but she slaps my hand away. Then, she grabs ahold of my hands and slowly and deliberately slides up and down my cock.

"God, you're so sexy when you take control."

She bites her lip as she sinks back down on top of me. I lock my eyes with her beautiful sea-blue eyes, and then I meet her rhythm. I watch as she pants harder with each thrust and movement against her clit. I watch as her eyes grow darker and more intense, as they always do before she comes, until my own eyes intensify right along with hers. We both close our eyes at the overwhelming sensations, but that's not what I want. I want us to come together and to feel as close as we can. I open my eyes.

"Look at me, princess," I say.

Her eyes open, and we connect our souls, perfectly aligned and matched as we come together.

Kinsley is panting hard, most likely exhausted from being on top and from the intense orgasm. I pull out and then pull her to me, still needing to feel close to her body. I feel complete and whole with her lying on my chest.

I want to stay like this forever. I want to have this moment forever in my memory because I'm afraid it won't last. I'm terrified I will never be able to connect like this with her again. And I need to tell her exactly how I feel in case I don't get the chance again.

"I love you, princess. No matter what happens, this was the best. The best I've ever had. The closest I've ever felt to another person."

She moans against my chest, obviously seconds away from falling asleep. "I love you, too, Killian," she whispers against my chest.

I smile. "Sleep now, princess."

Tomorrow, we will figure out what we do now but not today. Today, we will sleep and fuck until there is no way to pull us apart, no matter what happens to us.

15

KINSLEY

I WAKE up with strong arms wrapped tightly around me. I open my eyes and glance around a bare room that is bare, the morning sun blinding me through the shades.

"Ow," I moan softly as I roll over to face Killian.

My whole body aches from last night. We had sex three...or four times. Each time was more carnal than the next until we no longer had any energy left to do anything but wrap our arms around each other and sleep. Each time, I felt myself falling more and more in love with this man.

A man I'm not even sure I know.

I don't know his parents' names or where he grew up. I don't know if he has any siblings. I don't know why he chose to become an FBI agent. I don't know if he truly sucks at poker. I don't even know if what he told me the other night was true. I don't know if his favorite movie is *The Hangover*. And I know he lied about his family growing up in Las Vegas. He might have even lied about not liking Justin Bieber.

All I know is how his eyes look when they watch me come, full of intense appreciation. I know how every muscle in his body flexes when he's thrusting inside me. I know he can make me come with just a touch.

And I know I have a connection with him that runs deeper than sex. A connection that caused him to protect me from going to jail and brought me here despite the consequences.

I take a deep breath, trying not to worry about what I do or don't know about Killian. I relax while I watch him sleep. He looks so happy and content, lying next to me. His breathing is steady, like he could sleep this way forever.

"What are you thinking about, princess?" he asks without opening his eyes.

I have no idea how he knew I was awake.

"Just watching you sleep."

I stroke his hair, needing to touch him, and I watch as his lips curl up at my touch. I lift my head so I can softly kiss him on the lips. Killian grabs the nape of my neck and holds the kiss for longer than I was planning, but I don't mind as he slips his tongue into my mouth, asking me for more than just a kiss. The soreness in my body immediately melts, and I feel the wetness already forming between my legs. Even though we had sex multiple times last night, I didn't get enough to satisfy my need for him, and he obviously hasn't gotten his fill either. I don't know if either of us ever will.

My stomach growls.

Killian laughs against my lips. "I guess fucking will have to wait until after I feed you."

I groan. "My stomach can wait." I wrap my hand tighter around his neck and kiss him again. "My need can't though."

He kisses me back, and I quickly lose myself in his body, but he pulls away again.

"Food first, and then sex."

I pout, which just makes him laugh again. Killian rolls out of bed before I can protest further. I stay in bed and watch his muscular body contract as he walks to the closet and comes back with a pair of sweatpants on. He has a T-shirt in his hands I don't want him to put on, along with his phone.

He tosses me the shirt though, and I smile and put it on before climbing out of bed. I watch his eyes travel over my still visible legs. Then they move up to my nipples poking through the thin fabric.

Killian runs his hand through his hair. "You should put some pants on."

I laugh and walk by him, making sure to wiggle my butt as I go into the hallway. "You're the one who is making us eat before sex. I want you to be just as tortured as I am."

Killian grabs ahold of my arm and pulls me back to him in the bedroom. "Trust me, I am." His hand goes to my neck, and he pulls me into a passionate kiss that ends way too quickly.

"Let's get out of here before I change my mind and become the worst boyfriend in history." He grabs ahold of my hand, pulling me out of the bedroom and toward his kitchen.

I smile blissfully as I follow behind him. He just said he was my boyfriend. Killian is *my boyfriend*, and maybe soon, he will be more.

Killian drops my hand when we make it into his small kitchen. He walks over to the small fridge. He opens the door, pokes his head in, and begins pulling random things out.

"Do you know how to cook?" I ask.

He shrugs. "Sort of. Not well. I haven't had much opportunity to practice since I lived in a hotel room for five years."

I nod.

"You?"

"No, I didn't get much practice either. I loved living in hotels, and when I was home, we always had a cook. Spoiled rich-girl problems."

Killian laughs. I walk over to him, and that's when I see what he is pulling out of the fridge—salmon, yogurt, some weird-looking bread. Health nut—that much he wasn't lying about.

He pops bread into the toaster and then scoops some yogurt and precooked salmon onto a plate. The toast pops up, and he puts one on each of our plates. He carries the plates over to the bar where barstools sit underneath. I take a seat at one, and he sits next to me.

I wrinkle my nose at the food in front of me, causing Killian to laugh.

"Just try it. I'll get you a cheeseburger or something for lunch later. It's all I have though, so if you want to have sex anytime soon, then eat."

That's all it takes to get me to shuffle the first few bites of yogurt into my mouth, which I assume is a safe bet. From the corner of my eye, I watch him smile at me before he digs into his own food.

We both eat in comfortable silence, and I find the food isn't that bad, although it wouldn't be my first choice. But after a night like last night, and what I plan to do with Killian today, I'm going to need my strength and energy. So, I'm going to make sure to eat every bite.

"So, what do you want to do today, princess?" Killian asks.

I give him a wicked glance. "What do you think?"

He laughs. "We have to leave the apartment at some point. I don't have enough food for you to stay here for more than a few hours."

"I don't need food to survive. Just you."

Killian's phone buzzes. He pulls it out of his pocket and frowns. "I have to take this," he says.

He doesn't look at me. He just gets up and walks back toward his bedroom, so I can't hear the phone call, which can only mean one thing. He's talking to the FBI.

I take a bite of the bread as I try to listen to him speaking in the other room, but I can't hear him. His voice is too deep, and the walls are too thick. I try to eat more, but I just end up pushing the salmon around on my plate with my fork.

I hear the door to the bedroom open again, and Killian walks back and takes his seat next to me, like nothing happened. I'm going to have to work on getting him to talk more openly with me.

"Who was that?" I ask, trying not to sound too nosy.

He doesn't answer. He doesn't have to. We both know I already know whom he spoke to.

"A trial date has been set for your grandfather. It's two months from now to give your grandfather time to recover from his heart attack."

I nod. "I guess I was hoping, after the charges against me were dropped, the same would happen for Granddad."

Killian bites his lip as he looks at me. I want to know what is going through his mind, but I don't ask.

"They want me to take my break now instead of after the trial. That way, I can come back with a clearer mind, and they can decide an appropriate punishment for my actions. I have a month off." He seems anxious. "I should really go home and see my parents. I haven't been home in five years."

"Where is home?"

"Kansas."

My mouth falls open just a little at his response. I don't know where I was expecting him to be from, but I wasn't expecting Kansas. That means he will be leaving me here for a month.

"You must miss your parents terribly."

He stares off into the distance. "Yeah, I guess I do. I don't really know how I feel."

With my fork, again, I push the food around on my plate, trying to distract myself. I try to think of a topic to get off the fact that Killian will be leaving me for a month to be with his family while I have to stay here to take care of my grandfather.

"You don't think my grandfather's trial will be canceled though? You don't think the charges will be dropped now that they know it was just a mistake?"

Killian freezes but quickly recovers as he looks down at his plate. "No."

"Why not? Granddad didn't do it. He didn't do anything wrong. He's innocent, just like I am. There was just a mix-up with numbers. That's all this is."

I watch Killian's chest rise and fall. Once, then twice, and then three times. Each breath he takes seems painful.

"What is it?"

He grabs ahold of my hands. "Princess, you're wrong."

I shake my head and laugh cautiously, trying to break the tension between us. "I'm wrong about a lot of things. You're going to have to be more specific."

"Your grandfather, your father—they did everything the FBI is accusing them of."

I shake my head. "No."

He grabs ahold of my cheeks and moves his face closer to me. "Kinsley, you have to listen to me. You have to believe me. Your father did whatever it took to keep the company afloat and make as much money as possible for his family. That included several criminal things. He lied to the IRS. He lied to investors and stole money from them. He hid money from the company and kept it for himself. I was there for five years. I was his closest employee. He was grooming me to take over. He told me everything. He showed me how to follow in his footsteps, just like his father showed him and your grandfather's father showed him."

I push his hands off my face and fall back in my chair. "You're wrong. My father wouldn't have hurt anyone. He wouldn't have stolen." I feel a tear fall down my face while my face reddens in anger because he believes a family member of mine would have done such a thing. "You're wrong," I say, my voice shaky.

"Princess..."

"Don't *princess* me. Don't lie to me." I get up from my chair and go to find clothing to put on, so I can leave.

I walk into Killian's closet and find a pair of sweatpants and a sweatshirt. I quickly put them on with tears falling down my face as I realize we will never work. He will always be with the FBI, always looking to find something my family did wrong even if there isn't anything there, and I will always be defending my family against him. I can't be with him and be loyal to my family.

I grab my clothes and phone and storm back into the living room. I find Killian standing with one hand in his pocket and the other holding a stack of papers.

He puts the papers in my hand. I look down at them in confusion. The top paper is the paper from the courtroom. I quickly flip through the pages. They all look similar in that they have my name, my father's, and my grandfather's, and some even have Killian's name. All of the papers look familiar. They all have my signature on them. I remember signing lots of papers like this every summer when I was home. I was told it was just for my inheritance, so that's what I assume most of these are.

"Read them," he says.

"These are just my inheritance papers. They are nothing." I hold the papers up in the air.

"Read them," he insists.

"I already have."

"Kinsley, I'm so sorry this is hard for you. I hate that I'm right. I never wanted to be right."

"You're not right. My father was a good person!" I scream.

"Your father was a good person. He was also a liar and a cheat."

I can't be here anymore. I can't be with someone who would think that way about my father.

"How dare you! He trusted you. He loved you like a son."

"I loved him almost as much as I love you."

"You don't love me. If you did, you would listen to me. You would realize I'm not related to a monster." I take a deep breath, hating the next words I have to say. "We can't be together, can we?"

Killian looks at me with sad, dark eyes, but he answers automatically because he has already come to the same conclusion, "No, we can't."

I hate that he doesn't fight it. I hate that he doesn't say we will find some way to make this work. Some way to get around the fact I'm loyal to my family and he's loyal to the FBI. He doesn't try to fight it. He thinks it's hopeless, just like me. I can't love him while I hate him. And he can't change his loyalty for me.

"I should go."

He nods, looking like a sad, hurt puppy. He walks me to the door and holds it open for me.

"Good-bye," falls from my lips. Then, I turn to leave him.

He grabs my arm, stopping me. "It doesn't change how I feel. I still love you. I never faked my feelings for you."

"I still love you, too, but that love is quickly turning into hate."

"Stay," he says in almost a whisper.

Even though he knows I can't, it still feels good to see him fighting for us, even if this is the only time he ever does it. I can't stay, and I can't bear to say good-bye to him again. So, I don't say it, but my body tells him my answer as I walk out the door.

16

KILLIAN

THE FLIGHT to Kansas City was short and easy. The flight wasn't what I was dreading. The next part is.

It's dark by the time I see the Marysville water tower come into view. I drive past it, trying to decide what to do. I could stop at my family's house, but I never called to let them know I was coming home, and I'm not ready to deal with them yet. Just coming back to this godforsaken town after five years is hard enough. I can't face my parents and the town all in one night. That leaves me only one other choice. To stay at the only hotel in town. My family's hotel.

Five minutes later I walk toward the hotel that is the only reason I got the assignment to go undercover in Las Vegas in the first place. Because I had hotel management experience.

I chuckle to myself. It might be true, but this isn't a hotel—at least, it is nothing like the hotels in Vegas. My experience helping to manage this hotel did nothing to help me with my undercover placement. It's a wonder I did as well as I did. I expected someone in the Felton Corporation to fire me during the first week. I never expected to last five years there and to uncover what I found in the process.

Chris, the manager, is asleep behind the desk when I arrive. I shake my head at his incompetence. I reach across the desk and grab one of the keys. I slide it into the machine to activate it, choosing a room by random. Guessing by the two cars in the parking lot, my odds are good I won't select an already occupied room.

I take the key up to my room and slide it in. But the red light never turns green. *Shit.*

I head back downstairs to try to fix the key. This has happened every fucking time I've stayed here. It happens to so many guests that several of them will leave the door propped open when they leave. I guess it's the small-town trust.

I make it back to the first floor when I hear him. My father is speaking to Chris. I wait in the hallway just around the corner so that neither of them can see me.

"Killian's here?" my father asks.

"Yes," Chris answers. Apparently, he was awake when I entered. "Do you want me to go get him?"

"No," my father answers immediately. "I don't care to see him. I am just stopping by to pick up the package that was dropped off earlier."

I hear Chris hand my father the package, and then shortly after, I hear the creak of the door as it opens and closes. I wait a few minutes longer before I go back behind the counter and try the key again.

I have to repeat the process two more times before I can get the damn key to work.

When I finally make my way inside the hotel room, I crash onto the bed. "I hate this godforsaken town."

———

I found it hard to sleep after having Kinsley in my arms just a night ago. *Was it really just the other night when she was lying in my arms? It feels like a lifetime ago.*

I yawn as I pull into my family's gravel driveway, and turn off the engine. I stare up at the house I grew up in and that will forever haunt my memories. The blue paint on the siding is coming off in long flakes. The house needed a new paint job long ago. Weeds are growing in the flowerbed at the side of the house, so much so I would say it's a weed-bed instead of a flowerbed. I look at the door where the same old sign has hung for fifty years. *Byrne Family*, it reads.

I climb out of the truck and leave my suitcase in the bed. I'm not sure if I'll be welcomed to stay, and I'm not sure I want to stay. I walk up the cracked sidewalk. I knock once on the door, and then I wait. I wait a long time before the door opens, and my father stands, looking at me, with the same frown and grimace that always marks his face.

"Can I come in?" I ask.

He doesn't answer. He just turns from the door and walks back inside. I push the door open and walk inside. I walk through the hallway to where my father is now sitting in the living room. Nothing has changed in any of the rooms. Not a picture on the wall or rug on the floor or furniture in the house. Nothing has changed. It still feels like death and pain in this house. Even before it happened, it wasn't a happy place to grow up in—at least, not for me.

I take a seat on the couch, opposite my father in the chair. As if I'm not here, he glances back to the TV where a baseball game is playing. It doesn't feel like I'm really here; it feels more like it's a dream than reality.

I watch the game with him in silence, hoping if enough time passes like this, then it will somehow make it easier when we do speak. But, instead of relaxing and doing something normal with my father, I just feel more and more anxiety creeping into my body until I can't take it anymore.

"Are you going to even acknowledge that I am here?"

His response is turning up the sound on the TV.

"Dad!"

He doesn't respond.

I get up and walk over to him. I rip the remote from his hand. I turn the TV off. "Talk to me!"

He glares at me, his face reddening more and more with each second that passes. "What do you want me to say, Liam? That I forgive you? That you've made me proud? That I welcome you home with open arms?"

I wince as he calls me Liam. He never calls me Liam.

"Yes, that is exactly what I want you to say. I want you to say, *Son, I forgive you.* I want you to say that you're proud of me for the work I've done for the FBI. I just got promoted after doing such a good job with my last assignment." Maybe I shouldn't have mentioned the promotion since it has now been rescinded, but he needs to know I'm doing better.

He gets up from his chair until he is looking eye-to-eye with me. "I could never say that. All of my sons are dead." He looks at me for a second longer, walks out of the living room and down the hallway to his bedroom where I hear him close the door.

It was a mistake, coming here. I should have gone on a vacation. To Florida or Hawaii or Mexico. Anywhere warm for a couple of weeks. Anywhere but here.

I turn and storm out of the house.

I climb in my truck. I'm tempted to immediately drive all the way back to the airport right now, but I'm hungry. I haven't eaten since lunch yesterday, and I need to at least see my mother. Her car wasn't in the drive, which means she has a shift at the hospital. I'll have to wait until she gets off.

So, I drive down to the main street where I have only two options, other than fast food. The local diner and the local Chinese restaurant. I choose the Chinese, hoping there will be less people for me to run into.

As soon as I walk in, I realize I chose wrong, and I even consider walking back out before I'm spotted, but it's too late.

"Liam?" the older hostess says.

I turn and smile at her. "Hi, Mrs. Mapston. It's good to see you," I say as I lean in and give her a hug.

"It's good to see you, too, son. How long has it been? Four—"

"Five years," I say.

She nods and smiles at me, like she is trying to comfort me from something bad. "You should get in line for the buffet, or there will be nothing left if you let old Mr. Capers in line before you." She nods toward the man who has just pulled into the parking lot.

I smile at her. "Thanks."

She just winks, and I get in line for the buffet. When I've made it through without being spotted again, I sigh a little in relief as I make my way toward a table at the back where I won't be spotted.

I almost make it to the table before I hear a meek, "Killian?"

The voice might be meek, but I would know it anywhere. I was in love with that voice for almost fifteen years until Kinsley shattered those feelings.

Summer Hirst.

I turn and look at the woman who just spoke. "Hi, Summer," I say with a smile on my face.

Her face lights up just a little. "It is you."

I place my plate on the table behind me and then embrace her in a hug that lasts far longer than a hug between just friends should. When I release her, her face has brightened even more.

"Join me for lunch."

She glances at her watch. "I really shouldn't. I have a meeting in half an hour to decide if we are going to order a new MRI machine or not at the hospital."

I try to hide my disappointment. "Well, it was good seeing you, Summer."

Her lips curl to one side as she thinks for just a second. "What the hell? I'm the boss. I can be a few minutes late if I want to."

I nod as she takes a seat in the booth opposite me. She places the take-out box with her lunch on the table and opens it to begin eating.

"How have you been?" I ask before digging into my plate of food.

"Well, really well. I just got promoted to medical administrator."

"Congrats. You always were ambitious."

"What about you?"

I glance up when she tucks her long blonde hair behind her ears. That's when I see it. Something that I never realized before. She looks just like Kinsley. Both have long blonde hair. Both have slim, tall figures. Both flush a bright shade of pink whenever they feel embarrassed.

But that is where the similarities end. Summer is strong and determined. She knows exactly what she wants and goes after it.

Kinsley, on the other hand, has no idea what she wants. She's indecisive and naive.

But both women have let tragedy keep them from moving forward.

Is the similar look to Summer the only reason I am attracted to Kinsley? Is it the only reason I fell at all for her?

"Killian?"

I startle and look back at Summer. "What?"

"How have you been?"

"Good. It's always hard to come home though."

"It's hard for you to come home. It's hard for me to leave."

She glances down and moves her food around in her takeout box with her fork. I narrow my eyes at her. Maybe she's not as strong as I thought.

"Where would you go if you could leave and go anywhere?"

She shakes her head. "I can't think like that. My life is here."

"Because of your family?"

"No, because of me." She glances down at her watch. "I should go, Killian. How long are you going to be in town?"

I shrug. "I don't know. I don't plan on staying much longer."

Her eyes sadden.

"You should try for a job in a new hospital. Start a new life. I think it would be good for you."

She nervously tucks her hair behind her ear. "I can't."

"Yes, you can. You just won't."

"Maybe," she says.

And my heart stops. It stops at hearing her say the word that reminds me so much of Kinsley. And I realize how much Kinsley really means to me even though it can never happen. I wish my heart could still beat for someone like Summer, but it doesn't. My heart is completely taken by Kinsley, and there is no way to get it back.

"Are you really happy here? Driving the same streets. Having the same conversations. Going to the same two restaurants. Does that really make you happy?"

"It's safe here. That's all I need to be happy."

I frown but understand.

The only way I could ever be with Summer is to stay here. To live here. I could never do that.

It makes me wonder if I really love Kinsley if I'm not willing to give up my job for her either.

"I have to go." She stands and walks to me. Then, she softly kisses me on the cheek. "See you around," she says as she always says.

"Yeah, see you later."

After Summer leaves, I realize I can't wait to see my mom after she gets off her shift. I can't stay in this town any longer. I tried. I'm just not strong enough to stay here and face my mistakes.

I head out of the restaurant and back to the damn truck. I drive it the three blocks to the hospital. It is rather large for a hospital in this size of a town, but it also has to serve all of the surrounding towns for miles and miles. This is the only place they can go to without having to drive to Kansas City for care.

I pull into the parking lot and make my way inside the hospital. As I walk through the hospital, I know everyone is staring at me, wondering why I've returned after all these years. I ignore their stares and unsaid words and keep walking until I make my way to the hospital's emergency room.

I walk to the front desk where a woman who was a year or two younger than me in school sits behind the desk.

"Hi, Alisha. Is my mother around?"

The woman looks up at me in surprise, the same reaction I have gotten from everyone else who has seen me in town. I guess I'm not surprised they are surprised to see me since the last time anyone here saw me, I made it pretty clear that, when I left, I wouldn't be returning. I still don't know why I chose to return, other than I thought it would give me clarity. I thought my father could forgive me.

"Give me a second, and I'll see if I can find her for you," Alisha says.

"No need," I say as I look over Alisha's head.

My mother is standing in her scrubs with a pen in her hand. She doesn't wear the same shocked expression everyone else in town has given me. Instead, she looks at me with love and joy in her eyes.

"Alisha, I'll be taking my break now. Page me if you need me," my mother says.

I glance around the empty waiting room, except for one man who shows no obvious signs of illness.

My mother walks to me and embraces me in a hug. I feel tears falling from her cheeks and onto my shoulder. I hold her tighter. For the first time since I returned, I'm happy I came home, if only to make my mother happy.

When she releases me, I wipe the tears from her face.

"Come on. Let's go take a walk outside," she says.

I nod and follow her outside the hospital. I fall into step next to her as we walk the sidewalk around the hospital. The sidewalk was a fundraising venture she created in order to try to improve the health of the employees and patients of the hospital. As we walk, we don't run into anyone, despite the warm weather, so while the idea was a good one, I'm afraid it isn't being utilized in the way she imagined.

"I hoped you would come after your undercover assignment was over."

I raise my eyebrow at her. "How did you know my assignment was over?"

She smiles. "I've kept in contact with the FBI, just checking in from time to time, to ensure you were okay. Of course, they never told me what your assignment was, but they told me when it was over."

I nod. "I'm sorry I didn't contact you."

She shakes her head. "I know why you didn't."

"I wasn't even sure I should come back. Father hasn't forgiven me, and I wasn't sure if you had either."

She stops and looks me straight in the eyes while holding on to my shoulders to force me to look at her. "What happened to your brother was not your fault. How you reacted afterward was not your fault. What you choose to do with your life now does not mean I love you any less. I love you for doing what is best for you."

I look down at my mother, afraid I'm going to lose it. That I'm going to break down, crying in front of my mother because I can't handle the pain or the guilt.

"I'm sorry though. For all of it."

"Don't be sorry for living your life."

I nod, and we keep walking. I haven't seen my mother in five years. *Who knows how long it will be until I see her again?*

I can at least be honest with her about how I feel now. "I don't know what I want anymore."

"What do you mean? You don't know if you want to still work for the FBI anymore?"

I shake my head. "I still do. No, I have to, but..." *God, how do I tell my mother this?*

She knowingly smiles at me. "There's a girl."

I look at her in shock, and her smile just brightens.

"Finally, you've moved on from Summer."

I look down, trying not to meet her gaze.

"Please tell me you have moved on from Summer. That girl was never good for you."

"I thought you liked Summer?"

"I like Summer, but she's not right for you."

"Why?"

"She would have held you back, and I don't just mean physically keeping you in Kansas. She wouldn't have pushed you to go after your dreams. She wouldn't have challenged you."

I nod although I'm not sure if she's right.

"Tell me about her."

I sigh. "I can't. Not really. I don't even know how I feel about her."

That's not true. I love Kinsley. I just can't. I keep walking as I rub my neck in frustration. "I can't have her. She was arrested because of me. I was investigating her and her family for the last five years. I can't...I shouldn't even be thinking about her."

"Oh, Killian"—she places her hand on my cheek—"don't deny yourself if she will make you happy."

"You don't understand, Mother. I can't. I have to choose. Either I stay with the FBI, or I pursue her and give up everything I've worked for at the FBI. I can't do both."

"Then, I guess you need to figure out what or whom you can't live without. You need to figure out if working for the FBI really makes you happy or if you are just doing it out of obligation. You need to figure out if you really love this girl."

"She hates me though. Her family is ruined because of me."

"She might hate you for that, but hate doesn't stop a woman from loving." My mother glances at her watch. "I should get back before we get any critical patients, and I leave Alisha to handle them."

"I doubt that will happen in the middle of nowhere Kansas."

She smiles. "Glad your love for this town hasn't changed. I guess distance doesn't always make the heart grow fonder."

"I guess not, but I don't know when I'll see you again. I tried talking to Dad. I don't think he will ever forgive me, and I can't stay here any longer when I'm not even welcome in my parents' house."

"Your father is still mourning. He's not ready to forgive himself, let alone you, yet. Give him time."

"I did give him time. I gave him five years."

She smiles weakly. "Where will you go?"

"I still have most of my month left. I'll go somewhere warm to sort things out. Then, I'll be given a new undercover assignment. I'll try to stay in contact better than last time, but it will just depend on the assignment and how long it lasts."

She nods and hugs me again. "Just make sure you invite me to your wedding, if that is the future you decide."

I laugh. "I don't think you have to worry about that."

She releases me. "Maybe not, but I won't think anything less of you if you choose this girl over the FBI."

I force my lips into a tight smile. "I love you, Mom."

"Love you, too, son."

I watch her walk back into the hospital. She might not think anything less of me if I chose a girl over the FBI, but I would. I would think less of me.

17

KINSLEY

"WE WILL NEED to do the commercial soon, Ms. Felton, to ensure we can get it going in full swing before Mr. Felton's trial starts," Catherine, our marketing director, says on the other end of the line.

"I have the perfect model to do the commercial. Leave it to me to schedule her. Schedule the shoot for tomorrow."

"Will do."

I hang up the phone and go to call Scarlett to ask her to do the commercial, but the stack of papers Killian gave me is drawing me toward them. Every second I've had them in my possession, I've been tempted to read them, but I'm too loyal to my family and my own feelings to give in. Instead, I brought them to my father's office with me and placed them on the desk where they have been tempting me ever since.

I grab the papers and place them in front of me. I don't want to read them. I don't want to know who is lying—my father or Killian. I can't stand the thought that either man is a liar. I'm not even sure if these papers will prove it either way. I just have to read them.

I flip the page and begin reading. That's when I realize every page has my signature, my actual signature that isn't forged. I know because I was there. I signed them. I just didn't know what I was signing. I was always told the papers had to do with my inheritance. But I realize now that's not what these papers are. My father had me sign them as a way to keep his criminal activities in the family. As a way of tying them to me because he wanted to pass the company off to my future husband, to Killian, and he wanted insurance we wouldn't go to the police ourselves. That we would continue the criminal activities.

The papers are all lies my father and grandfather told the IRS, investors, and employees. Money transfers that don't show where they got the money and money that just suddenly disappeared. Every single page is a lie. A lie they told to make more money.

I drop the papers when I realize the truth and watch them scatter on the floor. Killian is right. My father and grandfather are criminals.

I expect tears to fall, except my tears are gone from crying all night because I had to say good-bye to Killian. I expect he is halfway to Kansas by now. Instead of sadness though, I feel anger. I'm angry at my family for what they have put me through, but most of all, I'm angry at my father because I thought he loved me above all else.

I shake my head. He wasn't a father. Not a real father. Real fathers don't lie to their daughters and then drag them into their criminal activities.

I swipe all the frames of the family off my father's desk and watch them fall to the floor, but it's not enough to satisfy my anger. I go to the wall and pull every picture and magazine photo of me off the wall and throw them to the floor.

And then the tears fall, as if my anger found a way to turn them on, like a faucet. I collapse onto the couch, a couch I used to love just like my father, and I cry.

Killian was right, and he ruined my life. No, that's not fair. Killian didn't ruin my life. He just exposed it, and now, I don't think I can look at him the same way again. It doesn't change the fact he is an FBI agent who investigated my family. I'm still pissed at him.

I shake my head. I don't have a family anymore. They are all dead to me now that I know the truth.

I want Killian. But I don't know if he still wants me. I don't know if he will take me back after I didn't trust him and then called him a liar. I don't know if I can mend that, especially when I have no way to get in contact with him while he's away for a month. And I'm still the daughter of a criminal. He wouldn't risk his job for me. And even if his job is no longer at risk, he wouldn't want to date someone who could easily follow in her father's footsteps.

I glance around the room covered in papers and broken glass. The room used to hold so many good memories of me and my father, but now, it holds nothing but my broken despair. I can't stay in here.

I walk out of the office and glance down the hallway to the office doors of the other executives. Tony's office is next to this one. And then down a couple is what used to be Killian's office. I don't want to be reminded of him either. The rest of the offices in this hallway are taken, as far as I know.

I turn the other way and walk down the hallway. I glance in door after door, trying to find an empty office. I walk to the end of the hallway before I find one that's empty.

I push the door open and step inside. The office is small and feels more like a closet than an office. A desk is pushed up against the one small window with a small stationary chair pushed under the desk. There isn't room for anything more than just the desk in this office.

I smile. This office will do perfectly. There is no room for pictures or decorations that would remind me of my family. There is no room for lies or anger. There is just enough room in here for me.

I walk back to my father's office. I grab the laptop and leave all the rest. I switch the light off, and I walk out the door and lock it behind me. I don't plan on going back in there again.

I walk back to the office I've claimed and place the laptop on the desk. I take a seat at the desk and look out the window to the Las Vegas strip below. I feel calmer now that I'm in my own office. Even if it is smaller than my father's, it's my office, and I can run the company my way—that is, if I don't sell my shares and just decide to leave this godforsaken city. I'm not sure I want anything to do with my family anymore. And I don't give a shit what happens to this company. But I don't want all the people working for us to suffer because of what my father and grandfather did. So, until I decide what is best for them, I guess I'll keep running the company from here.

I take a deep breath, and then I take my cell phone out of my pocket and dial the number for Scarlett.

"Hey, Kins," she answers on the second ring.

"Hey, I need a favor."

"Anything."

"I was hoping you would say that. I need you to do a commercial for the Felton Corporation tomorrow."

"Done," Scarlett says brightly.

"Awesome. Be here at six in the morning to get in hair and makeup."

Scarlett moans when I tell her the time. She's not a morning person. "Fine. But you owe me one."

I smile. "Deal."

When I hang up, my smile is gone. I have to spend the rest of my day in meetings before I resign to spending my night alone in one of the hotel rooms upstairs because there is no way I'm going to go home and face my grandfather. I don't know if I can ever look at him again.

I'm a woman without a family. Without a boyfriend. And without a future.

18

KILLIAN

"ANOTHER DRINK?" a waiter says.

I lift my ball cap up to see the waiter standing at the edge of my beach recliner. The sun streams down on my face, immediately drenching me sweat not even the ocean breeze will be able to cool. Only the taste of another fruity frozen drink will be able to cool me off.

"*Sí*, another piña colada," I say, even though I would much prefer a dark whiskey or scotch. But neither of those would stand a chance at helping me cool off, not as long as I sit on the beach with the sun beating down on me.

"*Sí, señor*," the waiter says before scurrying off toward the resort.

He'll be back in several minutes with my drink, along with ones for everyone else scattered on the beach.

I wipe my brow, trying to get the sweat off of it. I can't wait for him to come back. Needing to cool off, I get up from my chair where I've been sitting all morning. It is now getting into the late morning sun, and the heat is almost unbearable. The women who were just chatting incessantly suddenly stop when they see me walking down the beach.

The blonde woman at the end blinks at me. I would usually be all over someone like her but not now. Now, I want nothing more than to spend my vacation with Kinsley in Las Vegas, not alone on a beach in Mexico. But I don't have a choice. Kinsley hates me for ruining her life, and I can't be with her and keep my job.

I run down the few feet to the ocean until I feel the cool water crashing against my legs, slowing to a walk until my shoulders are covered by the salty ocean. Then, I go underwater, and a wave crashes over me, immediately clearing my head of the blonde with the long legs and replacing it with images of Kinsley.

I picture her here, on the beach with me, wearing a bikini like she wore in the photo shoot. Her long blonde hair blowing in the breeze. Lying on a lounger with me.

I shake my head. I can't go there. I can't be with her, but I won't be able to shake her image from my mind, not even if I did something stupid, like take the blonde from the beach upstairs.

I'm fucked.

I see the waiter making his way back through the other beachgoers, heading toward my recliner, so I make my way out of the ocean and back to my lounger. This time, when the woman bats her eyes at me, I look away, trying to turn them away from me instead of drawing them in.

I take my towel and dry off my skin.

"Piña colada, *señor*," the waiter says, handing me my drink.

"*Gracias.*"

I lie back on the recliner, planning on spending the rest of my day repeating the process of soaking up the sun, drinking fruity beach drinks, and dipping into the ocean when I get too hot. All the while, I try to push Kinsley out of my head.

I sip the drink and immediately feel the liquid cool my body. I try to relax and not think about anything. About work or my family or Kinsley. I try to just think about the sun and the ocean and the drink.

I close my eyes and try to slow my breathing to the same speed as the ocean waves until I feel calm and relaxed. This is the main reason I came down to Mexico, but it's not the only reason. I don't have to worry about that reason though until later this week. Today is all about relaxing.

"*Señor!*" the waiter says just as I begin to relax.

I open my eyes in frustration. "*Sí?*"

"*Teléfono, señor.*"

I sigh and grab my towel. I follow the waiter into the lobby. This call can't be good. I shouldn't be getting a call when nobody knows where I am.

"Señor Byrne," the waiter says to the man in the lobby.

The man nods at me, grabs the phone, and hands it to me without another word.

"Hello?" I say into the phone as I glance around the crowded lobby, wishing for privacy.

"Killian, you need to get a flight back right away," Agent Bisson says.

I sigh. I should have known the FBI would know where I went. I can never really get away. I've been on duty every day for five years. You would think I could get a month's vacation without being interrupted.

"Why?"

"We moved up the trial date for Lee Felton, and we need you back to prepare your testimony. We don't want to take any chances you are going to blow it, like you did at the girl's trial."

"Wait...what? I thought I had a month off. I thought his trial wasn't for another two months."

"Things change. You know that better than anyone. Just get your ass back here."

I sigh in frustration. "Give me another week, and then I'll be home."

"Not good enough. We want you back by Thursday."

"That's tomorrow."

"Yep."

Shit. I pace back and forth.

"Just book a flight home, Byrne."

I hang up the phone, and I walk back to my room without

speaking to anyone. I push the button on the elevator to get me to the top floor where my room is and wait for the elevator. The doors open and I walk in. I turn, but I'm no longer alone. The blonde from earlier joins me in the elevator.

I press the button for the top floor since I am closest to the elevator panel. I ask, "What floor?"

She smiles at me and bats her eyelashes. "Top floor, same as you."

I frown at her. I highly doubt she is on the same floor, but I don't argue with her. She can ride the elevator back down by herself when she realizes she isn't going to get anywhere with me.

The doors shut, and she waits to make her move until we're closer to the top floor. She drops her towel on the floor, which forces my eyes to look at the sudden movement. She seductively walks to me in her white bikini top and thong bottom. I notice she's wearing heels for some reason. The only reason I can think that she would be wearing heels is to seduce men in elevators.

Normally, I would jump on the chance she's offering me.

She walks until her body is just inches from mine. She smiles at me and then confidently runs her hand down my chest, like she has done this hundreds of times and has never gotten a no. I hate to disappoint her, but she is about to get her first.

I glance over to see the elevator is just two floors below the top.

I smile. She thinks I'm smiling at her. The doors open, and she holds on to my arm, like I'm her escort.

I shake my head. "Sorry, *señorita*, but I'm not interested."

I step out of the elevator and she follows me with confusion on her face, and that's when I realize she doesn't speak English very well. I'm not sure what language she does speak. Spanish? French? Russian? I don't know, and I'm not going to wait around to find out. So, instead, I guide her back to the elevator. I shake my head again and then leave her there alone to ride back down. I feel bad, but I'm sure a woman like that doesn't have any difficulty with finding a warm bed and a man to keep her comfortable at night.

I walk to my room and unlock the door with my key card in hand. I glance around the luxurious room I paid to relax in for the week, but now, I won't be spending more than one more night here. I walk to the bathroom and flip on the faucet in the large stone shower. I take off my swim trunks and hop into the shower, not waiting for the water to warm up.

The cool water is refreshing as I let it pour down my face, washing away the salt and sand from the beach along with my sweat. As I shower, I try to decide what I'm going to do because I know, as soon as I step out of this shower, I'm going to have to decide.

Do I just go back to Las Vegas tomorrow, like the FBI wants?

Do I stay here and say fuck the FBI so I can finish what I came here for?

My gut tells me to stay—at least long enough to follow this last lead. I need to find out whom her father met with here the week before he died. Once I know for sure this is a dead end, then I can go back home. Then, I will know I did the best I could as an FBI agent. Then, I will know I kept my promise to Kinsley's father.

I get out of the shower and towel off. I wrap the towel around my waist before pulling my cell phone out of the safe in the room. I walk out onto the balcony, trying to enjoy the last bit of sunlight as I make the first of two phone calls.

"Hello?" Juan says on the second ring.

"I need to meet tonight."

"That's not how this works. *Señor* Clavé will be available tomorrow night. He can't just change to tonight. He has other business and other clients he works with."

"I am no longer available tomorrow night. It's got to be tonight, or you can forget my business."

There's a long pause.

"One thirty then. We will call you to tell you the place."

I glance at my phone, seeing that it's already a quarter till one. "Just tell me now. It will take me thirty minutes to get there."

He laughs. "No, no. Not one thirty p.m. One thirty a.m."

I roll my head back and forth. It's going to be a long night if I agree to this.

"Fine."

"Done."

I end the call and then immediately call to schedule my flight for tomorrow afternoon. When that's done, I climb into bed for an afternoon nap. I'm going to need it if I'm not meeting these guys until one thirty in the morning.

———

I climb into the cab at one a.m. They still haven't called me back to confirm where I'm supposed to go.

"*Adónde*?" the driver asks, wanting to know where to drive me.

"Downtown."

"Downtown. More specific?"

"No, just drive me toward downtown." I assume that is where we will be doing business. In the heart of Cancún, not near the tourist hotels and resorts where I am staying.

The driver begins driving, and I hold on to my phone in frustration. I have no idea what I'm getting myself into or what Mr. Felton was doing here before he died. It doesn't make sense.

My phone rings five minutes into the drive.

"Hello."

"Tell the driver to take you to Fourth and Juárez."

The line then goes dead. I tell the driver more specific directions, and as I do, I know I'm going to regret this. I reach for my gun, making sure it's still hidden away in my pants leg. As the driver takes me further into the shadier part of town, I'm afraid I'm going to need it.

The taxi suddenly comes to a stop outside an abandoned-looking building. I read the meter and hand the driver the money.

"*Señor*, are you sure this is the correct address?"

"*Sí*," I say, stepping out of the car.

I walk toward the abandoned building, and the cab speeds off the second I'm out of the cab. All of my training as an FBI agent is telling me to run, to run fast and as far away from this building as possible, but I ignore my instincts and keep walking.

I get to the door, and then my hand reaches to push the cracked door open. It is less of a door and more of a piece of wood lying against the doorframe.

Voices stop me from entering. The voices are saying all the wrong things and confirming suspicions that, if I'm honest with myself, I have had for at least a year, possibly longer.

I was very wrong. Kinsley isn't safe. She's the furthest thing from it.

I slowly back away from the door and begin walking down the alleyway, away from the building. I couldn't go into that building without backup, and I'm not sure I can trust the FBI with the information I just heard, not if I want to keep Kinsley safe.

So, instead, I keep walking away from the building and hope I'm not followed. Not because I care about my safety. My life means nothing, but Kinsley's life means everything.

19

KINSLEY

"THAT'S A WRAP," the director says.

Scarlett walks over to me but not before she winks at the director first. If I weren't here, she would be all over him.

"Thank you so much for doing that. You looked great in the commercial."

Scarlett flips her brown locks back over her shoulder as the director walks by. "It was my pleasure." She's not looking at me.

"Come on," I say, grabbing her shoulder and oversized purse. I lead her out of the lobby of the Felton Grand hotel where the shoot took place. "Let me buy you lunch."

"But..."

I shake my head. "That man is twice our age. You are not sleeping with him."

"But he's hot," Scarlett whines.

I roll my eyes. "No."

She pouts. "Since when did you get so bossy?"

"Since I've been stuck running a multibillion-dollar company and finding a way to keep my family from ending up in jail."

Scarlett sighs. "Well, that is a depressing answer."

"Just get changed and meet me for lunch at..." I glance over at Scarlett, but she isn't listening to me.

Instead, she is flirting with some frat boys who are eyeing her boobs beneath her bikini top.

"Scarlett, go change," I say, pushing her toward the restrooms just outside of the lobby and handing her her purse where she put her clothes in.

She looks down at her bikini top and ripped jean shorts, but doesn't take her purse from me. "Why?"

"Because the restaurant won't let you eat without a shirt on."

"You own the restaurant. They will let us do whatever we want."

"Change," I say sternly, holding her purse out to her again.

Scarlett rolls her eyes at me but walks back to the lobby and over to the rack of wardrobe clothes. I watch from the hallway as she grabs a sheer tank top. She pulls the shirt on.

"Ready," she says, bouncing back over to me. She, finally, takes the purse from my hands. "Come on, bitch. I'm starving." She grabs my arm, and we walk to the Mexican restaurant in the hotel.

The restaurant is calm. Only a couple of other people are here since it's a quarter after two in the afternoon. It's not late enough for the evening crowds to start yet, so we easily get a nice booth. We take a seat, and I look over the menu.

"Can I get you two something to drink?" our waiter asks.

"I'll have a water," I say.

Scarlett's eyes widen at my order, and she shakes her head. "We will each have a grande margarita. Thanks."

"I have to go back to work after this. I don't need a buzz when I'm dealing with figuring out how to implement the new marketing plan."

"It's exactly what you need. You need to relax. Who cares if the company goes under? Your grandfather deserves to have his company destroyed after what he did."

My mouth drops open.

"I'm sorry. I didn't mean that" Scarlett immediately says when she realizes what just came out of her mouth.

She's always been honest though, and I won't fault her for that. Not again.

"No, you're right. My grandfather doesn't deserve to make any more money off the company, but the employees here don't deserve to lose their jobs because of my grandfather."

Scarlett nods. "I guess that makes sense. It doesn't mean you have to give up your life to run a company you don't even want to run. You can hire someone else and make it their problem."

I nod as the waiter places the margaritas in front of us.

"Are you two ordering any food or just drinks?"

"Definitely food," Scarlett says, glancing at the menu. "I'll have the steak fajitas."

"I'll have the nachos," I say.

Scarlett and I hand the waiter our menus.

I glance back to Scarlett. "I just don't know what I want to do, Scarlett. I've never had to decide before. I've never even thought about it. And until I decide, I want to do a good job here."

"Have you heard from Killian?"

I take a sip of my margarita. The alcohol immediately calms my nerves. Scarlett was right. I needed this.

"No, Killian hasn't called. I don't expect him to. I told him I couldn't handle dating someone who hurt my family, but I was wrong. I don't have a family. I want him, but I think I pushed him away."

"He'll come back."

I nod. "He'll come back for my grandfather's trial, but that's exactly why he won't date me either. He can't date me and work for the FBI. They are still investigating my family."

Scarlett sucks down half of her margarita. "God, your life is so messed up. I don't know how you deal with it, Kins. The hardest decision I have to make is what clothes I'm going to wear in the morning."

I remember that life. I remember not having to decide anything, but I wasn't happy. I asked for this. I asked to run the company. I asked to make decisions about my own life. And, now that I get to do that, I've made even more of a disaster out of my life.

Our food quickly comes out and is placed in front of us, but suddenly, I'm no longer hungry as I'm faced with more choices and decisions than I ever thought was possible.

"Eat," Scarlett says when she notices I'm not eating.

I pick up a chip and force it into my mouth, but it doesn't taste good. It's not what I want.

"Forget this. I'm tired of seeing you mope. We are going out tonight."

I frown. "No, we are not. The last time we went out, I almost made a terrible decision by going home with a random guy and my father died."

"Well, that's obviously not going to happen again."

My mouth falls open a little.

"Oh God! I didn't mean to be insensitive, Kinsley. I just really think we should have a good time. I think your mind will be clearer after we go out. You'll be able to decide what you really want to do."

"Maybe."

"I'll take that as a yes."

A tear falls as I hear her say the words that Killian always says.

"Oh, honey," Scarlett says, getting up from her side of the booth.

She quickly climbs into the booth next to me. She wraps her arms around me, and I rest my head on her shoulder. She rubs my back, trying to stop the tears, but they keep coming. I glance around the restaurant because I'm sure the wait staff will notice me crying. A CEO who cries in one of her own restaurants—that's got to be a first. I don't care though. I'm tired of caring about what other people think of me. I need to cry, so I do.

"I miss him so much."

"I know, sweetie. It's not fair that you lost your father. It's okay to miss him."

I sniffle. "Him, too."

A small smile creeps up her lips. "Killian will be back. He would be crazy not to come after a hot, strong woman like you."

"But what if he doesn't?"

"Then, you go after him and don't take no as an answer."

"He's in Kansas though. That's all he told me. I don't have an address. I don't even have a city. He could be anywhere in Kansas."

Scarlett laughs. "It's not like Kansas is that big. I'm sure we could look up his family's address and find him, but he'll be back in town for your grandfather's trial. When does it start?"

"I don't know."

"What do you mean? They haven't set a date yet?"

"I'm sure they have. I just haven't spoken to Granddad since I found out the truth. I've been sleeping at the hotel, and I hired extra staff to take care of him at home."

Scarlett looks at me, confused. "You need to go see him. You're the only family he has."

"No, I don't. He did this to me. I'm not his family. Not anymore."

Scarlett nods and holds me tighter.

"Let's go out tonight," I say.

She pulls away from me, so she can look at me in the eyes. "You sure?"

I hesitate for just a second. "Yes, I'm sure. I just want to have fun. No guys. No drama. No family. Just drinking and fun."

She nods. "Sounds perfect."

It does sound perfect. It sounds like exactly what I need.

———

I press the button for the elevator and wait for it to make it up to the eleventh floor where I'm staying. I pull some lip gloss out of my purse and apply it to my lips. I feel good in my skintight black dress, but I'm interested to see what Scarlett thinks of the change I made. After she left, I couldn't spend the day working on the marketing plan. I needed to spend time on me, on figuring me out. And, while I don't feel any closer, I do feel more like a woman and less like a girl.

The elevator doors open, and I step onto the empty elevator. I press the floor for the lobby where I'm meeting Scarlett before we walk over to a nearby club. The ride is long. The elevator stops on almost every floor as it goes down until it is completely full. It does make me happy to see the hotel running at full capacity and getting so much business, despite my indecisiveness with how I feel about running the company.

The doors open to the lobby, and everyone files out. I step off and smile at the passersby as I walk to the center of the lobby where Scarlett is supposed to meet me. She isn't here yet, not that it surprises me. She's probably still napping after I made her get up so early to do the commercial.

I plan on taking a seat on a bench in the lobby to wait for her when I see a family arguing with one of our managers behind the desk. I sigh. I guess I might as well make use of my time and see how I can help.

I walk over to the lobby desk with a smile on my face. In my current apparel, I'm afraid people won't take me seriously. But I'm not going to let it stop me from doing my job.

"Hello, I'm Kinsley Felton, CEO of this hotel and casino. Is there anything I can help with?" I surprise myself by saying CEO although it's technically true. *I'm the CEO.*

The man standing with his family doesn't even question me, like I expected.

"Yes, we booked a weeklong stay here over six months ago. We live in Mississippi and came here for a family vacation, but somehow, this man is saying that you lost our reservation and are booked solid."

The manager standing behind the desk frowns. "As I told you before, we didn't lose your reservation. We don't lose reservations. You will have to go—"

"No, I apologize for losing your reservation. I will get it fixed right away," I say, moving around the desk so I can access the computer.

I frown at the manager. I'll need to have a discussion with him later. He has to learn to speak politely to our customers if he wants to continue working for us.

"Excuse me," I say to the manager as I take control of the computer.

I scroll through the bookings and realize the manager is correct. We are completely full. There is one room though I can give to them.

"Okay, so we are almost full, but I do have one suite available."

"We booked a single room with a rollaway bed for the kids. We don't want to pay for a suite," the man says.

I smile at him. "Not a problem. We will give you the upgrade to the suite for free as a thank-you for being so patient with us after losing your reservation. We will just need an hour to get the room clean. I'll also give you some restaurant vouchers so you can have a nice dinner while you are waiting in the meantime." I grab some vouchers for our best restaurant and hand them to the man.

"Thank you," he says in surprise with a smile on his face.

"You are welcome. I will leave you to"—I glance at the manager's name tag—"Sean, so he can take your information and bags."

I smile at them and then turn to Sean. I lean over so that only he can hear me. "Put them in the room I'm staying in and have it cleaned immediately. Have my stuff packed and put into my office. And we will have a discussion later about how to handle customers."

He nods.

I glance back to the young family. "Enjoy your stay."

They smile at me, and I hand the two young kids each a lollipop before I leave. I see Scarlett walk into the lobby just as I make my way back around the desk. I smile at her, but she doesn't see me. Her eyes continue scanning the room for me.

"Scarlett!" I holler.

She turns her head in my direction, and when she sees me, she gasps, followed by a squeal I'm afraid everyone in the hotel hears. She runs to me and grabs my now much shorter blonde hair that stops just above my shoulders.

"Oh my God! I can't believe you cut your hair. I've never seen you with anything but flowy long hair." Scarlett takes a step back and takes in the full picture of me with my new lob hairstyle. "I love it!" she squeals again. "It makes you look so much..."

"Older," I say, finishing her sentence.

I flip my hair back, loving how the lighter locks make me feel.

"Yes, and sassy," she says, smiling. "You look so grown-up now. Maybe I should try a new do."

I widen my eyes. Scarlett's hair is long and gorgeous. Sure, she could pull off a shorter hairstyle, but why should she when her current hairstyle is so perfect for her?

"Really?" I ask.

She thinks for a second. "Nah."

I giggle. "So, where are we going?"

"A new club just opened two blocks down. It's supposed to be slammin'."

I laugh at her language. "What's so slammin' about this club?"

"It's on a rooftop."

———

"Wow," I say when we make it up to the rooftop. "This is…"

"Slammin'," Scarlett says.

"That's one word for it."

Scarlett and I begin the long journey of pushing our way through the crowd to one of the bars located in three of the corners. The fourth corner contains the stairs we just came up. The rooftop view is incredible. It has lights along the railing. The whole rooftop is just one giant dance floor. A DJ is playing loud music against one side. It's chaotic and loud, and honestly, it's exactly what I need to distract myself.

I see an opening in the crowd and push through toward the bar closest to us. Scarlett follows as people dance around us. I push my way up to the all glass bar. The bartender sees us and holds up a finger, saying he will be over in a minute. I turn to ask Scarlett what she wants to drink when I notice everyone at the bar has some sort of bright blue-colored drink that looks good. When the bartender comes over, I ask for two of them, and he tells me it's their specialty drink with vodka and fruit juices.

He quickly makes it, and I hand one of the drinks to Scarlett.

"Thanks, hon," she says. "To having fun." Scarlett raises her glass.

I raise mine and clink it with hers before taking a sip of my drink. It's good.

I take another sip and feel better already. I grab Scarlett's hand. "Let's dance."

"I love the new Kinsley," she says as we begin dancing in the crowd.

The music is loud and fun. I enjoy dancing with Scarlett. I enjoy just dancing by myself and feeling free while not having to think or talk. I get to be a normal woman going out on a Friday night.

Two more times, we repeat the process of getting drinks and dancing with each other, with ourselves, or just with the crowd around us. There are a couple of pee breaks in there as well, but mostly, we're just relaxing and having fun.

"Thanks for this," I say to Scarlett between songs.

She smiles. "Happy to help, friend."

I feel a drop of rain hit my face, and I look up just as rain begins pouring down on top of us. It's beautiful up here, seeing the rain fall from the sky as the lights from the bar shine up. When the two of them meet, it's magical.

"Wanna get out of here?" Scarlett asks as several of the people dancing begin making their way back inside the hotel.

"No, not yet."

I love the feeling of the rain falling on top of us. Scarlett and I keep dancing as the rain falls. Many of the people around stay as well. I love it and hope this never ends because, as long as I'm here, dancing, my world is good. I don't have to make any decisions here.

I hear thunder in the distance, followed by several more lightning and thunder strikes nearby. That's when they begin shutting down the bar and making everyone go back down into the hotel where it's safe from the lightning.

When we make it downstairs, there are several employees waiting with towels, handing one to each of us. I use it to wring out my hair and dry off as best as I can. Scarlett does the same before we give the towels to another employee who is collecting them.

"Ready to head home, or should we try another club?" Scarlett asks.

The sound of the slot machines in the casino draws me in. "Actually, I want to…"

Scarlett sees me eyeing the casino. "Get in a game of blackjack?"

I nod.

She sighs. I know casino games are not her thing. Her eyes instead follow a group of men who were dancing up on the rooftop earlier.

"Go with them. I just want to get a game or two in, and then I'll head back." Although, I don't know where I'm staying tonight since I gave up my hotel room and I don't want to stay at home.

She glances from the men and then back to me. "Are you sure?"

"Go," I say, waving her on.

She doesn't hesitate again. She struts up to them, and within seconds, she is welcomed into their group.

I run my hand through my short hair to get the wet strands off my face, and then I make my way in. The lights and sounds welcome me into the casino that I haven't been in before, despite trying out most of the casinos on the strip. It's smaller and older than the one in our hotel at the Felton Grand. There are only a fourth of the number of tables and only half of the number of slots. This casino is themed like a beach. It's simple and consistent throughout the casino.

I slowly walk through until I find an open blackjack table and take a seat. Two men about my age sit on the other end across from me. I quickly fall into the rhythm of the game almost automatically. Even when the men across from me try to draw me into polite conversation, I'm still able to count the cards and keep track of the running total.

I win more times than I lose, but it's not the winning or losing that makes the game enjoyable for me. It's the weird enjoyment I get from being around people while not actually having to talk with them. It's the sounds of the slots mixed with the quiet intensity of those playing the table games. It's the flashing lights that energize me. It's the subtle smell of alcohol and cigarettes. Even though this side of the casino is a nonsmoking section, it still lingers in the air. It's my father.

I bite my lip in frustration, knowing that at least half of the reason I love casinos so much is because of him, but now, that reason is gone. But there are still enough reasons left to make me enjoy this, and as difficult of a journey as it's going to be, running the company, I'm not sure I can give it up—at least, not yet.

I sit here for a while longer, playing more and winning more. I sip the same wine Killian ordered for me the first time we officially met. I feel my eyes begin to grow heavy after a while, and I pull my phone out of my purse to see what time it is, but it's dead. I frown and look around the casino, but I know it's no use. Casinos don't keep clocks or have windows. It helps to keep people playing the games if they don't know what time it is.

I could ask the other players, but there is no one left at the table, except for me, and the dealer isn't wearing a watch.

I ask anyway, hoping she has a phone hidden away in her pocket, "What time is it?"

"It's one fifteen," Killian says from behind me.

20

KILLIAN

KINSLEY SUCKS in a breath at my unexpected voice. I smile, glad I still affect her like this because she still affects me. She stands and turns to face me, and that's when I get a good look at her much shorter locks. She would have been unrecognizable from the back if I hadn't run into Scarlett and she hadn't told me where Kinsley was.

I suck in a breath at the sight of her dripping short locks.

"What are you doing here?"

I reach out, not being able to stand not touching her any longer.

"I thought I would try something shorter. I've had long hair all my life," she rambles in a nervous voice, which just makes me smile brighter at her.

"Beautiful," I say because she is. She's even more beautiful than she was before. "Strong and beautiful."

She smiles, and a flush forms on her cheeks.

"God, I want you so bad," I say, my eyes traveling over her dress, her curves, and then back to her bright blue eyes. "But there is so much to say, and you still hate me."

Kinsley bites her lip. "I used to hate you. Now, I realize who I should be hating."

I stick my hands in my pockets to keep me from doing something stupid. "And now?"

"Now, I sorta love you."

I grin and do something stupid. Despite trying as hard as I can to keep my hands firmly in my pockets, they fly out and grab Kinsley. One hand tangles in her newly cut hair, still wet from being out in the rain too long. The other wraps around her waist where I can see her skin through the see-through portion of her dress, but I can't touch it. My lips touch her soft lips while my tongue tangles with hers in a desperate kiss. A kiss I was afraid I would never get again.

I thought she would still hate me. I thought she wouldn't believe me, but somehow, she does. Now, I just have to protect her from the truth I just discovered. A truth that is a million times more hideous than what either of us knew to be true.

But, before I figure out how to protect her, I have to have her. I can't stand that I left her when she wasn't safe. I can't stand that I left her feeling like I didn't love her. I can't stand that I hurt her. And I can't stand that, within a minute of seeing her, my cock isn't already buried inside her because I need to feel close to her. I need to forget what I just learned. I need to forget that, if I choose to be with her past tonight, I'll be jeopardizing a career that I've worked my ass off for.

"Excuse me, ma'am. Would you like another glass of the Margaux you were drinking?" the cocktail waitress asks Kinsley.

Kinsley reluctantly pulls her lips away from me. "No, thanks."

"Sir?"

I smile, seeing that Kinsley ordered the first drink I ever got her. "No, I'm good."

Kinsley grabs her glass of wine from and finishes the last sip before handing the empty glass to the waitress. "Thank you," she says, her eyes trained on my lips.

Before the waitress even leaves, Kinsley's soft, plump lips are on mine, torturing me. I can kiss her, but I can't get what I want right now, no matter how hard I get for her. I press my cock against her stomach to show her how much I need her, and her eyes open. They are filled with need, showing me the same thing, that she needs me. Now.

I pull away, so my lips are just resting on hers. "Fuck, that look is the sexiest thing I've ever seen."

She grins. "You haven't seen sexy yet."

She grabs my hand, and then we are walking instead of kissing. I let her lead me a few feet when I tug hard on her hand until she is spinning back toward me. I grab ahold of her neck and kiss her again. She gives into the kiss as I sweep my tongue into her mouth.

She moans just a little, and then she pushes me away, laughing. "You have to stop that if you want more than just a kiss."

"What?" My eyes widen at her words.

She leans forward until her mouth is at my neck. "If you want to fuck me, you have to stop kissing me, so I can take you somewhere that is not swarming with people." And then she sucks my neck before pulling away.

I've taught her well.

She grabs my hand again, and then she's leading me off the casino floor.

I frown when she doesn't lead me to the lobby to get a room. "Where are we going? Shouldn't we head to the lobby to get a room?"

She bites her lip as she flashes me a wicked grin. "I can't wait that long. Can you?"

She cocks her head to the side, and I realize I was wrong. This is the sexiest thing I've ever seen.

She pulls on my hand again, and we are walking faster down a long hallway and then another. I have no idea how she knows where she is going, but she does. She slows when she gets to the end of a hallway, and then she pushes me into a restroom.

I grin. "You naughty girl."

Her tongue hungrily slips inside my mouth as her arms go around my neck. It's the most desperate kiss I've ever felt from her, and I match her hunger, kiss for kiss.

"God, I want you," I say.

"Then, take me."

I lift her legs, and she jumps into my arms, wrapping her legs around my waist. I slip my hands under her dress, and I grab ahold of her bare ass.

"Fuck, you're so naughty, princess. Naughty enough to not even wear underwear," I say as I carry her to the last stall. I push her inside just in case anyone walks into the restroom.

I push her against the wall and kiss down her neck. I listen to her moans as I kiss each perfect spot on her skin.

"I've missed you so much, Killian."

I kiss her neck again.

"I know it's only been a couple of days since I last saw you, but it seemed like years. Each day, I wasn't sure if I would ever get you back," she moans.

I move back to her lips, kissing and sucking. I pull her bottom lip into my mouth and gently bite down before slowly letting it go. "I could never stay away from you."

"Good," she says just before she grabs my cock over my pants.

"Fuck," I moan.

"I missed your cock."

I raise my eyebrow. "Just my cock?"

She smiles. "I missed you, too."

She rubs my cock again, and I lose it. I can't wait a second longer. I can't breathe if I'm not buried inside her.

Kinsley must agree because she pulls at my pants to unbutton my jeans. I let her undo my pants as I slide one of my hands to her pussy that is already dripping with her need for me.

"You're so wet for me."

"Yes." She reaches into my pants and pulls my cock out before guiding it to her entrance. "Fuck me."

I pull a condom out of my pocket and slip it on before I push inside her and am rewarded with her moan.

She arches her head back as I push inside her and hold her ass tighter to keep her from falling. I grab her hair, pulling her to face me so I can kiss her as I fuck her. She claws at my neck as my thrusts get harder and faster. She gives up complete control to me as I fuck her. She has to since her feet are off the floor, and the only thing she can really do is hold on to me.

I thrust faster and let go of her hair to reach one hand down between her legs to her clit.

"Killian…" Her voice gets louder this time as I touch her. Loud enough I'm afraid we are going to get caught.

I consider slowing down so she can control herself, but that's not what I want. If she's giving up control to me, I want to prove her trust is warranted. I want to hear her scream my name, so everyone in this hotel knows she is mine.

I thrust inside her faster as I rub her clit in tight circles.

"Killian…I'm…going…to…" She pants harder until she explodes in a scream that is too loud to be appropriate. And then I come right after, my moan equaling hers.

I lower her to the ground just as I hear the door to the restroom open. Kinsley's face turns a bright shade of pink.

We wait as the woman who entered runs the faucet.

Kinsley looks at me and starts giggling. I put my hand over her mouth so she doesn't give us away, but that just makes her giggle even more.

Finally, after what seems like hours, the woman finally leaves. I unroll some toilet paper and clean between Kinsley's legs.

"You didn't have to do that," she says, curiously looking at me.

"Yes, I did."

I move to tuck my cock back into my pants.

"Let me."

I move my hands away and watch as she drops her head to my cock. She licks and sucks me clean.

"Careful, or we will never get out of here," I say as I begin to get hard again at her touch.

She smiles and finishes cleaning me off with her tongue before tucking me back into my pants. She walks out of the stall, and I follow her. I grab ahold of her hand, and we walk out of the restroom.

"How did you know about this restroom?"

"I took a wild guess. All of our hotels have a restroom near the back that only employees use. I took my chances."

"You're naughtier than I thought."

She grins a smile I don't think has left her lips since I returned.

We walk back toward the casino floor, both unsure of where to go or what to do next. The sex was about connecting, but we have so much to talk about, and I'm still not sure if we are going to wind up agreeing. I'm not sure if she's going to walk away from me again. It's a thought I can't bear to face, but I have to talk to her, so I'm going to have to face that possibility.

When we make it back to the casino floor, we just stop and look at each other, trying to decide what we do now.

"Can I sleep at your place tonight? I gave away my hotel room," Kinsley says.

My grin returns to my face. I love the words that came out of her mouth even though I don't understand why she gave away her hotel room or why she isn't staying at her home.

"Yes."

———

We don't talk on the drive to my apartment. We don't talk as we walk from the car to my apartment. And we don't talk as I hold her in my arms on the couch.

"I'm sorry," we both say at the same time.

I narrow my eyes at her as she scoots over on the couch, so we can look at each other, face-to-face. "You have nothing to be sorry about," I assure her.

"Yes, I do. You told me the truth, and I didn't believe you. I blamed you for what happened when you were just doing your job. I gave up on us."

I grab her hand to try to comfort her. "You have nothing to be sorry for. You trusted your family over a man who had lied to you before. That's one of the reasons I love you. You are so connected to your family."

"Not anymore."

I sigh. "It kills me to see you hurting. It kills me to know that I destroyed your relationship with your family."

She shakes her head. "You didn't destroy my relationship with my family. My father did."

"You shouldn't hate your father. He loved you."

"Yeah, he loved me so much that he lied to me."

I sigh again. "It's going to take a lot of time for you to forgive your father. Just give it time." I realize I'm repeating the words my mother said to me about my father.

"Maybe."

I take a deep breath before I say the next part, the hard part. "There's more, Kinsley. More I just found out."

"What do you mean, there's more?" she asks, dropping my hand.

I look away, unable to hold her gaze as I further destroy her world.

"Whatever it is, just tell me. It can't be worse than finding out my father and Granddad are frauds and money launderers," she says in a joking manner, trying to make light of the situation.

I slowly look at her as I press my lips together.

She sucks in a breath. "It's that bad, huh?"

I nod and take her hand in mine again. "You're not safe here."

She sits back. "What?"

"You're not safe. Your father and grandfather weren't just involved in money laundering and fraud. They were involved in something more."

She bites her lip but doesn't speak. That's when I realize I can't tell her everything I know. It would just be putting her in more danger. I just need to tell her enough, so she knows it's not safe here.

"While I was away, I went to Mexico. Your father went to Cancún, alone, on a business trip the week before he died. I decided to check it out to see where it might lead. When I got there, what I found..."

"What did you find?"

I shake my head, and I decide to lie, to give her just enough of the truth so she will listen to me. "Drugs. Guns. I don't know yet why your father agreed to meet with criminals. I don't know if he was working with them or if he even knew who he was doing business with, but those people aren't safe," I say, my voice speeding up as I talk.

She closes her eyes and then slowly opens them. "It's a lot to take in, knowing that my father might have been involved in worse than what I already know. I'm just having a hard time accepting it."

I nod. I try to give her space, but I can't, not when I see her struggling so much with this. I pull her close to me until she is lying back on my chest.

"I don't want you going anywhere alone. Either I go with you, or you hire security. Understand?"

She nods but doesn't say anything.

"Good."

At least I know she will be safe until I can figure out how to keep her safe permanently. I just don't know if that means going to the FBI with what I have, even if that indicts her grandfather or her in further crimes.

Do I gather more evidence first before I tip the FBI off? Or do I just try to convince Kinsley to get as far away from here as possible?

Right now, all I have to think about is that she is safe.

I hold her tighter against my chest.

"I have to know the truth," she says suddenly. She doesn't move from my chest.

"You will. But let me or the FBI investigate. Don't go searching for information on your own. It's too dangerous. Promise me?"

"I'm not talking about investigating. I just want to hear the truth from Granddad. He owes me that much."

"I don't think he will tell you anything if he hasn't even admitted to the money laundering and fraud."

"Maybe, but I need to hear whatever he'll tell me. He needs to explain why. It's the only way I'll be able to move on from them."

I hold her tighter. We don't talk for a long time. I just lie here and listen to her breaths until they're steady. Then, I pick her up and carry her to my bed. I wrap my arms around her, and I promise her I will never let her go.

21

KINSLEY

I WAKE up in Killian's arms, feeling more exhausted than when I went to sleep. Finding out that there are worse things my family has done took all of my remaining energy away. And listening to Killian lie to me again last night almost destroyed me. I knew he was lying.

Everything about him changes when he lies. His speech gets faster, and his eyes dart away from me as he lies. And he was lying last night. I just don't know about what part or why he would lie.

I want to go talk to Granddad today. I need to know what the hell is going on, and I need to hear it from him. Then, I can decide what I'm going to do with my life. All I know is that I want it to involve Killian, but every time I begin to trust him, he lies to me.

I roll over and look at Killian, who is snoring next to me. He's still asleep. But I can't stay in bed any longer. I'm restless and hungry. So, I get out of bed, and that's when I realize I'm still wearing my dress from last night. I go into his now familiar closet and find a pair of his shorts and a T-shirt. I change clothes and head to the kitchen.

I walk over to the small fridge and open the door. There's the same food as last time. My stomach growls, and my head hurts a little from the alcohol I drank last night. It's not going to be fixed by gross salmon and yogurt. I remember we passed a doughnut shop about two blocks from here. I grab my phone and realize it's still dead. I consider writing Killian a note to let him know where I'm going, but I can still hear him snoring in the bedroom and don't think he will wake up before I get back.

I slip on a pair of his tennis shoes, grab my purse, and head out the door. In the hot Las Vegas heat, I begin the two-block walk in the oversized shoes and clothes. I'm sweating a lot after I make my way to the doughnut shop, which just makes me wonder more about why the hell I'm living in one of the hottest places in the country. And it's not even for a good reason, like a beach.

I make it into the doughnut shop as my stomach begins to growl, which is probably why I order a dozen doughnuts instead of just three or four, like I should. I eat one of the glazed doughnuts as I carry the large box back to Killian's apartment. I open the door and—

"Where the hell have you been?" Killian asks when I walk inside.

I hold up the box of doughnuts, and he takes a deep breath, but it's obvious from his face that he was worried.

"You promised me you wouldn't go anywhere without me or security. That includes going to get breakfast that will give you diabetes in five years."

"I'm sorry."

I realize now that he wasn't lying about fearing for my safety. Whatever is going on, he is scared. I walk over to the kitchen counter and place the box of doughnuts on it. I pull out a chocolate-covered doughnut with sprinkles and bring it to him.

"Peace offering," I say.

He reluctantly takes the doughnut from me and takes a bite. His eyes roll back in his head a little as he eats it, which makes me smile. I walk back, take out an apple fritter, and begin to eat it. I take a seat on the couch, and Killian sits next to me, continuing to eat his doughnut. I wonder, if we dated for real and didn't have to worry about my family's criminal activities, if this is what every morning would be like. Contently snuggling on the couch while eating fattening doughnuts before heading back to the bedroom. I smile. I could imagine at least every Saturday starting that way. But that might never happen.

"I still want to go speak with Granddad today."

Killian frowns but nods. "I agree. That is probably where we should start before we decide if we should go to the FBI with the info I have."

"I thought you were the FBI?"

He smiles. "I am. I just haven't reported the evidence to them yet because I don't trust them to keep you safe."

I take the last bite of my doughnut and then get up to get another. "We will go after we finish breakfast."

———

Killian parks the car in my family's driveway and turns the ignition off. He climbs out, but I stay frozen in my seat. I can't move. If I go in there and talk to Granddad, I don't know how I will handle it. I don't know how I'll be able to control myself. I watch as Killian begins to walk toward my house and then freezes when he realizes I'm not with him.

He turns and patiently walks back to my side of the car. He opens the door and squats in front of me so we are eye-to-eye. "You okay?"

"No."

He nods. "Just say the word, and I will get back in the car and drive you anywhere you want to go. You don't have to face your Granddad, but if you do want to face him, you don't have to do it alone."

I gently blow air out through my pursed lips. "I can do this."

He smiles. "Yes, you can, but you don't have to."

He holds his hand out to me, and I take it. He pulls me into a standing position.

We walk slowly and deliberately to my house that is full of lies. On the outside, it looks beautiful with its large expansive doors and windows covering the front. Not to mention, there are beautiful views out back, but I would trade it all right now if I could. I'd trade my privileged life, every drop of money, every piece of designer clothes, and every sports car. I would trade it all away for a family that loved me. For a family that earned their money honestly, but I guess that's easy for me to say when I grew up with all of this.

We get to the door, and I push it open and walk into my family's house. A house I was told I would someday inherit. Now, I don't care. Now, I just want to sell everything that had anything to do with my family.

"I'm going to go shower and change quickly."

Killian steps toward me with a gleam in his eyes. "Want any help?"

I smile and softly kiss him on the lips. "No. If you come with me, we'll spend the day in my room instead of talking to my grandfather."

He grins. "And what's wrong with that?"

I just shake my head. "Make yourself comfortable in the living room. Or grab a cup of coffee from the kitchen and sit out on the terrace. It is really nice out there."

He nods. "I will. I have a couple of phone calls to make while you are getting ready."

"I won't be long."

I run upstairs to the bedroom I grew up in. I begin stripping off Killian's clothes even though I love how they feel and smell. They bring me incredible comfort, as I feel closer to Killian when I wear them, but I have to change. I can't face the world in an oversized T-shirt and shorts. So, I leave them in a pile on the floor, and I walk into the shower.

I try not to think about the fact that Killian is probably outside right now, talking to the FBI. And, every time he does, I have no idea how I feel. I feel horrible that he is discussing ways to send my grandfather to jail for the rest of his life while I also feel happy that he will be brought to justice for the lives he hurt.

I let the cold water washing over me wash away my thoughts about my family. The water slowly begins to warm up. After I let the water warm me, I step out of the shower and dry off. I put on the sexiest underwear I have before I put on jeans and a simple black T-shirt. I towel-dry my hair and don't bother blow-drying it. I put a hair tie around my wrist in case I need to put my hair up later, and then I run down the stairs to check on Killian before I find Granddad.

I walk to the kitchen and find Paige standing there, cleaning the countertops.

"Good morning, Kinsley. Can I get you a cup of coffee?"

"Yes, please."

She pulls a coffee mug out of the cabinet and pours me a cup. "Killian is outside on the terrace," she says, handing me the cup. "Good pick. He's hot."

I laugh. I should formally introduce her to Scarlett. They would get along well with their same sense of humor and single-mindedness when it comes to guys.

I pick up the cup of coffee, and that's when I see which cup Paige chose. It's the one that says *World's Greatest Dad*. I hold the cup up to my lips but hesitate to drink from it, as if it would mean I believe the words on the outside of the cup. They are the furthest things from the truth. When I finally take a sip, Paige realizes her mistake.

"I'm sorry. Let me get you a new cup."

She doesn't know the reason this cup affects me so. She thinks it is because it brings up painful memories of missing my father, and it does, but it also brings up all the hatred I have for him as well.

"It's okay." I take the cup and turn to go find Killian on the terrace.

He isn't sitting in the chair, relaxing and enjoying the view and gorgeous weather out here, like I expected. Instead, he is pacing with his phone to his ear.

"I understand, sir," he says before ending the call.

I smile at him when he faces me, but he isn't smiling. I walk over and softly kiss him on the lips, but he doesn't kiss me back.

"What is it?"

"Is your grandfather here?" he asks slowly, carefully looking at me, like I know something I'm not telling him.

"I think so. I assume he's in his bedroom. He's still too weak to do much walking by myself."

Killian brushes past me, and I follow after him.

"What is it?" I ask again.

But he doesn't answer. He just keeps walking. He opens the door to the kitchen where Paige is still cleaning. She smiles at us, but it falters when she sees the look of anguish on my face at not knowing what the hell is happening.

"Is your grandfather's room this way?" Killian asks, pointing down the hallway toward his bedroom.

"Yes. You're scaring me. Tell me what's wrong."

He ignores me and runs down the hallway to Granddad's bedroom door. He pushes it open without knocking and then runs inside. I follow, but when I walk inside the room, I find Granddad is gone. I take a step back, not expecting him to be gone. I turn slowly to face Killian, making sure to look him in the eyes.

"They arrested him, didn't they? He's in prison," I ask.

I find my legs are growing weak, and I have to sit down on the bed. I didn't expect the news that my grandfather is in jail for crimes he committed to hit me so hard, but it does. It just goes to show I still love my grandfather, despite everything. I still love my family. It just makes me feel weak and makes me hate myself even more.

Killian runs his hand through his hair. "No, he's not in custody."

"Then, where is he?"

His eyes slowly and reluctantly meet mine. "He fled the country."

"How can you be sure?"

His lips tighten together. He's not going to tell me.

I close my eyes, hating the pain that comes with loving someone who lies to me and keeps things from me, but that has been my whole life.

"The FBI wants me to bring you in."

I open my eyes. "What? Why?"

"Because they think you helped get him out of the country, and if they have you in custody, they think it will compel your grandfather to return to the country."

My eyes widen when I realize Killian is going to have to choose between the FBI and me. His pained expression tells me everything. That the decision is painful instead of being simple.

His work as an FBI agent means something to him. It means as much as a relationship with me, but he can't have both, and I hate that I have to make him choose. If he chooses the FBI, I will spend my life hating him and missing him. If he chooses me, he will spend his life resenting me for making him give up his career. There is no good choice; there is no right choice. That's what I have learned; there is only the best choice among bad choices. It makes me never want to have to choose anything at all.

"What are you going to do?" My eyes meet his, and I see his need for me reflected in his eyes. But I also get a glimpse of his loyalty to the FBI.

"I don't know."

I fall back on the bed, closing my eyes. I just want to curl up in bed and go to sleep. Sleep until this is all over. Until I know for sure if Killian and I can be together. This ache, this pain at constantly being pulled together and then ripped apart, is slowly killing me. I wish I could find a way to let go of the love I feel for him. I wish I could just find a normal man who knows nothing about my family, so I could love freely without consequence. I don't get to choose who my heart falls for though.

I open my eyes and watch Killian pace back and forth in the room, like he always does when he's anxious. I shake my head. I'm not going to let him make this decision. I'm going to figure out where my grandfather is and get him to turn himself in. That's the only way Killian and I can be together—if I help the FBI.

I abruptly stand up. "Take me to the Felton Grand."

"Why?"

"If Granddad fled the country, he would have had to stop at the casino. There is a safe where my family keeps things, like passports. Maybe he left a clue as to where he went. And, if I can find him, maybe I can convince him to turn himself in."

"You don't need to do that."

"Yes, I do." I walk past Killian. "Let's go."

22

KILLIAN

WE STAND IN AN ALLEYWAY, just outside Kinsley's family's casino.

"No fucking way. You are staying here," I say.

"I'm going. You don't even know what you are looking for. I need to go."

"You are staying here. If I have to handcuff you to that pipe to keep you here, I will. You are not going inside. It's not safe. I will not have you arrested. Not again. Not until we figure out a plan."

Kinsley pouts at me, but I'm not giving in. I agree that her grandfather might have stopped here first before leaving, and if we can find him before the FBI, then we can possibly convince him to turn himself in and plead guilty, putting an end to all of this.

"Stay here. Promise me."

She looks down and then back up. I catch her gaze with my eyes.

"I'll stay. I promise," she mutters.

I blow out the breath I was holding. I'm not sure I believe her, but I'm going to have to. I don't have another choice. I'll just have to be quick so she isn't tempted to follow me.

I grab her face and plunge my tongue into her mouth. I know she is worried that I love my job more than her. That I can't give it up. She has every right to worry, but she needs to know it doesn't change how I feel about her. I love her, and the only way I can show her right now is with a kiss. So, I try to tell her everything with the kiss.

I try to pull away, but she bites my lip, holding me in place, making me want to stay, but I can't stay. I have to protect her, and the only way is to put an end to this.

I gently pull away. "I'll be right back."

Her lips pull into a tight smile, and then I walk away from her and into the casino. I look straight ahead as I walk. I don't look any employee in the eyes. I don't scan the crowd to see if there are other FBI agents here. I just look forward, hoping no one will notice I'm here. Although, if the FBI decides to pull the security camera tapes to see if Lee came back here first, they will know I was here as well, even if no one spots me.

I walk until I get to Robert's office, and then I pull the key Kinsley gave me out of my pocket. I unlock the door, and I push my way inside. And then I stand, frozen, looking at the mess of an office. It looks like someone was rummaging in here, searching for something. Papers are scattered on the ground. Frames are shattered on the floor. I walk over to the desk, and am surprised to see none of the drawers are open, making me throw out the theory someone was searching for something in here.

I bend down and pick up one of the papers off the floor. It's one of the papers I gave Kinsley. That's when I realize what this is. Kinsley did this. Her grief did this. I pick up the pile of papers that have the evidence I shouldn't have even shown Kinsley on them, and I put them into the shredder. I walk back to the desk and pick up a picture of Kinsley and her father when she was probably six or seven years old. She's sitting on his shoulders, and they look happy. They loved each other, and now, thanks to a lie, that love is broken. Just like my lies have prevented her from trusting me, her father's lies have prevented her from loving his memory.

I inspect the rest of the office, but I don't think her grandfather came in here. I walk out the door, careful to lock it behind me.

"Looking for Kinsley?" Tony says as he walks out of his own office.

336

"Yes," I lie.

"She moved to an office down the hall. I haven't seen her yet today, but she is usually in within the hour. You can wait for her there."

"Which room is her office?"

"The last one on the left, down that hallway," Tony says, pointing down the hallway.

"Thanks, Tony. I figured you would have been mad at me for what I did," I say.

"I am, but I still think you and Kinsley belong together. And I still think you are a good person even if you are working for the other side."

I nod and begin walking down the hallway toward her office. Kinsley didn't mention that she had moved into her own office. I guess she didn't think her grandfather would go to her office. I don't think he would have either, but I will check it out under the guise of looking for Kinsley. And, before I leave, I will have to check downstairs to see if anyone in the lobby saw him coming in.

I walk to the last door on the left and test the doorknob. The door is unlocked. I push the door open and step inside. That's when I realize why Kinsley didn't bother locking it. There is nothing here but a desk and a cord that connects to a laptop that isn't here. Next to it is a scribbled note and an envelope.

I pick up the note and read the shaky handwriting.

To Kinsley,

I'm sorry, but I had to leave. I've gone to make things right. I couldn't put you through a trial where the FBI would bring out false evidence against me and use it to send me to jail for the rest of my life. I couldn't put you through that.

I know this is a lot for you to understand. I know you don't understand why your father and I did the things we did, but in time, I hope you understand.

I've left the company to you with no strings attached. I won't be coming back to claim any right to it. It's yours to do with as you wish although my only wish is that it stays in the family.

337

I'll contact you when things are safe, and we can talk.

I love you, sweetheart.

~Granddad

The envelope is also addressed to her, and I go to open it when I hear a knock on the door. I put both into my jacket pocket and turn to see who is at the door.

"Killian, I wasn't expecting to see you here. I thought you were going to look at Kinsley's house. Any sign of her yet?" Agent Liddell asks.

"No. I tried her house and then here. I was thinking of trying her friend Scarlett's house next."

He nods. "Good thinking. I have a team in place here searching for evidence and they will be on the lookout for her."

I walk past him. "I checked this room. There is nothing here."

"Do you need backup to go with you to bring in the girl?"

I smile. "No. She trusts me. I will have better luck if I go alone."

"Be careful. These people are dangerous."

I nod. "Are we sure she didn't travel with her grandfather out of the country?"

"The video surveillance of the airport just showed her grandfather, so that's all we have to go by for now."

I walk past him without saying another word.

"Agent Byrne"—I stop walking as he walks to me—"Make sure you bring her in. Your standing with the FBI depends on it."

I glare at him, and then I walk away. I know where her grandfather went. I think I had known before we came here, but now, I'm positive, and I know, even if we found him, there is no way to convince him to come back to the U.S.

I walk through the busy lobby floor but stop when I hear a deep voice that stands out in the crowd. It's the same voice I heard in Mexico. I turn to try to catch the man's face that matches the voice, but he's gone, and I have to keep walking. I have to protect Kinsley.

I only have two choices. As my heart races faster while I get closer to Kinsley, I realize it's really not a choice at all. I can either turn her over to the FBI and deal with the fact that Kinsley could end up in jail again or...

I turn the corner and find Kinsley still standing where I left her in the alleyway. She has her cell phone in her hand, and she is mindlessly scrolling through it. She stops when she sees me. I run to her.

"We are leaving the country. Right now."

23

KINSLEY

I NOD. "You found out where my grandfather is?"

"No. But it's not safe here."

I cross my arms over my chest. "I'm not leaving with you. Not until you start telling me what's going on."

He frowns. "I will tell you, but I can't tell you here. When we get somewhere safe, I will tell you."

We both hear a loud popping noise, which makes me jump. Killian jumps in front of me and pulls a gun out from his waistband I didn't even know he had. He's pointing the gun at the alleyway, but I'm no longer concerned with whatever the noise is.

"You have a gun."

He scans the area one more time, and then a slow grin forms on his face as he puts the gun back into the waist of his pants. "I'm an FBI agent. FBI agents have guns."

I nod slowly, but he pulled it out, which means, for whatever reason, he really doesn't think we are safe.

"We need to go."

I open my mouth to answer but then bite my lip.

"Trust me," he says.

I don't trust him. I know at least half of the words coming out of his mouth are lies. The problem is, if I want to find out what the truth is, I'm going to have to trust him—at least temporarily.

"Okay."

He grabs my arm, and then without another word, we are moving, not running but more than simply walking. We are moving through the strip of Las Vegas to the parking garage where his rental car is. He doesn't look at me. He doesn't speak. His eyes are intensely focused on the task at hand.

When we get to his car, he holds the door open for me, and I climb inside. He goes around to the driver's side and immediately begins driving.

"Where are we going?" I ask.

He doesn't answer. Instead, he pulls out a cell phone. "I need you to meet me at the airport in half an hour with two passports—one for me and one for the girl—plenty of cash, and a flight out of here."

I try to listen carefully to hear the other side of the conversation, but it's a useless endeavor.

"Dang it, Hayes. I am doing this to protect her."

He pauses.

"Fuck the FBI! They would just arrest her, which is as good as a death sentence."

I shake a little when he raises his voice and when he talks about me dying if I went to jail.

"I'll tell them after. We just have to get out of here right now."

He pauses.

"Don't give me that bullshit! Just get us out of here. Now!"

Killian ends the call.

I take a deep breath and ask again. "Where are we going?"

He grabs my hand. "I don't know, but let's try to relax and enjoy this. Pretend we are going on a surprise vacation somewhere."

I smile, liking the idea that I will get to spend some quality alone time with Killian, but I hate not knowing where we are going. I hate not understanding what is happening.

He parks the car in front of the airport and gets out. He is pulling me into the airport, and I have no idea how to handle this. I have no idea what's happening. All I know is, I'm trusting a man I love, despite his lies, and I have no idea if it's the worst or best decision I've ever made.

24

KILLIAN

I DRAG Kinsley into the airport while doing my best to ensure her safety. I scan crowds for faces, listen for voices, and look for anything suspicious. I scan for anything that could be used as a weapon against us. I know I've been trained as an FBI agent, but I haven't had to use any of the physical training in over five years. I've been strictly focused on investigating this family, not on using any physical combat skills. I've barely even fired a gun in five years. I feel my senses are a bit rusty when it comes to sniffing out immediate danger.

Kinsley's hand is warm and shaky as I move her into the airport terminal. I try to be her rock, to keep her calm and steady, but if I'm honest, I'm just as nervous as she is. I've been an FBI agent for ten years now, but if she knew how many times I fucked up, she wouldn't trust me so easily.

I spot Agent Hayes sitting at a table in Starbucks. He has a ball cap and shades on to make it harder to be seen on the security cameras. I'm asking a lot of him to be here. Too much even for a friend whose ass I've saved, which was the only positive thing I've done while working for the FBI. I see him, but we walk past him to the restroom. I'm not going to put him further at risk by having him being seen plainly on security tapes, handing me what I need to escape. I'm at least going to make it difficult for the FBI to convict him.

I turn to Kinsley. "Go into the restroom. Wait five minutes, and then meet me here. Understand?"

She nods and looks at me with concern, but she does what I ask without question. I think she finally realizes it's useless to ask me questions right now when I won't answer her. When we get to wherever Agent Hayes is sending us, I don't know if I'll tell her then either, but she'll have a better shot of convincing me then.

I head into the men's restroom and wait.

"Byrne?" Agent Hayes says about five seconds after I enter the restroom.

"Did you get the stuff?"

He glares at me and hands me a bag. "It's all there."

I unzip it and see the cash, passports, and tickets along with some basic clothes and toiletries to make us look more like average travelers.

"Thanks."

"We are even now. Are you sure you know what you are doing? If you do this, you will never be able to step foot in this country again without being arrested. You are risking spending your life in jail for her. Why?"

"I couldn't protect my brother. I couldn't protect Summer, but I can protect her. I can't live with myself if I don't do it."

"The FBI can protect her here if you would just tell us what's going on."

"I will tell them just as soon as she is out of the country and safe. I don't trust them. I don't trust that they won't arrest her."

"They won't."

"I need you to do one more thing for me."

Agent Hayes glares at me. "You already got your one thing."

"I want you to run facial recognition software on the security tapes at the Felton Grand."

He narrows his eyes at me. "And what are we looking for?"

346

"Anyone involved in criminal activities in Mexico. I'll let you know more soon. Just do it."

He sighs and then pulls me into a quick hug. "Be safe."

And then he's gone. I walk back out of the restroom and find Kinsley waiting. She watches Agent Hayes leave, who doesn't even acknowledge she is standing there. And then she looks curiously at me.

"Let's go."

We walk quickly and efficiently through the crowd and get in line at security. I dig out our fake passports and hand one to Kinsley. "I'm Justin Briggs, and you're Megan Slade."

Her eyes widen.

"What's wrong?"

"Nothing. Just…"

I look at the passport again. "The last name."

"You know about Tristan Slade? You know what happened that night?"

"Yeah, it was the reason the FBI started investigating your family."

She looks down at her feet. "So, it is my fault."

"No." I pull her chin up so I can kiss her soft lips. "It wasn't your fault. You didn't do anything wrong."

The line moves, and we are forced to move forward, closer to TSA. I need to make sure she understands how serious this is before we get up there, and I need to get her mind off of feeling guilty, thinking she is the reason her family was investigated in the first place.

"You need to make sure you memorize everything on the passport. You need to know your name so that, if someone says it, you answer automatically. You need to make sure you know the birthday and birthplace. You need to have a back story so that you aren't flustered if people ask."

"Megan Joy Slade. Born May 3, 1994, in San Diego, California. I just graduated with a degree in mathematics from UCLA. Before teaching high school math this fall, I'm spending some vacation time in"—she glances at her ticket—"Tokyo, Japan, with my new boyfriend, Justin Briggs, who was born September 19, 1986, in Nashville, Tennessee. You teach business class at the local community college."

I smile at how she is able to remember everything after one glance of the passports. "Wow. Impressive. You even came up with a good story. If I didn't know better, I would suspect you of being in the FBI."

"Nah, I'm not FBI. I'm CIA," she says, which makes us both laugh. Her face brightens more as a thought enters her head. "Wait...when you went undercover for the FBI at Felton Corporation, you were given a new identity, but somehow, you ended up as Killian Browne —your name with only a slight variation on the last name. You fucked up, didn't you?"

Now, I'm laughing at how she said the word *fuck*, like a five-year-old who doesn't know the real meaning.

"Yes, I fucked up. I said the wrong name the first time I met your father, and then all I could do was change my last name, which is just a small change from my actual last name."

She laughs, and it's beautiful, seeing her laugh, even if it's at my expense.

"So, what was the name you were supposed to say? What name would I have known you by if you hadn't fucked up?"

"Harry Andrews."

She wrinkles her nose and then laughs again. "That's a terrible name."

I laugh. "Well, I'm glad I said the wrong name then. You might never have gone for me if you thought my name was Harry."

We step up to the TSA agent and hand him our passports.

"Have a nice trip, Justin," the man says, handing back my passport.

"Enjoy your trip, Megan," he says to Kinsley.

I take a deep breath. One step down and a million more to go before we make it to our destination. And I won't be able to breathe normally until we make it to our final destination.

25

KINSLEY

WE HAVE cramp coach seats on the airplane. I'm sitting next to the window, and Killian is in a middle seat. A teenage girl with earbuds in is sitting in the aisle seat. I want to ask Killian what is going on, but I know he won't answer as long as she is sitting next to us, even with the earbuds on. I also don't know if he will even talk to me after she gets up since other passengers are near us. I don't think I can wait to get more answers until we get to Tokyo.

But I have to wait.

I wait almost three hours into the flight before the girl gets up and goes to the restroom.

"I need answers now," I say in a hushed voice to Killian.

"I can't tell you here," he says, glancing around the plane.

"Killian..."

He eyes me.

"I mean, Justin. I need to know. I deserve to know."

He reluctantly leans in closer to me until his lips are right at my ear. "There isn't much more to say. All I know is that your father met with drug traffickers in Mexico. I don't know if he knew who he was meeting with or what the connection was, but I don't want to wait around and possibly put your life in danger if those men thought you were ratting them out to the FBI."

He's hiding something, but I don't know what it is.

"So, what is the plan now?"

"We are going to go somewhere safe where the drug traffickers can't find us. And then I will contact the FBI to explain why I did what I did."

"And do you think the FBI is going to be okay with you harboring a fugitive? You don't think they will take your job for this?"

"I think they will understand when I explain the circumstances."

I nod although I'm not sure if he believes the words he said. He seems worried although maybe that's just because he's trying to protect me.

"Where are we going? How long will we have to stay there?"

But I realize my time is up. He's not going to answer any more of my questions as the girl takes her seat next to him.

"Sleep, princess. Let me worry about everything."

I force my lips into a tight smile, and then I lean back and close my eyes. I try to sleep, but I can't. All I can think about is everything I don't know. Everything he isn't telling me.

I glance over at Killian. He has a little drool running down his chin. I smile and wipe it off him. I snuggle into his shoulder. Even though I can't sleep, I'm glad I can at least be with him.

When we finally land in Tokyo, I'm exhausted and in need of a bed. Killian holds my hand as we get off the plane and walk through customs. I've been to Tokyo several times with my father. I love the city. I love the architecture and the food, so I'm excited to spend some time in Tokyo with Killian.

We walk out to the curb, and Killian gets a taxi. He tells the driver an address, and I yawn and lean against his shoulder, barely keeping my eyes open. We drive thirty minutes before the taxi stops outside an old abandoned building.

"I'll pay you double if you wait for us here for five minutes," Killian says.

The driver agrees, and we step out of the car. I look around at where we are, but it doesn't look like any of the hotels I have ever been to.

Killian grabs my hand. "We need to get new passports, and then we will go."

"Why do we need new passports?"

"Because I don't want anyone to have any way to track where we are."

I look into the abandoned building. "How do you know this place will be able to get us new passports? How do you know about this place?"

He frowns at my questions.

"The FBI has connections."

I sigh when that's all he says. We enter the building, but I can't see anything. It's so dark in here.

"You know how you said you wanted to protect me? I'm not sure if dragging me into an abandoned building is the best way to do that."

He laughs at that.

Lights come on, and an older Japanese man walks into the room.

"Do you have the passports?" Killian asks. I don't remember Killian calling anyone on the plane, but he must have when he went to the restroom or when I dozed off.

The man nods and hands him the passports.

Killian walks over to him and pulls out some cash to hand to the man. He inspects the passports and then nods his thank-you.

"Let's go," Killian says to me.

"Where to?"

"Airport," is all he says.

I sigh as he leads me back to the taxi. He hands me the passport, which I study. I am now Erin Buffet. I glance at Killian's that reads Scott Foss. I lean my head back on Killian's shoulder and try to sleep. *Who knows when I'll get to sleep in a bed?*

26

KINSLEY

WE HAVE BEEN FLYING for more than thirty-six hours now. I haven't slept in over forty-eight hours. My eyes are red and dry. My back aches from sitting in cramp plane chairs. I'm exhausted. We have been to Tokyo, Berlin, Paris, London, and now Dublin. I have no idea when we are finally going to settle somewhere or if this is my life now.

"When's our next flight?" I ask as we get off the plane.

"We are here," Killian says, smiling.

"Oh, thank God," I say, which just makes him smile brighter.

He grabs ahold of my hand as we walk through customs in the busy airport.

"Are we staying in Dublin?"

"No."

I want to ask him where then, but I'm tired of getting ignored. If he ignores me one more time, I swear, I'm going to lose it, so I'll be patient until we get to wherever we are going. Then, when we are safe, I'll ask all the questions he promised he would answer.

I follow Killian onto a bus, but it is no more helpful in telling me where we are going since there are a billion stops on this bus route, according to the man we bought our tickets from at the ticket counter. I take a seat, and Killian sits next to me. He immediately puts his arms around me so I can rest my head on his shoulder and try to sleep.

"Are we Erin and Scott here, or Killian and Kinsley?"

He sighs and kisses me on the forehead. "Erin and Scott."

I nod sadly. I'm tired of being Erin and Scott although I already answer to the name. I don't like Erin. Erin is tired and grumpy and hungry all the time. Erin wears crappy clothes and doesn't do her makeup. Erin doesn't have a future. If I think too much about it though, Kinsley didn't have much of a future either.

"Just sleep, princess. We still have a couple of hours' drive ahead of us."

I sigh in frustration and close my eyes, but I don't sleep. Instead, about twenty minutes into the ride, I open my eyes and look out at the green countryside as it passes by. It's beautiful here. There are rolling hills covered in green grass with an occasional herd of sheep or goats. I glance up and notice Killian has his head rested on mine and is sound asleep. I envy him. He's been able to sleep on every plane ride and now bus ride while I haven't slept an ounce yet.

I continue to watch the beautiful countryside as we drive down the curvy roads. About an hour into the ride, it begins to rain, which somehow makes the landscape even more beautiful, but unlike everyone else on the bus, it still doesn't put me to sleep. So, instead, I count the raindrops on the window.

About two and a half hours into the ride, the bus driver comes to a stop outside of a city called Galway.

"This is us," Killian says, grabbing our one bag that only has one spare item of clothing for each of us but is mostly filled with cash.

I don't know what we are supposed to do when we run out of cash.

We step off of the bus and out into the rain.

"This way," Killian says, taking my hand and leading me down a city street.

I shiver a little as the rain pelts down on top of me. We walk for twenty minutes in the cold rain until I can't take it any longer.

"Where the fuck are we going? I'm exhausted. I'm hungry. I'm wet and not in a good way. And, I swear, we already passed that same pub ten minutes ago. If you don't find us a place to sleep in the next five minutes, I swear, I'm going home. I don't care if it's safe or not."

Killian's mouth falls open a little at my words. "I'm sorry. I have a cousin who lives around here. I thought we could just stay with him, but..."

"You are clearly lost, so let's just see if that bed-and-breakfast back there has any availability tonight, and we can try again tomorrow."

I begin walking in that direction without waiting to see if Killian agrees or not. It's a freaking bed-and-breakfast, for goodness' sake. It's about as safe a place as you can get. Plus, if anybody followed us and took that crazy schedule, there is no way in hell they have enough energy to come after us tonight.

So, I walk, and Killian follows me. Within five minutes, we are being escorted to our gorgeous room in the bed-and-breakfast. I open the door to our room, and it's fantastic. A huge white canopy bed sits in the center of the room with a few blue and green accents scattered throughout the room. There is a balcony leading out to the city street below and a large bathroom off the room. I don't care about all of that though. All I care about is the bed. I immediately walk over to it and crash onto it.

I blow out a breath as my body sinks into the heavenly bed. "You have to come try this bed. It's amazing."

Killian walks over to me and leans down so his mouth hovers over my ear. "I have some phone calls to make."

I frown.

"You sleep. I'll make some phone calls, and then I'll join you in a few minutes. I'm going to be out in the hallway if you need me, okay?"

I nod although it's not okay. After the trip we have had, I want his arms wrapped around me. I want to feel his warm breath on my neck as he softly kisses me until I fall asleep. I don't want to be alone, but I don't tell him any of that. I let him kiss me on the cheek. Then, he walks back out the door while I do my best to sleep alone in a strange place, in a strange country, and I still don't know what or who we are running from.

I'll ask him tomorrow, I promise myself. Tonight, I need to sleep.

————

I wake up the next morning and roll over, expecting to see a sleeping Killian. Instead, I find an empty bed and a note.

Morning, princess.

Went to find my cousin, so we will have a place to stay on a more permanent basis. They have doughnuts downstairs for breakfast, so you should be good until I get back. Don't leave the bed-and-breakfast. Be back soon.

~K

I crumble the note and toss it toward the trash can in the corner of the room. I miss, and I watch it bounce once on the floor before coming to a stop. I hate his note.

I look at the clock that says it's almost eleven a.m., and Killian still isn't back yet, although I don't know how long he's been gone. I get out of bed and realize I'm still wearing the same clothes I was last night. I walk over to the corner of the room where Killian laid out my clothes but took the bag, leaving me with no money, no ID, nothing.

He left me stranded.

I take a shower, and then I change into the new clothes, which consists of a pair of jeans that's a size or two too big and a white cotton T-shirt. I don't look great in them, but at least I am clean.

I head downstairs, but I am guessing that whatever breakfast was served is now long over.

"Good morning," one of the owners says when I make it to the lobby.

"Good morning. Are you still serving breakfast?"

She smiles at me. "Breakfast usually ends at ten thirty, but I think we have some leftover doughnuts."

"That would be great. Thank you."

The woman scurries into the back and pulls out a basket of doughnuts.

"Thank you," I say again as I take a couple out of the basket.

"Are there any places in this area that you recommend I see while I'm here?"

She smiles. "Well, just walking around the city of Galway is beautiful. I'd recommend seeing the nearby castle and cathedral along with the Spanish Arch. I would also stop in a jeweler and get a Claddagh ring, especially if you are here with a special someone. And if you haven't made it to the Cliffs of Moher yet, I highly recommend them."

"Thanks," I say.

I take my doughnuts with me and then head out of the bed-and-breakfast. I walk down the street to the main city block and begin walking, taking in all of my surroundings. The town is beautiful, just like she said. I instantly fall in love with the beautiful colors of the storefronts. The stores are quaint and small, compared to the large and bright casinos I'm used to in Las Vegas. It's so much calmer here. Everyone smiles and says hi to me here. No one is in a rush here. It's nice. The only problem is, Killian isn't here with me.

I spend the day exploring many of the places the woman suggested, including the beautiful cathedral and Spanish Arch. I go into several jewelers and admire all of their Claddagh rings. And, every few hours or so, I check back into the bed-and-breakfast to see if Killian has made it back. Each time, I come up empty until I am starting to worry that something might be wrong.

I head back to the bed-and-breakfast around dinnertime. I don't have any cash and am thankful to find a small dinner of tea and shepherd's pie is included. I fall in love with the tea that I sip on when Killian finally comes back.

I glare at him when he walks in.

"I'm sorry," he says when he walks over to me.

"I don't want to hear it."

"I'm sorry. My phone calls took a lot longer than expected, and I found out my cousin doesn't live here anymore."

I narrow my eyes. "Where does he live?"

He grimaces. "Dublin."

I shake my head in frustration.

"We can take a bus tonight if you want."

"No. I want to stay here. At least for a few more days."

I can tell Killian wants to argue with me, but he doesn't.

He leans down to kiss me, but I brush him away. I can't. I'm too angry with him for leaving me alone all day and for still not telling me the complete truth about why we are here. I thought today would be full of answers about why we flew around the world, but instead I got nothing but worry.

I yawn.

"Come on," he says. "Let me get you to bed."

I stand and follow him back to our bedroom. We walk inside in silence and then begin undressing, both preparing for bed without speaking. I just take my jeans off, and climb into bed.

"I still have lots of questions," I say to Killian.

He removes his shirt, revealing his body that I immediately want to jump. I bite my lip and look away while he continues to undress. I will not fuck him, not after leaving me alone to worry. Not after lying to me time and time again.

"And I want to hear all of them."

I look at him, and my eyes brighten a little. He begins climbing into bed when his phone vibrates on the nightstand next to the bed, stopping him. He looks at the number and then to me, but I already know what he is going to say.

"I have to take this."

I feel him climbing back out of bed, and he puts his jeans back on. I close my eyes and roll over as he walks out the door. A single tear rolls down my cheek. I don't understand how I'm here with Killian, but have never felt more alone.

How did forty-eight hours change the course of our relationship so severely? How is it possible to feel so distant from someone I thought I loved?

If this is the real Killian, I'm afraid I made a terrible mistake. I want the man who stood up for me in the courtroom. The man who couldn't keep his hands off me in the bedroom. Not the man whose work and own needs come before me.

27

KILLIAN

I watch Kinsley sleep. Her lips are pursed, and her now short locks curl around her flushed cheeks. I watch her chest rise and fall in a steady rhythm. I want to kiss her, but I don't think she would like that, not after leaving her alone and not telling her the truth of why we are here.

I didn't plan to spend the day away from her. It just happened. To contact the FBI without them tracking me, I had to go route the call through different locations, which required a computer and internet access that I didn't have at the bed-and-breakfast. I had to drive an hour away to get a laptop, and then I spent most of the day in various cafes using their internet.

I spent the whole day getting my ass chewed out by the FBI, but I think I finally convinced them that I did the only thing I could. The only problem is, they couldn't identify any criminals in the Felton Grand casino, which means the men don't have a record. And it means, we will be here for quite a while as they try to figure out who the men are that I overheard in Mexico and then again in the Felton Grand.

It also took me much longer to track down my cousin whom I haven't seen in twenty years. It required me getting ahold of my father since he was the only one who knew my cousin's address. He finally gave me the address, which I guess was progress since the last time I saw him.

Today though can't be about the FBI or my cousin. Today has to be about fixing things with Kinsley. Since I told her in the alleyway that we had to leave the country, I have felt her slipping further and further away. I have felt the distance between us grow instead of us getting closer and closer together. And I can't stand to be growing apart when I have nothing left in my life, except for her.

She stirs, and her mouth opens in a cute yawn as her arms stretch over her head.

"Wake up, princess. It's a big day today."

Her eyes pop open and immediately glare at me.

"Why? Are you planning on leaving me again today?"

I smile at her feistiness. "No. I don't plan on leaving your sight today. Not for a second. Even when you have to go to the bathroom, I'm going to be there."

"Ew, I think that is taking it too far."

But she is smiling, which was the point.

"So, what are your big plans for today?" she asks.

"Well, since you explored the town, I thought I would take you to my favorite place in the world today."

Her eyes light up. "And where is that?"

"The Cliffs of Moher."

She firmly kisses me on the lips, but then she quickly pulls away when she realizes that she isn't really ready to be happy with me. Or at least she's not ready to show me she is happy with me again, but I'll take what I can get.

"I had our clothes laundered, but if we find a place, we should pick up some new clothes tonight or tomorrow."

"Thanks."

"Go get your cute butt dressed. I'll get dressed and call a cab to take us. I think it's about an hour away from here."

"Sounds good."

I watch her roll out of bed and walk in just a T-shirt to the bathroom. I can't keep my eyes off her bare legs as she walks. I'm desperate to have her. I'm desperate to feel close to her again. But I guess I'll just have to wait.

————

"Thanks," I say to the cab driver.

I hand him money for the fare and then climb out of the taxi. Kinsley follows me. We haven't spoken much today. Instead, we've just focused on being content with sitting next to each other. But I know her questions are coming, and I try to prepare myself for them as best as I can.

I take her hand and walk her to the edge of the cliffs. She doesn't speak as she takes in the awe-inspiring view, but I can see the amazement on her face. Her hand goes over her mouth to cover her shocked expression. Her eyes slowly shift left and right, trying to take every drop of beauty in. I let out a breath I didn't realize I had been holding when I see that she loves this place as much as I do.

I guide her to my favorite peaceful spot, and we sit so our legs dangle over the edge. I wrap my arm around her waist, and we just sit. We sit in the amazement of this place, and that alone makes me feel closer to her.

"Were you born or raised in Ireland?"

"No. I was born in Kansas, but my family is from Ireland. The only person left who lives here is my cousin. Every year, up until I was in high school, we would save up money to come back here for two or three weeks."

"It's magical here."

I nod. "This is my favorite place in Ireland. I could spend all day here, just sitting and looking out at the blue water and the cliffs."

"Me, too."

And that's exactly what we do for an hour. We just sit in peace.

"What do you imagine for our future?" she asks.

I curiously look at her. Of all the questions that I know are burning inside her, that is what she asks. I try to answer but then stop because it's the one question I have no idea how to answer.

"Me, too," she says, smiling at my non-answer and turning to look back at the water. "I have no idea, and when I'm sitting in a place like this that makes me feel so small, it makes me feel like whatever I choose to do with my life, whatever we choose to do together, it's not big enough to matter. It's not big enough to make an impact on the world."

I reach up and tuck her breeze blown hair behind her ear. I rub my thumb across her cheek. "You are big enough to matter to me. And, as for our future together, I don't know, but I do know my future will always involve you in some capacity or another. I can't imagine a life without you."

She nods, satisfied with my answer.

"What made you decide to become an FBI agent?"

I stare off into the distance. "It's a long story."

"I want to hear it."

I turn to face her to show her how hard it is for me to tell her this, the worst mistake of my life. But when she looks back at me with such hope and purity in her eyes, it gives me the courage to tell her. After all, I know her worst mistake. She should know mine.

"I grew up in Marysville, Kansas. A tiny little town in the middle of nowhere. It was just the four of us living in a modest house. My mother worked as a nurse. My father ran the only hotel in the town. So, most of the time, at home, it was just me and my older brother."

She smiles. "I didn't know you had a brother. I always wished I had a sibling."

I nod. "Kieran, my brother, was the best. He was seven years older than me, but he was never ashamed of me. He was always protecting me. My name was Liam up until I was six or seven. I was an awkward child who got made fun of a lot. Lame Liam was practically my nickname.

"When Kieran found out, he started calling me by my middle name Killian. He said that it sounded like kill 'em, and he thought it fit me better since I was so tough. It stuck, and that has been my name ever since."

Kinsley looks at me with concern in her eyes. "You said your brother *was* the best."

I nod. "When I was seventeen, I was a bit of a wild child. By then, Kieran had been away from Marysville for several years while I was stuck alone in the town. I was girl crazy. I was bored. I was unfocused. I started smoking marijuana and skipping school."

She looks at me intently, listening to my every word.

"One day, me and Summer were hanging out after school, smoking marijuana and bored out of our minds in the cornfields."

"Summer?"

"She was the girl I wanted."

I see Kinsley grimace when I say Summer was *the girl*.

"I mean, I was seventeen, so I was attracted to any woman who gave me any attention."

She smiles. "Continue your story."

"Anyway, my dumbass was restless and trying to impress Summer. Kieran was working for the FBI. That was always his dream. He was always so focused. He always had such a clear idea of what his goals were while I was clueless and wild.

"That night, I got the idea to go find him. So, I drove Summer in my pickup truck from Marysville, Kansas, to Chicago, where he was working undercover. We drove all night, but when we got to Chicago we had no idea where Kieran was. So, I called him. Told him we needed somewhere to stay."

She nods while biting her lip in the cute way she does.

"Kieran came, of course, but by then, we weren't in the best part of town. I was looking to show Summer a good time, and my stupid young self thought we could score some good party drugs while we were in Chicago. The people we were buying from just so happened to be some of the people Kieran was investigating. He showed up; I blew his cover. I joked with the drug dealers that he worked for the FBI, but not to worry he was my brother. We were cool. The men opened fire."

Tears sting in my eyes, but I have to continue. I have to tell her. I have to show her one little part of my world that I can tell her. "The image of my brother, the person who cared about me most, getting shot in the heart is an image that haunts me every day of my life. He was shot twice in the chest because I blew his cover. The guys shot at me and Summer, but they quickly took off when sirens sounded in the distance."

I remember running over to him and pressing my hands to his blood-soaked chest. I tried to stop the bleeding, but there was just... just so much blood. It was impossible to stop. I remember just telling him to hang on, to just hang on, but of course, he was already dead.

"I got my own brother killed."

Kinsley wraps her arms around me and holds me while we cry together in his favorite spot that later became my favorite spot. She doesn't try to tell me that it wasn't my fault because it was my fault. She just shares in my pain with me as tears fall down both of our faces.

"So, that's why you became an FBI agent? For him?" she asks when she is able to speak through her tears.

I nod when my tears run dry. And then she kisses me on the lips, so softly and so carefully, like she thinks she will break me if she kisses me harder.

"You can kiss me. I won't break."

She smiles. "I'm afraid if I kiss you harder, we won't make it back to the bed-and-breakfast before things get out of hand, and we get arrested for public indecency."

I press my lips hard against hers and slip my tongue into her mouth until she's moaning crazily against my lips. She pushes me away though before I can get her really riled up. She bites her gorgeous lip that I want back in my mouth.

The skies open now, as it almost always does in Ireland, and little droplets of rain begin pelting down on top of us.

"Thank you," Kinsley says through the rain.

"For what?"

"For telling me a truth."

I smile and kiss her again until the rain is beginning to soak through our clothes. Even then, I don't want to pull away because I've never felt so connected to someone in my life.

"We should head back."

She looks at me, reluctant to get up, but she shivers. So, I put my arm around her, and we walk back to catch a cab to the bed-and-breakfast.

28

KINSLEY

I'M STILL SHIVERING from the wet cold rain when we make it back to our room in the bed-and-breakfast.

Killian lets go of me and walks to the bathroom. I hear him turn the water on in the shower, and I walk in.

"It should be warm soon. I laid out a towel for you as well. Are you hungry? I can go get us some food while you are showering," Killian says.

I shake my head at this incredible man. A man who is so selfless that he chose a career based on the love he had for his brother. The guilt of thinking he's the reason his brother is dead is overwhelming him. I understand that feeling.

"I'm not hungry."

He nods. "I'll let you enjoy your shower then."

He starts to walk past me, but I place my hand against his chest, stopping him. He raises one eyebrow at me. I grab the hem of his shirt and lift it over his head. I place my hand on his bare chest to feel his heart beating rapidly, matching my own heartbeat.

"Join me."

A wicked grin forms on his face.

He peels my shirt, and then my pants, off of me. His appreciative gaze travels over my body, warming me with just his look. Suddenly, I'm not cold anymore. I unhook my bra and slip out of my panties, and his gaze somehow intensifies.

I smile and then step under the warm shower. I crook my finger, indicating for him to join me. He doesn't even wait to remove his jeans. He just steps into the shower with me, making me laugh. I quickly push his jeans down because I can't stand not to feel completely lost in him any longer. I need our bodies connected after such an emotional day. I might not have gotten any answers about why we traveled halfway across the world, but I don't really care anymore. I got so much more than answers. I got his feelings. I got one little piece of his soul, and that piece is more than enough to keep me sane until I find out more.

Killian reaches behind me and grabs a bar of soap. He begins running the soap over my shoulders, washing me. He moves slowly down each of my arms, sending shivers all over my body. He notices and presses his body against me as he continues to wash me. He slowly washes my breasts in circles. He moves the bar down my stomach and then between my legs.

I let out a gasp at his touch. And then he is moving down each of my legs, making sure to wash every inch of me. When he is finished washing me, he spins me around so my back is to him. He grabs my arms and moves them until I'm holding on to the wall of the shower, and his cock is pressing against my ass.

"I need you, princess."

His cock presses at my wet entrance.

"I'm yours."

He finds a condom in his jeans that are still in the floor of the shower, puts it on, and then he gently pushes inside me, slowly stretching me, taking his time, like he never has before. I can feel every inch of him as he moves further and further inside me until I gasp when he stretches me fully. One of his hands grabs my breast while the other moves liquid around my clit. His touches are slow and deliberate and emotional.

I feel the water falling down my face, and I'm taken back to the cliffs we were just on. Killian thrusts into me, but each thrust isn't about sexual need; it's all pure emotion. Each thrust is Killian giving a little of himself to me. Each touch is him sharing his pain and love until I'm feeling everything he is feeling, the love and the pain, until I'm not sure which one is a stronger emotion.

"I love you," he whispers against my ear.

"I love you, too."

But this, whatever we are making, is more than love. It's trust.

Killian moves faster, and I match his rhythm until we are coming together, each screaming the other's name, connected in a way we have never been before. We're connected in a way that can never be broken.

Killian hesitantly turns the water off and slides out of me. His moves are slow, as if he's afraid the connection will be broken, but nothing can break the connection we just had.

I step out of the shower and begin to dry off. I hand him a towel, which he wraps around his waist before wrapping his arms around me.

He stares at us in the mirror. "God, I could take you again right now."

I laugh. "I know. I feel the same way, like I can never get enough of you."

He nods. "We should at least try. All night if we have to."

I bite my lip. "Okay, but first, we should eat. Then, we should do that again and again."

I watch him walk out of the bathroom. I finish drying off and then meet him in the bedroom. He's already dressed when I get there. I walk over to grab my clothes out of the bag, but he puts a hand on my arm, stopping me.

"Don't get dressed."

"How will we go get food if I don't get dressed?"

"I want you to stay here, naked. I saw a pizza place across the street. I'll bring back some pizzas."

I smile.

"You stay naked. I'll be right back." He leans over and softly kisses me on the lips, and then he leaves me alone in our room.

I sigh, not sure about what I should do now. I walk back to the bathroom and gather our wet clothes. I take them back to the small closet and begin hanging them to dry. We really need to get more clothes tomorrow. I hang up Killian's jacket, but it keeps falling off the hanger. I pick it up again, and that's when I feel something stiff in the pocket. I reach my hand into the pocket and pull out a note and an envelope that I assume contains some cash. I read the note quickly that Granddad wrote but learn nothing new other then he was saving his own skin.

I flip the envelope over and am shocked to see my name on it. I carry the envelope with me as I take a seat on the bed. I don't know what this envelope contains, but whatever it is, it is something Killian was hiding from me. It's the same feeling I got when I opened Tristan's bag of cocaine.

I shiver and decide to climb under the covers, but the covers don't stop my shivers. My shivers won't stop until I open the envelope, so with shaking hands, I do. I open the envelope and pull out the thick piece of paper it contains. I unfold it until it's a flat piece of paper.

Then, I look at the handwritten words my father wrote me. I read word after word. My eyes skim faster than my mind can even read. This is what Killian was keeping from me. In this one piece of paper, I learn everything I need to know about my grandfather, my father, and even Killian.

My body shakes, and my cheeks turn red. I was wrong when I thought the connection Killian and I shared couldn't be broken. It was just broken with one lie and one secret.

I fold the paper back up and put it back in the envelope. I turn off the lights before I climb back into bed just before I hear Killian fumbling at the door. I close my eyes and pretend to sleep as Killian walks in and flicks on the lights.

I hear him walk over to me.

"Princess," he says, kissing my cheek.

"Mmhmm," I moan but keep my eyes closed.

"You should eat."

"Too sleepy," I moan.

He sighs. I hear him take off his clothes. The lights flicker back off, and then he climbs into bed. His arms go around me, and somehow, that motion still relaxes me, even after knowing that he lied to me.

"Sleep sounds good." He softly kisses me on the neck. "We can eat and fuck later."

I pull his arms around me tighter.

"When I was getting the food though, I thought about what you asked me earlier. About what I see for our future. When I was standing in line, they were selling these little Claddagh rings that represent love, loyalty, and friendship. I realized then what I wanted. You. Just you. I want to be married to you. I want to have those kids you told me you wanted. Nothing else matters."

I try to keep my breathing normal as a tear falls down my cheek.

"I know it's too soon to be thinking like that. And I'm not going to officially ask you to marry me. Not until we have a lot more answers, but I just wanted you to know that. I see my future, and I'm married to you. What do you think? Could you see yourself married to me someday after all of this is over? Would you marry me if things were different?"

"Maybe."

I feel his lips curl up into a smile. "I'll take that as a yes."

He holds me tighter, and then his breathing slows as he drifts to sleep.

But more tears fall down my cheeks. Because that *maybe* doesn't mean yes. That *maybe* wasn't me hesitating to answer him. It was me deceiving him. Because a future where we are married and living happily ever after will never happen.

29

KILLIAN

I WAKE up and reach across to touch Kinsley after not having her again like we talked about last night. I'm feeling desperate to have her, but my hand comes up empty. I sit up and look around the room, but I don't see her. I get out of bed and check the bathroom, but she isn't in there either. If she went exploring again without me, I'm going to kill her. She doesn't understand that it's just not safe for her to go out by herself.

I walk back to the bedroom to put clothes on to go find her. When I see a note written on a napkin lying next to the bed, I pick it up to read it.

Maybe...never. I read my father's letter that you hid from me. I'm sorry, but I can't be with you. I can't be with someone that lies and hides so many things from me. I'm going home. I'll face whatever charges the FBI have for me, but I'm done running. I'm sorry that I no longer love you. I hope you can find happiness with the FBI.

—Kinsley

"Fuck!" I scream when I finish reading the note. "Fuck! Fuck! Fuck!"

I crumble the napkin and throw it onto the floor. I grab my clothes and quickly put them on. Then, I run out the door and out onto the street. I have to find her. I don't know what the hell she is doing.

How can she not love me anymore when I was inside her last night? How can love disappear so quickly?

I run a block down the street before I realize this is useless. She's not just wandering down the main street of Galway.

I run back to the bed-and-breakfast. I ring the damn little bell at the entrance and wait for the owner to come downstairs.

"The lady I was traveling with, have you seen her this morning?"

The owner looks at me for a second. "Yes, she was down rather early, around six. I hadn't even put breakfast out yet, and she was already out the door. I figured she had an early sightseeing day."

"Thanks," I say before running up the stairs to our bedroom.

I look through the bag and find most of the money along with her passport are gone. "Fuck!"

I go to the closet and grab my jacket. I feel inside and find that the envelope her dad wrote her and the note her grandfather wrote is gone. She really did find it. She knows the truth. And she is turning herself into the FBI because of it. She just doesn't realize that going home isn't safe either. The men that were working with her father and grandfather are dangerous and they are in Las Vegas. They will kill her. The FBI won't be able to protect her.

I pace back and forth in the room. I pick the napkin off the floor and reread it, but none of it makes any more sense than the first time I read it. I'm still just as lost as I was before. The only thing I can read from the note is that she doesn't care about me anymore. She doesn't love me.

So, instead, I do the only thing I can do. I take my cell phone out of my pocket, and I call Agent Hayes.

"Byrne?"

"Hayes, I need..."

"You are in a lot of trouble Byrne. Bisson is furious. Just tell us where you are. Come home and then we can straighten everything out. There is a protocol you have to follow if you think a witness is in danger. This isn't it. If she really is in danger she should be in witness protection."

"I know Hayes. I just couldn't leave her with you. I don't trust anyone but myself right now. But listen! I need you to see if a Megan Slade or Erin Buffet has booked any flights out of Ireland today. And then I need you to assemble a team to pick her up if she did."

"What is happening?"

"I think Kinsley is turning herself in to the FBI. I think she's had enough of the running."

"What?"

"I'm going after her. Just tell me where she is headed, and I'll be on a flight to go after her. Can you do that for me?"

"Yes. I'll text you."

I grab a cab to the Dublin Airport, and I'm an hour away before Agent Hayes texts me, saying that she's on a flight to New York and then has a connecting flight to Las Vegas. I text back, saying I'm taking the next flight and I will be wherever she is going soon. I just hope that we get to her before her grandfather's men. She's turning herself in to the FBI, but that won't stop his men from trying to get to her first. She's in danger, and I have to protect her. I promised I would.

––––––––

The flight to New York takes forever, and it feels longer than forever when I don't know what the hell is going on. I run off the flight and am surprised to find Agent Hayes standing just inside the terminal. I figured he would have been with Kinsley.

"Did you get her?"

"No."

"No? Why the hell not?"

"Killian Byrne, you are under arrest," a man says from behind me.

Then, I'm surrounded by agents who grab ahold of me, and handcuffs go around my wrist.

"I'm sorry," Agent Hayes says.

Then, he walks away, leaving me to be arrested.

I'm sorry, too. I'm sorry I failed to protect Kinsley Felton. I failed her father. I failed Kinsley. I failed the FBI. And I failed myself. And I don't know who else is going to have to pay for that mistake.

And, now that I'm being arrested, I won't even have a chance to fix my mistake.

30

KINSLEY

I WIPE a tear from my eye at the thought of never seeing Killian again. I hate that I broke his heart, but it was the only way to protect him. What I hate worse is that I lied to him, I'm not going to turn myself in. I'm doing the only thing I can do after reading my father's letter. I'm making things right and fixing my family's mistakes.

"Boarding group three can now board," the gate agent says over the speakers.

I stand from the blue seat I'm sitting on in the terminal with my plane ticket and bag in hand. I wait in a short line until I reach the gate agent. I hand her my ticket, which she scans, and then hands back.

"Have a good flight to Cancún," she says.

I nod and force my legs to move forward. I force my body to move toward what has been my destiny all along. I force my legs to board a plane to Mexico.

The End

Keep reading for Maybe Always...

MAYBE ALWAYS

1

KINSLEY

"MA'AM, can I get you anything to drink?" the flight attendant asks.

I open my eyes and then immediately yawn. I've been flying for over twenty-four hours with minimal sleep.

"Coffee," I say. I have only about an hour left on this last flight. I need to start waking up.

"Here you go," she says, handing me the coffee.

I take it and set the cup on the tray table in front of me. Next to the coffee are my new passport and the letter my father wrote to me.

I flip the passport open again and read the name, Hannah Grove. I got the passport from the same abandoned building Killian got our previous fake ones from in Tokyo. It was risky. I didn't know if Killian or the FBI would check there. Even if they do, I paid the man almost ten times the amount the FBI usually does to ensure loyalty to me and not them. They can't know where I am or where I'm going. Although I know they will figure it out soon.

I told Killian I was going to turn myself in. When I got to the airport, I called the FBI and told them the same. I even bought a direct flight from Dublin to New York.

I just didn't get on it.

I learned from Killian the best way not to be found was to get good and lost. Change passports. Change planes. So that's what I did.

I'm not going to turn myself in. I'm going to Mexico. I'm going to end this. I'm not going to let Killian get hurt for my family. I'm not going to let him lose his job for me. I love him, and I know he loves me, but he can't keep harboring a fugitive. He can't keep protecting me and keep the job that is so important to him. I just hope the FBI will believe Killian is loyal to them and not me.

I shake my head, thinking back to my conversation with Agent Hayes.

"Hello, this is Agent Hayes."

I nervously hold the pay phone in my hand and take a deep breath. I have to tell him. I have to do this.

"This is Kinsley Felton."

Agent Hayes sucks in a breath on the other end of the phone, but his voice is calm when he speaks, "Where are you?"

"I can't tell you that. All you need to know is that I'm buying a flight back home. My flight gets in at eight tomorrow morning at LaGuardia, and then I have a connection to Las Vegas at nine. I'll cooperate. I'll do whatever you want."

"Is Agent Byrne with you?"

"No. He's been tracking me. I saw him in London, but he didn't find me. He's the reason I'm turning myself in. I can't keep living my life, running from the law."

"That's good, Kinsley. Just get on that flight. We will meet you in New York and fly back with you to Las Vegas. Then we can talk. You aren't in any trouble. We just want to talk."

I know he's lying. He doesn't just want to talk. He wants to arrest me and my grandfather. If only he knew how much bigger this is than just money laundering and tax evasion. It's much bigger. And I'm the only one who can put a stop to it.

"I'll be on the flight," I say.

. . .

I sip on my coffee. I don't know if Killian has a chance at staying in the FBI's good graces, but at least he will be safe in the US and not here, trying to protect me. No one can protect me. As much as my father thought he could, no one can. My family is too involved. And as much as I want to just abandon my family, I need to make things right. After I figure it out, I can save Killian's career by making him seem like the hero.

I unfold the letter my father wrote and begin reading it for the hundredth time.

My dearest princess,

If you are reading this, I am no longer with you, and I'm so sorry about that. There is nothing more I wanted than to spend forever with you, protecting you from what I now must tell you. I need you to know, even after you've read the last word on this page, I love you princess. I love you more than everything else in my life even if I wasn't always able to show you.

I don't know how to tell you this, but I have to. I'm not a good person. Your grandfather is worse. Your great-grandfather might have been worse than him. We aren't casino and hotel owners. Not at our hearts. We are criminals. We like greed and money above everything and will do anything to keep it.

By now, you might have found out we are money launderers. We don't pay our fair share of taxes. We have lied and cheated our investors out of money. And, while that is all true, it was just a cover for what we really do.

I can't believe I'm even going to tell you the worst of it because you will never forgive me after I do. You will hate me, and your hatred for me will be valid. I won't be there to defend myself, but you deserve to know who your family is. You deserve to know the truth.

So, here it is. We are smugglers. It started off small. Drugs and guns in small amounts, but it quickly grew. We realized we could make more money doing that than we ever could running hotels and casinos. Then, we found reinvesting the money into our casinos and hotels would make us even more money and keep our real activities hidden.

But the smuggling of drugs and guns soon grew so large, we got even greedier. We wanted more. Always more and more. We never had enough.

So we grew to smuggling jewels, diamonds, anything of value. And that satisfied us for a while until we found out what our partners really wanted, what they would pay top dollar for.

People.

They wanted us to smuggle people.

Our immediate response should have been no, but we couldn't say no because we were in too deep. And, to be honest, we didn't want to tell them no. We wanted the money and excitement that came with smuggling. So, it made no difference to us if we were smuggling drugs, guns, diamonds, or people. They were all the same to us.

I realize now it was a mistake. But, at the time, it was just our next adventure, an adventure we passed down from generation to generation. From son to son.

I didn't realize how wrong it was until I had you, and my world changed. At first, I thought I could pass the company to you along with all of our illegal activities, but we quickly realized that wouldn't be a possibility. You were too delicate to take over. You would have ruined everything we worked so hard to build.

So, instead, we thought we could pass it on to your husband. But we would have to choose your husband very carefully to ensure we could pass the company on to him.

Finding you a husband became our new mission. Tristan was horrible. We knew he was a druggie and couldn't be trusted around drugs, so we set him up. Of course, that turned into a mess when you were caught with the drugs instead of him. But, in the end, it all worked out. He was gone from your life, and you gave us the deciding power to choose your next boyfriend and who your husband would be. It couldn't have worked out better.

We let you date Eli because he was harmless, but we knew he would never work out.

And then I met Killian. Killian was perfect. Strong, decisive, and loyal. He would do anything I asked of him without a second thought. And I asked a lot of him.

He was strong enough to run the company and keep up with the illegal activities, while still protecting you from them.

We thought we had found the perfect solution.

Except we hadn't. I found out he was FBI. I was going to have to kill him, a man I had grown to love as a son. I was going to have to shoot him in cold blood.

Now, you need to know I've killed before, so it wouldn't have been an unusual thing for me to do, but I've never killed someone I thought would one day be my family, someone my daughter would someday marry.

But I had no other choice. The day came when I had to kill him. I had the gun. I had Killian alone, but I couldn't do it. I couldn't kill him, but if I didn't, we were all as good as dead. You were as good as dead. I couldn't have that.

I had to protect you. That became my obsession. I would do anything to protect you.

So, I made the decision to sacrifice myself and your grandfather to keep you safe. I told Killian I would give him everything he needed to put us away in prison if he swore to keep you safe. He promised, and I believe him.

I haven't told him everything yet, but I will. All he knows about is the money laundering. He's gained my trust though, so I can now tell him the rest. Now, I can tell him everything, and he can help me nail these guys, but it will be at the cost of me and your grandfather going to jail. We deserve it though. And I would do it all again to keep you out of harm's way.

But, if for some reason I die before I get a chance to tell Killian everything, you have to tell him. You have to give him this letter. You have to let him protect you. Promise me, princess, that you will be safe. Your safety is the only thing that matters to me.

I included the address to our main smuggling facility in Mexico at the bottom of this letter. I've already laid the groundwork to make sure Killian will be accepted as my successor. He will be able to gain access, and call in the FBI to arrest everyone involved.

I'm so sorry, princess. I hope you can forgive me someday, but I don't know if you will be able to. I'm sorry, but you will be safe.

. . .

All my love,
  Dad

I wipe away a tear. I cry each time I read the damn letter.

I didn't even know my father. I knew nothing about him at all. He wasn't a nice, caring father. He was a criminal who ruined who knows how many people's lives.

If he thought I was going to just let Killian come in and fix all my family's problems, he was wrong. There is no way I'm going to let the man I love risk his life to protect me. Not when I know there is a real chance Killian could be killed if he tried to arrest any of these men. I can't let him die while protecting me, even if it is his job as an FBI agent. I won't let him do that. Not on my account. Not when his cover has been blown.

No, I have to find a way to infiltrate them myself. Once I have evidence that we really do smuggle people, then I can call in reinforcements to arrest everyone.

I fold the letter back up and put it in my pocket. I put the tray table up and sit in silence as the plane lands before I go through the long process of exiting the plane and going through customs. Then, I'll be off to form a plan in a nice hotel; the last nice hotel I might ever stay in.

If only I could find a way to contact my grandfather, then I could easily put an end to this, but I don't even know if he will be in Cancún when I land.

I don't have a choice though. Even if he isn't there, I have to go to the address my father provided. And, when I do, I will be the criminal. Despite my good intentions, there will be no distinction with the law. The FBI will arrest me if I make it out of there alive. And being with Killian will no longer be a possibility. But at least he will be alive and free to continue working as an FBI agent while I pay for my family's sins.

2

KILLIAN

I FEEL the cold metal handcuffs go onto my wrists, and then it becomes real. I'm being arrested. My career is over, my life is over, and all because I fell in love with a woman I was never supposed to love.

Agent Hayes grabs my arm and begins leading me through the airport.

He's talking to me, but I'm not listening to him. I'm too worried about Kinsley to listen to the meaningless words coming out of his mouth. I already know why I'm being arrested. I'm being arrested for helping her when I shouldn't have.

I made a promise to Kinsley's father that I would protect her above everything else. I would have protected her anyway. And, now, I've failed. I failed the second I let her out of my sight.

Hayes leads me outside to an unmarked black SUV, the same type of SUV I've driven criminals in before. I climb in and realize how uncomfortable it is to sit in a car with my arms stuck behind my back. Hayes buckles me in before climbing into the front seat. I'm surprised when he begins driving without a partner in the seat next to him. He's not following protocol.

I sit up straighter. "Where are we going?"

Hayes glances up to the rearview mirror to look at me. His eyes look sad. "FBI office."

My shoulders slump. "Hayes, you have to listen to me. Kinsley is in trouble. We have to—"

"I know she's in trouble. She said she was going to turn herself in, and then she didn't. Now, she is officially a fugitive. She's facing a lot of jail time."

"That's not what I'm talking about. She isn't safe. You have to let me go. She could die."

Hayes shakes his head. "You don't understand, Byrne. You are in a lot of trouble, too. The office thinks you were harboring a criminal. A criminal you were supposed to be prosecuting. Under the Patriot Act, you could go to jail for life without a trial."

I glare at Hayes. "I thought you were my friend. I thought you were going to help me and keep silent about what you knew."

"I tried. Kinsley called me when I was in Bisson's office. With our boss over my shoulder, I didn't have a choice. He heard everything. And then you called. I had no choice. If I didn't arrest you, they would have arrested me."

"Why aren't you following protocol then? You know you will be reprimanded for not having a partner when arresting a fellow FBI agent. What is the point?"

Hayes's eyes drift down to the steering wheel. "I wanted to talk to you alone. I know I'm the only person who might be able to talk some sense into you. This girl isn't worth losing your career over. You barely know her."

"She's worth protecting though."

"Only because you love her."

"No..."

"No, you don't love her?"

"No, that's not the reason she's worth protecting. She's naive yet strong. Loving yet ruthless. A princess and a warrior. She is a perfect contradiction. But, most importantly, she is innocent and in danger. I don't know about you, but I took an oath when I took this job. I promised to protect the innocent and those in danger."

Hayes sharply turns the wheel. We turn the corner before pulling to a stop in an alleyway. For a second, I think maybe he is letting me go, that I've convinced him, but when he turns to face me with anger on his face, I know he's not going to let me go.

"She's not innocent, Byrne. She's a criminal, just like her family. If she were innocent, she would have been on that flight back home. If she were innocent, she wouldn't have lied to me about where she is going."

"She was lying to protect me!"

"Why would she protect you? She's the one who supposedly needs protection, not you."

"Because that's what she does. She protects the people she loves, no matter the cost."

Hayes sighs.

"You have to let me go, so I can go after her. She could die if I don't."

Hayes narrows his eyes at me. "I can't."

I drop my head, knowing he is my last chance to get free. My last chance to save her.

"Why does she need protection?"

I raise my head again. "Because her family is involved with dangerous people, and she is going to try to stop them. She feels responsible for her family's actions and feels she has to be the one to resolve them even though she carries none of the guilt herself."

"What are you talking about? You went undercover with this family for five years. You never found out anything other than the money laundering, did you?"

"No," I lie. "I never found anything else out."

"Then, what makes you so sure now? She could be lying to you. She could just be setting you up so she and her grandfather have time to hide somewhere we will never be able to find them."

I shake my head. He doesn't get it. He will never get it. I have to find another way to save her.

Hayes' eyes study mine for a long time. The longer we sit here, the angrier our boss, Bisson, is going to be when we finally get to the office. He will think Hayes did something. He will think Hayes is helping me. I can't let that happen. Hayes doesn't deserve to be punished because of me.

"Just take me to the FBI office."

Hayes runs his hand through his hair. "I don't know why I'm going to say this, but I believe you. You obviously believe the girl is in trouble, and I believe you. I can't let you go though, but I can go after her myself. Where is she?"

I stare back into the eyes of the only friend I have at the Bureau. My only friend. But I don't trust him. I can't tell if he is using a technique just to get me to confess where she is or if he is genuinely concerned and will go after her without telling the FBI. So, I keep my mouth closed. I can't trust him. I can't trust anyone but myself when it comes to Kinsley's safety.

"I'm disappointed in you, Byrne," Hayes says. Turning back to the wheel, he begins driving again.

We drive the rest of the way to the FBI office in silence. Hayes parks the car in front of the large building and then walks over to my door. He unbuckles my seat belt and helps me out. He holds on to my arms as he pushes me inside the office building I have walked into countless times of my own volition, but now, I am walking in while under arrest.

I watch the stares as we walk to the elevator. Each person who sees me is one more person I never want to see again. Each person's face wears the same expression—disappointment. Everyone is disappointed in what I did. In their eyes, I let the Bureau down, and I'm a criminal.

Everyone has always thought I am a mess-up. Since the day my brother died, I have been trying to fight the stereotype, but today, I've proven them right.

God, I can't think about what my father is going to say when he finds out I've been arrested. He will really think he has no sons left. It's preferable to thinking your only child left is sitting in jail, possibly for the rest of his life.

The elevator doors close, and then it's just me and Hayes in the elevator. Hayes presses the button for the third floor. He doesn't look at me, and I don't look at him. When the doors open, Hayes pushes me out in a stern and forceful way that is all business. I'm nothing to him, just like every other criminal he has arrested.

He leads me into the interrogation room where I know I will sit for the rest of the day. The FBI will then put me in the holding cell overnight and bring me back to the interrogation room in the morning. I'll go back and forth until they think they have gotten all they can from me. Then, I'll be sent to prison where I'll have no chance at escape, no chance at saving Kinsley.

Hayes removes the cuffs before leaving me alone in the room. I rub my sore wrists, just like I've seen the criminals who have been brought into this room before do.

I can't think about me though. All I can think about is where Kinsley is and what she is doing. She must have found the letter. I searched everywhere in our room in the bed and breakfast and couldn't find it. I was stupid enough not to read it earlier, so I have no idea what it says, but it must have said enough of the truth to make Kinsley feel like she has to go set everything right.

I just don't know if it gave her a clue as to where she should go. If it did, I'm afraid it's going to send her to Mexico, to the one place in the world she shouldn't go. It isn't safe. And I can't do a damn thing about it.

The door opens, and my boss is standing there—well, my former boss. I'm sure, at the very least, I've been fired for my actions. He walks slowly over to the table. He sits down across from me, and I see a cup of water in his hand.

I smirk. I wasn't sure if he was going to be the good cop or the bad cop. I guess he is going with the good cop routine, which will make Hayes the bad cop. The idea of that makes me laugh.

Bisson pushes the water across the table to me. "It seems you have gotten yourself into quite a predicament, Byrne."

"Yes, sir," I say automatically before I realize all the niceties in the world won't help me now.

"I want to help you, Byrne. You are going to let me help you, aren't you?"

"I don't think you can help me."

He smiles. "I can. See, this whole thing boils down to one simple question and one simple answer. Do you want to be an FBI agent, or do you want to help a silly girl? If you want to be an FBI agent, you will answer anything I ask you, which is simple really. Where is the girl?"

"I don't know where she is. She lied to me, the same as she did to you."

Bisson narrows his eyes at me, trying to determine if I am lying or not.

I don't want to do it, but it might be my only chance at gaining his trust. So, I reach into the back pocket of my jeans and pull out the note Kinsley wrote. I hand it to him and then stare down at my hands while he reads the short letter.

On the surface, the letter makes it seem like I am nothing to her. At the heart of it though, it says how much she really loves me because she wouldn't have lied to me if she didn't love me. She thought she was giving me my life back and keeping me safe.

She's wrong though. I don't have a life without her. I don't care about being an FBI agent anymore, no matter how much it hurts to think that. I feel like I no longer care about my brother every time I think that, but it's the truth. I'm not meant to be an FBI agent. I suck at this job. All I care about now is keeping Kinsley safe.

"You don't know where she is?"

I shake my head. "No. I thought she was coming back here. I thought the same as you—that she was turning herself in."

In the back of my mind, I know where she is. I know what her father's note said without reading it—the truth.

Robert Felton loved his daughter above everything. That is the one thing I know to be true about that man. So, that note told her the truth.

I know exactly where she is—Cancún, Mexico, the last place I ever wanted her to go—and there is nothing I can do about it.

I look up at Bisson, who is intently staring at me. He's trying to determine if I am lying or not, but I know he can't read anything but my desperation for a girl I love but can't save.

He gets up from the table. "Think about it some more. Think long and hard about where she could be. Then, I'll be back."

I watch as he walks out the door, leaving me alone in the gloomy room. Its only goal is to make me feel so depressed that I tell them everything I know. I can't though.

Instead, I think about Kinsley. I think about her red lips and short locks that somehow embody the strength that now encompasses her. I miss the naive girl who was so innocent and sweet that she would do anything for her family. After she faces what I know is coming, there won't be a drop of that girl left. She won't survive if I can't find a way out of here.

3
_____

KINSLEY

I FEEL the warm light shining into the room despite the dark shades. I open one eye and realize the shades don't close fully, allowing the sun to peek through the cracks. I sigh. So much for sleeping the day away.

I pull the white linen sheets over my head and roll over, but that lasts all of five minutes. When I can't fall back asleep, I get up. I grab a robe hanging in the closet and put it on over the tank top and underwear I slept in. I haven't bothered to buy any additional clothing, so I'm stuck with just two outfits and two pairs of underwear.

I walk over to the shades and pull them open before walking out onto my balcony. I take a deep breath, smelling the salty air that comes from being so close to the ocean. The waves are calm this morning, as calm as I feel even though I should be a wreck.

I don't know what time it is. I could walk back inside and see, but the time doesn't really matter. I know I can't go to the address in the middle of the day. I have to wait until darkness settles in. That means I have all day to enjoy the beach, the drinks, and the food. I have one last day to enjoy the beauty of the world before I experience how dark it truly can be.

I walk back inside and find the room service menu. My eyes

immediately go to the pancakes, doughnuts, and muffins, but then I think of Killian. He wouldn't order any of that crap, especially not if he needed to feel strong and fearless later. I need my strength. I skim the menu, looking for something Killian has fed me, but I don't find anything. The healthiest item on the menu is an egg-white omelet with spinach and goat cheese. I order it and a coffee.

I walk into the bathroom and decide to take a quick shower to wash away all of my travels while I wait for my breakfast. I turn the hot water on and take off my robe and underwear. By the time I'm done undressing, steam has filled the large bathroom.

I step inside and am immediately filled with memories of the last shower I had with Killian. I suck in a breath as I remember his hands traveling across my smooth stomach before grabbing my breasts. As the water streams down my chest, I can practically feel his hands there, torturing me and turning me on with his touch until I'm panting hard with need.

I close my eyes and let my hands travel over my body. I massage my breast, doing my best to imitate Killian's strong touch that drives me wild. I let my hands slide down my stomach to my pussy.

I find my clit, just like he would, and I massage myself in torturous circles, slowly letting my body grow with lust, before I move my hand faster in tight circles.

I picture his strong smirk, his lips on my neck, his thick erection pressing up against me, begging for attention but not giving into his own needs until I'm satisfied first.

And then he whispers something dirty in my ear just as I come all over his hand. I come as I picture it.

I keep my eyes closed after I come, trying to keep Killian with me for as long as I can. But I know I have to open my eyes and let him go soon. I have to focus on what I need to do. I set him free. I can't bring him back into my mess of a life.

A knock on the door forces my eyes open and requires me to say good-bye to the Killian I brought back into my life through my dreams.

I turn the water off, despite the fact I didn't shampoo my hair or wash my body like I'd planned. I grab the towel and quickly dry off before putting the robe back on.

"Coming!" I yell toward the door as I exit the bathroom. I run my hand through my newly cut short locks before I open the door.

One of the hotel employees is standing with a cart of food. "Where would you like it?"

"On the balcony," I say.

I hold the door to my suite open while he carries a tray of food in. I then find my purse to pull out a couple of dollars.

"Gracias," I say, handing the tip to the man before he exits my room.

I walk out to the balcony and take a seat in one of the two chairs. It's hard, seeing an empty chair sitting right next to me. Killian should be here. No one comes to resorts like this alone. People only come here with their significant others or families.

I sigh and pull the lids off the two plates of food. A single tear falls down my cheek at the sight in front of me. One of the plates is the omelet with fruit on the side, like I ordered. And the other plate has an assortment of pastries I didn't order.

It's like Killian is saying it's okay to have a little sweetness with my healthy breakfast. It just makes it all the harder to do this without him. I have to though. I want him to be happy, and he would never be happy with me if it meant giving up his job with the FBI.

I pick up the plate with my omelet and then add a doughnut to it. I smile at the food that is a little bit of me and a little bit of Killian. It's perfect.

I spend most of the rest of the day eating on the balcony, napping, and looking at the calm ocean that brings me even more peace the longer I stare at it. I wish this were my life—just sitting on the beach, enjoying the warm weather without a care in the world. If I survive this, I'm going to spend least a month on the beach. Even if I have no money after all this is over, I don't care. I'll find a way to just sit here until I forget every horrible thing my family did.

When the sun slowly begins moving closer to the horizon, I get up from my chair and head back inside. I find my new cell phone I bought when I first got here. It's a pay-as-you-go phone no one should be able to track. At least, I don't think anyone can track this number to me. I dial my grandfather's cell number and wait, but no one answers.

It was a long shot. I wasn't expecting him to answer. He wouldn't have known it was me. He doesn't know I'm here. I just hope he is here. I need to convince him I'm on his side, or my plan will never work.

I end the call and try calling Killian's cell. I'm not going to speak if he answers. I just want to hear his voice. I just need to know he is okay and back in the US, back with the FBI. I did everything I knew to do to make that possible. I just need to know my scheming didn't go to waste.

I wait though, but there is no answer. I try his number one more time, but there is still no answer. *Damn it!*

I need him. I need to know he is okay, that he is going to move on. Instead, I got no answers. Instead, I just have to hope he will find a good life without me. I expect the FBI will continue the investigation, but I don't expect him to come running in here, like he would have before. He thinks I hate him. He wouldn't go out of his way to help someone he hates. I gave up on us. I just hope my words were strong enough he won't come after me, not beyond what his job requires anyway.

I walk back outside and watch the sunset. It's beautiful here. I could just stay here. No one would find me, not for a long time anyway. I would be safe here, but the world wouldn't be. Not as long as my family is out there, smuggling and killing.

I walk back in and put on the same clothes I wore the last night I had with Killian. I grab my purse with my cell phone and leave the rest of my belongings. I won't need them, not where I'm going.

I head downstairs. I try my best to soak in the beautiful modern lobby full of color and life, but I can't. I'm too focused on my mission to enjoy the last beautiful thing I might ever see.

I walk outside the hotel into the muggy air and dark sky that is getting darker by the second. The streets are still busy with people—

some heading in from the beach, others just beginning to go out for a night of partying. I envy them, all of them—the families, the couples, the kids. I would easily trade my life for any of theirs.

I walk three blocks to a shopping mall I saw when the cab dropped me off at the hotel. I duck inside the first store. I don't know why, but I feel like I have to change. I can't wear the torn jeans and ratty shirt. I have to make a good first impression. I have to come off as strong and independent if I want them to believe me, and I won't be either of those things if I feel weak or if I'm thinking about Killian.

I walk up and down the racks of clothes. There are several things that would do, but I don't pick any of them up. I realize I'm stalling. I know this is the last step before I call a cab and walk into what is most likely going to be a suicide mission.

So, I force myself to pick up the next suitable outfit—a pair of black leather pants and a black halter top that will make my boobs look good.

I take them into the dressing room and slowly strip out of my jeans and T-shirt. I take my bra off and then slip on the pants and halter top. I was right. I look good in this. I'm lucky my body type looks good in most anything since designers make clothes with my body type in mind.

My ass looks good stuck in the tight pants, and just enough of my nipples is pushing against the thin fabric to make any man who looks at me melt in my hands.

I fluff my hair, pull my red lipstick out of my purse and apply it. I look hot and strong. It's the best I will be able to do. All I need now are some heels.

I gather up my clothes and head back out to find some heels. I easily find some and then check out, paying with cash. I'm still carrying my old clothes when I leave the store. I hold the clothes up to my nose and take a deep breath. I can still smell Killian's scent on them—a mix of expensive cologne and sweat I couldn't mistake for anyone but Killian. It's the last thing I have of him, but I have to let it go.

So, I walk over to the nearest trash can and reluctantly toss the clothes into the bin. And then I walk away before I change my mind and dig the clothes out of the trash. Before I change my mind and put Killian in danger.

I pull my phone out to call a cab. I'm surprised my hands aren't shaking as I dial the number. I expect to have butterflies swarming around in my stomach, but there are none. Whatever happens, I know I'm doing the right thing.

Ten minutes pass before the cab pulls up, and I climb inside.

"*Adónde*?" The cab driver looks to be in his early forties.

I pull up the address I have saved on my phone and hand it to him.

"Here," I say, pointing to the screen, knowing my Spanish isn't good enough to communicate where I need to go. And I don't know if his English is good enough for me to communicate with him either.

The man immediately begins shaking his head. He pushes the phone back into my hands. "No, no, no, *señorita*. I can't take you there. No safe."

I frown at him. "I have to go here."

"No. You go there, you never come back."

I sigh. I know the man is right, but I don't have a choice. I need him to take me there. I dig in my purse and pull out enough money to triple what the fare will be.

I hand the money to the man. "Take me there."

He shakes his head again. "No, no." He shoves the money back into my hands. "Stay at one of these hotels. Whatever your troubles, the hotels will fix them. Not that place. That place only brings pain."

I don't know how I'm going to get through to this man, but if he knows so much about this place, there is a good chance all the cab drivers know about it, and none will take me.

"*Señor*, please. I have to go there. My family has done some bad things there. I don't believe anyone will hurt me. Not if they know who I am. My name is Kinsley Felton, and I have to make things right."

When I say my last name, I watch as his eyes widen with fear, and it rips through my heart. I didn't think we were bad people. I thought we were a good business family. Maybe that's what we are known for in the US, but here, it is clear we are known as vile, vicious people who deserve to die for what we have done.

He begins driving and doesn't say another word. I stare out the window and watch as the sky grows from dark to complete blackness. I watch the pretty lights of the hotels disappear as we drive farther and farther away from the tourist area and into the heart of the city.

The city seems nice, just like any other city I have ever been in, but then we turn, and my worst fears come true. We drive into what looks to be an abandoned part of the city, except I know it is anything but abandoned. It is full of a dark evil I never imagined existed.

The cab driver slows as we grow closer to our destination. His eyes glance into the rearview mirror, showing sorrow, pain, and hatred for me and for what my family has done to these people and this town.

He stops outside the worst building of them all. It's tall and dark and looks completely uninhabitable. The door is barely hanging on the hinges. The windows are mostly boarded up. The roof looks like it could collapse at any second.

I get chills just from looking at it. This is where my father, my grandfather, and my great-grandfather would come to do unthinkable things. This is where they came, so this is where I shall go.

I hand the money back to the cab driver, but he shakes his head. He doesn't look at me. Instead, his eyes are focused on the door in front of us. A door I will soon enter and might never return from.

"Please, take it," I say, my voice strong.

"No, *señorita*. I can't take your money."

I sigh, but I leave the money in the backseat. Surely, he will take the money after I leave.

I slowly get out of the car. My feet in heels are unstable while walking on the gravel, but I walk steadily anyway toward the door, my destiny.

I think about my father. I hate him. I hate him for what he did. I hate him for writing me the letter I left in the hotel room. I couldn't bring it with me.

He supposedly wrote the letter to protect me, to keep me safe. He wrote it to ask for forgiveness.

It's all bullshit. He didn't write the letter to protect me. He wrote the letter because he knew I was the only one who could put a stop to everything. And he knew if he told me not to go, I would. He wrote it because he thought I could save him from his sins. He was right.

I take a step forward and then another and another. My anger overtakes any fear and keeps it buried deep inside me.

I glance up and only see the moonlight shining down on me. The cab driver drove away the second my feet hit the ground. I'm all alone.

I walk up to the abandoned building. I don't have to do this. It's not my responsibility to put an end to this. I don't even know if I can put an end to this. I don't even have a very good plan. My plan is based on convincing everyone I want to follow in my family's foot-steps. Then, I'll either convince my grandfather to put an end to it or call the police once I've infiltrated them, know who all the players are, and have evidence against them. It's a terrible plan, but it's all I have. And I'm not turning back now.

I walk to the door and press my ear against it, trying to hear anything inside. I hear nothing but silence. *Is anyone even here? Could I be wrong? Could this address be an old one?* It might be too late. They might have already moved on to a new address I might never be able to find.

I try to decide if I should knock or just open the door and head in. Neither seems like a good option, but I decide it is better to be invited in than to walk around a dark building until someone finds me.

I just need to tell them my name. As soon as I do, they will have to listen. I don't know who is the boss in all of this, my family or someone else, but I do know if they want to continue working with my family, they will have to hear me out.

So, I move my ear from the door and force my hand to form a fist.

Then, I knock as loudly as I can against the wooden door. I wince when the sound echoes in the alleyway. I glance behind myself to see whom I might have pissed off, but I don't hear a sound, and I don't see anyone. I turn back to the door and don't hear any movement inside.

I wait a few minutes and try knocking again.

Nothing.

Damn it!

I was wrong. I'm out of clues. I'm at a dead end. If they aren't here, I have no idea where they are. I have no idea where to find them. Everything I just did was for nothing.

I turn and walk away from the door while digging in my purse to pull out my cell phone. Now, I have to convince a cab driver to pick me up here. *Yeah, that's going to happen.* I glance down at my heels that now look like a terrible choice now that I have to walk to a safer area before I can get a ride back to my hotel.

"Don't move," a deep voice says.

My heart skips a beat at the sound. I drop my purse. *Shit.*

I steady my breathing and open my mouth to speak. "I'm—"

"Shut up, bitch," the man says as he presses a gun into my back.

I close my eyes. I'm going to die before I even had a chance to speak.

I gather myself and try again though because I know it is my only chance at surviving long enough to get inside. "I'm Kins—"

"I said, shut up!"

That's when I feel something hard come into contact with my head. My last thought is of Killian and his beautiful grin that is only for me. How I yearn to see it just one more time, but now, I never will.

4

KILLIAN

"BREAKFAST!" the officer yells as the door to the cell opens.

I don't move though. Instead, I close my eyes and turn over in bed. I've been in this jail for three days now. And, for three days, I've barely existed. I haven't eaten. I haven't showered. I haven't shaved. I haven't watched TV or read. And I haven't heard anything from anyone.

The only time I even seem alive is in the afternoon when I get an hour to make as many phone calls as I want. And, even though I know my calls are being monitored, it hasn't stopped me from trying to call Kinsley and her damn grandfather who got us both into this mess. It hasn't stopped me from calling my parents or Hayes. I've tried them all, but none of them answer. None of them give me any answers or peace.

So, when my time is up, I slump back to my bed and spend most of the day thinking.

I think about how the hell I'm going to get out of here. How the hell am I going to fulfill my promise to Robert Felton if I'm in here? How the hell am I going to protect Kinsley? I can't lose another person I love because I was stupid or too weak to save them. I won't survive. If Kinsley dies, even working for the FBI won't bring me any comfort or purpose in my life, not that they will take me back.

I just don't want to keep living if she is dead. I've already thought about ways to end my life in here if she dies. There are so many ways. It would almost be too easy. There's hanging. I could get into a brawl with one of the gangs. They would easily seek their revenge on me. I could overdose on drugs. I could slit my wrists with a razor. Or I could starve myself to death. I have so many choices.

I realize now what jail does to people. I've been here for only three days, and I'm already choosing death over living in here. Just three days without her. That's all I can bear.

I shouldn't be thinking about death. I should be thinking about how to get out of here and how to save her. But the truth is, even if I find a way out of here, even if the FBI lets me go today, there is a good chance she is already dead.

I grab my head as the painful thoughts overtake it, bringing such sharp pain that it is almost impossible to tolerate. I try to wait for the torment to disappear again, like it always does, but each time I think about her, it takes my brain longer and longer to push out the pain. I can't keep living like this much longer.

She's dead. I know it. She's dead, and I will be, too, as soon as someone confirms it. I'll be gone.

I just don't know when or if I'll ever find out the truth. I haven't even been told how long I will be in here. I don't know if I will have to face a trial or if the FBI are just going to use some national security law to keep me locked away. I know nothing, so I choose to do nothing but sleep.

I've tried talking with the FBI. I've tried reasoning with them. I've tried to explain that Kinsley isn't guilty, that I'm not guilty, and that we have to save her because she isn't safe. They won't listen to anything. All they want to know is where she is so they can bring her in, but they don't understand that by moving in, it would let the criminals that work with Kinsley's family know the FBI is there, and they would kill her before the FBI had a chance to save her.

"Here," my roommate says, tossing some things onto my stomach.

I open my eyes, despite the pain I still feel in my head at the thought that Kinsley is most likely dead. If she went to Mexico, she's dead. Even if her grandfather is there, it won't matter.

I look at what the man threw me. A protein bar, a bag of Doritos, and a banana now lie on my stomach.

I sit up in my bed and look at my cellmate. I still haven't asked his name, despite sharing a cell with him for three days now. I run my hands through my hair, not understanding why he is giving me any of his food.

"The breakfast here is shit. Just tasteless oatmeal." He nods in my direction. "Eat. You'll need your strength if you are going to survive in here."

I unwrap the protein bar and take a bite. I know I can't turn down the food he paid for even if the food he's offering me isn't much better than what the jail serves. Who knows what he did to get this food in the first place.

The first drop of the protein bar hits my stomach, and my body roars to life. I feel the ache in my core for the first time since I've gotten here, and I feel each bite of food ease the pain. It just makes me eat faster. I finish the bar and quickly move on to the banana. And, when I'm finished with the banana, I tear into the Doritos despite the fact they have no real nutritional value. They might as well be little pieces of cardboard. But when I taste the first bite of the cheesy goodness, I forget about that. It tastes better than any vegetable or healthy piece of meat I've ever eaten.

"Thanks," I say with a mouthful of Doritos.

The man nods but doesn't say anything. He just sits in the chair across from my bed, waiting until I'm finished chewing. That's when I realize maybe I shouldn't have taken the food. He might think I owe him something for consuming his food.

"I'm Santino Marlow," the man says when I'm finished.

"Killian Byrne," I say, extending my hand.

The man just stares at me like he has no idea what I'm doing. I pull my hand back. *Fuck, I'm an idiot.*

"I'll pay you back for the food."

He smirks at me. "No need. That was nothing to me."

I nod.

I have no idea what this guy wants. He looks like a majority of the other men in here. Tattoos cover his muscular body. His head is shaved. He looks like he belongs in here. So unlike me. I stick out like a sore thumb in a place like this.

"It's not what you think," he says.

"What?"

"The reason I'm in here. I'm not a druggie. I don't sell drugs. I didn't steal shit. I'm not in a gang."

"Then, why are you here?" I ask, risking getting punched.

But hearing this guy's story might just be the distraction I need to get me through today. At the very least, it would reduce the pain I feel right now.

"I'm in here because of a girl."

My eyes widen.

"And I suspect it's the same reason you are in here."

I nod.

"The key to surviving without the girl you love is to talk about it. It will kill you if not. I tried to keep it buried inside. I thought, if anyone in here found out, they would think I was a pussy, and I'd get jumped. The opposite happened though. They understood because every guy in here has a girl at home. Everyone has a bitch they miss."

He pauses and takes a bite of an apple I didn't see he was holding in his hand.

"I'm in here because my girl disappeared. Vanished. Nobody knows where she is." He shakes his head. "They think I did it just because we fought. I didn't do it. I wouldn't lay a finger on her." He looks up at me. "The key to not thinking about her is to keep busy."

He stands and motions for me to follow. So I do.

"We have time in the yard this morning. You play ball?"

I shrug.

"Good."

I follow Santino out to the yard and find a concrete basketball court with two hoops that are barely standing upright. A dozen men or so are already involved in a game. One man shoots but misses the hoop entirely.

"Get out of there, Kenny," Santino says to a scrawny man that can't be much older than eighteen.

The man obediently walks off the court, like he's too afraid not to do exactly what he was told. I understand the feeling. Outside, I felt powerful and in control. In here, I have no powers. I barely even understand the rules.

"Who's this?" a man double my size says to Santino.

I'm not going to let Santino answer for me.

"Killian. Here to play," I say.

He glares at me. "Can you?"

I take the ball from his hand, and then I dribble and shoot what should be a three-pointer. The ball goes in with ease.

I turn back to him. "I'll be taking Kenny's place."

I spend the next hour on the court. It feels good to be running and sweating again. Although I'm not the best player on the team, I pull my weight enough not to get treated like Kenny. My team easily wins.

Santino was right. Distraction is the best way to spend my time here. As long as I'm doing something, I'm not thinking about Kinsley. I'm not living in constant agony.

I grab a cup of water and take a seat at one of only two benches near the court.

Santino walks over and takes a seat next to me. "Tell me about your girl."

I sip on the water. "She's the same as your girl. She disappeared. The only difference is, I know where she is. I just can't tell the FBI. If I do, she will die." I take another sip of my water. "She might die anyway if I don't get out of here."

Santino nods, staring straight ahead, as he sips his water. "I might be able to help you with that," he says without looking at me.

"What? How?"

He shakes his head as a guard walks onto the court.

"Tomorrow," Santino says, getting up.

But I don't think I can wait till tomorrow. If he has a way out of here, even an illegal one, I need to take it now. I can't wait till tomorrow. Tomorrow, she could be dead.

The guard walks over to me. "Killian?"

"Yes."

"Come with me. You have a visitor."

I follow the guard even though I don't want to, not now that I have hope.

5

KINSLEY

I OPEN MY EYES, but it is still as dark as when my eyes were closed. I try to grab my pounding head with my right hand but find it handcuffed to something large and metal behind me. My left arm is free though, so I use it to massage my temple, trying to ease the pain. It helps a little, but I know I'm going to have a headache for weeks from where the man hit me in the head with the butt of his gun.

I try to look around the room to get a bearing on where I am or how long I was knocked out. I don't have a clue though. It could have been minutes, hours, or days. The room tells me nothing. There are no windows to let me know what time of day it is.

I shiver and move my arm away from my head, wrapping it around my body to try to warm myself up. I wish I had brought a jacket, but I never thought I would need one in the heart of summer in southern Mexico—that is, if I'm still in Mexico.

My heart rate increases at the thought, instantly warming me just a little. I could be anywhere. They could have taken me anywhere. And, if I'm not in Mexico, then I'm completely and truly fucked.

My grandfather knew about the place in Mexico. Killian knew about the location. Somebody could have helped me if I needed them. But not now. Now, I'm on my own.

My eyes slowly begin adjusting to the darkness, and I start to make out a little bit of my surroundings. There is a door across from me—wood and sturdy. It couldn't be easily kicked in, like the main door to the building. The rest of the room is small with four walls and a wooden floor.

I'm attached to a heavy metal pipe. I test the strength of it, but I know there is no way my scrawny arms could bend it. I test the handcuffs, but I don't have a clue how to pick a lock or get them off. I'm stuck where I am, sitting on the wooden floor with one arm attached to the pipe that juts into the wall.

There are no windows. There is no other exit, other than the door. There is no way out for me. I'm entirely at these people's mercy until they decide what to do with me. Until they decide if I get to live or die. I swallow down those thoughts though. I can't think about them. I have to be strong.

I try to think of all the times I've been strong. None come to mind. All that comes to mind is when I've been weak, naive, and gullible. Even Killian said I was naive.

I shake my head. But he also thought I was strong and capable of running the company. He loves me. He wouldn't love someone he saw as just a meek, little girl. I've grown. He's helped me, and I've grown stronger than I ever imagined I could.

I can do this. I will survive this. I will put a stop to this.

A man's voice yells, followed by another man's even louder voice. Both are muffled, just beyond the doorway.

I startle at the sudden sound, as I got used to the silence. I strain my ears, trying to listen, but all I understand is the men are mad and arguing. I hope they aren't arguing over whether to let me live or die. I strain my ears trying to listen, but the voices quickly fade into the distance.

I try to close my eyes and sleep. Despite having been knocked out, I'm still exhausted, and my head is pounding. There is nothing else to do but sleep anyway. I move until I'm lying down on the hard floor and then force my eyes closed, despite the fear that I will never get the chance to open them again.

———

The door is thrown open, blinding me with light from the hallway and thrusting me from my dreamless sleep. The light just makes my head hurt worse.

"Eat," a deep voice says.

I hear two things drop in front of me.

The man immediately turns.

"Wait!"

The man doesn't listen. He keeps walking.

"Wait! You need to know, my name is Kinsley Felton."

The door closes though. He didn't hear me.

A tear rolls quickly down my cheek. I wipe it away with the back of my hand. I will not let my fear overtake me. Next time that door opens, I will shout my fucking name over and over until the message sinks in.

I look around the room again, but the darkness is too much. My eyes need time to adjust before I can see again.

I reach forward into the darkness, trying to feel what the man brought me. I feel a bowl and pull it to me. I feel around in the bowl but don't find any silverware. From what I can tell, it's rice and beans.

I scoop some into my hand and bring it to my mouth before I realize this might not be the best idea. It could be poisoned. I could die if I eat this. My stomach growls, letting me know it hasn't been fed in a long time. I could die if I don't eat it. And it doesn't make sense for them to poison me, not when a bullet is so much easier.

I force the food into my mouth, like an animal would. The food is cold, but despite the temperature, it tastes amazing. It's just beans and rice, like I suspected. I don't care though. It's food, and with each bite, I feel my strength coming back.

I quickly eat every morsel in the bowl. My stomach feels full and satisfied as the last drop of food goes down. That's when I realize how thirsty I am. I reach forward and find a bottle of water sitting next to where the bowl was. I unscrew the top of the bottle and gulp the whole thing down.

I glance around in the darkness. Now that I'm finished, I wish I had taken my time because there is nothing left to do but sleep or stare into the darkness while plotting all the ways I want to kill these men.

The door bursts open again, and from what I can tell, the same man from before walks to me.

I don't hesitate this time. "I'm Kinsley Felton! Kinsley Felton!" I repeat over and over. "I'm the daughter of Robert Felton. The granddaughter of Lee Felton. They sent me here."

The man bends down and releases me from the handcuff holding me in place. My immediate thought is to run, but I can't. I'm supposed to want to be here. I need them to trust me, not think I'm going to run away. I wouldn't make it far anyway—not in my heels, with my pounding headache, or with this man's strong hand holding my arm so hard I want to cry from the pain.

I don't though. I just keep repeating, "I'm Kinsley Felton." It's almost a battle cry against the pain now pulsing through my body.

"Shut up, bitch," the man says, hitting me hard on the head again.

I immediately shut my mouth as the room begins spinning. I don't know if I could chance saying another syllable. If he hits me on the head again, he could do some permanent damage, I'm sure.

The man begins walking, dragging me through the door, before I'm steady on my feet.

"Walk," the man says, shaking me like I'm purposely struggling to walk instead of doing my best to walk through the dizziness and headache.

I try to steady myself and keep up with his pace, but I can't. So, instead, I stumble as he drags me down the bright hallway. I try to glance around the hallway to figure out where the exits are. To figure out where I am. I look around the building that seems less broken on the inside than the outside, but I have no idea if I'm in the same building I knocked on.

The man turns left, heading down another hallway. I turn my attention to him. I need to study every person here. When the time comes to turn them over to the FBI or police, I need to know who is involved and what their jobs are. This man is tall. It's hard to tell how strong he is, but the grip on my arm tells me he has plenty of strength. His skin is whiter than mine, and his hair is blond and unkempt. Honestly, when I look at him, he looks like a typical American man in his jeans and T-shirt that fit a little tighter than they should.

We stop in front of a door that he knocks on calmly and steadily. It seems out of character for the man who seems to have no patience.

"Come in," a deep voice says.

The man holding on to me opens the door, pushes me in the room, and then steps in behind me.

"Sit down." A man sitting behind the desk in front of me points to the chair in the center of the room.

I quickly take a seat, thankful not to be standing in my dizzy state any longer. I glance around the room that is much larger than any other office I have been in before. At least a dozen men are standing against the walls, smirking, grinning, or glaring at me.

I try to remain calm and strong as I turn my attention back to the man behind the desk. He's tall, his skin is darker than mine, and his hair is almost as long, but it's his piercing, ruthless eyes that have me trapped. He's only wearing a dark T-shirt and jeans, nothing that says he has any authority here, but his eyes command the attention of the room. He walks around the desk and then leans against it while he curiously looks at me.

I open my mouth to speak, but then I think better of it, as the man who hit me before is still standing right behind me, and I can't take getting hit again.

"My name is Nacio Marlow. I run this organization you see here." He gestures to the men at his sides. "These are my men."

My eyes drift from side to side to the men who are intently listening to him while staring at me. Each one of them looks like he could kill me with just his bare hands.

"We have never had an uninvited guest here in the ten years we have been working from this location." His lips curl up into a psychotic-looking grin as he walks to me. He grabs my chin as he looks into my eyes. "So, what is a pretty girl like you doing here?"

This is my chance to tell him. To convince him I am on his side. To convince him I am a ruthless Felton, just like my father and grandfather before me. This is my chance to save myself, to keep myself breathing for another day, but instead of speaking, I freeze. I open my mouth to speak, but nothing comes out—not one word, not even a breath.

Nacio frowns and walks back to his desk. "Persuade her, Seth," Nacio says to the man standing behind me.

My eyes immediately close as I wait for another knockout hit that will leave me feeling like a vegetable when he is finished with me. It never comes though. Instead, I feel the end of a gun pushing into my temple. The feel of the cold metal pressed against my head is enough to knock me out of my frozen spell.

I take a deep breath. I have to play this right. I can't seem like a scared, naive girl begging for her freedom. I try to channel all of my inner Scarlett, my best friend that has all of the confidence in the world. I stare straight ahead at Nacio, ignoring the gun pressed against my head. "I suggest you have your goon remove the gun from my head."

Nacio cocks his head to one side with a smug grin on his face. "And why would I do that, sweetheart?"

"Because I'm Kinsley Felton, daughter of Robert Felton, granddaughter of Lee Felton. And, if you don't remove the gun from my head right now, I will make sure the Feltons never work with the Marlows ever again. I will make sure that we destroy the Marlows."

Nacio's eyes read fear for just a second, not long enough for his men to notice. Not long enough that I'm even really sure of what I just saw, but enough that I know the fear was there. His family fears mine.

I glare at him, my eyes focusing intently on his, even though I want to smile because I know I'm not going to die today. Today, I'm going to live. Today, I'm going to become the next one in charge. Today, I'm going to take over a smuggling ring.

But Nacio doesn't give the signal for Seth to lower his gun. The gun is just as firmly pressed against my head as it was a second ago.

And my fear returns.

I don't let it show though. I can't. If I do, I know I'll be dead.

A wry smile appears back on Nacio's lips. "Excellent. Now that we have found all of the Feltons that are left, it's time to kill them."

6

KILLIAN

I DON'T KNOW who is going to be sitting across the table from me when the door opens to the visitation room. The guard guides me into the room. Hayes is standing in the corner, and I'm not surprised. Not at all. I didn't expect my family to travel out of Kansas. I don't have any other friends, other than Hayes. I'm not sure I'm allowed visitors even if I did. I think a small part of me was hoping it was Kinsley. Even if it had meant her going to jail, it would have meant she was still alive. Still safe for another day.

Hayes looks at me as I enter. His eyes are red and puffy, like he's been crying. His body looks worn down, almost broken. He's wearing his typical suit all FBI agents wear when not undercover. If I didn't know any better, I would think he just came from a funeral instead of the office.

"Who died?" I ask sarcastically as I sit down at the table.

Hayes doesn't sit. Instead, he looks out the small window for a second. "You can leave," he says to the guard.

"I have to stay, sir. It's protocol," the guard says.

Hayes pulls out his FBI badge. "I have classified FBI business I need to discuss. Leave," he says.

The guard frowns at Hayes. "At least let me handcuff him to the table."

"That won't be necessary. He will be leaving the jail in an hour or two anyway."

The guard hesitates for a second longer and then leaves.

"I'm leaving, huh? Found me innocent or taking me to a high-security prison? Or maybe you think you can get me to talk about Kinsley in exchange for my freedom?"

"Shut up, Byrne."

"Why am I here, Hayes?"

Hayes runs his hand through his hair and then takes a seat across from me. "Because you were right."

My eyes widen. "What do you mean, I was right? You found Kinsley? Her grandfather? What else do you know?"

"Yes, we found them. And we probably know about as much as you do now."

"Where are they? Is she safe? Do you have her in custody?"

Hayes looks down at his hands. He won't meet my eyes. And I know it's bad. They have her—the drug lords, the smugglers. The monsters have her. And the FBI is breaking me out, so we can go after them.

He finally glances back up at me, somberly, and I swear, I see a tear in his eye.

"She's dead, Byrne. They both are."

I fall back in my seat. My hands go to my hair, grabbing my pounding head. I can't process what he just said because she can't be dead. She can't be.

"She's not dead," I say.

"Killian..." Hayes never calls me by my first name, making me wince. "She's gone. We found her body this morning along with her grandfather's and mother's. Well, what's left of their bodies."

"Show me."

Hayes shakes his head. "I can't do that. You wouldn't be able to get that image out of your head if I showed you."

"Show me," I demand. "I need to see what they did to her. I need to see that she is actually gone to believe it."

Hayes reluctantly reaches into his pocket and pulls out his cell phone. He scrolls until he finds the picture and then slides the phone across the table to me. I pick it up.

I thought I could handle it. I've seen enough crime scene pictures of bodies that are more horrifying than this. But this rips me apart— seeing Kinsley, her grandfather, and her mother burned to pieces. They almost look unrecognizable, but I know it's Kinsley. In my heart, I knew they would kill them once they knew the FBI was investigating them. It gets too messy for them to keep Kinsley and her family alive. I just don't know who *them* is yet. But I plan to.

I can't hold it together any longer as tears streak down my face while I look at what is left of my beautiful princess.

"How did she..."

"Gunshot wound. She must have died instantly. They burned her body after she was already dead."

I know his words are supposed to comfort me. That she died instantly. That she wasn't in any pain. It doesn't comfort me. Nothing ever will again.

Nothing.

Tears fall faster now, and I wish Hayes wasn't here. I hate feeling weak in front of someone else, especially him, but as I glance up through my tears, I see he is almost just as torn apart by her death as I am. So, we both just cry across from each other. Not connecting or trying to comfort the other. But still sharing her death all the same.

Hayes stops crying. My tears stop long before I have come to terms with my grief. Still, when my tears dry up, Hayes takes the time to talk. Like that is something I am capable of right now.

"I'm going to get you out of here."

Hayes waits for me to respond, but I can't. I don't care if I live the rest of my life in here or out there. It will feel like a prison to me either way.

"You can't work for the FBI again. They don't trust that you will follow their commands, which is all they care about. They think you'll go rogue again. In fact, they want to give you a security detail until we close the case and make sure you are safe. You can't go after them though. You would just get yourself killed, too. You have to let us handle it."

Hayes pauses to allow me time to promise him to let the FBI handle it. I won't promise him though.

"You should go home. Your family is worried about you. Even your father is worried."

I look at him now, not understanding. "My father?" I croak through my dry mouth.

He nods. "They are at the FBI office, waiting for you. Both of your parents are a mess. They just want you to come home. Your father said he couldn't lose another son."

I nod, although I can't believe my father still cares about me. I thought going to jail would effectively end our relationship, not be the thing that brought us back together.

"Killian, are you listening?"

"Yes."

"Good."

"I should go. I have a lot of paperwork to do to make sure you get out of here this afternoon."

I nod.

Hayes walks over, picks up his phone from the table, and pats me on the back. He doesn't say anything as he walks away. He doesn't have to. I can feel how sorry he is. And this isn't his fault.

This is my fault. I was the one who promised to protect her. I was the one who failed. I am the one who failed. She's dead, and it's my fault. Just like it's my fault my brother is dead. I bring death to everyone I meet. That is why the world would be better off if I were dead. Then, I couldn't cause anyone else to die. Then, those I loved would be safe.

The guard comes back into the room. He reaches down and grabs my shoulder, and I stand as he pulls me up. He puts the handcuffs back on and guides me back to my cell where my handcuffs are removed. Then, I'm left alone. Santino is gone.

Now is the time to kill myself. To get rid of the pain I know I'll never be able to escape from now that she is really gone.

But that's no longer what I want. Those thoughts are completely gone from my mind, despite the pain being worse than when my brother died. When he died, I wanted to kill myself, but I realized quickly that dying wouldn't help my brother. My penance was working for the FBI and taking over his role. But the real reason I took the FBI job was to go after his killers. I thought working for the FBI would let me get my revenge. It didn't.

Now, that's all I see. *Revenge.*

I have to go after her killers. I have to end their lives. It's the only way I will find peace. I can't protect her any longer, but I can protect the future Kinsleys of the world from a few less monsters.

My anger overtakes my body. I grab the bedding off my bunk and rip and tear it apart until it's a pile of shreds on the floor. I grab the pillow and rip it open, pulling the stuffing out and ripping it apart. I try to calm my anger so I won't start a fight with someone while I'm still in jail. If I do that, I might never get out. Or I might end up killing an innocent man.

My blood is pumping fast and warm through my veins as I grab Santino's bedding as well. He might kill me for this, but I don't care. I don't think. I tear his bedding to pieces, just like mine. The fabric so easily bends to my will. Just like the men who hurt Kinsley will as soon as I find them. They will be wishing they were dead pieces on the floor by the time I am done with them. Because death is not something I will give them, not until they have experienced every pain known to man. Because that is the pain Kinsley experienced. That is the torture I am going to face every day until I die.

"She was yours," Santino says as he leans against the door to our cell.

I narrow my eyes as I toss the last piece of stuffing onto the floor. "Who?"

"The girl who is all over TV. The daughter of the billionaire casino owner. She was your girl."

"Yes."

I glance past him, and that's when I see the TV showing nonstop coverage of Kinsley, her grandfather, and her mother. It will be all over the news for weeks. A beautiful girl like Kinsley will be hard for the news crews to just drop the story without answers and outrage from their viewers.

I watch Scarlett in tears on the TV. And I see that the news outlet even have Kinsley's ex-boyfriends, Eli and Tristan, coming on next. They'll have any person who ever spoke to her on. Every grocer, mailman, and neighbor who ever spoke to her will come on and speak. It brings me some comfort to know she won't easily be forgotten. Even though she's dead, she won't fall from everyone's memory. She will live on. That's why I have to live—to keep her memory alive when the media has moved on to the next scandal.

"Still want a way outta here?" Santino asks.

I incredulously stare at him. I have a way out now. A way out where I can see my family. Where I can find out what the FBI knows about what happened to Kinsley even if they won't let me stay on. A way where I will be watched like a hawk and have no chance at ever getting my revenge.

But, if I go with Santino, I will be a fugitive. The second the FBI finds me, they will send me back to jail. But, if I get my way and end the men who killed Kinsley, I will be a fugitive anyway. Either way, I will end up back in this jail—no, in prison for the rest of my life. At least, if I kill them, my heart will be able to rest.

I look at Santino. I have no idea why he is offering to help me or what payment I will have to pay for my freedom. I don't even know if he can get me out of here. But I know I have to take the chance.

"Yes, get me out of here."

A slow grin curls up his face. "Wait here," he says before he vanishes.

I look at the mess I've made and begin tossing the torn sheets back onto the bunk beds. If any of the guards see this, they will think something is up and reprimand us. I can't take the chance, not when I'm so close to freedom and revenge.

I toss the last piece of stuffing back onto the bed when Santino returns.

"Let's go."

I follow him out of our cell, but I wish I knew what the plan was instead of just blindly following him. Now, I am completely at his mercy, and I have no idea who else might be involved in the plan.

As we near the edge of the main room where we all hang out, a fight breaks out across the hall.

"Shit," I say under my breath. Now, we will never get out of here. The place will go into lockdown for the rest of the day, and we won't get a chance again because Hayes will be getting me out.

But, when I look at Santino, he isn't fazed at all. It's part of the plan, I realize. But who would be willing to pose a fake fight and possibly be in here for longer just to help two other men escape? It makes no sense.

Santino ducks inside the kitchen, and I do the same. The kitchen is crazy with people pushing carts of food in and out of the building. It's shipment day. The one day a week when the food for the whole jail is brought into the building, and everyone is busy pushing carts in and out as fast as they can. Prisoners and guards and chefs are all busy with moving things around. No one is paying us any attention.

Santino walks to the far side where a large empty crate sits, ready to be moved out of the building.

He opens the door to the large crate. "Get in."

I climb in without a word, and Santino climbs in right after me. We don't say a word as he closes the lid, and darkness covers us.

We both sit in the darkness, not moving, not speaking, barely breathing, for fear we will be found. Eventually, the cart starts moving. We are rolled out of the building and up a ramp to what I assume is a truck. We stop for a while, and then I hear the truck moving.

We drive for hours. We drive so long that the tears at losing Kinsley come back. I let them out, knowing Santino can't see me in the darkness.

The truck eventually comes to a stop. To my surprise, Santino climbs out. He doesn't wait until whatever man driving the truck is gone.

I climb out after him.

He lifts the door to the back of the truck and jumps out. I follow.

"Thanks, man. I owe you one," I say.

Santino stops and looks at me. "I was hoping you would say that. Because I'm supposed to deliver you to my brother."

Fuck, I think as I realize where I know Santino from. It's the last thing I think before losing consciousness.

7

KINSLEY

FUCK. I was wrong. They are going to kill me.

I close my eyes and wait for the trigger to be pulled. At least the pain in my head will be gone when I'm dead. And at least Killian will be safe.

I wait one...two...three seconds, but nothing happens. The trigger isn't pulled, and the gun isn't lowered.

Maybe I'm already dead? Maybe this is an illusion?

I open my eyes, expecting to be floating above my body that must be broken and bloody on the floor. Instead, I'm sitting in the same position. I glance up at Nacio, who is grinning wildly at me. He's won, and he knows it. I gave him a drop of fear, and he ignited it. He had no intention of killing me—at least, not yet—but he's just proven he has the upper hand here. Not me.

He laughs, and then all the men in the room are laughing along with him. My cheeks flush in embarrassment.

I push the gun away from my head and stand, finally able to breathe again. I walk over to Nacio with a tight glare on my face, showing I don't appreciate his games. I can't let him win this fight, not when my life and the lives of those I love are on the line.

He stops laughing and smugly looks up at me.

"I didn't come here to play games. I came here to take my father's place in the company."

Nacio grabs the neck of my shirt and jerks me forward until my face is inches from his. His grip around my shirt tightens, making it hard for me to breathe.

"I don't play games either. Don't threaten my life, and I won't threaten yours."

He releases me, and I can breathe again. My heartbeat has just gone through a roller coaster of ups and downs in a matter of minutes, and I'm not sure it can survive much more without suffering a heart attack. It's no wonder my dad died from a heart attack if he had to deal with people like this on a daily basis.

He begins walking to the door before he turns and looks me up and down. His eyes lust over the curves of my chest then ass in the tight clothing. "Follow me, princess." His voice is harsh.

I don't react when he says, princess. At least I do everything in my power not to react when I want to cringe in disgust. I don't want it to become his pet name for me.

I walk toward him as confidently as I can in my heels as I toss my grungy hair behind my shoulders. I feel every man's eyes in the room on my ass. If it weren't for my time modeling, I would be completely disgusted by the thought. Now though, I know it's my greatest power to control these men, and I'm going to use it.

I pause for just a second when I reach Nacio. "It's Kinsley. Not princess. Not sweetheart. Not baby. I am none of those things to you."

I strut past him out the door and into the hallway. I don't wait for him. I just keep walking down the hallway, hoping I will be able to find my grandfather or find out more information about the operation.

I hear Nacio yell at his men to get back to packing.

And then he is right at my side. "Slow down, sweetheart," he says in his slick voice.

I roll my eyes at his childish games. "I thought we weren't playing games with each other."

His grin widens until it covers his face. It's a grin that might usually make my knees weak if I didn't know what kind of monster lies beneath the wicked smirk. And if my heart didn't still long for another grin. A grin that puts Nacio's grin to shame. A grin that only I cause on Killian's face. Not like Nacio's that is probably given out to every girl he sees.

Just thinking about Killian makes me want to run out the door and forget why I even came here, but I can't.

"Not games, but if we are going to work together, I think we should be on friendlier terms than first names, sweetheart."

Nacio touches my neck, and I freeze. He's flirting. He's known me all of five minutes, and he's already flirting. He doesn't even know if he can trust me yet. I suck in a breath, trying to decide if I should let him flirt or if I should flirt back. It might make it easier to get him to tell me everything, to get him to trust me. But, as his slimly hand strokes my neck, I know I can't. I can't fake attraction for him. I'm not a good enough actress. So, instead, I go for controlling bitch.

I slap his face as hard as I can. I watch as his face turns away from me, and his hand goes from my neck to his cheek. He turns back to me. But his face doesn't wear a surprised look. Instead, he's grinning like he was expecting that reaction all along, and somehow, being hit makes him more attracted to me.

"I think you and I will get along well, sweetheart."

"Show me around, and take me to my grandfather. And don't touch me again without asking, or I will cut your balls off in your sleep."

His grin widens. "This way, sweetheart."

I sigh. At least he decided to settle on sweetheart instead of princess. It still sounds disgusting falling from his twisted lips, but at least he doesn't get to taint the term that is Killian's and my father's name for me. At least I can still have that.

"These rooms serve as our offices. At least the men who are high enough to need an office and aren't just doing the grunt work."

"Should I be introduced to the other men in charge?"

Nacio stops walking and sternly looks at me. "No, I'm in charge. You've already met my right hand, Seth. And my younger brother will be here soon. Other than that, you don't need to worry about getting to know the other men."

I nod although I don't like it. I need to know the name of every man who has any power in this company. If not, when I call the police to move in, some of the men could run and start this over again somewhere else. I won't let that happen.

"Still, if I'm going to be running the company, don't you think I should know all the names of our employees?"

He shrugs. "Not really. I don't even know most of their names. The less we know about each other, the better. Most don't stay long anyway."

I pause at a cracked door as chills roll through my body. I feel a connection to this room. I don't ask Nacio for permission as I push the door open. He doesn't say anything as I walk into the large office. I switch the light on and watch as it flickers to life.

A desk sits across the way, just like in Nacio's office. Several chairs sit in front of it. I look to my left and find a nice leather couch against that wall. I hesitantly walk over to the desk, afraid of what I'm going to find, as every nerve in my body ignites.

I pause when I get to the desk and run my hand along the solid wood surface. A computer and two picture frames are all that sit on the desk. I reach out and touch one of the frames. I know whose office this used to belong to before I glance at the photo.

I turn the frame so I can see the photo of me riding on my father's shoulders. It is the same frame sitting in my father's office in the casino in Las Vegas.

This office was my father's. I immediately want to scream and cry. I hate that my father has an office in such an awful place. I want to destroy this office, just like I did to his office in Las Vegas. I can't though, not without letting Nacio know I hate my father instead of love him.

Nacio puts a hand on my shoulder in what is meant to be a comforting manner, but it just creeps me out. I haven't even seen the man do anything horrible yet, but it still gives me the creeps.

"Your father was a good man. He's been missed. I hope you can fill his place. I would hate to lose you, too."

I suck in a breath at his threat. "You won't be disappointed."

"Good."

"Will this be my office now?"

"No."

He walks out the door without another word, leaving me confused. I follow him out and try to keep pace as he picks up speed until we reach the staircase.

"Where will my office be?"

He shakes his head. "You haven't earned an office yet. Nobody gets to the top without doing the grunt work first. Nobody, not even if they have the last name Felton."

He begins up the stairs two at a time, and I follow at a more leisurely pace, not liking what he just said.

"Where is my grandfather?"

"He's not here."

I narrow my eyes. "What do you mean? Where else would he be? He's not in Las Vegas."

"They are at a different location."

"They?" I stop in my tracks, wondering if my father isn't really dead.

"Your grandfather and mother."

I try not to react, but I know my eyes widen just a little. I didn't think my mother was involved. I thought she might have been the most moral person in our family. But nothing truly surprises me anymore about my family. My father and grandfather are rotten, horrible, vile people. So, why not my mother, too?

I nod, as if I remember now. "And where is the other location?"

He shakes his head. "You haven't earned that information yet."

I frown.

Nacio turns from me and begins walking again. "These are the men's barracks." He gestures to the rooms on either side.

"We haven't had a girl stay with us in quite a while." He stops and smirks. "Well, not one we didn't plan on torturing, raping, or killing."

I frown in horror. *God, I'm not going to be able to keep this up.* He is going to find out that I'm not up for this. That I'm only here to destroy him. He doesn't seem to notice my reaction. Instead, he turns back and walks to the door on the far end.

"But since we have already started moving several of our men to the other location, this room is empty. It's yours while you are here."

The door is already open, so I step inside the large room that contains six sets of bunk beds. They don't appear to have been occupied for a while. But there is a stench that hovers about the room. The sheets on the beds don't look like they have ever been laundered, and dirt and mud cover the floor. At least I will have my own room though. At least I won't have to worry about one of the men getting too friendly in the middle of the night. I doubt Nacio sleeps in anything this bad. From the looks of him, he is accustomed to nicer things.

"If it isn't up to your standards, you can always sleep in my bed, sweetheart."

I shudder at that thought. "I'll make do."

"Good. Now, let's get down to business."

I nod. The sooner we get down to business, the sooner I'll be done.

He gestures for me to follow him, and we begin walking again.

"As you probably already know, our operation has been compromised. The FBI found out about the money laundering, and there is a good chance they know about our operation as well."

I nod.

"We are working to put a stop to the FBI coming after us."

"How?"

He ignores me and walks back to the staircase. He begins walking higher and higher up the stairs until I'm sure we can't safely climb any higher in this rickety building. He leads me down another dark hallway that has men standing outside each of the doors.

"We need to fake your deaths."

I twist my hair as we walk. I hate this hallway. Chills inch over my body with every step we take. I don't understand why, but I know something dark is here. Something that brings more pain than I can even understand.

"Why?" I ask, turning my attention from the hallway and back to Nacio.

"So the FBI will stop investigating. We will give them bodies. We will lead them to this place where they will catch some lowlifes we have left behind, who they'll think were in charge. But then it will lead to a dead end. Meanwhile, we will be safe to move our operations elsewhere."

My mind is spinning as he talks. I'm trying to understand why we need to fake our deaths. "How is it even possible? Even if we give them bodies, won't they know with DNA testing those bodies aren't us?"

Nacio sighs, like he has been explaining something very simple to a three-year-old. "No."

He turns his attention away from me. The man guarding the door we have stopped outside of moves to the side as Nacio grabs ahold of the doorknob.

Everything inside of me is screaming not to go through that door. To run. To go anywhere but here.

Instead, I watch as Nacio pushes the door open, and I force my legs to walk in after him.

The first thing I notice is the stench. It's not the same as the one I smelled in what will be my room for the next few nights. This room smells worse, if that is possible. It smells of urine, vomit, and...blood.

It's a dark, small room, much like the room I was held in earlier. It just makes me even more nervous.

Nacio stops a step or two inside the room. I stop just behind him, too scared to look around him, at what I'm sure is on the other side of him.

Nacio looks from the floor to me and then back to the floor. "Yes, you will do perfectly," he says to the floor.

He looks back at me, and I can see it. I can see excitement and lust in his eyes. I don't understand what has gotten him so excited, and I have to know. I have to understand what I'm really dealing with.

I take a step forward and to the side so I can see what Nacio was looking at. My body must turn white at the sight. My hands are cold and clammy. My heart stops beating at the sight that proves such evil exists. Evil I didn't think could ever exist, not even in the darkest corners of hell.

The sight before me is not something I ever imagined seeing.

A woman lies naked on the floor—or what is left of a woman. She doesn't try to cover her nakedness when she sees that other people are here, looking at her. Instead, she just lies on the ground with emptiness in her eyes.

One of her arms is tied to a post in the corner of the room, but I don't see the use in tying her up. She looks far too weak to even lift her head, let alone try to break out of this place.

Her body is thin, far too thin, with bruises and blood covering most of her body. From the amount of blood and bruises covering her, I suspect at least her ribs and one of her arms are broken. Her hair is dirty, but I guess it was a beautiful shade of blonde at one time.

I stare into her eyes, hoping I can give her hope if I can get her to look at me. She doesn't look at me though. I'm not even sure if she notices I am here. Instead, her blue eyes are glazed over to the point I'm not sure if she is really even here.

Nacio turns to me. "Ready for your first test?"

Alarmed, I look at him. I don't know what he is going to want me to do to this woman, but I can't hurt her. She's so broken anyway.

I open my mouth to tell him that when I see a dark piece of metal in his hand. He lifts the gun until it's pointing at the girl, and he pulls the trigger.

8

KINSLEY

I STARE at the woman who now has blood pooling from her head. It's an image I will never get out of my head for as long as I live. She will forever haunt me.

I don't remember what I did when he pulled the trigger. Did I scream? Or freeze? Or cry?

I don't know as my feet follow his down the hallway that holds more people. Any of whom could be killed in an instant. On a whim. Just because Nacio wants them dead.

I hate myself for not doing something to stop him. To save her. I should have realized why he brought me to that room. To kill a woman who looked like me, so he could leave her for the FBI to find. I should have known. I should have stopped him.

My only solace is maybe that is what the woman wanted. Maybe she was ready to die. Maybe he put her out of her misery. She was beyond saving. But, even if that were true, it wouldn't make my part in all of this any better. I could have stopped him, and I didn't. I might as well have pulled the trigger myself.

I continue silently following Nacio until we reach his office. I watch his body bubble with the excitement from a kill. I watch him crack his neck when he reaches the door of his office, as if killing helped to release whatever tension he was feeling.

I hate him.

I should kill him.

I can't though. There is no way I could kill anyone, not even him. I'm too weak to handle that. But I already did, and the thought creeps into my head. I didn't pull the trigger, but I let that girl get killed. I didn't even know her name. I will never know her story, and now, she's just gone, and her family will never know what happened to her.

He walks into his office and picks up a cell phone from his desk. He dials a number and waits. He's not looking at me. He must have forgotten I'm even here.

"I need you to go up to room eight. Take the body and prepare it with the others to be dropped off at the location." He pauses and listens to whoever is on the other end of the call. "No! I need it done within the hour."

He pauses again as he turns. He sees me, remembering I am still here.

"Just get it done." He puts the phone down.

"Sit," he says to me.

I look at the chair in the center of the room. The chair I sat on with a gun pointed at my head. There is no way I'm sitting in that chair again. Instead, I pull a chair from against the wall up to his desk and take a seat. He takes a seat in his expensive-looking large leather desk chair across from me.

He stares, studying me. I try to remain as blank as possible. I know, if I don't, he is going to put a bullet in my head, just like he did that girl.

"You didn't react how I thought you would."

I try to force a smile onto my lips, but it is no use. I don't think I'll ever find a reason to smile again. "How did you think I would react?"

"I thought you would scream. I thought you would cry. Or I thought you would pass out from the shock. I didn't expect you to react so..."

"So?"

"So unfazed by it all. Like you knew it had to be done and just accepted it."

I tuck my hair behind my ear. "I'm not the naive girl you think I am. My father taught me to be stronger than that." None of the words leaving my mouth are true.

I don't know how he's drawn the conclusion he has. I am anything but unfazed. I'm a mess. I'm very fazed, but I can't let him know that.

He cocks his head to the side, like that is going to make a difference in how I look, and he studies me for further clues.

"The first kill I saw was when I was twelve."

My eyes widen. "Why so young?"

"My father began grooming my brother and me to take over when I was ten. He thought that was a good age to get started." He chuckles. "I didn't have a clue what was happening when I was ten. I was a punk who thought it was cool, smuggling drugs and things that gave us lots of money to have the best cars and the best houses. I didn't understand, not until I was twelve."

I watch his eyes glaze over as he goes back to wherever he was that day.

"It was a building, much like this one, that we were operating from at the time. I was being a smug punk, like always. A new guy, who was working for us, came in, and I harassed him to no end even though he had already been punished and was barely clinging on to life. Told him he had to do whatever I said because I was the boss's son. My father wasn't in the office that day. Your father was the one watching over me. He saw me harassing this man.

I had no idea why this man was on the verge of death. All I knew was that he had to do whatever I said, or I'd get to kick him. It was fun. It was a game to me. I didn't understand I was messing with someone's life.

"Your father, he couldn't stand it any longer. He took his gun out right in front of me and shot the man square in the head. I cried at the sight of the lifeless man lying on the floor."

I raise my eyebrows at him.

"I was twelve, so, yeah, I fucking cried like a baby. I didn't understand why your father had killed the man. When I finally settled down, he told me the work we did wasn't a game. It wasn't fun. We took from people's lives in order to better our own, and the sacrifice of those who had to die along the way deserved respect. That if I wanted to be the boss, I would have to face death on a daily basis, and until I was ready for that, I shouldn't order people around. That day, I stopped being a punk and became a man."

Tears stain my face. I can't hold them back. Nacio can just think that seeing someone die right in front of me is finally catching up to me. Or that I'm crying over missing my father instead of crying over the man my father was.

"I guess he prepared both of us to take over the roles we would one day have to do here. It was just in different ways. He showed me the truth while he protected you for as long as he could."

To my surprise, he hands me a tissue. I take it and wipe my eyes.

"It gets easier, watching it happen. It gets better and better until you begin to find death as beautiful and enjoyable as life. And then, after the first time you kill, it gets hard again. And then so, so much fucking better."

I can't listen to his words. His words suck. I can't imagine watching someone die getting any better. I will always think of it as horrible. I don't want killing someone to get any better. It should never get better.

"I have some more arrangements to make. You can head to the first floor and grab some dinner."

I stand, ready to get as far away from Nacio as possible.

I make it to the door before he speaks again, "The first test isn't over. You've done well so far. Don't fuck it up."

I don't give him a response. I just turn from the door. I don't know what he means, that my first test isn't over. I know he doesn't trust me. But I don't know what he expects me to do.

Run. He expects me to run. That is my first instinct as soon as I leave his office. No one is here. No one is watching me. I could run. I could run away. I could go to the police and tell them where the location is and hopefully put an end to as much as possible.

But, if I ran, the next location would be safe. My grandfather wouldn't have to pay for what he did. My mother wouldn't have to pay. Nacio's brother and all of the men who have already moved wouldn't pay. And all the people at the next location wouldn't be safe. I can't run.

I glance to the corner of the hallway and see a security camera sitting in the corner. I couldn't run even if I wanted to. There is no way they would let me. I would end up dead. Just like the girl.

I catch my breath and then begin making my way downstairs. I'm surprised by how few people are moving around the building. I guess they have all moved on to the next location. All the more reason to stay.

My stomach growls as I make my way toward where I assume the kitchen is. It smells like tacos. It smells like heaven.

I stand just outside the door to the kitchen and listen to the men talking. I don't know how I'm supposed to go in there and eat with them like this is just a usual night for me. *How am I supposed to do that when every man in there has smuggled drugs and people? When they have killed or at least watched people being killed?*

I shake my head. *How am I any different?* I just watched a woman die. And I'm here. The only difference is, I'm not going to let them keep getting away with it.

I step into the kitchen, and the voices stop as everyone's eyes turn to me. My initial reaction is to smile politely at them, like I would if I were entering a boardroom. But I don't know how I'm supposed to react to a bunch of killers.

I smile politely at them and then walk over to the kitchen where there is a pot of meat and a tray of taco shells.

I grab a paper plate from the stack at the end and then place three shells on it. As I put meat in the shells, I feel everyone's eyes on me. I turn from the kitchen to the long table only a third filled with men.

I don't want to sit at that table. I want to take this food back to the room that is mine and eat in peace. That won't help me earn Nacio's or the men's trust though.

So, instead of going and hiding in my room upstairs, I march over to the table and sit in an open seat in the middle of the men. I ignore the surprised looks plastered on most of their faces. I honestly don't care, not when my stomach is growling loudly, signaling for me to eat the large plate of food I prepared myself.

I take a bite of the first taco, which practically melts in my mouth. It is a million times better than the slop they fed me when they were holding me in the room in the basement.

I scarf down the first taco as fast as I can, ignoring the roomful of men who are all looking at me. Usually, I would be too self-conscious to do anything, but today, I don't care. I scarf down the second taco before I look up at their stares.

The man sitting across from me is smiling brightly. "See? I told you all I could cook. If the girl likes it, then it must not be that bad."

"It still sucks balls," a man further down the table says. "I don't care if the girl likes it. It doesn't mean anything."

"Hey, first of all, the girl's name is Kinsley. And, second of all..." I look down at the plate of food and realize the meat is barely cooked. I have been consuming almost entirely raw beef. "And, second of all, this is terrible. I'm just starving, and I would eat anything right now."

The men all chuckle.

"See, Karp? I told you it was bad." The man sitting next to me grabs my plate with the one remaining taco on it. "Let me see if I can find you some real food."

I smile at him, thankful he is getting me more food that won't make me sick in the morning.

"Sorry, Kinsley," Karp says to me. "I was never taught to cook. I didn't think it would be that goddamn hard."

I smile. "It's okay. Just maybe leave the cooking to someone else in the future."

Karp smiles back. He looks young, at least a couple of years younger than me. His hair is dark and short. His body is short but fit.

He doesn't look like a hard-core killer. He looks like a kid who has lost his way and doesn't know what to do.

"Here you go, *Kinsley*," the man says, emphasizing my name, as he places a new plate of food in front of me.

Tamales, I recognize immediately.

I dig in and realize this food is much better than what I was previously eating.

"Much better, right?"

I nod as I consume another mouthful.

The man smiles. "I'm Raul."

"Thanks Raul," I say through a mouthful.

Raul looks scary with tattoos covering his body and face, and he's almost double Karp's size.

"That's Samuel," he says, pointing to the man to my left. "You already met Seth." He smiles, pointing to the man who was my guard and held the gun up to my head earlier.

"Sorry about that," Seth says before taking a long drag of his beer.

I frown at him.

Raul continues, "The guy who cooked you the questionable food is Karp. And the quiet one over there is Ricardo. He doesn't speak much English."

I nod at Ricardo, who seems to be the oldest man in the room. I take another bite of my tamale and moan a little at how good it is until I see Raul looking at me with lust in his eyes. I force a smile and then return to eating without moaning.

"So, what do you guys typically do around here at this time of night?" I ask.

The men glance around to each other, not sure of what they are supposed to say or not say in front of me.

I stop eating. "Oh, come on, guys. I'm a Felton. You can tell me what you guys do."

The men continue to stare at one another, none of them wanting to speak.

Finally, Seth opens his mouth. "We are all on night shift tonight. None of us usually work nights, but since most of the men have moved to the other location, we have to cover more shifts. We are in charge of making sure no one gets in or *out* tonight."

I smile at him. "Good to know I'll have such strong men protecting me tonight." I take another bite. "So, where is the next location?"

Raul answers, "We don't know. They don't tell us shit."

I look around at all the men who are grumbling about not knowing where the next location is and that they should get to know something since they have all worked here long enough.

Seth looks at his phone. "We need to get going. Shift starts in five."

The men grumble some more but all begin to get up.

"Thanks again for the food," I say to Raul.

"Karp is also on cook duty tomorrow night. So, come to me, and I'll get you something edible."

"Thanks," I say.

I watch as the men all leave before I finish my plate of food. I get up from the rickety old table. I pick up the other empty plates the men left and throw them in the trash. I hate that these men made me feel anything for them at all. But they just seem like men. Not killers. Men who need a woman to pick up after them. Men who need a woman to teach them that what they are doing is wrong.

I yawn. I have no idea what time it is, other than knowing it is late based on how tired I feel. I should ask Nacio if they found my purse. That way, I can at least get my phone back.

I head upstairs through the old corridors until I find Nacio's office. I don't bother knocking. I just open the door and head in, just like Killian used to do to me.

His words, "*You find out the best information if you don't knock,*" ring in my ear. He's right.

As I enter Nacio's office, I hear Nacio use Killian's name, and I freeze. I glance around the room to see if Killian is here, but I see no one. *Please, God, don't let Killian really be involved with these people instead of the FBI. Please. Please just let him be an FBI agent.*

Nacio glances up at me with a frown on his face. He looks worn and worried for just a second at the sight of me, but then it disappears just as quickly. He ends his call without saying good-bye. Without any warning.

I walk over to the chair I pulled up to his desk as casually as possible, trying not to seem too interested in what he was saying. Trying not to seem bothered, but it is difficult. I take a seat in the hard chair and run my hand through my short locks.

His eyes focus intently on my hand as I do so. I let it slowly fall down my exposed neck. His eyes never leave my hand. His weakness is my sex appeal. That's the best way to get this man vulnerable enough so he trusts me. I just don't know if I can stomach flirting or doing more with this man.

"Who was that?"

He cocks his head to one side and shrugs. "I don't know what you are talking about."

I moisten my lips and watch as his eyes fall to my mouth. I take a guess. "Why were you talking to your brother about the FBI agent?"

Nacio's eyes darken, and he snaps out of the spell my body was drawing him under. "You'll find out soon enough."

I shake my head. "I'm not a very patient person. I want to know why, now."

"The FBI agent is in jail. His own people put him there. Just discussing if he is still a threat to us or not now that he is in jail."

I don't react to the news that Killian is in jail. In fact, I'm happy. It means he can't come after me. He can't try to save me. He's safe as long as he is there. After this is all over, the truth will come out. The truth that he is innocent.

"That's too bad. I would have liked to have seen him suffer more than that after what he did to me."

Nacio smiles at my harsh words. Words that are all a lie.

"Glad to hear you say that. I agree. The traitor deserves to suffer a lot more for what he has done."

I nod even though I don't know why Nacio hates Killian so much. He never did anything to Nacio. That's not true though, I realize.

Killian knew this location, and my father trusted him enough to tell him some things.

Nacio stands from his chair and walks around his desk until he is leaning against it right in front of me. His legs are inches from my own. He reaches down and grabs my hand. He begins slowly massaging it.

I let him. He's just touching my hand, I reason. It's harmless although the look of lust on his face tells me he wants so much more. That he wants to fuck me. Or rape me. That he would take either one. That's not something that can happen. It's something I won't let happen.

"When are we going to the next location?" I ask, hoping to suck as much information as I can from him.

"In two days. We have a package arriving late tomorrow. We will leave the next night."

I nod. "How are we traveling?"

"Plane."

"Private or commercial?"

He shakes his head. "So many questions. No need to worry your pretty little head about issues like this. Everything is all taken care of. You don't need to worry about a thing. The plans have already been made."

I pull my hand out of his grasp. "I need to know if I'm going to help run things. I deserve to know."

"Not really. You don't deserve to know anything. Not yet. I already told you nobody becomes a part of this organization without paying their dues first. Even a Felton. Your father paid his dues. Your grandfather and his father before him. The same rules apply to you. Once you pass the tests, then you get to know. Not before then."

He crosses his arms and studies me now that he can no longer touch me like he wants to. Although, if he really wanted to, he could do whatever he wanted to me. He's stronger than me. He could overpower me in a second. That means, the only reason he isn't, is because I have something he needs. I just don't know what that is yet.

What power, other than his desire for me, do I hold? Is there something my father told me that Nacio wants to know?

"You know, sweetheart, if you would just give in to me, I could make the rules disappear. You wouldn't have to pay your dues. You wouldn't have to wait for answers. I could tell you everything if you were mine. If you let me claim you. If you let me fuck you and marry you, then you wouldn't have to wait."

I raise my eyebrows at his absurd proposal. I stand up, and he straightens his body just a little until his body is pressed against mine.

"Really? You would do that for me? You would fuck me and marry me?"

Nacio grabs my ass, tightly pulling me against his growing erection. "Yes, I would do that for you. It's what any princess like you would want. To be taken care of by a strong, competent man like me. I have money. I have power. You would never have to worry about a thing again."

"We would run the organization together, fifty-fifty?" I ask, letting him keep his hands on my ass, despite wanting to rip his arms off for what he is doing.

He shrugs. "Not fifty-fifty. The organization has never been run that way. There always has to be one person in power and one person who has less. But you wouldn't have to get your hands dirty. Admit it; this isn't the life for you. You don't want to kill people. That's not what you want. You just want the benefits that come from this business, just like you have always had. Marry me, and you would never have to worry about getting your hands dirty."

He grabs my neck. "And you would never have to worry about not being satisfied again," he whispers in my ear.

I try not to flinch as shivers travel throughout my body. But, this time, I'm not turned on by sexy words being whispered in my ear. My body shivers out of revulsion and tries to shake him off my body.

"Who's in control now? Who has the power now?"

"Me," he says.

I know he's lying. His eyes dilate, and his nostrils flare. He needs me to marry him and give him whatever power I have in this organization. It would give him the power he desperately seeks.

"What about your brother, my mother, my grandfather? If we married, what would we do with them? Wouldn't they be upset that they'll lose out on having the power in the organization?"

He smiles and then licks his lips, like a tiger would just before it pounced on its meal. He thinks he's won, and I'm the meal.

"I wouldn't worry about them. They couldn't protest if we were already married."

I glance over his shoulder, unable to look at his lust-filled eyes any longer. I have to keep a look of disgust off my face. I look at his desk, trying to decide on what I'm going to do. *Do I say yes? Would that be easier? Or do I say hell no and try to find another way to gain his trust?*

That's when I see it. My purse is sitting on the corner of his desk. He's known who I am the whole time. The whole time he had me locked in the basement, he knew who I was, and he still kept me locked up like I was a dog. He thinks he can control me and do whatever the fuck he wants with me.

He's wrong.

I glance back to Nacio, who has a smug look on his face.

"So, what do you say, sweetheart?"

Nacio leans down to my neck to kiss me, but I don't let him get that far. I take my knee and knee him in the groin as hard as I can.

He releases me and grabs his groin as he writhes in pain. I walk around to the other side of his desk and grab my purse.

"I told you I would remove your balls if you touched me again without my permission. Don't do it again."

He looks at me with a deep grimace. His eyes have turned darker, and I know I shouldn't have done that. He will make me pay for hurting him. I don't think anybody gets away with hurting him without paying. But it was worth it. Whatever he does to me, I can take it just to see the look of shock and pain on his disgusting face.

I hold up my purse to him. He doesn't say anything. He just keeps grabbing his balls.

"You knew who I was the whole time. You had my purse, and I'm sure you went through it. You knew, and you still kept me locked up." I glance down at his crotch. "Call us even now."

I check that my phone, ID, and money are still in my purse before I walk around the desk and head toward the door. I pause and turn back to Nacio when I reach the door.

"I'm going to sleep now. Alone. And, if anybody enters my room tonight, I will do much worse than just kick them in the balls. Tomorrow, I will need a car to go into town to get some new clothes. I can't keep wearing this forever."

I turn back, thinking I've won. I grab the door and begin to open it when the door suddenly gets slammed shut in my face.

"No. You will not get a car to go into town. You will not leave without permission. Like I said before, you have not passed my tests yet. You don't leave the premises until then. I will have someone go into town and get some clothes that are more revealing than the granny clothes you have on now."

He glances up and down my body, but I know he is lying and just trying to get under my skin. My halter top and pants are plenty revealing enough.

"And, if you think about leaving, I will know. There are video cameras in every hallway. You can't leave without me knowing. Tomorrow, you will have your second test, so get some sleep, sweetheart. If you don't pass, you won't get out of here alive."

I narrow my eyes at him. I hate him. I hate the tone of his voice as he threatens my life. It's so casual, yet I can tell it excites him, thinking about killing me. I realize I might have chosen wrong. I don't know what the next test is. I don't know if I can do it. If one of the tests involves killing someone innocent, I don't think I'll be able to do it. It might have been easier to marry him and sleep with him. And, if that is the case, I might as well take his gun and pull the trigger myself because I can't let that happen.

Instead, I grab the doorknob again, and I leave without another word to Nacio. He doesn't get to see my fear. He doesn't get to know I'm already dead.

I walk back to the room that Nacio told me was mine. I open the door and step inside the smelly, dark room. I don't bother turning on the lights when I enter. I prefer the darkness right now. I close the door behind me, and I lock it, but I know the flimsy lock will be useless. If any of the men decide they want to come in, they can do so without putting a drop of effort into it.

I walk through the room, passing bunk bed after bunk bed. I only stop when I bump my leg against the corner of one of the bunks in the far corner of the room. I look at the sheets on the bottom bunk that I know have never been washed. This is as good as it is going to get right now.

Unless I say yes to Nacio. Then, I could sleep where he sleeps. I could sleep in a nice, plush bed I'm sure is fit for a king instead of this dank, dark room.

I try not to think about Nacio as I lie down on the bed. I don't bother to crawl under the covers. I just lie right on top. I don't take my clothes or shoes off either. I can't stand to take my clothes off— not in a place like this, with men like this. I need to be able to make a quick escape even though I know a quick escape doesn't exist, not unless the escape is at the end of a gun.

Tears begin falling in cascades now. Tears that should have fallen long ago now make their way down my face until my eyes are burning from the smeared mascara and eye shadow stinging my eyes from not washing it off in days. I need to shower. I need clean clothes. I need makeup.

But my needs seem silly compared to what I just witnessed today. I saw a girl die because of me. She died simply because she looked like me. That's a terrible reason to die. And that's a terrible reason to watch someone die.

I close my eyes, trying to push the woman out of my head, but her blue eyes and blonde hair keep coming back to haunt me. There is nothing I can do about it. I will never be able to sleep again.

9

KILLIAN

I OPEN MY EYES. I don't see anything but darkness. My head hurts like a motherfucker. I try to rub my head to ease some of the pain, but my arms are met with resistance. Rope is wrapped tightly against my arms, keeping them tied behind my back. I try to slip my hands out of the rope, but it is no use. Whoever tied my hands behind my back has done this a time or two. They knew what the fuck they were doing. I won't be able to break free. Houdini couldn't break out of these ropes.

My shoulders begin hurting from being in an awkward position, and I feel the ropes burning into my wrists. I don't care though. The pain actually makes me feel better. It reminds me of my mission. It reminds me that I have to seek my revenge for Kinsley. I just have to figure out how to get out of here first.

The box truck bounces as we go over a bump. My head bounces hard against the truck wall.

"Fuck," I moan as the pounding in my head gets worse.

I try to figure out my surroundings in the back of the truck, but it is hard in the darkness. It's not the same truck Santino and I rode in when we broke out of jail. This truck is much smaller than that one, and as far as I can tell, I am the only one or thing back here.

My legs aren't tied, just my hands, so I adjust them to push against the wall until I'm in a standing position. I walk slowly to the back door of the truck, trying not to fall, despite the truck bouncing at every curve. If I could get the door open, then I could jump and make a run for it. It would be risky, but what other option do I have? My only other option is to stay in the truck and wait for them to kill me. Even if they don't kill me, whatever they have planned for me can't be good. I know that much. And I'm not going to just sit on my ass and wait to find out.

I just wish I knew where I am. Somewhere rural? Urban? The middle of nowhere?

If I'm going to make a break for it, I would much rather do it somewhere urban where I can get to a phone. To people. If I break out in the middle of nowhere, I don't stand a chance. They could take their time in tracking me down with guns. They could run me over with the truck. I'd be fucked.

I can't focus on that though. There are no windows, so I have no idea where we are. All I need to focus on is getting this fucking door open and then running as fast as I can. And, if I die, so be it.

I put my foot down where the latch is and pull hard until it turns over. I'm a little shocked that it actually worked. I thought for sure they would have put a lock on the outside of the door. These guys aren't as experienced as I first thought.

I regain my balance as we round another corner, and then I put my foot back under the latch. My heart is beating fast. This is it. As soon as I lift it, the door will make a loud noise, alerting the driver that it is open. So, no matter what I see on the other side, I have to be ready to run as soon as I open the door.

The truck slows a little, and I know this is my chance. I lift my foot hard and fast, trying to give as much momentum to get the door moving upright. It moves about halfway open. It's enough for me to jump out.

Buildings. I see large buildings. *Thank God. I have a chance.*

I don't have time to decide which building is my best bet to run toward. I don't have time to make a plan. I jump from the truck, somehow landing my feet on what I realize is a rocky dirt road instead of the pavement it should be in such an urban area. I don't have time to think about it though. I just run.

I run straight ahead for a block and then duck down an alleyway. I don't hear the truck turn around behind me. I don't hear footsteps either, but that doesn't mean someone isn't there. I keep running down the alleyway, trying to get as far away as possible, before I decide to duck in somewhere to get help.

But, as I run, I begin to lose hope I'm going to find anyone who can help me. As I run, I realize where I am—the one place I never wanted to return to, yet knew I would have to one day.

Yet this is the one place I wanted to be. This is where I'll get revenge for Kinsley. This is where I'll make things right. But I won't find help here because there is no one here who can help. There's only darkness and hatred. Only danger.

I keep running though, hoping I can find someplace to hide until I can get these ropes off and find a weapon to kill them.

But I don't get the chance.

I turn the corner, and Santino is standing with a gun pointed at me. I freeze. I consider turning and running in the opposite direction, but I was wrong. These guys are experts. They do this for a living. If he pulls that trigger, he won't miss, so I don't move. This isn't my chance. I will have to try again—if I get another opportunity.

Santino walks slowly toward me, the gun pointing straight at my head. I don't focus on the gun. I don't know if it's my training or what that tells me to keep my eyes on the shooter and not the gun. The gun isn't what is going to kill me; the shooter will. The shooter's eyes will tell me if he is going to shoot or not. By the time his finger pulls the trigger, it is too late to react.

And Santino's eyes are telling me he doesn't want to shoot me, but he will if I run. I don't understand what he needs me for, but I'll be patient long enough to find out. So, I stay in place as Santino moves closer and closer.

He grabs ahold of my shoulder to turn me around as he presses the barrel of the gun to my head. "Walk," he says.

I walk. When we make it out of the alleyway, another man comes over and holds on to my other arm, but Santino doesn't remove the gun from my head.

The buildings become more and more familiar as we walk through the city until the one I recognize comes into view. The door is still barely hanging on to the hinges. We don't pause at the door though. Santino doesn't knock. He just pushes me inside where I know I will never return. There are only two reasons they would bring me here—to get some info out of me and to kill me. There is no other reason.

I just have to find a way to kill as many of these motherfuckers as I can before I go. That way, Kinsley's death won't be for nothing.

Santino walks next to me, the gun still firm against my head, as the other man trails off behind me. I can't tell, but he most likely has a gun on me as well.

We walk down a hallway, and I hear voices. One voice in particular sounds familiar. It's the same voice I heard that night when I came here. The same voice I heard at the casino. It's almost identical to Santino's voice. It's a wonder I didn't recognize Santino's voice before.

We round a corner, and the voices get louder.

"In here." Santino grabs my arms and jerks me into a large room full of people.

The contrast between the dark hallway and the light room blinds me at first. I close my eyes and then open them again, trying to get them to adjust quickly.

"Good job, brother. I wasn't sure if I could count on you to do this job, but you've proven your worth," a man says in a similar voice to Santino.

I see the man stand up from the table of men who have now grown silent. The man walks over to us, and I see he is definitely Santino's brother. He has the same coloring and facial structure, although this man is a little taller and slightly older than Santino. And his hair is long, compared with Santino's buzzed head. But I realize now they both have the same eyes. Eyes that are out for blood.

"I'm Nacio," the man says. "Glad you could finally join us."

I glare at him but don't say anything. I don't know what his role is here yet. I won't disrespect him and get myself killed until I have killed the person responsible for Kinsley's death.

The man turns to the far side of the room. "Sweetheart, will you come here?"

He motions to the side of the room. My stomach churns as I think about whatever vile woman would think so little of other women to be with a man who treats women like property, like dirt. I can't imagine such a woman.

A woman stands at the far side of the table. She doesn't look at me. All I can see are her dark pants and black lacy bra. She doesn't even bother to wear a shirt. My eyes travel up though and then stop at the chopped off blonde locks.

It can't be...

The woman turns to me, and I see...

"Kinsley?" the word falls from my lips as she walks to Nacio's side.

She barely looks at me though and then turns her attention to Nacio.

She's alive. My heart beats wildly as I see her here, alive. I don't know how it's possible, and I don't really care. All I know is, my heart has a reason to keep beating. My lungs have a reason to keep breathing.

Somehow, the universe has answered prayers I never asked because I thought it was impossible.

She's alive. Kinsley is standing no more than five feet away from me, and I want nothing more than to run to her, tackle her to the ground, and kiss her like crazy.

I feel a tear welling up in my eyes. A tear of pure joy. It drops quickly down my cheek, so fast I'm not even sure if anyone notices.

"You know how you told me you wanted to kill the FBI agent who destroyed your life?" Nacio says to Kinsley. "Well, I had my brother get him for you. I agree he deserves a lot worse than just going to jail. I want him to really pay for what he did, too, so I brought him here for you."

Kinsley doesn't look at me as he's talking. Instead, she looks at him. A slow grin forms on her face at his words. A smile I have never seen before. A smile I don't understand.

"What do you think about that, sweetheart?"

Every time he calls her that, I want to hurt him. I want to bring him as much pain as he brings me when he calls my girl that. I can't stand it.

"Thank you," Kinsley says simply, a smile still on her face.

"Really? I break him out of jail for you, and that's all the thanks I get? If I had known you didn't really mean what you said last night, I wouldn't have bothered."

When he finishes speaking, she doesn't hesitate. She walks straight to him, grabs his neck, and solidly kisses him on the lips.

I lose it. I move toward them, intending to put a stop to it, when Santino grabs my arm.

"You move, and I'll kill you," he says.

I stop moving. But I can't fucking look at her kissing another man. I close my eyes and wait until she finishes the kiss.

I can't believe her. I can't believe she would willingly kiss another man. I thought I was her life. I was wrong. I'm a fucking idiot.

I should have chosen the FBI, not her. She's willingly working here. She could have left at anytime, but instead, she's staying here. For all I know, she's been participating in the smuggling, in the rapes, in the killings. She is a monster, just like everyone else in this room.

"Thank you," she says.

I open my eyes to a smug Nacio beaming from the kiss, like he just won.

He won.

I lost.

Now, I just want them to get this over with and put a bullet between my eyes.

"It doesn't change anything, Nacio. I'm not going to marry you," Kinsley says.

Nacio's face drops a little.

The men around the room are all staring at the exchange

between the two of them. I suspect that was not something Nacio wanted Kinsley to share with everyone. He didn't want her to share that she had turned down his proposal, but it makes me feel better to know she isn't going to marry the smug fucker—at least, not yet.

He raises his eyebrows at Kinsley, but she stands defiantly next to him, not backing down. I don't quite understand the relationship between the two, but if I know anything about Kinsley—which I'm not sure I do—I know she is stubborn as hell and won't back down, not when she decides on what she really wants.

Nacio walks over to her and whispers something in her ear. She frowns but doesn't say anything further.

Nacio pulls a gun out of the back of his jeans and hands it to Kinsley. "Kill him," Nacio says to her while motioning to me.

"What?" she says, frozen with the gun in her hand.

Kill him, I think. *Kill Nacio.*

We won't survive, but at least the ringleader in all of this would be dead, too. At least the man who forced Kinsley to kiss him would be dead.

"Kill the FBI agent. After all, he's the reason your father is dead. Kill him, and avenge your father."

10

KINSLEY

I HOLD the gun in my hand. It's heavier than I thought it would be. For such a small thing, it feels bulky in my hand. I can't stop staring at it.

This tiny object is the cause of so many people dying. So many lives have been lost all because of this weapon. Those lives might not have been lost if the person hadn't had a weapon that so easily separated them from the crime they were committing. If they'd had to use a knife instead of a gun, would so many killings have happened? If they'd had to get their hands dirty with the victim's blood, would they still have done it? If they'd had to really think about it and plan it with a bomb, would they still have done it?

I hold the gun in my hand. How easy it would be for me to aim the gun at Killian and pull the trigger. It wouldn't even feel like I'm really killing him because this gun doesn't feel dangerous. It doesn't feel any different than holding any other inanimate object. But it is. This object is the most powerful of all.

I could do it. I could kill Killian and secure my place here. I would have all the power if I did. I know Nacio thinks I can't do it. He's still suspicious of why I'm here. He thinks I still love Killian.

He's right. I do.

The second I saw Killian walk into the cafeteria, my heart stopped. The one thing I was trying to prevent from happening has happened. And, now, everything I have been through over the last few days without Killian has been for nothing. Now, we are both going to die.

I tried to hide behind the table of men blocking Killian from me. I thought if I hid, nobody would be able to see my feelings so clearly plastered all over my face. There's no way for me to hide how I feel about Killian.

When Nacio called me to the center of the room, I couldn't bear to look at Killian for more than one second. If I did that, the whole room would know I still love Killian, I always did. They would know and shoot us both without a second thought. So, I tried to remain frozen. I tried to remain careless. I tried to look at anybody but Killian, tied, standing in front of me.

When I saw him so broken and in so much pain at the sight of me, I almost couldn't stand it myself. I couldn't stand remaining by Nacio and not running to Killian. Even if it meant we would both die, it meant I could die wrapped in his arms. I could die loving him. Death might be worth one final embrace. One final kiss.

I didn't though. I stayed by Nacio's side. And I did the only thing I could think of that would make Nacio less suspicious about my relationship with Killian. I kissed Nacio.

It wasn't a gentle, chaste kiss either. I forced my tongue into Nacio's mouth as our lips collided together. I grabbed the nape of this neck, keeping his lips firmly against mine. I moaned just a little as his tongue pressed against mine. I put everything I could into the kiss.

And, now, I won't be able to live with myself for doing it. I won't be able to live with myself for kissing anyone but Killian. I won't be able to forgive myself for kissing another man in front of Killian, especially since that might be the last image of me he ever sees. I hate that I put a small drop of doubt into Killian's head, making him think I don't love him. But I already did that with the note I wrote him. I already planted that seed in his head. With the kiss, I just confirmed he means nothing to me.

I shiver from the cold draft in the room, bringing me back to the present. I resist the urge to wrap my arm around my chest to warm myself. I hate that I'm basically wearing a bra in front of a dozen men, but I can't let Nacio see me as weak. He has to see me as an equal, so I won't let him know he has won with the clothing he bought for me, considering this outfit was the most covered one he bought. I should be thankful for the clothing. Revealing clothing makes it easier to control these men. It makes it easier for them to think I am only a sex object and not a person who schemes and plans and wants power of her own.

"On your knees," Santino says to Killian.

I glance up in time to see that Killian hasn't moved. He's standing tall in front of us, just like he always does. Santino forces him into a kneeling position. I don't know why it matters whether he stands or kneels if he is going to be shot and killed either way. I guess kneeling makes it easier for me to shoot him. If he's standing, he might run at the last second.

I take a chance and look into Killian's eyes as he kneels in front of me. They're dark and intense, like always. When I look at them, I realize he's in a lot of pain, not necessarily physical but just pain. I've hurt him in unforgivable ways, but I still see love there. When I see it, I look away, back to the gun in my hand, hoping I am the only one who can see the love still there in his eyes.

"Kill him," Nacio commands again from behind me.

What I really want to do is kill Nacio. He deserves it for what he's done. If I did that though, all the men sitting at the table on either side would shoot me next before I even had a chance to react.

"Kill him for what he did to your father," Nacio says.

I have to know. Before I figure out if I have any options other than killing Killian, I have to know what Nacio is talking about.

"What do you mean, Killian killed my father?" I ask Nacio.

"Killian is the reason your father is dead. Your father didn't die from a heart attack. Killian killed him."

"Why? Why would he do that?"

"When your father found out Killian was FBI, Killian did the only thing he could to save himself. He killed your father first before your father could kill him, before his cover was blown and we found out he was FBI."

Nacio smirks at Killian. "We found out anyway."

"Lies!" Killian screams suddenly from the ground. "It's all lies!"

I glance from Nacio to Killian in time to see Killian getting kicked in the back by Santino.

"Shut up, or I'll shoot you myself," Santino says.

Killian squeezes his eyes shut, most likely dealing with the pain from being kicked hard in the back. I watch his breathing become uneven as he tries to deal with the pain.

I turn back to Nacio, unable to watch Killian in agony without feeling it myself. But, when Nacio speaks about Killian killing my father, he doesn't seem to be lying. He's telling the truth—or what he believes to be true. Killian was involved in my father's death. I just don't know in what way exactly.

A week or two ago, that would have hurt me to find out Killian might have been the one who killed my father. Now though, it barely stings since I know my father got what he deserved. He probably deserved even worse.

I turn back to Killian. He lied though. Again, he lied. And I have to make it known I'm not happy about it.

I walk toward him, my eyes focused on his. I can't show him anything but the anger I let surface from another lie he told me. Another lie that hurts me. That's all I get—lie after lie after lie from him. Never the truth. With him, there is always something more hidden.

I walk until I'm standing right in front of him. I'm fuming. I feel everyone's eyes on me, all unsure of what I'm going to do. Kill him? Question him? Forgive him?

I try to feel the anger as best as I can as I look Killian in the eyes. All I see is love and truth. Truth I never expected to see. He thinks I've moved forward to kill him. He thinks these are his final seconds alive, and with those seconds, he is going to love me.

I hate that he thinks that. I hate that I could kill him, and he would still love me with his last breath.

I bend down, so I can look eye-to-eye with Killian for what he thinks is going to be the last time. I glare at him with my blue eyes while his soften with more love. He's trying his best to tell me it's okay, he understands why I'm doing this.

I stand back up. "This is for killing my father," I say. I raise the gun and hit it against Killian's head as hard as I can.

I hear a gasp from someone behind me. I watch as Killian's head whips to the side, and I am surprised to see a gush of blood spill from his lips where I hit him instead of the side of his head where I aimed.

I glance up and see Santino smiling smugly behind Killian, happy I'm on their side instead of Killian's.

I watch Killian put his head back upright, and I'm scared at how much blood covers his face. I can't hit him in the head again, like I was planning. It would cause too much damage. Too much pain.

He opens his eyes, even though one is bloody, despite the torment I know he must be feeling.

I kick him hard in the stomach with the heel of my shoe. I watch as he falls backward. He hits his head again on the hard concrete floor.

I take a step forward so I'm standing over him. "That was for me. For lying to me about who you were and pretending to love me when all you were really doing was framing my family to meet your own needs."

I spit on him in disgust and then turn away, hoping I didn't give him a concussion or cause any other permanent damage.

"Kneel, you motherfucker," Santino says.

Killian moans as he is forced back into a kneeling position.

I try to ignore the pain I hear coming from him. Instead, I focus on the wicked gleam in Nacio's eyes. He's impressed by what I've done. If I shot Killian now, he would believe I was on his side. Even if I didn't kill Killian, one shot would be enough.

I can't though. I can't shoot him, and I can't let anyone else either.

So, I think of the one thing that might give Killian one more day to live even if it means I'm risking my own life to do it.

I lift the gun and place it in Nacio's hands. "We can't kill him," I say.

Nacio frowns at me in disappointment. "Don't you mean, *you* can't kill him? I'm disappointed in you, sweetheart. After the performance you just gave, I thought putting a bullet between his eyes would be the easy part."

Nacio takes the gun and begins walking toward Killian with the same intensity he had when he walked me to the room with the blonde girl he killed. I grab his arm and turn him back to me.

"You can't kill him either. We still need him, baby," I say, adding the term of endearment to the end, despite how much it kills me to.

"And why not?"

I stroke his cheek, buying myself more time to figure out a reason.

I smile when I finally have an answer. "Because the FBI might already know where our next base of operation is. They could follow us or get here before we leave. He's our only insurance. We need to figure out what he knows and then keep him alive until we are sure the FBI is no longer invested in going after us. Then, we will get rid of him. The FBI will simply think we turned him. They saw him leaving the jail of his own accord with Santino, after all."

Nacio smiles and then tangles his hand in my hair before pulling me into a wet, hungry kiss. He releases me a few seconds later. "Beauty and brains. Who knew?" Then, he says, "Seth."

Seth stands from the table.

"Take him upstairs and see what he knows. After you find out what he knows, keep him upstairs and get him ready to be transferred tomorrow. Understood?"

"Yes, sir," Seth says.

Seth signals for two other men to follow him and then goes over to Killian. I watch as they force him back into a standing position. Killian doesn't take his eyes off of me though. Not until he is forced to turn away from me and walk out the door.

I don't know what kind of pain I've just subjected Killian to. I don't know what torture they will use to get him to talk. I just hope he talks. He needs to survive long enough for me to find a way for him to get out of here.

I don't know how much time that is. One night? Two? I don't know how much time I have left to keep him alive. But that is my new mission. Keep Killian alive, and then I can worry about the rest.

When Killian is no longer in view, Santino walks over to where Nacio and I are still standing.

"So, you're the infamous Kinsley Felton," Santino says to me.

"Yes. And you're Nacio's younger brother, Santino."

Santino smiles brightly, showing off his sparkly white teeth. "So, my brother did talk about me while I was gone. I wish he had talked to me about you. I would have gotten here faster if I'd known how beautiful you were. You think you can kiss me like you did my brother? After all, I deserve a kiss, too, for breaking Killian out of jail for you."

I don't have to answer though because Nacio throws a punch in Santino's direction. Santino ducks, expecting the punch. He laughs as Nacio's face reddens and darkens at the thought of Santino kissing me.

"Chill, dude. I was just joking. You know I would never mess with a girl you already claimed. Not when a dozen more just like her that I could fuck with less trouble are upstairs right now. I'm just messing with you. Lighten up, man."

Nacio's face lightens, but his eyes stay dark and angry. "I'm heading into town for a couple of hours to pick up some things. Want to come, baby?" he asks me.

Santino interjects, "Or you could stay with me, and I could show you around. I know my boring brother didn't do that great of a job." He smiles at me, expecting me to take Nacio up on his offer.

But I don't want to leave the premises, not now that Killian is here. I can't take a chance that whoever remains behind will change their mind and just kill him. I also don't know why Nacio will let me leave the premises with him when, earlier today, he was so stern about me not being able to leave.

"I'll stay with Santino," I say to Nacio. "I need to get to know both of the people I will be working with."

Santino slings his arm around my shoulders in a way I wasn't expecting. "Don't worry, brother. I won't do anything you wouldn't do."

I smile. I can't help it. Santino's smile is infectious.

Nacio glares at the pair of us. "Fine. I didn't show her how the men get paid. You can start with that."

"Boring," Santino says flatly.

"Do it. I'll be back in an hour, and then we can discuss transportation plans for tomorrow."

Santino rolls his eyes but nods at his brother.

Nacio walks to me, stopping too close for my comfort. "This doesn't mean you have passed yet. When we arrive at our next location you will still have to kill him to pass the test. Until then, the same rules apply."

I nod. "I didn't think they wouldn't apply."

"Good." Nacio says to his brother, "Behave," before he walks out of the room, leaving me along with Santino.

Santino pulls his leather jacket off and hands it to me. "Here. You look cold."

I notice the goose bumps covering my arms and torso. "Thanks."

"My brother can be a bit of a jackass. Don't let your opinion of him influence your opinion of me though. I'm much nicer and a lot more fun than he is."

I smile as I slip into his jacket, thankful to be more covered up.

He holds out his arm, and I take it, like he's my prom date.

"Come on, I can show you the boring paperwork to appease my brother, and then we can find something more fun to get into before he gets back."

I nod, and he guides me out of the cafeteria and up the stairs to the offices. He leads me into an office next to Nacio's. This one is slightly smaller than Nacio's, but otherwise, it looks exactly the same.

"Pull up a chair next to my desk," Santino says as he takes a seat behind his desk.

From his desk, he begins pulling out envelopes with names written on them. He starts typing on his computer, and I pull up a chair next to him behind his desk, so I can see what he is doing.

He has a spreadsheet with names pulled up. But they aren't regular names. They are code names, I realize. Even if someone took this computer, no one would have any legal names or any way to track the business. That basically means, if I or the FBI took it, the computer would be useless.

"These are all code names we use for the guys who work for us. We also use this system to tag all the people, drugs, and money, but we will explain that part of the system later when we get..."

I suck in a breath, waiting for him to tell me where, but he catches himself.

"Anyway, only the people at the top know how to read the code names. It is a boring, tricky process to assign men code names and remember them since we don't have any sort of key written down anywhere. You just have to remember. Once you start meeting all the guys, we will help you memorize them."

"Do the men know their own code names?"

"No. We call them by whatever first name they tell us. I don't even think the names they tell us are their real names, and it honestly doesn't matter to us. We find out their real names anyway and then do extensive background checks on all our men regardless of what they want to be called. This is just a system to keep their real names off the books."

I nod.

"Anyway, you don't need to worry about any of this right now. All you need to worry about is the hierarchy of the men and how they get paid."

I nod again.

"Our men get paid every six months."

I raise my eyebrows. "Why so long? Don't the men get upset with having to wait that long to get paid? How do they pay their bills?"

"No, they don't get upset. They know up front how long it will be until they get paid. And all of their living costs are paid for as long as they work for us."

"What about their families?"

"Their families are taken care of—if they survive six months. If they survive, we will pay for basic expenses for their families as well. And the money they make is more than most of these men would make in a lifetime. We are very generous employers."

"But why make them wait six months until they get paid?"

He smiles. "Loyalty. We want loyal employees who will stay with us forever. Doing what we do, we need people who will be devoted to us for life. We don't want people who are only in this for a quick paycheck. That's why we reward loyalty, not position. The longer you are with us, the more you get paid."

"There aren't higher and lower positions?"

"There is us and them. There are the Marlows and Feltons, and then there is everybody else. Everybody else does whatever position we ask them to do. Sure, there are people we trust more than others, but everybody gets the same, depending on how long they have been with us. Tomorrow, we could have different needs. For example, our most trusted person who is responsible for shipping might have to be responsible for night-shift guard duty the next night. We reward loyalty above everything else."

"But what motivation do the men have for doing a good job if they aren't going to get paid accordingly?"

He cocks his head to the side in the same way that Nacio does, except Santino has a small dimple on his cheek. I notice it when he smiles, making him seem less harmful than Nacio.

But, as he leans forward and pulls his gun out from his jeans, I know he is equally as dangerous, despite the dimple.

"This," he says, holding his gun. "This is why the men listen and do what they are told without question. They know they will be eliminated if they don't. We don't give second chances."

I nod slowly as he puts the gun back in the back of his jeans.

Santino turns his attention back to the screen. "So, as you can see, we mark off six-month periods, and for every period they last, they get a five percent increase."

"How long do the men typically last?"

He shrugs. "If they make it six months with us, they usually last a lifetime. But less than twenty percent make it to six months."

I gulp, not wanting to know the answer to my next question, but I ask anyway, "Do you kill them if they don't make it to six months?"

He actually laughs at my question, like it is the most bizarre thing I could have ever asked.

I stare blankly at him. I have no idea what I said that was so funny.

He stops laughing suddenly when he sees my face. "Sorry, but I thought the answer to that would have been obvious. Yes. If they don't make it to six months, then they have to go. Once you start working for us, it is a lifetime commitment. We can't chance them telling someone about what we do."

I want to ask for exact details. I know they smuggle, but from where to where? Why? How? I want to ask all the questions, but I don't.

"We have two men coming up on six months, so it's time to pay them."

"Why do most of the men that make it to six months last?"

"By then, they have seen the worst. They have killed people. They have gotten their hands dirty. And because of this..." He points to the screen.

When I see the large number, my mouth drops open. I stare in disbelief at what these men make in six months if they last that long. It's half a million. They make half a million US dollars if they can last six months.

"Once they get that first large paycheck, they are hooked."

I nod, understanding now. "How do we pay them?"

"Cash."

"How do we give them that much cash at one time?"

"We don't. At the six-month mark, we give them the cash in a few increments over the next month or two. When you see an envelope full of cash, it does something to you. The men will suddenly do anything for you. Things they wouldn't do before, they do now."

"But why wouldn't they just quit after that first paycheck?"

"First of all, nobody quits, remember? And, second of all, they get hooked. They get used to that money and want more and more of it. They can't stop."

I still don't understand fully, but I guess it makes sense because our families have been getting away with this for years without getting caught, so whatever they are doing must be working.

I hear a knock on the door, and we both look up.

Santino exits the program on the computer. "Come in," he says.

The door opens, and Seth walks in.

"I have the info the FBI agent told us."

"Good. Proceed," Santino says.

Seth looks to me and then back to Santino, unsure if he should be speaking.

"It's okay, Seth. Kinsley is one of us now. If she messes up, she'll be dead. Anything you have to say, you can say in front of her."

Seth hesitates for another second, shifting his weight from side to side, before he finally speaks, "He says the FBI found the bodies. They are investigating what happened and believe they can figure out the location based on the evidence at the scene. They are assembling a team to move in."

"Excellent. Anything else, Seth?"

Seth looks down at his feet and then to me. "He's still in love with her," he says, looking at me.

Santino raises his eyebrows. "Anything else?"

"No, sir."

"Good."

Seth turns to leave, passing Raul who stands hesitantly in the doorway as Seth passes him.

"Come in." Santino sighs, like this is how he spends most of his day and he hates it.

I hate that Seth said Killian still loves me. It means that at least one person was observant because I know Killian would never admit to that and put me at risk on his own. It makes it even more important for him to get out of here.

Raul comes in next. He's out of breath and panting hard. He holds his chest, trying to slow his breathing so he can speak. It takes him several seconds, but he is finally able to get the words out. "Security system...it's down."

"Shit," Santino says, quickly getting up from his chair.

I watch as the chair falls over, and then I quickly get up, too. I run after Santino as he walks out of the office. I'm not going to miss a chance to check out how the security is set up.

I follow Santino down the stairs, past the cafeteria, and into a small dark room.

"I don't know what happened," Karp says, pointing to the screens. "I didn't do anything."

"Out of the way," Santino snarls at Karp, pushing him out of the way.

Santino sits down at the computers that are black instead of surveilling the building. Santino begins pushing buttons and turning things off and on, trying to get the screens to work again. But it doesn't work.

"Go get Seth," Santino says to Karp. "And, Karp, you'd better hope we can get this back up and running."

Santino's threat is obvious. Karp's job and life depend on getting the security systems back up and running.

I stand, watching Santino try thing after thing, but nothing happens. I glance to the cord behind Santino and see the easy solution to the problem. I shouldn't tell him. It is to my advantage if the security systems stay down. But I can't let Karp die for a simple mistake. Maybe it will earn me some points to fix the security system.

I bend down and plug the cord back into the wall. I watch as the screens roar to life. I watch as Santino's lips curl back into a smile of relief. I doubt Nacio would be happy to return to find the security systems down. Santino stares at me.

"The outlet is flimsy. If we were staying here, I would recommend it be replaced. You should let whoever is on security duty next know the cord could fall out of the outlet again."

Santino just stares at me until Seth comes into the small room.

"Sir?"

Santino stops staring. "The security system was down, but I got it up and running again. It seems the cord fell out of the outlet. You are on duty tonight, so I just wanted you to know how to fix it if it happened again."

Seth nods.

Santino turns back to the screens and begins checking that everything is in place. I look over his shoulder, trying my best to see where the cameras are located.

I take a deep breath when a screen switches to the hallway. The hallway that will forever haunt my dreams. I wait for the cameras to switch to one of the rooms. I wait to come face-to-face with the room where I watched the woman die. I wait for the cameras to show me Killian tied up in a room somewhere. I wait for the cameras to show me all of the other broken people who are trapped in the rooms upstairs. I wait, but the cameras never go into any of the rooms. Instead, they just skim the hallways and exits.

There are no cameras in any of the rooms.

The thought sounds over and over again in my head.

There are no cameras in any of the rooms.

That means, I can visit Killian. My heart beats rapidly in my chest at the thought of having a few seconds alone with him. I could do it. I could go to his room. I just need to find out which room he is in, and I need an excuse for being in his room. But that is all details. Because I can go see Killian. And that is all that matters.

11

KILLIAN

I DEEPLY BREATHE OUT, trying to rid my body of the pain that has inched its way into every corner of my body. My arms are sore from being tied up on either side of my head, making my muscles ache.

I can barely think straight due to the pounding, stabbing pain continuously nagging my head. Blood still drips from my lips and eye where Kinsley hit me. My back stings from being whipped multiple times, and my stomach is bruised from Kinsley's kick.

Overall though, the physical pain is nothing compared to the emotional pain I'm dealing with. I'm lucky really. The pain I endured after I was brought to this room was nothing. The simple whipping stopped as soon as I started talking. It wasn't real torture. The men who were whipping me, their hearts weren't in it. They were just doing their job.

Real torture only happens when people truly care about what they are doing. When they aren't trying to get information out of someone but instead doing it because they enjoy the torture themselves. That's not what I experienced.

If I'm lucky enough to live another night, I have a feeling I will get to experience real torture at the hands of Nacio or Santino. They hate me. They have a reason to torture me. They have a reason to make me pay for the trouble I've put them through.

But the discomfort they have dealt with is nothing compared to what they have put me through these last few days. The misery from thinking Kinsley was dead was unbearable. I shouldn't have survived it. Somehow though, I'm still alive, barely hanging on. Somehow, I've managed to live long enough to see Kinsley alive again.

It's enough, seeing her alive. It's enough to make all the pain I went through worth it. It's enough to make my death worth it. My death that I know will be coming soon.

Kinsley barely kept me alive today. She found a way to keep me alive, but I don't know if she is keeping me alive for my benefit or hers. I don't even know if she still loves me or just wasn't heartless enough to kill me—yet.

But, either way, the only way she will survive more than a couple of days is to kill me. And dying to keep the woman I love alive is more than worth it. I would give my life a hundred times if it meant she would get to live. It's all I care about anymore. All I care about is that she lives.

That is my only mission—to keep her alive at all costs.

I don't care why she is here. To join them. To bring them down. To protect her family. I don't care. She must survive this.

My eyes grow heavy with each second, so heavy that I must sleep, but sleep won't come easily. Not when my hands are tied up above my head and I'm stuck sitting on a cold floor. Not when the headache is worse than I want to admit. I try anyway though. I close my eyes, think of Kinsley and hope dreaming of her will be enough to lull me into a deep sleep.

I let the image of her standing in front of me when I thought she was dead fill my mind. I see her standing there, strong and unbreakable, in her tight dark pants that show off the curve of her ass. I let my mind move up her body to her bare stomach, smooth and perfect. Up to her bra that shows off her perky breasts that fit so perfectly in my hands. To her hair that somehow still shines, despite not being styled in days. To her plump lips that I want to claim with mine.

I imagine a different meeting. A meeting where the second I see her, I run to her and never let her go. I run to her, and I don't ask questions about what she is doing here or who she has become. I just take her in my arms and love her.

I imagine ripping her clothes off and not caring who is watching because I need to be with her more than anything. I imagine her moans at the first touch of my hand on her bare breast. I imagine her screaming my name as I thrust inside her, expanding her, until she is more than full. I can practically feel her wetness covering my cock, more and more with each thrust. I feel the tight walls of her pussy contracting as I make her come hard and fast. I hear her screaming, but as soon as she gets the release out, it turns into barely a whisper that she repeats over and over, like a quiet plea for more.

"Killian...Killian...Killian," she says in her soft, perfect voice.

I moan softly, loving how she says my name.

"Killian," she says louder.

I grin wildly as she begs me for more, even when I know she isn't ready for another round so quickly after we just finished.

"Open your eyes, baby," she says softly to me.

I moan. I can't open my eyes. If I do, she will be gone. I'm not ready to let the image go.

"Open your eyes," she says again. This time, she's stroking my cheek so softly that I'm not sure if she is actually touching me.

I begrudgingly open my eyes and expect her to disappear, but instead, I find her crouching in front of me. Her brow is wrinkled as she looks at me, biting down on her lip.

I look around the room and realize I'm still in the prison they locked me in, except Kinsley isn't just an image of my imagination. She is kneeling down in front of me.

I reach my hand to touch her face, but the rope keeps my hand in place. I can't help but smile at her, even though I know she is risking her life to be here.

"You shouldn't be here," I say.

"I couldn't stay away." She reaches her hand up and gently touches me on the cheek.

It stings wherever she touches, but I don't tell her to stop. I can't tell her to stop. I need her touch too much to let a little pain get in the way.

"I'm sorry," she says as she stops rubbing my cheek.

"Don't stop."

My eyes meet hers, and I see a tear fall down her cheek. A tear I can't wipe away, despite how much I need to.

She slowly reaches her hand back to my cheek and touches me so softly that all I feel is the pleasure from her touch.

"I'm so sorry I hit you. I didn't know what else to do. I just couldn't kill you. I couldn't live if you were dead. I'm sorry I kissed Nacio. It was the only thing I could think of. I would have done anything to gain his trust and keep you alive. I couldn't kill you. I couldn't kill you," she says as her voice turns to sobs.

"Shh," I say, cursing the ropes for not letting me touch her. "Stop it. You have nothing to be sorry for, princess. Nothing at all."

She wipes the tears, but as soon as she does, more tears fall. "Yes, I do. I hurt you. I never wanted to hurt you. Ever."

I sigh. "You didn't hurt me tonight. Seeing you alive brought me back from the brink of death. That's all I care about. That you are happy and alive even if..." I can't bear to say the next words. *Even if you don't love me anymore. Even if you never did.*

She stops crying immediately and looks up at me. "You think I hate you, don't you?"

I can't look at her, so instead, I look at the cold, dark ground. I can't answer her. I don't want her to pretend she doesn't hate me when she does.

I feel her hand reach around to the nape of my neck. She slightly lifts my head, forcing me to look at her. She bites her lip again as she looks into my eyes, trying to read my expression, but in my swollen state, I don't think she is able to read any of my emotions.

She pauses for a second longer, studying me, trying to understand, and then her lips are on my lips. Her tongue is in my mouth. Her hand is tangled in my hair. Her kiss demands me to kiss her back, and I oblige as best as I can. I push my tongue further into her mouth until it is tangling with hers. She moans loudly as I do, and as she deepens the kiss, I know there is no way she hates me. There is no way she could feel anything other than love for me. And I hate myself for doubting that love. I hate myself that one word—*never*—made me think that she hated me when I read the note she left in the bed and breakfast in Ireland.

She slowly, reluctantly moves her lips from mine. She places her cheek against my cheek. "I love you. I could never hate you. I love you. I've always loved you. I always will," she says.

"I know, princess. I know. I love you always, too."

She kisses me hard against my cheek, holding the kiss for a long time, like she is preparing to say good-bye, but she isn't. She is just leaning away from my face so we can look at each other again, eye-to-eye.

"You should go." I force the words out of my mouth even though it is the absolute last thing I want.

"I can't. I need you too much first."

I suck in a breath, not able to stand the torture she is putting me through when she promises me something that can't happen. I close my eyes, trying to break the connection between us. "You have to go. I need you to stay alive."

"I will. I will stay alive, but I won't without having you first."

I shake my head and keep my eyes closed, ignoring what she is telling me she wants.

"It's not safe, Kinsley. There are cameras everywhere. There are guards. They can't find you in here. You need to go. I need to know that you are safe. That you are alive."

Her lips touch mine, and I can't keep my eyes closed anymore. They open automatically as she runs her tongue across my bottom lip. I could let her suck me. I could let her fuck me. I wouldn't last. It would be over in a matter of seconds. I've missed her too much to last longer than that.

"No," I say sternly. "No."

"I am safe. I told Karp."

I narrow my eyes in confusion at the name.

"The man who is on guard duty. I told him I wasn't done with you. That I needed to make you pay for what you did. I needed to make sure you weren't hiding anything else. He thinks I'm in here, torturing you, beating you up. There are no cameras in here. We are safe."

"Thank fucking God."

She smiles brightly at me, but the brightness soon fades as more blood drips down my face. She moves closer to me, and I freeze as I watch her tongue move out of her mouth. I anticipate her running it across my lip again, but this time, it moves to the corner of my lip where blood is spilling. She slowly, hesitantly licks up the blood, and I can't do anything but stare at how sexy she is as she laps up the blood.

I can't grab ahold of her with my hands, but it doesn't matter because I grab her lips with my mouth and pull her into mine. I suck hard, tasting the mix of my blood and her in my mouth. Nothing could taste sweeter than the taste of us together.

She suddenly pulls away, far enough away that I can't pull her back in with my lips, and I hate that I'm tied up. She keeps her eyes closed, most likely reliving the kiss, just like I am.

She opens them, and I see the somberness that has formed there.

"What?"

"I need you, but the only way I can have you is if they think I am hurting you. I can only have you if they think I am torturing you."

I nod. "Then damage me, torture me. I would do anything if it meant I got one more chance to love you."

"I'm not sure I can though. I don't think I can hurt you again."

"You can only harm me by walking away and not giving me what I need."

"What do you need?"

"You. I need you."

She thinks for a moment, and then I can see her desire for me overtake any reluctance at the thought of causing me more pain.

"Go get the whip in the corner."

She turns from me and looks reluctantly in the direction where I nod. She doesn't move. She just tucks a strand of hair behind her ear.

"Go."

She slowly walks over and picks up the whip that brought me so much pain earlier at the hands of Seth. And, now, it will bring me pleasure because it means I get to have her.

She picks it up, and it looks awkward in her hand. I know I'm going to have to convince her it's okay for her to wound me. It's more than okay. It's what I want.

My eyes turn dark with desire for her to claim me. My throat turns dry as I think of her taking me. My cock stirs as I think of her riding me, destroying me for any other woman in the world.

She slowly walks back with the whip in her hand. She looks up at my tied-up hands with tears forming in her eyes.

"At least let me untie you."

She walks to my hands and tries to untie me, but I know it's no use. She won't be able to untie the knots—not without spending hours doing so, and that's time we don't have.

"No."

Her hands freeze midair. "Why not?"

I shake my head. "I don't want you to untie me. I want you to hurt me. I want you to dominate me. I want you to make me pay for ever letting you go."

She steps back for a second, and I see her lust for me grow as she looks into my eyes to see I am telling her the truth.

"You're wet for me, aren't you?"

She sucks in a breath.

"You're wet for me at just the thought of hitting me."

She bites her lip.

"You've had this fantasy before. You've always wanted to be in power. In control."

I watch a tinge of anger mix with her lust.

"But I never let you have control. Take it. Take control now."

I watch as the whip twitches in her hand, begging her to use it.

"Hit me. Claim me. Make me pay for lying to you. For not telling you the truth."

"Don't tell me what to do."

I smirk. I've gotten through. "Then, make up your mind already."

She hits me with the whip, and I feel the sting of it as it hits my exposed stomach.

My smirk widens. "Is that all you've got? I thought you wanted to claim me. I thought you wanted to punish me for what I put you through."

She hits me again, and this time, I feel the passion behind the whip as it hits my thigh.

"Stop talking. I'm the one in control."

She uses the whip again, and I feel it hard against my shoulder.

"You don't get to be in control anymore. Not after you lied to me again and again."

She walks forward and slaps my cheek hard with her other hand, causing me to moan loudly as my wound from her original hit re-opens.

But she makes up for the hit by grabbing my chin and forcing me to kiss her hard and fast until we are both panting.

When she releases me, she hits me square on the other cheek, and a grunt escapes my lips.

She smiles. "How does it feel, not having any control?"

She slides the end of the whip down my face, over my lips, and to my bare chest.

My eyes darken, begging for more, at her seductive speech.

"Princess, I'm not going to last if you don't take me soon."

She shakes her head. "You're not in control. I am."

I feel the sting of the whip hit my back, making me bleed, I'm sure of it. She doesn't know my back is already covered in sores from being whipped before. And I don't let her know. She needs to do this. She needs to injure me to stay safe, and I love letting her hurt me. I love letting her love me.

Her eyes drop to my pants. My jail jumpsuit barely hangs off my hips, and my cock presses against the thin material, begging her to touch me.

I watch with wide eyes as she lets the whip trail down my body until it is just over my cock.

"Don't," I say, my voice a little shaky.

She smiles and then lifts the whip above her head.

I squeeze my eyes closed, afraid of where she is going to hit me. I cry out when she hits me the hardest she has yet, but she doesn't hit my cock. She hits the inside of my thigh. It somehow electrifies me and makes me want her even more.

I open my eyes and am rewarded by a naked Kinsley. My eyes grow wide at the sight of her naked before me. I strain my arms in the ropes, hoping I can get out of them because I need to touch her so fucking bad.

She smiles, watching me squirm. She takes a second longer to run her hand down her body, across her swollen breast and down to her pussy.

I watch in anticipation as she moves her fingers in circles around her clit and her eyes fill with lust. I can no longer breathe when her fingers dip inside her dripping pussy. I can't think. It's the sexiest thing she has ever done.

Her grin grows larger as she sees me lose control when I suddenly call out her name.

She immediately takes the whip and hits me again. My moan turns from pleasure to pain so if anybody were listening in, they would hear her torturing me instead of loving me.

Her hand reaches down and touches my cock through the thin material of the jumpsuit, and I know I'm going to need her to hurt me a lot more if I'm going to cry out in pain instead of love.

I bite my lip, trying to hold back a moan.

"Hurt me," I whisper. "Make it so every time I move tomorrow, I'll think of you. I need more pain if I'm going to make it through this."

Her eyes intensify at my words. She releases me and walks back to the corner of the room. When she returns she has something behind her body, but I can't see what it is.

"Close your eyes," she whispers softly into my ear when she reaches me.

I hesitate for a second, realizing how much trust it takes for me to close my eyes. I do it though. I close my eyes and wait for the sting. It doesn't come though—at least initially.

Instead, I feel cold metal moving across my body. I feel her hand on my cock again, firmly gripping it. I bite my lip, causing more blood to spill out from the corner of my lip, to keep from calling out her name again.

And then I feel the greatest mix of pain and pleasure I have ever felt. I feel cold metal spikes drive hard into my back at the same time as when I feel her claim me with her pussy, straddling over me.

I scream loudly. Loud enough I'm sure the whole building can hear me. It's a painful scream, but at the same time, it's a beautiful scream. It's a scream that makes me love her even more because she knows so perfectly what we both need.

Her hand grabs ahold of my back as she begins moving up and down my thick cock, making the pain a faint memory until it is almost gone.

The second she feels the pain disappearing from me, she grabs my back, digging her nails into the sores on my back while picking up speed.

I scream again, but then she muffles my screams with her mouth as she kisses away the pain.

She picks up speed, and I match her. We both lose control together. We both moan together. We both claim each other.

When we are done, Kinsley grabs ahold of my body, and I know she's exhausted from what she just did. And I know it is going to take everything I have left to convince her to let me go.

I kiss her on the top of her head as my eyes grow heavy again. I need to close them. I need to get some rest. And she does, too.

"Get dressed, princess."

I nudge her with my head, and she stirs a little.

"Get dressed," I say again.

She slowly lets me go and gets dressed. Then, she moves back to my cock. Her eyes stay on mine, and I nod. She licks my cock clean while I do my best to stay quiet so nobody hears me.

She then pulls my pants back up to where they were.

"You need to go."

She nods this time, and it rips me apart to know this might be the last time I see her. Tomorrow, one of us might be dead.

"Do I look thoroughly beaten up?" I ask, trying to joke with her.

She glances down at my body, and I see the sadness return in her eyes, giving me my answer.

"Hey, it's going to be okay. You're going to survive this."

She shakes her head. "I don't want to survive without you."

"You have to. You have to survive."

"No, I will only survive if you do."

I try to speak again to tell her she has to survive, but she holds a finger up to my lips, silencing me.

"Tomorrow. They are moving everyone to a different location tomorrow."

"Where?"

"I don't know. They don't trust me enough to tell me yet." She pauses and then starts again. "My plan is, after we move to the other location and I find out as much info as I can, I will contact the police and the FBI."

"How?"

"They let me keep my cell phone."

I nod. "You should have called them by now. You can't risk waiting."

She shakes her head, and I know why she won't do it now. Her grandfather isn't here. He's at the next location. Most of the people they smuggled have already been moved. Saving them is more important. Setting things right is more important.

"Fine, but you call them as soon as you are moved. Don't wait."

She nods. "I'm not planning on waiting."

She looks down at her hands and then back up at me. "You have to promise me something," she says.

"Anything."

"Promise me if you have a chance to escape, you will take it. You won't wait for me. You will just go."

"No."

She raises her eyebrow. "Promise me. I need to know you are going to live. They are going to make me kill you. I need you to promise the first chance you get, you will run without me."

I take several deep breaths, trying to figure out how I can get out of promising her, but I don't see a way out.

"Killian?"

"I promise," I say even though it's a lie.

She knows I'm lying to her.

"But you have to promise me something, princess. You have to promise me if they make you choose between your life and mine, you will choose your own life. You will shoot me if you have to. You will kill me to survive. Promise me."

A slow tear drips down her cheek, and it kills me I can't comfort her, I can't hold her.

"Promise me?"

"I promise," she says in a whisper. She wipes the tear from her cheek. "I need to go. One last kiss."

She places her lips against mine, and I suck her in, trying my best to make her feel better. Trying my best to take away her pain, but I know the agony remains, just like it remains inside me. We both know this could be our last kiss. Our last touch.

I feel our tears falling down our cheeks and mixing together. Then, suddenly, Kinsley is pulling away.

"Stay alive, princess."

She nods and wipes her eyes.

We don't say anything else to each other. Neither of us can say anything more. We both know we love each other. We both promised we would survive, even at the cost of the other. We both lied.

Kinsley keeps her eyes on me as she walks to the door, and I keep my eyes on her, trying my best to take this memory with me forever. But I'm not sure I can take the memory with me.

I'm afraid, as soon as she walks out the door, I will lose her forever. I'm afraid the pain will return, and I won't survive. But maybe that's for the best. Maybe, if I die, she will live.

12

KINSLEY

I CLOSE the door behind me, and I lose all control of my feelings. My emotions all mix together, and I no longer know how I feel. Happy or sad. Hopeful or defeated. Satisfied or longing. Everything mixes the second the door closes to the only person left I truly love.

I look down the hallway to where Karp was sitting earlier, watching guard. He's still sitting there, but his eyes are no longer open. His head is drooped down, and I can hear him snoring from here.

My shoulders relax a little as I see him asleep. I should have a clear shot back to my bedroom. The only person who might see me is whoever is watching the security cameras tonight. That is, if they are awake enough to keep an eye on the screens.

I don't hesitate to wait and see if anybody is going to notice me. Instead, I walk down the long hallway that feels of death to the stairwell. I climb down the stairs to where my bedroom is.

I pull the door open to my room, but the door is slammed shut. My whole body jumps, and my eyes close automatically at the sudden movement. I turn to see who it is, expecting Nacio or Santino. Instead, I find Seth breathing down my neck, just inches from me.

"What were you doing?" he asks.

I cross my arms and give him a stern look. "I was getting my revenge on Killian. I didn't think he had been punished enough. I wanted him to suffer more. I wasn't sure about what you were able to get out of him. I wanted to see what other information he would tell us."

I turn to walk into the room that will be my bedroom for one more night, but Seth doesn't remove his hand from the door. He doesn't allow me access to the room.

"I don't believe you tortured him. I don't believe you could torture anyone. And you aren't supposed to leave your room without permission. It's not allowed."

"Well, I did. Go check him yourself, and you will see."

Seth grabs my arm and pushes me hard against the wall. He pulls a gun out from the waistband of his pants but doesn't aim it at my head. He just casually holds it, letting me know he could use it.

Except he can't use it. Nacio would be pissed. And Seth would be the next one to die.

I smile, looking at the gun. "You aren't going to shoot me. Don't even pretend."

His frown deepens, and his face turns scarlet red. "You don't get to give me orders. Not yet."

I smile wider. "Neither do you. Now, I suggest you let me go to bed if you don't want me to speak to Nacio about your actions."

Seth slowly releases me, still holding his gun by his side.

I walk past him and open the door to take my barracks and walk inside. I quickly close and lock the door behind me, not that it would hold anyone out. I wait at the door, listening silently, until I hear his footsteps walking away. Then, I walk through the dark room to the bunk that I have made into my bed.

I don't notice the smell anymore. I don't notice the dirt on the floor or the stains on the bed.

I don't even think about Seth. I don't think about the fact that he will report my actions to Nacio. I don't think about the fact that Nacio could kill me before I even have a chance to explain.

All I think about is Killian. I think about how it felt to have his muscles flexing beneath me. I think about how his lips devoured mine. I think about how his cock claimed me. I wish those were all the things I could think about. But along with the most pleasurable moments with Killian also come the most painful.

My body shakes as I remember seeing Killian tied up. His body was obviously broken from torture. His heart was broken at the thought that I no longer loved him.

That is what destroyed me worse than seeing any of the painful marks that crossed his body. I hate I was the one who caused him so much misery.

I hate I had to use the whip to bring him more injuries so we could both experience pleasure. Somehow though, the sting of the whip brought us closer together instead of further apart. I don't understand why, but I enjoyed the power the whip gave me over Killian. Torturing him turned me on. The power turned me on. I was afraid hurting him would make him hate me, but instead, it made him just as excited as I was.

If we both survive this, I will have to remember to bring more excitement into the bedroom. The only problem is, I don't think we will both survive tomorrow, let alone live long enough to experiment more with whips, canes, and bondage.

I try to push Killian out of my head. I try to think of anything else, but my thoughts keep coming back to him. I lie down on the bed, trying my best to sleep.

But I can't sleep. If I sleep, I'm afraid my dreams will be of the girl who died. Or of what Nacio said about Killian killing my father. Or I'll dream of having to kill Killian.

So, I won't dream. I won't sleep. I can't. Instead, I will just relive my last night with Killian over and over and pretend tomorrow will never come.

"Pull the trigger," Nacio says.

I hold the gun in my hand, but I don't understand why I would pull the trigger. Why would I want to kill anyone?

"Kill him. He killed your father. Kill him."

His words anger me. I want nothing more than to kill whoever killed my father. I loved my father. No matter what he did, he didn't deserve to die. I turn toward the man kneeling on the ground.

Killian.

"I can't kill him," I say.

"Yes, you can. Kill him. Pull the trigger. Gain our trust."

"No."

"Kill him, or we will kill you."

"No."

"It's you or him."

Tears threaten, but I don't let them out.

"Choose now."

I look at Killian, who nods, giving me permission to kill him.

I pull the trigger...

———

"Wake up, sweetheart. It's time to go."

I open my eyes and try to remain calm, but I can't stop my chest from rising and falling way too fast. I can't stop the panting or hide the sweat on my face.

I sit up, wiping the perspiration off my forehead caused by the dream I'm too afraid will become my reality.

"You okay, sweetheart?" Nacio asks.

I yawn, trying to calm my speeding heart. "I'm fine. Just thrown from being woken up so early in the morning."

"It's time to go."

"Go where?"

Nacio just smiles and walks away.

I groan and stretch before I get out of bed. I couldn't have slept more than an hour or two. I tried not to sleep, but somehow, sleep must have found me.

I rub my arms, feeling cold. I stand and walk to the bed across from mine where I piled up my clothes. I dig through the clothes, trying to find something suitable to wear. Something that won't make me feel like a complete slut.

I don't find anything. I change my bra into a white crop top that might as well be a bra. I grab the jacket Santino lent to me. I slip it on and then walk out into the hallway where Nacio is waiting for me.

He frowns when he sees the jacket. "Where did you get that?"

I shrug and yawn again. "Where are we going?"

"To our next base of operations."

I swallow hard, trying to calm my nerves creeping back up again. I don't know where the next place is or what it holds, which is what scares me the most.

"Let's go," Nacio says, holding out his arm to me.

I ignore it.

"Shouldn't I pack my clothes and things first?"

"No, I'll have the other men pack up your clothing and bring it when they come. We have a flight to catch."

I nod.

Nacio waits a second longer for me to grab ahold of his arm. When I don't grab ahold of it, he sighs and then walks to the stair-well. I follow. We climb down the stairs without saying a word before I realize I don't have my purse with my phone in it.

"One second, I need to go back to grab my purse."

"We don't have time."

"I'll be just a second. My passport is in there."

"You won't need a passport."

"We aren't leaving the country?"

"We are, but you don't need a passport."

"I would like to have my phone and IDs."

Nacio grabs my arm and leads me to the exit of the building. "We don't have time, and like I said before, you won't need them. We will make sure you have everything you need once we get there."

I want to protest again, but I don't. My phone was the only way I had to contact the outside world. It was my security to call in the police if I got desperate. Now, I have nothing.

I walk outside, happy to taste some fresh air after being stuck inside the building for days. It is still dark outside, making me suspect even more that it is very early in the morning. My best guess is three or four. The only sound I hear is the gentle humming of the two vans parked outside the building. The windows on both of the vans are dark, making it impossible to see inside.

Nacio opens the door to the first van. "Ladies first," he says to me, holding the door open for me.

I climb into the van and notice Seth and Santino are already sitting in the backseat. I take the middle, and Nacio climbs in after me.

A man I don't recognize climbs into the front seat and quickly begins driving. The car ride is silent. I suspect everyone is too tired to be up for any conversation.

I lean my head against the van window and watch the broken, old buildings roll by. The buildings quickly turn from broken down to shiny, new hotels that make up most of the city.

Nacio slings his arm around my shoulders. I turn and glare at him, but he isn't looking at me. His head is resting against the head-rest with his eyes closed. I sigh and surrender to having his arm around my shoulders for the rest of the van ride.

I'm tempted to close my own eyes as we drive. My eyes grow heavy with each sway of the van, but I can't close my eyes. Not with Seth in the back. At any moment, he might decide to tell Nacio or Santino of my actions last night. If I fall asleep, I could dream of Killian, and I can't take the chance I might talk in my sleep. So, I don't sleep. I stay awake as the van drives and drives.

The van slows as we reach an airport. I assume the driver will stop out front and drop us off. He doesn't though. He drives up to a metal gate. I watch as he rolls down his window.

A man speaks in barely audible Spanish over the speaker, but it must be audible enough to our driver because he says, "The Marlows are here."

A loud buzzer sounds, waking up Nacio. The gate opens, and the driver rolls us through and onto the tarmac of the airport. We drive a little farther, and then the van parks in front of a large private plane. My mouth drops as I realize this is how we are flying.

I've flown private several times before with my father, but I guess I didn't think a bunch of criminals would fly privately. It makes sense though, as there would be less questions. But, even with the size of the plane, I know the number of men I saw earlier will not fit on the plane. They also won't fit in the two vans that drove us here.

I turn to Nacio. "How are the rest of the men getting to wherever we are going? They won't all fit on the plane, will they?"

He studies me for a second and then opens the door. "No, they won't fit," he says as he climbs out of the car.

I quickly climb out after him, not satisfied with his answer. "Then, how are they getting there?"

"They aren't."

"What do you mean?"

"They are staying behind for the FBI to find."

I raise my eyebrows, not fully understanding. "Alive or..."

He smirks at me and then softly pats me on the cheek, like I'm a child. He doesn't answer. Instead, he walks over to the plane and climbs the stairs, leaving me standing on the tarmac alone.

But I have my answer. The men that I saw and had dinner with. The men whom I realized were just ordinary men. Nothing more or less, just trying to survive. Most of them are now dead or will be.

Santino grabs my arm, bringing me back to the present. "Come on. You won't get a good seat on the plane if you don't."

I smile and follow Santino onto the plane. The inside of the plane is large. Larger than most of the private planes I have been on before. The first area is made to look like a living room. Two large couches that could easily hold half a dozen men line each side of the living room. A flat screen TV sits in the corner. I walk past the living room and find a large bar already stocked full with food and drinks.

Past the bar is a business area with individual recliners, tables, and TVs. I count six large recliners. Past the recliners is a bathroom door and a second door, which leads to a bedroom, if I had to guess.

I'm not sure where I should sit—the living area or the reclining chairs in the business area. If I had my choice, it would be the large reclining chairs in the business area.

"Sit anywhere but the first on the left. That's Nacio's seat," Santino says.

I smile at Santino and then take a chair on the right, far away from where Santino said Nacio would be sitting. Santino smiles back at me and then takes the reclining chair in front of me. The chair I'm in gives a great view of the entire aircraft. I can see the bar, living room area, and even the edge of the cockpit.

I lean back, loving how comfortable the chair is. I plan on sleeping most of the flight to wherever we are going. I recline the chair, put my feet up, and close my eyes, preparing to do just that.

"What are you doing?" Nacio asks.

"Sleeping." I open my eyes and see Nacio standing over me with a frown on his face.

"Oh, leave her alone," Santino says, reclining his own chair. "She just wants to sleep. If you want to sit by her so bad, sit in that chair there instead of your usual chair." Santino nods to the chair just across the aisle from me.

Nacio's frown deepens, but he takes a seat across the aisle from me instead of where Santino says he usually sits. I sigh. I wanted to sit alone, but instead, I'm surrounded by the Marlow men.

I begin to close my eyes again when I hear more men getting on board. Men I don't recognize. I wait to find the men that I do know. I wait to see Karp or Raul climb on. But I don't see them. I watch as all the men fill the couches up front.

The only person I know left is Seth, as far as I see. I glance across the aisle and see Nacio pulling a computer out of his bag. I glance the other way and find Santino is already snoring.

I relax a little, hoping they won't bother me during the flight, so I will be able to get some sleep just as long as Seth takes the one remaining seat on the couches up front.

I close my eyes, trying to drift off, when I hear Seth's voice.

"Where do you want him, sir?" Seth asks.

I open my eyes and find Killian standing in front of me with Seth behind him, holding on to Killian's shoulder. Killian looks bad. Worse than the last time I saw him. He's still wearing the same jumpsuit he was wearing before, but it is now covered in dirt and blood. His chest is exposed, as the top half of the suit is torn. His chest is covered in whip marks, blood, dirt, and sweat. Marks I caused.

I feel a tinge in my chest at the sight of him in such a state. His arms are tied behind his back. I take a chance and look into his eyes that have deep circles under them from lack of sleep. His hair is matted on top of his head. Tape covers his mouth, but I still see a trickle of blood fall from a corner onto the stubble covering his chin and neck.

Still, even his current state doesn't stop the desire from creeping up inside me. I want nothing more than to take him into the back room of the plane and fuck him until we are both satisfied. Even though I just had him last night, it wasn't enough. It will never be enough. No matter how many times I have him, I will always want more.

Killian doesn't look at me. Instead, he looks at Nacio. I want him to look at me though. I need to see the love is still there. I need to see he still has fight left. That he hasn't given up yet. That he is going to live. But he doesn't look at me.

It doesn't keep me from staring at him. Even though I have to look at him with anger and disgust, I still stare because I can't *not* look at his strong body I fell in love with.

Nacio stands as he glances past him to the front of the plane and then sighs. "Put him in one of the chairs there," Nacio says, pointing to his usual chair.

Seth tugs on Killian's arm and shoves him into the chair. He buckles Killian in, so he can't move. The chair is facing forward, away from me, so I can barely see him unless he intentionally turns his head around. He won't. He's too worried someone will find out about what I did last night. So, he won't look at me. Instead, he will face forward and pretend he hates me.

I watch as Seth takes a seat behind Killian and in front of Nacio. Now, I won't be able to sleep. I can't leave Seth alone to talk with Nacio. I hope Seth will sleep himself so I can get some rest. But he seems intent on making sure Killian doesn't move. Not that there will be anywhere for Killian to go as soon as the plane takes off.

I close my eyes as the pilot comes over the intercom, telling us to buckle our seat belts and how long the flight will be. I don't listen, despite knowing the pilot could be telling me where we are going. I can't focus on anything other than Killian. I can't focus on anything other than the fact that whether or not I pull the trigger, I'm the reason Killian is going to die.

The plane takes off, and I know Killian and I's time is limited. Every second we get closer to our next location is one second less that Killian has to live. I must find a way to keep him alive. I have an entire plane ride to form a plan and to find any reason that he should live. I saved him once from death. I'm just not sure I can find a way to do it again.

13

KILLIAN

THE CHAIR FEELS LIKE HEAVEN, despite my hands being tied behind my back. I am able to rest my head on the headrest, and even though I can't recline the chair unless Seth reclines it for me, I am still able to get some sleep I desperately need.

Sleep might be the only thing that keeps me from thinking about Kinsley. The only thing that will keep my eyes away from hers. The only way to keep our love hidden.

I close my eyes, expecting sleep to come easily, but then I hear Nacio speak, and I know I won't be able to sleep.

"Paris," Nacio simply says.

"What?" Kinsley's beautiful voice asks.

I force my head forward instead of looking in her direction.

"We are going to Paris. I think it's safe to tell you now. You'll find out anyway as soon as we land."

"Really? Paris?"

"You sound shocked." He laughs. "It seems your grandfather found the perfect place to continue our work in plain sight, so we don't have to hide in a dark, abandoned building, like we did in Mexico." He pauses. "When we get there, we should go to dinner. I know the perfect place to take you. Of course, we will have to wait until after you pass the final test."

My heart beats rapidly in my chest. I won't be able to stand it if she says yes, but I know that is what she should say. Thank God I'm tied up. Otherwise, I would beat that man for even asking her out.

"That would be nice," she says sweetly.

I can hear the hesitation in her voice. I just hope no one else can tell she's hesitating. I hope no one else understands the disgust in her voice.

I'm glad it's Paris though and not another dark, dank city with no way for her to escape. If they are in the heart of a city, she will have a chance to live.

I close my eyes again when they stop talking, hoping everyone will settle in for the long flight. But, of course, that doesn't happen.

"Sir, I need to speak with you about an incident I saw on the security cameras last night," Seth says.

I freeze, knowing he is talking about Kinsley entering my room. My hands begin trying to untie the rope I know won't come untied, but it doesn't keep me from trying. My only hope is they won't kill Kinsley on the plane. I have to hope they will keep her alive at least until we reach Paris. By then, I might have a plan to keep her alive.

Nacio sighs. "Not here, Seth. If any of the men were involved, it can't be properly dealt with here."

"It doesn't involve the men," Seth says.

"Well, everyone else is dead or shipped off. I don't need to know the details."

"It involved Kinsley."

"Thank you, Seth, but I can tell the story from here. Like I said last night, it doesn't involve you," Kinsley says.

"I disagree. I think it does involve me," Seth says.

"I—" Kinsley says.

"What did you see, Seth?" Nacio says, silencing Kinsley.

"Kinsley decided to visit the FBI agent last night. She stayed for almost an hour and then went back to her room. When I saw her leaving his room, I approached her and questioned her. She said she was there to torture him more, but I don't believe her."

"Is that true, sweetheart?" Nacio asks.

"Yes, I went to see Killian." Her voice strengthens with each word. "I went to see him because I didn't think he had fully paid for what he did to my father. And I wanted more information. I wanted him to tell me why he'd killed my father. I wanted to find out if he was still hiding something."

"I don't think that's why she visited him, sir. I think she still loves him. I don't think we can trust her, sir," Seth says.

"Look at him! Look at Killian! His body is completely broken after what I did to him, and I still don't think it is enough. He hasn't suffered a fraction for what he has done. I should have killed him. I shouldn't have let him live."

"Sir—" Seth starts.

"Enough, Seth. It doesn't matter what Kinsley went in there for. It's obvious Killian has more wounds than he did before. All that matters is Kinsley kills him when it matters."

"But—" Seth tries to speak.

"Enough, Seth. Go check on the pilots to make sure we are still going to land on time."

I watch Seth get up and walk past me with a grim look on his face.

And then I hear Kinsley scream, and it takes every nerve in my body not to react to her pain. I can't when I know Nacio and Santino are watching me.

"Get off me!" she screams.

"No, not until you understand your life is in danger. Not until you understand you don't have a choice. You are either with us, or you are dead. You don't get to do whatever the fuck you want. Do you understand?"

"Get off of her. She can't breathe," Santino says, sounding bored.

I hear Kinsley wheeze, and I breathe a little easier myself, knowing Nacio is no longer holding her neck.

"That is your last chance, sweetheart. Fuck up again, and I will kill you," Nacio says.

No other words are spoken, but I can feel the tension between Kinsley and Nacio and even Seth when he returns. Still, none of them speak.

I wait. I wait until most of their breathing has turned back to the calm steadiness it was before, and then I turn my head just enough to see her out of the corner of my eye. I thought she would look weak or scared. She doesn't. She looks strong. She has a plan. I can see it in her eyes as she glances back at me. I just hope her plan involves her living. Because there is no use in saving me if she doesn't save herself.

14

KINSLEY

I'VE FAILED.

I know I've failed. I know Nacio is suspicious. I know I didn't convince him. The marks he left on my neck prove he doesn't believe me, he thinks I still care about Killian.

I've failed. I have no idea how to keep Killian or I alive any longer. We will both die. As soon as I prove I can't kill Killian, Nacio will kill us both.

I pretend to sleep for the rest of the flight, but it is a useless endeavor. I can't sleep. I don't think I will ever be able to sleep again.

I keep my eyes closed until I feel the plane land on the runway. I open them and find everyone else doing the same—slowly opening their eyes. It seems everyone was pretending to sleep rather than talk to each other. Or they were actually sleeping.

No one speaks as the plane pulls to a stop outside the Paris airport. I watch as the men at the front of the plane disembark. I watch as Seth exits the plane and then climbs back on. I watch him unbuckle Killian from the recliner chair. I watch Killian stand, and I see the bruises and lacerations covering his back. He doesn't glance back at me as much as I know he wants to. Instead, he walks forward, away from me. I try to look away, but I can't. My eyes stay on him until the last second when he walks off the plane.

I watch as Santino stands and begins exiting the plane, leaving me alone with Nacio. I stand, but Nacio grabs ahold of my arm, preventing me from moving off the plane.

I look at him, but the look in his eyes scares me. His eyes look red instead of their usual shade of green. All of the muscles in his face are pulled tight as he glares at me. He's going to kill me before I even have a chance to speak with my grandfather. Before I even have a chance to run to a phone and tell the FBI about our new location. He's going to kill me right here on this plane.

"I know your secret."

I suck in a breath, but I try to remain calm and not give anything away.

"I don't have anything to hide."

"Yes, you do. Since you first came here, I've suspected your intentions weren't pure. I'm still not entirely sure what your intentions are. But I do know you care about the FBI agent more than you should, so you can stop trying to hide it."

"I no longer care about how you currently feel. I care about how you *will* feel. What future you will choose. I intend to show you what you could have if you choose me, if you choose a life of running the company your father cared so much about. If you choose me over him."

"And if I don't?"

"You already know what will happen to you." He strokes my neck, still sore from where he choked me. "You will both die instead of just him."

He releases my arm, but I don't move. I watch as he picks up his bag and stands. He smiles at me as he grabs my hand and leads me off the plane. I let him.

He's giving me more time, I realize as we get off the plane. He doesn't want to force me to kill Killian. He wants me to *want* to kill Killian. He wants me to want to choose him over Killian. So, I have to make him think I'm open to the idea of being with him.

When I glance up I expect to see another crummy van waiting to pick us up like before, but I guess we only ride in luxury in Paris as a black luxury sedan is waiting. I climb into the backseat and see Santino already sitting in the front. Nacio climbs in after me. This time, when he puts his arm around me, I lean into him just the slightest, enough that I smell his cologne. It is much too strong, suffocating me with the stench. But I don't move away as much as my nose wants me to.

I glance out the window and notice two vans driving away. One of them must contain Killian. I try not to stare or think about him. I just try to pretend I'm open to giving Nacio a chance.

The driver begins driving off the tarmac. The ride is beautiful. I watch historic buildings pass us by as we drive to the heart of the city. We pass buildings I have been in several times while on trips here with my father. We pass restaurants. We pass the Eiffel Tower. We pass the Louvre. We pass everything that everyone cares about so much in this city.

It all seems so beautiful. I would give anything to go back in time and enjoy everything more. The food, the history, the people—I would have enjoyed all of it more. Appreciated all of it more.

But, now that I know a base of operations is here, I wonder if every visit here with my father was just another chance for him to smuggle. For him to meet with Nacio's father.

Every time he ran off to take a meeting or phone call, was he really taking a meeting with Nacio? Was he dealing with an employee he had to kill?

Now, every memory I have of him, every single memory I have of traveling the world with him, is tarnished.

The car finally stops outside of a building. Santino jumps out, seemingly happy to spread his legs. Nacio climbs out next and makes his way over to my door. He opens the door to my side of the car, and I climb out.

The warm sun shines down on me as I glance up at the building so typical of Paris. In fact, if I didn't know any better, I feel like I might have stayed at this building before. The building is four stories with white brick walls. Windows are scattered up the front with balconies protruding from each one.

I don't understand how they can smuggle people in a building like this. I don't understand how they think their men could go in and out of this building without others seeing it as suspicious.

I don't think my grandfather, mother, or I could leave this building without being recognized. Not when we are all supposed to be dead.

I follow Nacio into the building, hating that there is such darkness living in such a beautiful place. As I suspected, the inside is just as beautiful as the outside. The entrance is simple, full of white with colorful pops of silk flowers. The building looks like it used to be an apartment building, but now, it runs as our headquarters.

Nacio guides me to a row of doors. He points to the first door. "My office." He points to the second. "Your grandfather's." He points to the third.

"My father's," I say, already knowing the answer.

He nods and then walks to the second door. He knocks loudly on it.

"Come in," my grandfather's voice says.

Nacio pushes the door open, and I walk in behind him. I see my grandfather behind the desk. My eyes widen at the sight. I knew he would be here, but somehow, actually seeing him here makes everything real. It proves to me how horrible he really is.

Granddad looks at me but doesn't really look at me. Instead, he looks through me, like I'm not really here. He turns his attention back to Nacio, who walks over and takes a seat in the chair across from Granddad's desk.

"We have a new shipment coming in an hour. Are your men ready?" my grandfather asks.

"They will be. They are settling in the agent and the last shipment now," Nacio answers.

"Good. We need to discuss what the agent is doing here. That wasn't what we agreed to. He was to be killed and left for the FBI to find tomorrow when they raid our facility," Granddad says sternly. His face is already becoming flushed red.

Nacio pulls out the chair next to him, and I walk over and take the seat, but Granddad still doesn't acknowledge me.

"I realized the plan we discussed was flawed. We needed security, so if we did fuck up and leave a trail for the FBI to our location here, we would have a way out. A way to protect ourselves," Nacio says.

"We shouldn't need a way to protect ourselves! You should have made sure you wouldn't fuck up!" Granddad says.

"It was my decision to make!" Nacio says.

"No, it wasn't!" Granddad stands, his anger overtaking him.

All I can think is, if he keeps this up, he will have another heart attack, but I don't say anything.

"We need to change locations," Granddad says.

"Oh, not this again. We have been in this location for years. It is perfectly safe here. There is no need to move to a different location," Nacio says.

"No! It is not safe here. I've already looked into more suitable locations south of here."

Nacio shakes his head. "Maybe it's time I buy you out. You've lost your mind, old man. We can't shut down our two main locations, not at the same time. We would never recover."

"This is ridiculous! You don't have the power here. I have the final say, and you know it."

"No, you don't. That's where you are wrong. You don't have any more power than I do. Not now that Robert is gone."

Granddad glares at Nacio. "Perhaps it's time we go our separate ways then."

"Indeed, it is time. It is time for you to go, since that is what you want so much. The Marlows will continue running things here."

Granddad snarls at Nacio while Nacio leans back in his chair with a smug grin on his face.

"What are you doing here?" my mother's shrill voice says from behind me.

I turn slowly in my chair and watch as she glances from me to Nacio and then to Granddad.

"I'm here to run the Felton empire. To gain money and power, same as you."

"You..." She walks to me. "You shouldn't be here. You ruin everything."

"You must not be running a very good business here if one woman could bring down everything," I say.

Her cheeks turn bright red, and I can see the alcohol lingering in her bloodshot eyes. She should be in rehab, not here.

"You'll see, Nacio. You should have killed her when she showed up at your door in Mexico," Mother says before walking back out of the office with a bottle in her hand.

I should cry at my mother's words. I should feel sad or hurt or some sort of pain. I don't though.

I feel free, knowing I had every right to hate my mother all these years. I'm not her daughter, and she is not my mother. I feel a release at knowing I no longer have to feel anything for my mother because I never had a mother.

15

KINSLEY

Nacio glances down at his watch. "I need to go see that the new shipment gets settled." He stands and then turns to me. "Sweetheart?" Nacio waits for me at the door.

"I need to speak with my grandfather."

"You sure? I wouldn't waste your time with him if I were you."

"I'm sure."

I look at Granddad, who is still standing behind his desk, pretending like I'm not even here.

"I'll come find you when we are finished," I say.

I watch Granddad keep his eyes glued on Nacio behind me. When Granddad looks back down at his desk, I assume Nacio has gone.

"I think we have a lot to talk about."

Granddad takes a seat in his desk chair and leans back with his arms crossed in front of his body. His nostrils are flared, and his face is still red with anger. He finally looks up at me. "We have nothing to talk about. You shouldn't be here. You should leave before you get yourself killed."

I frown even though he's right. I probably will get myself killed. He should be protecting me though. He should be telling me he wouldn't let that happen. I don't have a mother, and it seems I never really had a grandfather. Or a father. I never had a family.

"No, I have to be here. I'm here because my family does horrible things. My family kills and rapes and tortures. And I want to be a part of it.

"I no longer have a life at home. You ruined it. If I go home, I'll be thrown in jail. My only hope for a real life is here, ensuring the family legacy lives on."

Granddad laughs. "You won't survive here. You would have more of a life in jail than here. Leave before you are too far in to be able to leave."

I raise my eyebrows. "No. You won't let me anyway. I already know too much to be able to leave. I want to do this. I want to understand my father. I want to work with the only family I have left."

Granddad runs his hand through his hair. "You can't do this work. You aren't suited for it. It will kill you if you try."

"It will kill me if I don't." I tuck my hair behind my ear. "I want to know the truth. And I want to be given a chance to be a part of the organization."

Granddad laughs again. "What makes you think I would let you help run this organization when I wouldn't even let you run the legal part of the Felton Corporation?"

"Because I don't think it's up to you to decide."

He frowns. "You think it's up to Nacio?" He laughs. "That boy isn't much better than you are. No, the decision is mine to make." He stands from his desk and walks to me. "You are right about one thing. You are in too deep now for us to simply let you go. You want to be a part of this organization? Then, prove it."

My eyes widen. I'm afraid I've woken a sleeping giant. I'm afraid he will take me to Killian right away to put a bullet in his head. I shouldn't have provoked Granddad.

I just want to understand why my family does this. I just want to find out the truth of what they do and how. As soon as I do, I'll make the call to the police, and this will be over.

I stand and follow Granddad out of the office. He walks to the elevator and presses the button. I should stand and wait and let him tell me whatever it is he wants to tell me, but I can't. I'm done waiting.

"I want answers. I want to know why. How? I think I deserve to know after everything you have put me through."

Granddad doesn't seem fazed by my questions. Instead, an elevator arrives and he walks in, pressing the button for the second floor. "Why is simple. We needed money to start the casinos."

The doors open to the second floor, and Granddad steps out and stops just outside of the elevator.

I follow him. "Why did it continue though after you got the money for the casinos?"

"We were hooked. The money was better and easier than anything the casinos could provide. We were good at it. The casinos were just a front and a means to find what we needed."

I scrunch my nose.

"What did you need?"

Granddad smiles. "You already know the answer to that."

"People to smuggle."

He nods. "People, drugs, diamonds. Anything of value, we learned to smuggle and make a profit. The casinos simply provided us with a large group of people to choose from to smuggle and sell."

I think back to a conversation I had with the executives at the Felton Grand casino after Granddad left. I remember something about employees not showing up to work. My eyes widen as I realize how they find the people. "You smuggled people from our casinos. That's why employees didn't show up to work. That's why guests disappeared unexpectedly. You were taking them."

"Just the ones without family. Just the ones who wouldn't be missed."

"Then, how are you going to find people to smuggle now?"

He smiles. "The same way we always have. Just because I'm not there in person doesn't mean we can't continue to find people and drugs from the casinos. But those aren't the only places we find them. We have our hands in various corporations involved in helping us find and sell them."

Them. I hate how casually he says the word. I hate how casually he speaks of ruining people's lives.

"Who do we sell the drugs and...people to?" I force the words out of my mouth.

"Mainly men with money. Men who want to party and have a good time without having to deal with the laws of everyday society."

"So, for sex? You sell the women to men for sex."

He nods. "Usually."

Granddad begins walking again, and I follow a step behind. He walks purposefully down the hallway and then turns right into a large room that most likely used to be a recreation room of some sort when the building was an apartment building.

There aren't any furniture or decorations in this room. The room is empty with scuffed white walls, except for a pole in the center that I can't keep my eyes off of. The pole has bloodstains dripping off of it, bearing the pain of who knows how many men, women, and children over the years. I don't know what it is for, but I have an idea.

I don't know why Granddad has brought me to the empty room. *To show me what they do to those who disobey? Or is he planning on tying me to the pole and beating me himself?*

I don't ask. I can be patient. I can wait. Because I don't like any of the answers he might tell me. I can't come up with one single answer that would bring me any peace.

I look up at Granddad, who is typing something on his phone.

"I should go find Nacio," I say as I begin to walk out of the room that scares me half to death.

"No. Nacio will be joining us shortly."

"Why?" I ask the question I have been avoiding.

"If you are going to stay here, I need to know which side you are on. You can't be on the Marlows' side. You are a Felton. You must be loyal to the Feltons."

"Why should I when all the Feltons ever did to me was lie?"

"Because, like it or not, you are a Felton, not a Marlow."

"What if I became a Marlow?"

Granddad raises his eyebrows at me. "I don't think you will."

"I might. The Marlows have treated me better than my own family ever has."

"Even if you married one of them, it wouldn't change anything. You were born a Felton. You don't have a choice."

"Here's the man who raped the woman," Nacio says suddenly from behind us without any warning.

I turn my attention from Granddad to Nacio. My mouth drops when I see Karp standing in front of him. I didn't think he had even made the trip. I thought he was dead in Mexico.

"Good. Make an example of him," Granddad says.

"My pleasure," Nacio says, smiling.

He begins walking Karp over to the pole in the center of the room. He locks eyes with me, silently begging me to help him. I look back at him but don't tell him anything. I don't know why he thinks I will be able to help him. He's the one who chose to work for these terrible men, even knowing the consequences. He was the one who raped a woman, despite knowing he wasn't allowed to.

I watch as Nacio makes quick work of tying Karp's arms above his head, attaching the rope to a loop at the top of the pole. Karp doesn't even fight him. I think he knows it will be worse if he does, but I can see the terror forming in his eyes.

I look back to the door when I hear more people filing past the room. Woman after woman walks past the room, each with a man who works for Nacio and Granddad. Each man holds on to a woman's arm or the rope tied around the woman's wrists. Each woman looks different yet the same. Most are wearing business-casual clothing, as if they just got off work. Some are wearing workout clothing. Some are just in casual clothes. But all show fear. All look to me with hope, like I'm the one who is strong enough to help them. They don't understand I am just as much a prisoner as they are. My life is just as much at risk.

One woman in particular catches my eye. She looks so normal in her black pants and business jacket. Her hair is dark brown and curled, landing halfway down her back. She doesn't look much older than I am. The only unusual things about her are that her arms are tied tightly together in front of her body and her eyes. Her eyes are wild with anger and fear. She was the one Karp raped without permission.

I don't know what the future holds for this woman. I don't know where they plan to ship her off to or if they will rape or beat her first. But, now that I've seen her, I know I can't let them do it. I can't let them hurt her. I won't be able to live with myself if I do.

I silently promise her I will save her, or at the least I will get the revenge from these men, something she may never get.

I turn back to the door when I see the children walk by next, and my heart stops. They can't be more than seven, eight, or maybe nine years old. All of their arms are also tied with a man holding onto the end of the rope. Each wears a look of fear. Some have tears falling fast down their faces.

The children are what kill me more than anything. Seeing them here, knowing my family has ripped them from theirs and plans to sell them to someone who only sees them as a sex object, it's too much to bear.

I watch until the women and children are gone. To be held in a room until they are sold. It's too much to fathom even though I just saw it with my own eyes.

I glance back to the door and see Killian walking in, looking even more badly beaten than before. Seth holds on to his arm with a gun pointed at his head.

"You'll be next if you don't behave," Seth growls to Killian.

Nacio steps forward with something black in his hand that I can barely see.

Then men who work for Nacio return after locking up the women and children.

"You didn't follow orders, Karp. You touched a woman who wasn't yours. And you don't have the money to buy her. You robbed us of money, and now you will pay."

16

KILLIAN

I STAND UNCOMFORTABLY against the wall. I try to keep my eyes off of Kinsley, but they automatically go there. Her eyes aren't on me though. They are on Karp. She's glaring at him for what he did to that woman. Even though, the woman would have been raped eventually by some man Nacio or her granddad sold her to. I know Kinsley still thinks she will be able to save them, but I'm not even sure if we will be able to save ourselves, let alone anyone else.

She looks strong in the center of the room with her granddad. She is wearing tight jeans and a jacket covering most of her bare stomach, but when she moves, I get a glimpse of it and her lace bra.

I watch as Nacio holds a whip in his hand and walks toward the man in the center of the room. I look closely at it, thinking it is the same whip used on me. The same one Kinsley used on me when she fucked me earlier. But, on closer inspection, I realize it is not the same whip. This whip has small spikes at the end. This whip is meant to inflict the most pain possible.

"You cost us a couple hundred grand when you raped her, Karp," Nacio says as he walks closer to Karp, firmly gripping the whip. "We could have easily gotten that much for the virgin. Now, we will get less than half for her initial purchase. We should make you pay with that many lashes, but I don't think you would survive, and unfortunately, we don't have the time to break in a new man yet."

Nacio thinks for a minute as he steps forward. "The last man we whipped only lasted thirty lashes before he begged for mercy. We gladly put a bullet between his eyes, releasing him from the pain."

I glance at Karp, the man tied tightly to the pole. Nacio rips his shirt open, exposing his back. I can't see Karp's face as Nacio lifts the whip, but I know it must read fear.

"If you can survive to thirty-five, your debt will be paid."

Nacio brings the whip down hard on the man's flesh. I hear him scream when the metal spikes dig into his skin. The rest of the men in the room tighten into stiff statues, but they won't interfere or try to stop this on behalf of their friend. The sight of the blood dripping down the man's back is bad, but his screams are worse. His screams reveal how bad the torture really is.

Nacio brings the whip down three times in quick succession, and Karp's screams become deafening. I close my eyes, but it only amplifies his screams.

I open my eyes and look at Kinsley, who is staring at Nacio. She doesn't look away. Instead, she watches intently as the man is whipped. Occasionally, I watch her eyes drift closed when it all becomes too much.

After fifteen lashes, Nacio stops. I glance at the man's back covered in blood. I don't think he will last much longer. I think he will ask for death rather than more lashes. Nacio walks away from him. Karp will only survive if Nacio decides he has had enough lashes.

Nacio stops in front of Kinsley. "Want a try?" he asks, holding the whip up to Kinsley.

I watch Kinsley's eyes widen as she looks at the handle of the whip Nacio is holding out to her. She doesn't react, even though I can see the conflict in her eyes. This could cement her place. Ensure that Nacio trusts her. Karp deserves to be beaten. Every man in this room deserves it. But I'm not sure Kinsley can inflict the justice. She just looks at the whip, almost studying it.

"You are going to have to finish yourself, Nacio. Kinsley doesn't have it in her to beat a man, even a man as guilty as Karp," Lee says.

Kinsley immediately grabs the whip from Nacio's hand. Nacio grins wildly while Granddad frowns. I wonder if her granddad was egging her on because he wants her to join him or because he wants her to prove him right, so he can get rid of her. From the look of disappointment on his face, I would guess it was the latter.

Kinsley walks up to the same place where Nacio was just standing. She turns back to Nacio, and I think she is going to change her mind. She can't beat another man, even a man as horrible and vile as Karp.

She can't do it.

And, if she does, she is going to regret it. So, as much as I know it will help her standing with these men, I don't want her to do it. Whipping *me* was one thing. Whipping *him*, drawing blood from a man who is getting no pleasure from it, is something entirely different.

She looks to Nacio. "How many are left?"

"Fifteen," Nacio says.

Kinsley turns back to the man and brings the whip up just like Nacio did. She brings it down hard and sharp against his skin. Karp screams out again, but it's not as deafening as his previous screams. The whip still struck his skin, but she doesn't have the same finesse or power that Nacio just used.

I watch her chest rise and fall as her adrenaline sinks in. I can see a hint of nerves bubbling under her skin at the thought of having to hit a man fourteen more times while listening to his bloodcurdling screams. She doesn't hesitate for longer than a second though before she brings the whip up and down again. This one is even weaker than the first.

I glance over at Nacio and her granddad. They are staring intently at Kinsley. Nacio has a large grin on his face as he walks over to her and stands behind her.

He holds on to her arm and shows her how to lift the whip. "Like this," he says as he helps her use the whip again.

This time, Karp's scream returns to the bloodcurdling one it was earlier. This scream makes the whole room shake again with terror.

Nacio steps back and watches Kinsley whip Karp again with the same speed and sharpness he just did. Nacio's grin grows larger. He thinks he's won. He thinks she is on his side now.

She isn't. She's mine. All mine.

I want to scream that to him. I want to punch him for touching Kinsley. For forcing her to do this. The only thing that stops me is that I know they would kill me in front of her, and I can't let her experience that pain. A pain I have felt before when I thought she was dead.

Kinsley glances up and I know she's imagining the woman who was raped, and I don't know what she sees, but something changes inside of her. She has renewed strength at what she must do, and this time, she hits Karp with all the power she has. As she does, her face seems content and satisfied.

She moves again, and I watch the satisfaction grow on her face. I watch the pleasure spread through her body as she hits him. I don't know what the pleasure is from. *Is it from inflicting pain on another person?*

I try to close my eyes. I try not to see the pleasure engulfing her body with each whip, but I can't keep my eyes off of her. Because I quickly realize what changed. In order to get through this, she shut out this room, and returned to the room with me in that cell. She's imagining my screams instead of Karp. She's riding my cock pulling my pleasure from me along with the blood.

She stops for a second to remove her jacket, exposing her bare stomach and black lace bra. Now, there is no way I will ever be able to take my eyes off of her again. She looks sexy, standing there, with a whip in her hand, and I suddenly want her fantasies to be true. I wish she were whipping me, not him. Even though the whip in her hand is a million times more painful than the one she used on me, I still want it.

I want to feel the sting of it on my skin as she looks at me with desire.

She whips again, but this time, Karp doesn't scream. I look at him, and I think he has passed out from the pain. She needs to stop. She could kill him.

But she doesn't stop. Kinsley lifts the whip and thrusts it forward again and again.

Each time she does, my cock grows harder and harder. Each time, I want to beg for her to touch me, to whip me. Each time she whips him, I see the desire growing behind her eyes as well. She's back in the room with me, not him.

We're twisted, so fucking twisted. We are both aroused by her whipping. If she touched me or even looked at me right now, I'd come. And I know she'd be right behind me.

Because at first, she whipped Karp to cement her place here. To further earn Nacio's trust. After seeing the woman Karp raped, she whipped him harder to extract the revenge the woman would never get a chance to extract. But now, she's whipping him because it is bringing her back to that cell with me.

I've brought her into the darkness with me.

I watch her pant with lust and need as she quickly hits him, each time going faster and faster. My breathing picks up, and my heart rate builds to an unbearable pace. My cock twitches and aches for her. I feel like I'm going to burst if I don't come soon. I'm afraid I will die if she doesn't touch me.

She whips again, and this time, she screams an orgasmic, harsh scream I haven't heard from her before. The scream is enough. The pressure that has been building in both of us is suddenly gone. It left when she screamed. It's gone, as simple as that, and it's replaced with Kinsley's anger. I see the rage forming the second the release disappeared. A anger caused by what her family did to countless people. Frustration with me for lying. Anger at Karp for hurting that woman. Everything in her world comes crashing down now that the high she felt is gone.

She becomes wild and lashes the end of the whip toward Karp, but her movements are no longer smooth and practiced. Now, they are wild and untamed.

Nacio walks over to her, barely missing getting hit by the whip himself. He tightly wraps his arms around her. "Enough. He's had enough, baby." He nestles his face in the crevice of her neck.

My face rages with so much anger as I see him touch her after such an intimate moment. I can feel the steam rolling off my bare skin.

Nacio tucks her hair behind her ear. "You did well, baby."

I watch her breathing slow at his words, and I hate him. I hate him for comforting her. I hate him for calming her anger. I know that, once the anger at Karp is gone, once the anger at her situation completely disappears, a new hate will form. I've felt the hate before when I caused my brother's death. When I thought I had failed Kinsley, I felt the same.

Kinsley will hate herself.

17

KINSLEY

I HATE MYSELF.

I should kill myself.

I should pull Nacio's gun out from his waistband and kill myself. I am a horrible person. I can't believe what I just did. I destroyed a man, and I enjoyed it. I'm just like Nacio. Just like Granddad. Just like my father.

I truly am a Felton. A monster.

I'm twisted. I just whipped a man, and I've never been more turned on. Once the whip got in my hand, the images of Killian came floating back. The need to bring the woman justice helped me start. The anger flowed, quickly turning to lust for Killian. But even if the man deserved it, I shouldn't have done it. And I definitely shouldn't have enjoyed one second of it. I deserve to die.

Nacio slowly releases me and looks to his men in the room. "This is what happens when you disobey an order. I don't care who you are or how long you've worked for us. Never disobey," Nacio points to Karp, who I swear must be dead against the pole.

His body is slack, and I don't see his chest moving. He's not breathing. *He's dead.* I killed him. I killed someone. I feel the butterflies I kept hidden forming in my stomach, making me queasy.

Nacio nods at the men. They begin filing out of the room. I don't chance a glance at Killian even though I can feel his eyes on me. I can't bear to look at him and see his disappointment in me.

The room empties, except for Nacio, Granddad, Karp, and me. Nacio, Granddad, and I stare at the man who is still bleeding in the center of the room.

Two men come back into the room.

"Get him down, and clean him up. Get him medical care if he needs it," Nacio says.

The men exchange glances and then walk over to where Karp's body is. *He's dead*, I think, as his body falls to the ground in a limp pile. They cut the rope, keeping his arms attached to the rope.

He's dead. I killed him.

The men reach under his arms, lifting him. Karp groans, proving me wrong. He is still very much alive—at least for now. The men begin dragging him out of the room.

I don't wait. I can't stand to be in here any longer.

I run past them before they get to the door. I need air. That is my only mission. I don't care if it is breaking the rules. I need to get out of here.

My stomach begins churning as soon as I make it out of the room. I won't make it down the stairs and outside before I lose it. I move to the hallway window a foot away from me. I try to push it open, but it doesn't budge. I try the latch, but it is frozen. My stomach churns again, warning me I don't have much time. I glance out the window and see a balcony. It looks to be down the hallway, to my right.

I run as fast as I can, holding my stomach and praying the contents won't come up. I can't let them see how I react. I have to get out of here. I push the door open to what used to be an apartment. I run across what looks to be an old living room to the sliding door of the balcony. I grab the handle to throw it open and am relieved when it creaks and opens enough for my body to fit through.

Breathe.

I finally breathe, and I taste the fresh air from outside. But the air isn't enough to settle my sick stomach. I grab the railing just as the contents of my stomach come up. Thank God the street is empty, and no one is walking below me.

"Here," Nacio suddenly says from behind me.

I come up for another breath between vomits.

I feel his hand on my back in a surprisingly comforting manner I didn't expect from him.

I turn to face him and see him holding a glass of water in his hand.

"Thanks," I say, taking the glass from him. I sip on the water, and it immediately relaxes my stomach.

Nacio's hand stays on my back, slowly moving in calming circles. Although this man became the monster that he is, I know there is something better inside him. He has kept some part of him buried for far too long. Maybe, if I can appeal to that part of him, he can help me put an end to all of this. I just need to find that small part of him again.

"You did amazing back there, baby. I'm proud of you."

I shake my head. "And then I puked. I'm not sure I'll ever be cut out for this job."

He laughs. "Sure you will. It just takes some time to get used to the blood, to the smell. We've all puked before. It doesn't take away from what you did back there."

I nod.

"How do you feel?"

"Queasy and guilty that I enjoyed torturing another man."

Nacio's grin widens. "That's what makes you cut out for this job. Nobody enjoys it if they aren't cut out for this."

I try to force a smile onto my own lips, but it's hard. I don't want to be cut out for this. I don't want to be tempted into this world. I want to put a stop to this.

"Does that mean I passed?"

"Yes, but you still need to kill the FBI agent. After that, you will have full access to everything."

"Have we heard anything about the FBI in Mexico?"

He moistens his lips as he tucks a loose strand of my hair behind my ear. "So impatient, baby. Don't worry. You will get to kill him soon. We haven't heard yet if the FBI has found our place in Mexico, but they will soon."

I nod.

"Come on." He holds his hand out to me. "I want to show you something."

I place my hand in his, despite my gut telling me not to.

We walk back inside. We walk past the room where I beat a man almost to death. I try not to look inside as we pass. I pray I don't run into Granddad or Mother. I pray we don't run into anyone as we make our way back downstairs.

We don't.

Nacio walks outside, still holding my hand, and that's when I realize I'm wearing a bra and jeans on the streets of Paris. Nacio notices my free arm curl around my stomach.

He pulls me to him in an awkward hold. "Stop. You're beautiful."

I smile, but I hate his words. I hate that a tiny butterfly returns to my stomach when he looks at me. I hate that I am even a little bit attracted to a man who isn't Killian. I hate that I'm affected at all. I hate that I get the tiniest tingling for a man whom I watched kill an innocent woman.

As soon as the image of the woman comes back into my head, the tingling disappears. The butterfly in my stomach disappears. I gently pull out of his arms, not able to stand being in them.

"Where are we going?"

"My house," he says, frowning at me as I stand two feet away from him instead of in his arms. "It's fifteen blocks from here. You able to walk that far?"

I nod.

He holds his hand back out, and I place my hand back in his, despite the urge I have to keep my hands firmly wrapped around my midriff.

We walk in silence down the beautiful streets of Paris. We pass other couples who are holding hands, and they smile at us with knowing looks on their faces. They think we are together. They think we are lovers, but that is something we could never be.

We turn the corner, and I begin to feel the pain as I walk in my black heels. My feet are sore with blisters I'm not used to experiencing, ones that shouldn't be there after such a short walk. I pause for a second to try to fix the heels, so they stop rubbing against my blisters.

Nacio pauses with me and then steps in front of me. "Climb on." He bends down a little, giving me his back.

I hesitate. I don't want to climb onto his back, not unless I get to slit his throat when I do. I climb onto his back anyway because I know I won't make it if I have to walk any farther. I don't understand why we are walking at all, other than Nacio wanting an excuse for me to climb onto his back.

Nacio stands back up, tightly holding on to my legs, while I reluctantly hold on to his neck. I can't help but breathe in his scent as we walk. The smell of his cologne makes me close my eyes as it reminds me of Killian. It's not quite the same scent, but it's close enough to bring me back to him. I remember he is locked up in a cell somewhere in severe pain while I complain about my feet hurting. I really am a spoiled princess.

Nacio walks several more blocks before we turn another corner.

"This is your house?"

He sighs, relaxing at the sight of his palace he calls his Paris home. A gate stands between us and his house, blocking some of the house, but I can tell from here his house is at least three times the size of ours in Las Vegas.

"How were you able to afford something so grand? My family's house in Las Vegas isn't even this large."

"I inherited it from my father," he says somberly.

I slide down his back, willing to walk the rest of the way to his house. We pause at the gate, and he enters a code. And then we take the quarter of a mile walk up the entrance gardens full of green trees and vines with just a few pops of color from the flowers. I don't understand how a monster lives here.

We walk up to the door, and he unlocks it with a key he pulled from his pocket. I expect to immediately be greeted by staff members welcoming Nacio home, but I don't see anyone rushing to us.

"Is anyone here?"

Nacio glances down at me, and his eyes widen. "You seriously think I would have staff here?"

I shrug. "Yes. Who cooks and cleans for you? Who does your laundry? Who takes care of the gardens?"

"Me."

Now, it's my turn to raise my eyebrows. "Really?"

"Yes. I don't like having other people cook or clean. I have two security guards, but that's it. I like my privacy."

I nod. I glance up, looking at the beautiful chandelier hanging overhead. I could stay here forever, just looking at it, but Nacio grabs my hand and pulls me through the foyer to a large room at the back. This room is a large dining hall with a ceiling at least two stories tall.

"Sit," he says, pointing to a chair at a long dark table that could easily seat twenty.

"You don't want to show me around the rest of the place?"

"No, you need to eat first."

On cue, my stomach growls, giving me away.

"Fair enough, but don't you need time to cook?" I grab my stomach that still feels a little queasy after being sick earlier.

"No, I'll have to cook for you another time."

Nacio walks through the door of the dining hall to what I assume is the kitchen. He returns a second later with glasses, a wine bottle, and a plate of cheese.

He places each on the table and then begins pouring us each a glass of wine. He then pulls matches out of his pocket and lights the candles nearest to us even though it's not dark out yet. I watch as he takes a seat on the end, kitty-corner to me.

He lifts his glass of red wine, and I do the same.

"To us," he says, clinking his glass against mine.

I take a sip but then immediately regret it. This wine isn't sweet. It's harsh and bitter. I won't be able to do more than sip it. It's nothing like the wine Killian has gotten for me.

I grab one of the squares of cheese on the tray in the center of the table and pop it into my mouth. This, on the other hand, tastes like heaven. I grab a handful of the cheese and continue popping several into my mouth until my stomach begins to settle a little.

"How did your father die?"

"He didn't die," Nacio says, frowning at me.

"Oh..." I pause between bites of cheese. "I thought you said you inherited this place from your father."

"I did, but he didn't die. He is running our location in Asia."

Fuck. There is another location. Another place for pain and suffering.

"Oh, where in Asia?" I ask casually before popping another piece of cheese into my mouth.

Nacio takes a bite of cheese himself. "I inherited this house and this location when my father chose to move to Asia. We will have to travel there at some point. I haven't visited that location yet. We have spent most of our time traveling between Mexico and Paris. But this location is my favorite. Santino prefers the darkness of Mexico. I prefer the light of Paris. My father prefers the excitement of Asia."

"What about my family? What did my father prefer? My grandfather?"

He thinks for a second. "Your grandfather prefers Mexico. It was hard for him to give up that location. Although we will start up a new location in South America soon. And your father, Paris. I think that's why he and I got along so well. It killed me to see him die."

"You were there when he died?"

Nacio nods.

"You were in Las Vegas?" I sit up straighter in my seat.

He nods again. "I was there when your father died."

"So, it really wasn't a heart attack?"

"It wasn't a heart attack. Killian killed him. He poisoned your father and made it look like a heart attack."

I feel a tear fall down my face. I know that Nacio isn't speaking the truth. I know that Killian didn't kill my father. But I still don't understand who did, and I might never know. Even though I hate him, I still care for him deep down, which kills me. It kills me that

I'm crying for my father when he was a monster. Maybe, now that I am one, too, I feel more for him than I should. I feel connected to him.

I glance to Nacio, who wipes the tear from my cheek. There's a softness, a kindness, in Nacio, just like my father. I didn't have the opportunity to turn my father from the darkness, but I can bring Nacio to my side. I just don't have any idea how to do that, other than to flirt and let him flirt back.

"I miss him," I say.

"Me, too."

Nacio tucks a strand of hair behind my ear, and I grab his hand, keeping it pressed against my cheek. I close my eyes, trying to imagine his hand is Killian's, but that won't work. Nacio is nothing like Killian. Nacio is selfish, ruthless, and intimidating. Killian is loving, selfless, and intense. Their strength and ability to lie to me might be the only similarities between the two men.

I open my eyes, no longer able to fantasize that Nacio is Killian. I place my hand on the nape of Nacio's neck and pull him to me until his lips are pressed against mine. He aggressively kisses me. His tongue thrusts in and out of my mouth, making it hard for me to breathe. I continue to hold on to his neck, trying to hold on to dear life, as he grabs my other hand and pulls it hard to his chest. Harder than what I'm comfortable with. A painful moan escapes my lips when he pulls my hair with his other hand. I try to make it sound sexy, but there is no mistaking my moan for anything other than pain.

I pull at his hair and hear his painful growl in return. Fuck, I don't know how to stop this. He must hear my thoughts though because he aggressively releases me. He wipes his mouth with the back of his hand. We both breathe hard and fast, trying to catch our breaths after a kiss like that.

He has a wicked, dirty grin plastered on his face as he looks at me, and I'm afraid I've ignited his lust for me. I'm afraid he is going to want to fuck me right this second, but I can't let him.

"You and I would make quite a pair. I don't trust you yet, not fully. But I will soon, and then we can take over everything together."

"How?" I ask when my breathing has returned.

"We will kill them. *All of them.*"

My mouth drops a little at his suggestion, but maybe I misunderstood him.

"What do you mean, kill all of them? Who exactly?"

"Your grandfather, your mother, my brother, and my father. We kill them all, and then we will be free. We kill all of them, and then we can do what we want with the organization."

His face brightens. This isn't the first time he has thought about this. I can tell from his excitement. This is what he really wants. I just don't understand why.

I sip on the bitter wine, trying to mask my disgust at what he is suggesting. I set the glass back down. "You could really do that? You could kill your father? Your brother?"

"Yes," he answers automatically.

I know he is telling me the truth. He's not lying.

"Could you? Could you kill your grandfather and mother?"

I don't have to think about it. I already know my answer. "Yes."

18

KILLIAN

I'VE BEEN in this dark room for hours. My stomach growls, letting me know how hungry I am, as if the ache isn't enough to let me know. My body is sore from being tied up, from lack of sleep, and from not eating in days. If they don't plan on putting a bullet in my head soon, I will easily die from lack of food and water.

At least, this time, I can move around. My arms are still tied behind my back, but they didn't tie me to anything. So, I could move around if only I found the strength to move from my position on the floor.

I glance around the small room I'm sure used to be a closet. The door looks weak, compared to the door that was keeping me in when we were in Mexico. I could try to kick it in. But then what? I would have to run, but I'm not sure I have the strength to do that, not without getting caught. If they caught me, there would be a good chance they would shoot me on the spot.

I try to sit up, but just lifting my head is painful and exhausting. So, I don't bother again. I just need to rest. Once I rest, I will have enough strength to form a good plan.

I close my eyes and think of Kinsley. I try to let her stay in my thoughts. But the darkness soon overtakes me.

"We can kill him soon," Seth says.

I open my eyes, expecting to see Seth standing in front of me, but he's not. The darkness is still covering me. He must be just outside my door though. That confirms that, even if I kicked the door down, I wouldn't be able to escape with Seth just outside the door.

"Good, I don't like keeping him alive," Lee says.

"The FBI has found our location in Mexico. It's all over the news. They seem to think they have found everyone who was behind your deaths," Seth says.

"Good. We just need to verify that before we kill him. I expect he will be dead by tomorrow," Lee says.

"What about Kinsley, Nacio, and Santino? They could ruin everything. What are we going to do about them?" Seth says.

"Santino isn't a threat. He will do whatever we say. And, as for Kinsley and Nacio…" Lee says.

My eyes grow heavier as they speak until I'm barely able to keep my eyes open. Until I can barely hear the words they are saying.

"We can handle them, just like…"

19

KINSLEY

I'M SITTING in Granddad's office with Mother, Nacio, and Santino. They are discussing what prices they are getting for the five children we just got in and where they will be going. The prices are insane, all in the millions, and they are throwing the numbers around like it is nothing.

What's worse is the way they talk about the children. As if they aren't children. Just objects to be bought, sold, and rented.

"So, it's agreed. Nacio and Santino will take the shipment to London," Granddad says.

"What about Killian?" Santino asks.

"We will take him with us. We can kill him and throw him over the yacht. He won't ever be found," Nacio says.

Everyone nods in agreement.

"Kinsley can come with us and do the honors," Nacio says.

"I'd love to," I say.

Nacio winks at me. After our last conversation, he thinks I'm on his side. He thinks I will do whatever he says, and I will. I will because getting close to Nacio might be my only chance at keeping Killian alive.

ELLA MILES

———

I watch as the five kids—two boys and three girls—are escorted from the bus to a private yacht. I watch them walk what could be their last walk where they are completely unharmed. They haven't been raped or tortured or murdered. This could be the last time they experience even a shred of happiness even if it is only from the warm sun beating down on us.

I can't let them get hurt. I can't let them be sold. I can't.

I watch the three men escorting them. They are so unfazed by what they are doing. Santino is escorting the first two, followed by two men I don't recognize. All of them seem calm and relaxed, like they are just going for an afternoon walk, not walking children to their deaths. I don't know what to do, but I know I can't let it happen. *I won't.*

Next off the bus are Killian and Nacio. Killian doesn't try to hide his stares this time. This time, he locks his gaze on me as he walks past where I'm standing on the base of the ramp of the yacht. I glance to Nacio, who is also staring at me. Both men are showing me how much they want me. Both men are devouring me with their eyes, and I can't give either of them the reaction they want.

I wait for them to walk past me, and then I follow them onto the large yacht that could easily fit twenty-plus people. I watch as the men take the children down the stairs inside the yacht. Nacio follows with Killian while I stay on the deck of the yacht. I can't stand to go downstairs with them. I wouldn't be able to keep my composure. I couldn't keep from trying to kill all of the men who are walking so calmly down the stairs.

I walk over to the edge and look out at the water that is so calm and beautiful. The sun is setting over the water. It's beautiful here. Riding on a yacht like this in such a luxurious setting should be beautiful, but all I can think about is that this might be the last beautiful thing I see as well because we might all be dead by morning.

"It's beautiful, just like you," Nacio says from behind me.

He wraps his arms around me, like a lover would do, except he is a monster and I'm far from a lover. Still, we stay like this for a while as the yacht begins moving away from the dock. I feel weirdly calm with his arms wrapped around me. Nacio has a weird way of making me feel like he's a good person who cares about me one second, and then the next second, he's the devil who wants to destroy people's lives. I can't understand him.

"We are going to play cards. You want to play?" one of the men asks from behind us.

Nacio looks to me.

"Sure," I say.

I follow the man down the stairs. A large kitchen, complete with marble countertops, sits at the bottom of the stairs with three tables. Past that seems to be a lounge area. A man is sitting at the first table with a deck of cards, tequila, and chips and salsa spread out on the table. I smile at the man, but he doesn't smile back at me as I sit down next to him at the table.

Nacio sits next to me, followed by the man who invited us down to play.

"Where's Santino?" I ask.

"Driving the boat," Nacio answers.

"And who is watching..." I can't finish the sentence. I can't say *kids* or *prisoners* or *shipment*, as they often call them. I can't say any of those words.

"No one. There is no need. We are in the middle of the ocean, and they are locked up. We don't have to worry about them until morning," Nacio says.

I nod.

"I'm Kinsley," I say to the two men whom I haven't met before. "What are we playing?"

"I'm Don," the younger man across from me says. He looks to be close to my age, and he has blond hair and green eyes. He doesn't have the monster look yet.

I glance to the other man who looks slightly older, probably because of his eyes. His glare makes him look more menacing than Don. His hair is darker, and his stubble is thicker than Don's.

"Maurice," he says somberly.

"Poker. That's all the men know how to play. You know how to play poker?" Nacio asks.

"Yes. I know the basics. What are we playing for?"

"We usually play for duties, but since you both are the bosses, I don't think that is the best idea," Don says.

We all nod.

"Strip poker?" Nacio suggests.

I roll my eyes. That isn't going to happen.

I glance around the room, trying to come up with something we could play for, but all I see are the tequila and tortilla chips. Tequila —that's my only hope. If I can win enough games and get them drunk enough, I might have hope at getting the kids safely off the boat. I might have a chance at saving Killian.

"How about shots? Everyone that loses each round has to take a tequila shot. And when you lose all of your poker chips, you have to take three."

The men shrug. I stand and pull four shot glasses out of the cabinet while the men pass out poker chips from a case beneath the table.

I watch as Maurice begins dealing out cards. I get a two and a seven. The men begin betting, only speaking to place their bets. I call and then watch the flop. None of the cards on the table go with the cards in my hand.

I am forced to fold, which causes me to have to take a shot. Don pours me a shot of tequila, and I down the glass. It burns down my throat. Nacio wins the hand and forces Don and Maurice to take a shot as well.

This isn't going to work unless I win a majority of the games. I need them to pass out from the drinks, but if I pass out first, I won't be able to save anyone.

Don deals the next round.

I lose. I drink.

After the third hand, I've had three shots while everyone else has split shots evenly among themselves.

I deal the fourth hand and finally win. I relax a little. But poker is a game of chance, especially with how the game is set up. The only way to keep from drinking is to win every hand, which is hard to do.

So, on my next deal, I make sure to make my own luck. I hide a pair of kings I'll use the next time I think I will lose a hand. It causes me to win three in a row, so all of the men have to drink. My head is spinning from the three shots I have had while most of the men at the table have had close to eight. Their heads must be pounding.

"I should go check on Santino," Nacio says after another loss.

I glance at his pile of chips. "Not until I've won."

He smiles. "Or I could just give you all of my chips now."

"No. I want to win fair and square."

"You've been cheating," Maurice says next to me.

I freeze. "Have not."

He smiles for the first time all night. "Relax. There is no way a pretty girl like you could cheat."

He slurs his words, and I know he's getting close to blacking out from the alcohol. So, instead of playing another hand, I grab the bottle of tequila that is almost empty, and I pour everyone a shot.

I lift my shot glass. "To Nacio, for the kick-ass yacht."

Nacio tries to smile at me but only one side of his lips curls up. "To you."

We clink glasses together, sloppily spilling half of our shots, before knocking them back.

I stand from the table and stumble as I get up. I've had more to drink than I planned on.

"You okay?" Nacio asks.

I nod and then sloppily kiss Nacio on the cheek. "Bathroom. Be right back to finish kicking your asses."

I stumble through the kitchen to the bathroom just before the base of the stairs. I take my time in the bathroom, hoping to God my plan works. I can't shoot Killian, and I won't ever be able to live with myself if I let those kids go. I wait almost twenty minutes and then decide I've waited long enough.

I slowly emerge from the bathroom and tiptoe to where the men are sitting. Maurice is snoring loudly. Don has moved from the table to the couch. His eyes are closed, and he seems to be asleep. Nacio has his head resting on the table, his breathing slow and easy.

I sigh and tuck a loose strand of hair behind my ear. They are asleep. I just don't know for how long or how deep of a sleep they are in. I slowly back out of the kitchen until I find the stairs at the back of the yacht. I pause at the stairs and glance back to where the men are sitting to see if any of them have moved. They haven't, so I take my chance.

I move as quietly but as quickly as I can down the stairs, knowing my time is limited, but I have to take this chance. It might be the only chance I will ever get. By the time I make it down the stairs, my head spins from the tequila, so much so that I can barely walk in a straight line. But I keep moving forward, regardless that it isn't in a straight line.

I get to the first door. I turn the knob and push it open. I find an empty bedroom. No Killian. No kids.

I leave the door open and move to the second door, hoping I find them soon. Every second I don't is another chance I take that one of the men could wake up. The second room is empty, too.

I glance down the hallway and count ten other doors. I don't have time for this.

"Killian," I whisper as I now run down the hallway, pushing every door open but not finding him.

I get to the last two doors. I try to push the second to last door open, but it doesn't open. The knob doesn't turn.

"Killian," I whisper again.

I wait a second.

"Kinsley?" Killian whispers back.

I sigh in relief from just knowing that I've found him.

"I need to get you out, but the door is locked. Can you unlock it from the inside?"

A second passes and then another as I wait for Killian to answer me.

"No, I can't open it. What are you doing here?"

"Getting you out. I don't have time to explain. We don't have much time, and we have to be quiet."

"You're going to have to find a way to unlock it from out there. I'm tied up, and even if I weren't, the door can't be unlocked from the inside."

"Do you know who would have the key?" I ask.

"No."

I think for a moment, trying to decide on what to do. I could try to search the men for the key, but that would be risky. They could wake up. I could pick the lock, but I have no idea how to do that or even if I could find the tools. I could kick down the door, but it would be loud, and I would risk waking them up, or Santino could hear us from where he is driving the yacht.

"Can we pick the lock?" I ask.

"Have you ever done that before?"

"No."

"Okay. I can try to walk you through it. Do you have a hairpin?"

"No," I sigh. I think back to all the bedrooms. If a woman or girl stayed in any of them, there is a good chance one fell on the floor. "Hold on though." I run through bedroom after bedroom, searching the bathrooms and floors to find a hairpin. I get lucky in the third room, finding a hairpin lying in the corner of the bathroom floor.

I run back to the room where Killian is locked inside. "I have a hairpin."

"Good. You need to break it in half."

I easily break it. "Okay, it's broken."

"One half, you need to bend, so it is curved like a hook," he says, his voice so calm.

My hands are shaking viciously. "Done."

"The other half, you need to bend the end just a little."

I bend it, but I must bend it too far because it breaks.

"It broke," I say in a panicked voice.

If I can't get him out, he's going to die.

"It's okay. Just try again." His voice stays calm.

I bend it slower this time, and it doesn't break. "Okay. Now what?"

"Put the hooked one in the bottom and the slightly bent one on top."

I do it.

"Then, slowly move the top one in to lift each barrel, keeping pressure on the bottom one. You have to lift each lever to get it to unlock."

I begin thinking this is never going to happen, that I'm never going to figure it out, but it unlocks easily with hardly any effort. I push the door open and see Killian standing on the other side of the door. His hands are tied firmly behind his back.

Tears streak down my face at the sight of him. I run over and throw my arms around him, and my lips go to his. Even though his hands are tied behind his back, he still sucks me in and holds me with his body, with his lips. It's a feeling I never thought I would get again. Every emotion I have been holding in every time I am around him comes flooding back as his lips kiss mine. Love, hunger, need. My desire overtakes my body and thoughts with each kiss. With each kiss, I forget more and more of why we are here. That we are in danger. That we have to stop.

All I can think about is my need for him. I need him filling me. I need him to keep devouring me like this. I need...

I hear a scream from the room next to us as the yacht rocks harder when we hit a rough patch. We are out of time.

"We have to go," I say as I force my lips off of Killian's.

Killian turns. "Untie me."

I try to untie him, but I can't. "There's a knife upstairs. I can use it to cut the rope off."

He nods. "Go. I'll start working on talking to the kids."

I run down the hallway, back to the stairs. I slow as I move my way up, trying to keep my steps quiet. When I get to the top, another wave hits just as I reach the door. I grab the handle to keep from falling over and to keep from squealing. The kids downstairs don't hold back though. I can hear their squeals from here.

I slowly walk to the kitchen, being as quiet as I can be, as I pull a knife from a drawer. The whole time, I keep my eyes glued on the men in the room, hoping they will stay asleep. Another wave hits, and I swear, Nacio opens one of his eyes. I freeze, trying to come up with a reason I would be holding a knife. But I can't come up with one. He doesn't move though, and when I look again, his eyes are closed. I must have imagined it.

I quickly run back downstairs to Killian, who is trying to calm the kids at the door.

"We are going to get you out, but you have to be quiet," Killian says through the door.

He sees me, and I know he isn't as sure they are going to get out. I walk behind him and immediately start working on cutting the ropes holding his hands together.

"They are still asleep upstairs, but I don't know for how much longer."

"There is a small boat on the back. We can all fit on it. We will head straight for the shore. It's a long shot because this yacht could easily outrun the smaller lifeboat, but it's our only shot."

"I agree. I'll try to stall them for as long as I can to give you a chance."

The ropes come undone just as Killian turns to me with intensity in his eyes. "You're coming with us." He firmly grabs my hands, and I know he will drag me on the boat if I don't convince him.

"I can't."

"Why the hell not?"

"Because there are more locations than just Paris. There is one in Asia."

"Where in Asia?"

"I don't know, but if I can earn Nacio's trust, he might tell me. And I need to make sure that when the FBI comes, they find them. That they don't run. The FBI will need someone on the inside."

Killian runs his hand through his hair. "I don't like it. I should be the one who stays, not you."

I shake my head. "They will kill you if you stay."

He raises his eyebrow at me. "And they won't kill you?"

"No, they won't. They have no reason to believe I helped you. Why would I help you and then stay? It doesn't make sense."

"Exactly, it makes no sense. I'm not leaving you."

20

KILLIAN

KINSLEY HELPS the last kid onto the boat.

"Get on. I'll give the boat a good push to get us going so we won't have to start the engine until we are far enough away we won't be heard," I say.

Kinsley nods as she steps on and begins untying the rope. She fought me, but I convinced her it wasn't safe for her here. That she has to come with. We will contact the FBI immediately. They will get here in time to save the women and find the other facility in Asia.

When the rope is loose, I push the boat as hard as I can and jump on, knowing my weight will propel the boat forward.

I exhale. We aren't safe, not yet, but we are together. And as close to safety as we've been.

I turn with a small smile to keep the kids calm, and then I move to Kinsley.

Fuck.

I turn completely around when I find the empty seat where Kinsley was supposed to be sitting.

Kinsley is standing on the yacht, staring at me stoically. With love in her eyes she mouths, "I love you."

Fuck, fuck, fuck.

I consider trying to turn around to go back for her, but that would require starting the engine. It would involve risking the lives of the five innocent children on this boat with me.

"I love you too," I mouth back, knowing I can't turn around.

Kinsley smiles at my words. She didn't give me a goodbye kiss, she gave me no warning she was going to stay. She's the strongest woman I know, and though I will worry for her safety, I have no doubt she will fight with everything she has to save every one of those women and children her family and Nacio has hurt.

"I will come back for you," I mouth.

She nods and then turns and disappears back into the boat.

When we are far enough away not to be heard, I start the engine, knowing I'm leaving the love of my life behind. And if anything happens, I won't survive without her. It's the hardest thing I've ever done.

We speed through the water most of the night. I try not to look back, but it is hard not to. It is hard not to think about Kinsley. That I left her to possibly be killed by Nacio as soon as he finds out we are gone. My only hope is that Kinsley is right. That she has Nacio tied around her finger and she can find the last location, so this never happens again.

I glance up at the sky beginning to light, and I know we are about out of time. The yacht was supposed to reach shore by seven in the morning, just an hour or so after sunrise. We need to reach the shore first. We need to get to the police first before they get to us.

I crank the engine, trying to get the boat to go faster, but it doesn't go any faster. I look over at the children who have somehow fallen asleep on each other, despite our situation. It's better this way. It's better if they sleep. Earlier, one of the girls, I think her name was Jill, puked off the side of the boat from seasickness. That caused all but one of the others to puke as well.

I spent the first hour after that trying to distract them, and I learned about all of them. I know all of their names—Jill, Stephanie, Brooke, David, and Jose. I know where all of them are from and how many siblings they each have. I tried to find out as much about them as possible, to distract not only them, but me. To keep me moving forward instead of considering turning back and risking all of their lives.

After an hour though, they all fell asleep, giving me too much time to think about Kinsley. About how it would feel if she died.

I look up when I spot the shore.

"Kids, wake up. We are almost there."

We are going to make it.

And, as soon as I get to shore, I'm going to call the FBI to have them move in as soon as possible to get Kinsley out of there.

Just hold on, Kinsley. Hold on.

21

KINSLEY

"Wake up, beautiful. We are almost there," Nacio says while gently shaking my shoulder.

I stir and am greeted with the worst headache possible and a crick in my neck from sleeping on the poker table. I grab my neck as I look up at Nacio. "I need—"

"Here's some Advil and coffee." Nacio hands me the coffee and pills.

"Thanks," I say, taking them from him. "I think we drank too much last night, but I don't remember."

Nacio smiles at me. "You'll feel better soon. We won't drink as much on the way back."

"Good." I sip the coffee, hoping it will cure my headache.

After Killian left, I came back and knocked back a couple more shots, so I could pretend I passed out, just like the rest of them. And also to get the image of Killian out of my head. I know I did the right thing forcing him to leave with the children, but the look on his face. The worry around his eyes and pain at being forced into leaving me here was an image I will never forget. I regret drinking so much now.

"Go check on them downstairs, and get them ready to be moved," Nacio says to Maurice and Don.

I try to remain calm, knowing they are going to find the bedrooms empty. But my heart flutters so loudly I'm afraid Nacio can hear me.

"Have you ever been to London?" Nacio asks me.

"Yes. A couple of times with my father."

Nacio nods. "I want to take you to one restaurant on the river before we head back tonight."

"Sounds wonderful."

"Um...sir?" Don says nervously at the door.

Nacio angrily glances up. "What is it?" he snaps.

"They're, uh..." He tries to get the words out, but he can't.

"They're gone," Maurice says, stepping up.

Nacio slowly stands from the chair next to me. "What do you mean, they're gone? Where could they have gone?"

"They took the boat off the back. The FBI agent must have helped them."

"Fuck! I knew we should have killed him in Mexico." He glares at me.

I glare back. "I'm sorry. You were right. I thought—"

He slaps me hard on the face. I grab my face. It stings where his hand touched me.

"If I find out you had anything to do with this, I will kill you myself," Nacio says to me.

I glare at him. "I didn't have anything to do with it. I was passed out from the alcohol, same as you. Maybe you should have made sure they couldn't escape. Obviously, one of you fucked up and didn't lock the door. It's the only way they could have escaped."

Maurice and Don turn to Nacio. It's obvious he was the one who locked the door. When he realizes he might have been the one who fucked up, he pauses for just a second.

Then, he starts yelling, "Search the boat, just to be sure, Don! Now!" He turns to Maurice. "Tell Santino to step on it, and keep an eye out for their boat."

He turns to me as he pulls out his phone. "I have to make a call. Help Don search the boat."

I nod and begin walking around the boat. I search downstairs in every bedroom even though I know they aren't here. I search the main deck and upstairs. I check in with Don to see if he has found any clues as to where they went, but he hasn't. When there is nowhere for either of us to look, we go in search of Nacio. We find him with Santino, who is steering the yacht.

"We didn't find anything," Don says.

Nacio turns to us as Santino turns the yacht around.

"They were spotted heading into a police station," Nacio says, his face bright red with anger. He paces back and forth in the small room.

"Are we going to go after them?" I ask.

Nacio stops and looks at me. "No."

Inside, my heart relaxes a little, as I know Killian is safe. He's actually safe, and we aren't going to go after him. We aren't going to bring him back. I can finally relax and let my heart go with him. It's the only way to protect what's left of it.

"So, we are heading back to Paris?"

"Yes. We are heading back, but we can't stay in Paris long. Just long enough to move everyone and destroy any evidence linking us to the other location. We will have to move to our Asia location or go into hiding for a while now that the FBI knows of the Paris location because of Killian."

I swallow down a gulp, seeing his anger because we can't stay at the Paris location. At his favorite location. Because of Killian and me.

"I'm sorry."

He walks to me. "You should be. It's your fault Killian is still alive. It's your fault we have to give up the Paris location. It's your fault we just lost over five million dollars in one day. Lee isn't going to be happy when we get back. And I'm not going to stand up for you. He can do what he wants with you."

Nacio turns back to Santino, and they begin talking about the best course to take back to Paris, effectively ignoring me. I look at Don, who is looking out at the water, ignoring me. I walk back inside to the living room alone.

It's going to be a long day of traveling back to Paris. Nacio might believe I didn't help them escape last night, but he still blames me for keeping Killian alive. And I know Granddad will agree with him. I don't know if Granddad will actually have me killed for that, but whatever he decides, it won't be good.

I just hope the FBI moves in before they have a chance to punish me. I hope the FBI moves in before they have a chance to scatter and hide. But, most of all, I feel like I can breathe for the first time since Killian arrived. Now, Killian is safe, and my heart is free.

22

KILLIAN

I CALLED THE FBI. They will arrive in the morning. I didn't think that was good enough. I wanted them to move in immediately, but they said they needed time to get their agents in location and to ensure all of the criminals were actually at the Paris location before they moved in. That means Kinsley is on her own for one more night.

It's already been an entire day since I left her. An entire day since I ripped out my heart and left it with her. That is why I couldn't go one more night without seeing her and making sure she was still breathing. So, the second I got off the phone with the FBI in London, I was on the next flight to Paris. I've been hiding out in the building across from the Marlows' and Feltons' organization in Paris for hours now, waiting for them to return. Waiting for the FBI to get here in the morning. Waiting to see if Kinsley is still alive.

Just waiting.

I'm tired of fucking waiting.

But I don't have a choice. So, I sit and wait. And pace and wait. And curse and wait.

Darkness begins to fall over the city, and I'm afraid they decided not to come back to Paris. I'm afraid they decided to move to their

Asia location or went into hiding now that they know the FBI and police are on to them.

I consider calling the FBI again and seeing if they tracked them elsewhere when I see a van pull up. I watch as Nacio, Santino, two men I don't know, and Kinsley step out of the van.

I exhale when I see Kinsley. She's still alive.

I watch them walk into the old apartment building, hidden by the cover of darkness.

I text one of the local FBI agents, saying I think they are all here. They text back they need five hours still and to stay where I am and text them if there is a change.

Fuck.

I can't stay.

I'm done waiting.

I don't have a plan. In fact, I have no idea what I'm doing at all as I walk down the stairs of the building that sits across from the one where Kinsley is. I just know I have to be closer to her. I know I have to keep her safe.

I walk out the side of the building into the darkness. I'm not worried about being spotted outside since the street is so dark. I'm worried about the cameras inside the building. The only way to go undetected is to cut the power. But, if I cut the power to just their building, then they might think the FBI is already here.

So, I take my phone out of my pocket and dial Hayes. He owes me one after he had me arrested and put Kinsley at risk.

"Killian, what's wrong? Have they already moved?"

"No, but I need you to turn the power off in the south part of the city."

"Why?"

"Just do it, Hayes. You owe me."

He sighs.

"Hayes?"

"Give me five."

I end the call and wait. Almost exactly five minutes later, the city plunges into darkness, and I take my chance. I cross the street to the building where Kinsley is inside. I walk to the side door, hoping I won't be spotted. I slowly open the door and slip inside.

Complete darkness is all I see once I'm inside the building. I feel around the walls and realize I'm in somebody's office. I move as silently as possible to the door and press my head against it. I hear people moving and yelling on the other side of the door, as they are trying to figure out what to do now that they have no electricity.

I hear Nacio yell at Kinsley and then nothing. I slowly open the door as Nacio begins yelling again, hoping the darkness will hide me. Nacio stops yelling and walks away. I know Kinsley must be here somewhere, but I can't see where she is. I take a chance anyway.

"Kinsley," I whisper.

"Killian?"

I hear her voice coming from my right, so I reach out in that direction. I feel her shoulder. I grab ahold of her arm and pull her toward me and into the office. I quietly close the door behind us.

Her arms engulf me, and I tightly squeeze her. I wasn't sure I was going to get to experience this again. I feel her body relax in my arms the longer I hold her.

"You shouldn't be here, but I'm so glad you are," she whispers.

"There is nowhere else I would be. Even the possibility of death couldn't keep me away."

She reaches up and grabs my cheeks, pulling me down toward her so she can firmly kiss me on the lips. A kiss we were denied when she decided to stay on the yacht instead of coming with me. Her tongue slips inside my mouth, and I tangle my hand in her hair and listen to her beautiful soft moans as I deepen the kiss.

"I've missed you, princess."

She moans again before pulling my lips back to hers. I try to let myself get lost in the kiss. It would be easy to just let go. Kinsley makes it easy for me to let go. I can't let go though. She's not safe, and I have to protect her.

I grab her shoulders and pull her lips from mine. "We need to go."

She takes a step back. "No, I can't leave. Not yet, not until they are all in FBI custody."

"You have to leave with me. The FBI will be here in five hours."

"By then, they could already be gone."

"Please, princess. You've done your job. Let the FBI do theirs."

"No. I need to be getting back. I'm supposed to be helping pack things up for our trip to Tokyo."

"Do you think that is where their other base of operation is?"

"I don't know, but I plan to find out. Nacio is talking to the city to try to get the electricity back. I guess we can't get into one of our vaults where they keep the money without electricity. As soon as we get electricity back, I'm supposed to meet downstairs to help transfer the money to the vans."

I lift her chin and kiss her hard on the lips. I'm hoping, if I tempt her, she will decide to come back with me instead of staying here. I feel her try to pull away from me, but I don't let her. I won't let her risk herself again. Instead, I walk us backward in the room that has been converted into an office. I kiss her, trying to make her forget about what she is here to do. She moans softly, but I know it's not enough for her to forget what she is doing here.

I feel the door I came in from behind me as I move my lips to her neck. I feel her purring against my lips. I need to make her moan. I need to make her scream, and she can't do that in here.

I grab the door handle, and I pull her outside.

"What"—she pants—"are"—she sucks in as my lips touch her neck again—"you"—she exhales deeply—"doing?"

I grin against her neck. "Making you change your mind."

She moans and grabs my head, forcing my lips on hers. Her tongue is on my tongue. My cock is pressed against her stomach.

"I don't think that's possible. I've already made up my mind."

I reach my hand under her bra and run my thumb over her hard nipple. I watch as her body convulses with just the touch. "I've made you change your mind before," I say into her ear as I squeeze her nipple again, making her pant.

She reaches into my jeans and grabs ahold of my cock that is already hard for her. "I need you now. It can't wait."

She slowly moves her hand up and down my thick cock. I grow harder, willing to give her anything she wants as long as it means I get to be inside her.

"Fuck me, and give me the courage to walk back inside this building. Fuck me against this building in the alleyway."

My brain doesn't register her words. It doesn't register that this is her saying good-bye. All that it hears is, *fuck me.*

"My pleasure, princess."

I spin her around so she can hold on to the building to keep her balance. I kiss her neck and listen to her groan as I reach my hand into her pants, feeling her wet pussy welcoming me in.

"Fuck me, Killian," she moans. "I can't wait."

I move to unbutton my pants and watch as she does the same to hers. Our need to have each other outweighs our need for safety. I hold my cock in my hand and press it against her bare ass now that her pants are hanging around her ankles. I glance to the right, trying to figure out what people might see if they walk by right now, but since I can barely even see the street in the darkness, I know noone can see us either—at least not until the electricity comes back on, and the darkness disappears.

"Fuck me," she whimpers again.

I press my cock against her again. I grab ahold of her ass and bend her further until I find the entrance to her pussy. My cock slides inside.

"You're so tight, princess," I moan as she tightens around me.

I begin thrusting slowly, enjoying being inside her, but her hips tell me it's not enough. She needs more. She needs passion.

"I need..."

But I already know what she needs. I grab her ass and begin thrusting into her harder and harder. My balls hit her clit with each thrust, and I grab her breast with my free hand.

I feel her building with each thrust. I feel her lose herself, which is exactly what I wanted.

I move my head to her ear. "Come for me, princess," I whisper into her ear before biting down on her earlobe.

"Killian!" she screams into the darkness.

That's all it takes for me to explode inside her.

I tightly squeeze her, refusing to pull out of her anytime soon.

This is what I need. This is what we both need for the rest of our lives. Without this, there is no reason to keep living. Without her, I have nothing. No job. No home. No love. No life.

She takes a step sideways though, and I am no longer inside her. I watch her pull her pants back on, and I do the same. By the time I put my pants back on, she is already turning back toward me. The streetlights flicker back on. She looks beautiful, standing there, in the light. Her lingering orgasm is still shining on her face. Now, we are exposed though, and it is no longer safe.

We both have to make a choice—to go back inside and put a stop to everything or run away together and never look back.

"Have you changed your mind?" I ask.

"No. Have you?"

"No."

She firmly kisses me. A good-bye kiss. A kiss that I refuse to even think about because it is *not* a good-bye kiss.

"This isn't good-bye. If you choose to go back in there, I'm going, too. I'll be hiding in the shadows. I will keep my promise to your father and to you. I will keep you safe, princess."

"You promise?"

"Always."

23

KINSLEY

I open the door to go back inside. I walk in, and Killian grabs the door, following me. I wish he would leave. I wish he were safe, but I guess it's not fair to ask that of him when I won't go somewhere safe for him.

I walk to the far door of the office and pause at it. I can't look back at Killian and still do what I have to do.

"I know. I love you, too. Go. I'll be watching you," he says.

I open the door and step out into the now lit hallway. I quickly close the door behind me. I look back at the door for just a second, and then I start walking. Away from Killian. Away from the only person left who is worthy of my love. And, this time, it feels more final. It feels like this could really be the last time I see him. The last time I kiss him. The last time both of us are alive.

I walk down the hallway to the stairs and down into the dark basement where Nacio told me to meet him. The room is large, and several of the men are already in the room, beginning to load up the money into bags, while others are carrying the bags out of the building.

I spot Nacio and Granddad directing them.

"What can I do to help?" I ask.

"About time you joined us. Where have you been?" Granddad asks.

"I was trying to help arrange transportation, like Nacio asked, but I couldn't find anyone who had a phone I could borrow."

Granddad motions with his fingers, and Santino and Seth grab ahold of my arms before I realize what is happening.

"What is going on? Let me go."

I struggle against the men's hold, but it is useless. Their arms are too strong, and even if I did break loose, there are half a dozen other men ready to grab me. I glance around and notice the whole room is frozen, watching me.

Nacio notices it, too. "Get back to work."

The men immediately snap to life and begin putting the money from the vault into bags.

Granddad walks over to me. "Nacio told me about your trip."

"It's not my fault Killian escaped with the children. I had nothing to do with it. I thought it was in our best interest to keep him alive."

Granddad smiles a smug grin. "I think you had everything to do with it."

I frown. "I was just as drunk off my ass as the rest of them. I didn't have anything to do with it."

"We will see if you have the same story to tell afterward."

"After what?"

My question is immediately answered though.

Granddad nods at Seth and Santino, who immediately have me on my face against a hard wall. My jacket is ripped off my body and then I feel the sting of the whip.

I cry out, unable to remain quiet.

It hits my skin again, ripping my skin, and causing blood to drip in long streams down my back.

Again.

Again.

Again.

The pain increases each time and I regret ever touching the whip to Killian. I regret what I did to Karp. And I can't help but think I deserve this.

For the hurt I caused.

For being so naive.

For not ending this sooner.

I begin to hear the crack of the whip, but no longer feel it. My back as gone numb. I've tuned it all out, and my screaming stops along with my breathing slowed.

I'm dying. I must be, it's the only reason the pain must be getting better instead of worse. Just a few more minutes of letting go and I'll be gone.

"Now, would you like to tell me what happened on that yacht, or should we try this all over again?" Granddad asks.

The men turn my body to face him, slamming my back against the wall as I scream from the intensity. The pain didn't stop, they just stopped whipping me.

"I didn't do anything. I was with Nacio the whole night. I'm on your side."

I glance to Nacio, who is standing next to Granddad. With my eyes, I beg him to put a stop to this, but he doesn't move. I glance over at Granddad, who nods, and then I'm being dragged back to the wall.

"Stop!" I try to scream, but my voice is no longer able to scream. "Stop!" I try again, this time much louder.

The terror I feel as the whip pierces my skin again intensifies. I understand now why most would rather die from a bullet wound then this slow torture.

I struggle at first, but it doesn't matter. I feel the same darkness coming back, this time much faster than the first time. A shadow casts over my body, I'm going to die.

24

KILLIAN

I SIT at the top of the stairs to the basement, listening, but I have a hard time making out what is going on.

Until I hear Kinsley scream. The second she does, I can't wait any longer.

I run down the stairs as I pull my gun out from the waistband of my pants. I know the gun won't be enough. Not against a dozen men with guns, but hopefully, it will be long enough to keep her alive until the FBI gets here.

That's all I need. More time.

When I reach the bottom of the stairs, what I see terrifies me.

I aim the gun at Lee's head, knowing he is the one giving the orders. "Tell them to stop."

He smiles and motions for Seth and Santino to stop. I watch out of the corner of my eye as they jerk Kinsley from the wall. She trembles in their hold, needing their arms to hold her up as blood pours down her back. Santino smacks her cheek, trying to wake her up more, but her seeing me does that for him. She tries to run forward, but they pull her back.

"So happy you could join us, Killian. It saves us the trouble of hunting you down. Now, we can kill you without the hunt."

"Let her go. You can have me. Let her go, and I will ensure the FBI won't find you."

Granddad shakes his head. "I don't think I'm going to have to let her go. We will be long gone before the FBI arrives."

"They will be here in half an hour. You need to leave now."

"I think you are bluffing. See, we have someone on the inside now, and he says they won't move in for another three hours at least."

My eyes widen because he knows the truth. I was bluffing about the FBI. They are most likely still hours away like they told me earlier.

"Let her go," I say again.

"Drop the gun," Seth says as he points a gun at Kinsley.

I immediately drop the gun.

"Kick it away," Lee says.

I kick it.

I watch as Seth forces Kinsley to walk with him over to where Lee and Nacio are standing.

"Give her the test," Nacio says. "Let her prove she is telling the truth."

Lee looks over at Nacio. "And if she doesn't do it?"

"Then, we'll have our answer," Nacio answers.

I look from Nacio to Lee to a broken Kinsley. I know what they want her to do. They want her to shoot me. I want her to shoot me. If she shoots me, she guarantees her life. They will think she is on their side, and they will keep her alive until the FBI moves in. I just don't know how to remind Kinsley of her promise to me.

Nacio pulls a gun from his waistband and hands it to Kinsley. "Shoot Killian. Avenge your father. Prove you choose us, not him."

Seth continues to aim his gun at Kinsley as she studies Nacio's gun for a second. Her eyes go to mine, and I tell her what I want. I tell her to shoot me. Her eyes tell me she loves me.

And then she lifts the gun and pulls the trigger.

25

KINSLEY

I WATCH Killian fall to the ground, and it is the worst thing I have ever watched. I tried not to aim for any vital organs, but watching him fall like he did has me worried. I know it's what he wanted. I know I promised to shoot him. I just never thought I would have to do it.

I feel like I betrayed my heart by shooting him. I feel empty, like I was the one on the other end of the gun.

Nacio grabs the gun from my hand and then tightly hugs me. I wince as his hands hit the wounds on my back.

"I knew you would choose correctly," Nacio says in my ear before releasing me.

Seth lowers his gun, accepting that I am on their side. I smile. This is now my chance to ask about the other locations. This is my chance to become a true Felton. And then I can do anything to keep Killian alive.

But Granddad's laughing distracts me. Nacio lets me go as I turn to face him.

"Is it funny now to watch a man die?" I ask, cocking my head to one side, as I look at my grandfather.

"No, watching you shoot someone because you thought he killed your father—that's what's funny."

"Killian didn't kill my father?"

"No." He laughs again.

"Then, how did he die?"

"I killed him. I had him poisoned."

"Why?" I ask, my voice shaky, as is my entire body. I don't have the strength to stand strong much longer. The adrenaline is the only thing keeping me up on my feet.

"Because he was soft. He grew tired of the business. He grew a heart. He didn't want to traffic people anymore. He didn't want to smuggle drugs. He didn't want to kill people anymore.

"From the second you were born, I noticed when he began to change. His heart simply wasn't in it anymore. Once we found a man to pass the company on to, I thought that would change, and for a while, having Killian there did give him new hope, new energy. Until he found out Killian was FBI. I think he took it as a sign we weren't supposed to be doing this anymore.

"He wanted out. But you don't get out. Not once you start. He had to go, or he was going to ruin everything. He risked everything for you. I had to kill him."

Tears fall from my eyes. "You killed your own son?"

"Yes."

More tears fall. They fall for my father who didn't deserve what he got. They fall for me for losing a father too soon. And they fall for Killian who is barely breathing on the floor all because he sacrificed himself, just like my father did to save me.

"I hate you! I fucking hate you!"

I begin to move toward him, but he pulls a gun and aims it at my head. I freeze. If I die, shooting Killian would have been for nothing.

"You are just like him. And, now, I get the pleasure of killing you, too," Granddad says.

I glance to Killian, who is lying on the floor. Blood pools around his body, but I can't tell where the bullet went. He's still breathing, just barely. He won't make it much longer.

"I love you always," I say under my breath as I close my eyes.

The last thing I hear is the bang of a gun being fired before the pain in my lungs overtakes me.

26

KINSLEY

I OPEN MY EYES, and all I see is white. White walls. White lights. White sheets.

I'm in a hospital room. I survived.

I test my arms and legs, trying to see what has been damaged, but the only thing that hurts are my lungs.

"Oh my God!" Scarlett squeals next to me before she tackles me with her body. "I was afraid you would never wake up. I flew to Paris as soon as I heard."

I smile, happy to see someone I love. Happy to feel safe. I just wish I saw another face in the room as well.

"Is Killian..."

"He's alive."

I exhale the breath I was holding while waiting for Scarlett to answer.

"Where is he?"

"He's here, at the hospital. They won't let him see you until they have questioned you first. And they couldn't question you until you were awake. He's been going crazy out there."

I smile. He's alive.

"Where was he shot?"

"The shoulder. Evidently, your grandfather didn't have very good aim."

I raise my eyebrows, realizing Killian must have said Granddad shot him instead of me. I'll have to remember that when I'm questioned.

"Did Granddad…"

"He's dead."

"How?"

"Nacio shot him. Nacio is in the hospital room next door. The FBI shot Nacio after they heard him fire at your grandfather. He's a rather good-looking…"

"He's a horrible person, Scarlett. I watched him shoot a woman."

"Nacio also saved your life."

"It still doesn't make up for what he did. He will still spend the rest of his life in jail."

Scarlett nods.

"Did they get everyone else who was there?"

Scarlett shakes her head. "No, I guess Nacio's brother escaped. And they haven't found their father or their other location yet. They are hoping Nacio will tell them in exchange for a deal when he wakes up."

I nod. I hope the FBI finds them, but for now, I'm glad the Feltons are no longer involved.

I'm safe. Killian is safe. That is all that matters.

"My mother?"

"She's in jail."

I nod, not really caring.

I hear a knock on the door, and I sit up, hoping it is Killian, but I see two men in suits standing at the doorway.

"We have a lot of questions for you. Are you up for it?" one of the men asks.

I nod. "I bet you do."

27

KINSLEY

THE FBI QUESTIONING WENT WELL. I told them Killian's lie about who shot him even though I'm not sure it mattered. We did whatever we needed to survive. They aren't going to arrest me or Killian. Although Killian will never be able to work for the FBI again. I'm not sure if it matters anymore though.

The doctor came in afterward and said I was in the clear and could fly home. I was suffering from a slight infection. They will keep me on antibiotics and have me check in later in the week to make sure the wounds on my back are still healing, but they don't expect any further complications. I just need to take it easy and not do anything too strenuous for a while. The scars that will remain on my back will be minimal.

Scarlett bought me some clothes. I asked for sweats and a T-shirt, but instead, she bought me a dress and underwear. It's a nice, simple black dress. Something I used to wear all the time but not something I want to wear on a long flight home from the hospital. I put it on anyway though because it is the only thing I have to wear. I pull a brush through my hair but don't bother with putting on the makeup Scarlett brought me.

A knock sounds at the door, and I perk my head up. Killian still hasn't come in to see me, so I assume it's him.

"Come in!" I shout.

I look up, and my heart stops as I wait for the door to open. When I see it's just Scarlett, I sigh.

"Ready to go?"

"Yes."

She walks over to me. "You look beautiful." She reaches into the overnight bag she brought me and pulls out the makeup bag.

"I really don't think I need makeup to walk out of the hospital."

"I want you to feel your best," Scarlett says. She applies some blush, lipstick, and mascara to my face, despite my protests.

Another knock sounds, and I perk my head up, but when I see it's just my nurse, my head drops.

She pushes a wheelchair into my room. "Your chariot," my nurse says.

I sigh and climb in. I'm too tired to protest that I can walk.

Scarlett gathers my things and then follows us out of the room. The nurse walks slowly down the hospital hallways while I really want her to hurry. I don't know where Killian is, but I need to find him. I need to see that he is still alive. And I need her to hurry up, so I can do that.

We finally reach the front door to the hospital when Scarlett says, "I can get her from here."

I'm shocked when the nurse nods and lets her push me.

"Thanks. I don't think I could stand for her to keep pushing me at that pace much longer."

Scarlett smiles and keeps pushing me. I expect her to push me toward the parking lot, but she doesn't. Instead, she pushes me around to the side of the hospital.

"Where are we going?"

"You'll see."

My heart flutters at the unknown but not in a good way. I don't know if I will ever be spontaneous again. Not after what I went through. I never want to have my heart racing that fast again.

Scarlett suddenly stops the wheelchair. "Do you think you can walk?"

"Yes. But where to?"

She shakes her head and holds out her hand to me. I take it, and she helps me stand in the small heels she brought me.

"Lean on me if you need to," she says.

I hold on to her arm as I get used to walking again. It's not too bad. It just hurts when I breathe.

We turn the corner of the building when I see him.

Killian is standing in a beautiful garden with candles everywhere. He's dressed in dark jeans and a button-down shirt. One arm is in a sling. The beard that started growing is now gone, and his hair is trimmed a little. I don't care what he looks like though. I'm just happy to see him.

Killian runs over to me. When he reaches me, he throws his free arm around me, and I wrap my arms around his neck after letting go of Scarlett. His lips sizzle against mine. His tongue finds mine, and then my world stops.

For the first time in forever, I don't have to think about anything else. Not family obligations. Not my future. Not my past. Not surviving. Or right or wrong. Or saving him.

For the first time in forever, I can just get lost in a kiss.

I don't know how long the kiss lasts, but when it stops, Killian reaches down to hold my hand. He leads me into the garden that looks so similar to my favorite place at the casino where he proposed earlier.

He stops when we are in the center of the garden.

"Princess, I know this isn't going to be perfect. We are in a fucking hospital garden. We both have a lot of healing to do, but after the last few weeks we have had, I don't think I can wait for perfect. I don't know if I will ever get perfect, so I have to do this now."

I watch as he kneels in front of me, and tears spring to my eyes.

"You are everything I ever wanted. I knew it from the first time I saw your picture, from the first time I saw you in person. When I promised your father I would protect you forever, I knew you were mine.

"You are a beautiful princess, but I've realized now, after really getting to know you, you are so much more. You are my warrior princess. My survivor. You have more strength in you than I ever thought possible. You even had the strength to risk your life for me. To save those children and women. You even had the strength to shoot me even though you didn't want to. You're everything I ever thought I wanted and more.

"I know I'm not worthy. I made a terrible FBI agent. I couldn't even figure out the trafficking and smuggling ring that was right under my nose. I'm unemployed. I don't have any money. I don't know what my future holds. I don't even have enough money to buy you a proper ring. But I can't wait until I do to ask you to spend forever with me. I can't wait because we aren't promised a tomorrow, and I want to start living tomorrow with you now.

"Kinsley, will you marry me?"

Killian opens a box, and in it is a pink plastic ring with a fake diamond on top. Most likely, he got it from a machine in the lobby.

I smile. "Maybe."

"I'll take that as a yes," he says, grinning widely.

Standing, he puts the cheap ring on my finger. A ring I know he will replace when he gets the chance, but this proposal is perfect, and I wouldn't have it any other way.

"Take it as an always."

EPILOGUE

KILLIAN

Six Months Later

I HEAR the front door to our one-bedroom loft in New York open and close.

Finally, I think.

I close my computer and meet Kinsley at the door. She quickly kisses me on the lips, but I can tell she's distracted.

"What's wrong?" I ask.

"Huh?" she says as she smiles at me.

She places her bag on the counter, and I see the shine of her stupid plastic ring reflecting in the light as she does.

I wanted to replace the ring right away, but after the proposal, we weren't sure what to do with the money she had, and I had practically no money. We weren't sure what to do with the Felton Corporation. With our lives.

It took us a couple of months to realize we didn't want to touch any of the tainted money from the Felton Corporation. We didn't want to run the company. Basically, we wanted a fresh start. So, Kinsley sold the company, and we gave all the money away to charity.

Now, Kinsley works for an organization that helps battered

women rebuild their lives. She's good at it, and she really seems to love it.

She didn't take long to figure out what she wanted to do, but it has taken me longer to decide what I want to do. I'm just not sure how I'm going to take the job.

"What's got you so distracted?" I ask, holding on to her waist and kissing her neck.

She moans softly. "Right now, you."

I grin. "Good." I kiss her neck again. "Seriously though, are you okay?"

"Yes. I'm just worried about this woman who came in today. I'm not sure she's ready to start over."

I nod. "Be patient with her. It takes time." I kiss her neck again.

"I know, but I don't want to talk about work anymore."

"Me neither. I want to fuck you."

She groans. "Fucking sounds good."

I move my hand under her T-shirt, feeling her smooth stomach. "I want to try something. Do you trust me?"

"Of course. What do you have in mind?"

I lift her up and carry her to the bed. I gently put her down, firmly kissing her on the lips. I walk over to the nightstand and pull out the items I bought today. I hold them out to her. She closely looks at the rope and whip.

"You want me to whip you again?"

"No. I want to use it on you."

Her eyes widen.

"I think it's only fair since you got to use it on me." I lean down and kiss her earlobe before sucking and pulling on it with my teeth, the way she likes. "I think you will enjoy it, but if I take it too far, I will stop."

I've been dreaming about doing this to her since she held the whip in her hand in Mexico. And knowing she needs to face her fears so the pain of it won't haunt her forever.

"Yes, I want it."

I smile. I remove her clothes, followed by mine. With her laying on her stomach, I tie her arms to the posts of the bed with rope, but I leave her legs free. I lift her legs onto her knees and then kneel behind her with the whip in my hand.

"Ready?" I ask, rubbing her ass.

"Yes," she breathes.

I let the whip come down on her ass. She whimpers, and I watch as her ass turns a bright shade of pink.

"That was—"

I don't let her finish. I use the whip again on the other cheek. She squeals, and my cock twitches when I see her body react to me. I hit her again and see hot liquid dripping from her pussy down her leg. I whip her again and again until—

"Fuck, Killian," she moans.

Then, I can't take it any longer.

I thrust inside her, and she screams. I thrust quickly, knowing how she likes it. I grab her breasts and hear her moans intensify.

"I'm going to—"

She can't speak, but I feel her clenching around me. It's the fastest she has ever come, showing me how much being whipped and tied up turns her on. I thrust faster until I'm filling her with my cum.

After we come together, we both collapse, exhausted and content just to be together. After a few minutes, I feel her wiggling, trying to get out from under me, and I laugh.

"Hold on," I say. I untie her hands and roll off her so we are lying side by side.

She smiles at me. She looks so beautiful, so content, lying naked in our bed. I don't think I will ever get used to the sight.

"What's wrong?" she asks when she notices I don't wear the same content smile she does.

I take a deep breath before I speak, "I accepted a job today."

"Really?" she asks excitedly, sitting up higher in bed.

"Yeah."

"Well...what is it?"

I take another breath, not sure about how she is going to react. "I accepted an executive job with a hotel chain."

Her smile brightens. "Really? That's awesome. That job always suited you."

"You don't think it's stupid, doing the same work I did for your family?"

"No. You were great at it. I don't care what you do, as long as you are happy."

I grab her neck and firmly kiss her, showing my appreciation. "You amaze me."

I turn back to my nightstand and find the box I bought after accepting the job and knowing how much money I will be making.

"I guess I can give you this then," I say, opening the box.

Her mouth drops. "Killian, it's beautiful!"

I smile and take the plastic ring off her finger. I replace it with the large princess cut ring. I go to throw the plastic ring away, but she snatches it back.

"You are not getting rid of that ring—ever," she says sternly.

I smile. "Whatever you say, princess."

"Does this mean we have enough money to start planning a wedding?"

"It does."

She squeals again. "I need to call Scarlett. We need to get to planning right away if we want a shot at a spring wedding."

She hops off the bed and begins walking away, mumbling to herself, but I don't mind. The view of her naked ass is worth her leaving.

She pauses at the door and looks at me. "Now that we are no longer broke, does this mean, in a couple of months after the wedding, we can start trying for kids?"

I laugh. "Maybe."

She smiles. "I'll take that as a yes."

The End

Thank you so much for reading! The series isn't over just yet, Scarlett has a story to tell that you won't want to miss!

You can get the first book in Scarlett's series, Definitely Yes, for FREE here—> Grab Definitely Yes for FREE Here

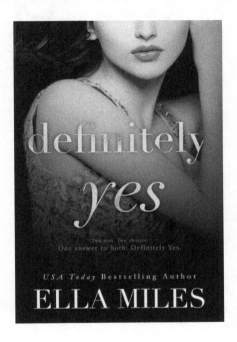

Or Grab the Definitely Boxset Here!

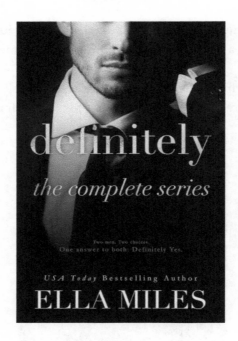

FREE BOOKS

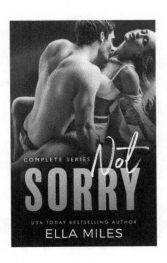

Read **Not Sorry** for **FREE**! And sign up to get my latest releases, updates, and more goodies here→EllaMiles.com/freebooks

Follow me on BookBub to get notified of my new releases and recommendations here→Follow on BookBub Here

Join Ella's Bellas FB group for giveaways and FUN & a FREE copy of
Pretend I'm Yours→Join Ella's Bellas Here

ALSO BY ELLA MILES

MAYBE, DEFINITELY SERIES:

Maybe Yes

Maybe Never

Maybe Always

Definitely Yes

Definitely No

Definitely Forever

Truth or Lies (Coming 2019):

Taken by Lies

Betrayed by Truths

Trapped by Lies

Stolen by Truths

Possessed by Lies

Consumed by Truths

DIRTY SERIES:

Dirty Beginning

Dirty Obsession

Dirty Addiction

Dirty Revenge

ALIGNED SERIES:

Aligned: Volume 1 (Free Series Starter)

Aligned: Volume 2

Aligned: Volume 3

Aligned: Volume 4

Aligned: The Complete Series Boxset

UNFORGIVABLE SERIES:

Heart of a Thief

Heart of a Liar

Heart of a Prick

Unforgivable: The Complete Series Boxset

STANDALONES:

Pretend I'm Yours

Finding Perfect

Savage Love

Too Much

Not Sorry

ABOUT THE AUTHOR

Ella Miles writes steamy romance, including everything from dark suspense romance that will leave you on the edge of your seat to contemporary romance that will leave you laughing out loud or crying. Most importantly, she wants you to feel everything her characters feel as you read.

Ella is currently living her own happily ever after near the Rocky Mountains with her high school sweetheart husband. Her heart is also taken by her goofy five year old black lab who is scared of everything, including her own shadow.

Ella is a USA Today Bestselling Author & Top 50 Bestselling Author.

Stalk Ella at:
www.ellamiles.com
ella@ellamiles.com